"Joseph H. Badal returns with another gripping page turner set against the backdrop of the 2004 summer Olympics in Athens. Filled with compelling characters and inside military knowledge, Badal has written another timely story that is intriguing and terrifying. You won't be able to put it down. Highly recommended."

— Sheldon Siegel
New York Times best-selling author
of *FINAL VERDICT*

"As up-to-date as today's headlines, *TERROR CELL* throws the reader slam-bang into the middle of a deadly struggle between the CIA and terrorists hell-bent on disrupting the Athens Olympics. Joseph Badal takes international intrigue to a whole new level."

— Steve Brewer
author of *BULLETS*

"Joe Badal takes us into a tangled puzzle of intrigue and terrorism, giving readers a page-turning mystery that gives readers a chance to combine learning of Greece and Greek politics with a tense, well told tale."

— Tony Hillerman
New York Times best-selling author

TERROR
CELL

TERROR
CELL

Joseph H. Badal

SEVEN LOCKS PRESS

Santa Ana, California

© 2004 by Joseph H. Badal. All rights reserved.

No part of this publication may be reproduced, distributed, or transmitted in any form or by any means, including photocopying, recording, or other electronic or mechanical methods, or by any information storage and retrieval system, without prior written permission from the publisher, except for brief quotations embodied in critical reviews and certain other noncommercial uses permitted by copyright law. For permission requests, write to the publisher, addressed "Attention: Permissions Coordinator," at the address below.

Seven Locks Press
P.O. Box 25689
Santa Ana, CA 92799
(800) 354-5348

Individual Sales: This book is available through most bookstores or can be ordered online or directly from Seven Locks Press at the address above.

Quantity Sales: Special discounts are available on quantity purchases by corporations, associations, and others. For details, contact the "Special Sales Department" at the publisher's address above.

Printed in the United States of America

Library of Congress Cataloging-in-Publication Data
is available from the publisher
ISBN 1-931643-45-8

Cover and Interior Design by Sparrow Advertising & Design

The author and publisher assume neither liability nor responsibility to any person or entity with respect to any direct or indirect loss or damage caused, or alleged to be caused, by the information contained herein, or for errors, omissions, inaccuracies, or any other inconsistency within these pages, or for unintentional slights against people or organizations.

DEDICATION

This book is a work of fiction. Although *Eleeneekee Aneexee* ("EA") (*Greek Spring*) mentioned here is a fictitious terrorist organization, it is based on the *17 November* terrorist group, which operated in Greece from 1975 to 2002, assassinating both Greeks and non-Greeks. Many of the victims of *17 November* mentioned in *Terror Cell* are real.

Suspected members of *17 November* were on trial in Athens at the time this book was written. The leader of the group was convicted in December 2003 of 2,500 acts of terrorism and sentenced to life in prison, which in Greece means that he will probably serve no more than twenty years. Other members of the group, if convicted, will also more than likely serve no more than twenty years. So, they will, in all likelihood, be free men someday.

I dedicate *Terror Cell* to the victims of *17 November* and to the victims' family members who have had to live with the memories of the crimes perpetrated against their loved ones and with the frustration of what seemed to be more often than not the incompetence and indifference of the Greek Government to the acts of *17 November*.

17 November's victims included:

1. Richard Welch, CIA Chief of Station, murdered 12/23/75.
2. Evangelos Mallios, Police Officer, murdered 12/14/76.
3. Petros Babalis, Police Officer, murdered 1/31/79.
4. Pantelis Petrou, Police Officer, murdered 1/16/80.
5. Sotirios Stamoulis, Police Officer, murdered 1/16/80.
6. George Tsantes, U.S. Navy Captain, JUSMAGG, murdered 11/15/83.
7. Nikolaos Veloutsos, Driver for George Tsantes, murdered 11/15/83.

8. Robert H. Judd, Jr., U.S. Army Master Sergeant, JUSMAGG, wounded 4/3/84.

9. Nicolaos Momferatos, Publisher, murdered 2/21/85.

10. P. Rousetis, Driver for Nikolaos Momferatos, murdered 2/21/85.

11. George Theofanopoulos, Public Prosecutor, murdered 4/4/85.

12. Demetrios Angelopoulos, Businessman, murdered 4/8/86.

13. Dr. Zaharias Kapsalakis, Physician, wounded 2/5/87.

14. Seventeen U.S. Air Force Personnel wounded in bombing 4/24/87.

15. Eleven U.S. Air Force Personnel wounded in bombing 8/10/87.

16. Alexandros Athanasiadis, Businessman, murdered 3/1/88.

17. William E. Nordeen, U.S. Navy Captain, murdered 6/28/88.

18. Konstantinos Androulidakis, Prosecutor, murdered 1/10/89.

19. Panagiotis Tarasouleas, Deputy Prosecutor, wounded 1/18/89.

20. Anastasios Vernardos, Deputy Prosecutor, murdered 1/23/89.

21. Giorgos Petsos, Minister of Public Order, wounded 5/8/89.

22. Savvas Bakogiannis, Member of Parliament, murdered 9/26/89.

23. Vardis Vardinogiannis, Industrialist, wounded 11/20/90.

24. Ronald Odell Stewart, U.S. Air Force Master Sergeant, murdered 3/12/91.

25. Four Turkish Diplomats wounded in bombing 7/16/91.

26. Cetin Giorgu, Turkish Diplomat, murdered 10/7/91.

27. One Greek Police Officer murdered and five wounded in rocket and grenade attack 11/2/91.

28. Two Greek Police Officers wounded in shootout 11/20/91.

29. Ioannis Palaiokrassas, Bystander, murdered in rocket attack 7/14/92.

30. Eleftherios Papadimitriou, Member of Parliament, wounded 12/21/92.

31. Mihalis Vranopoulos, Former Governor of Bank of Greece, murdered 1/24/94.

32. Nikolaos Griskpos, Driver for Mihalis Vranopoulos, wounded 1/24/94.

33. Omer Haluk Sipahioglou, Turkish Diplomat, murdered 1/24/94.

34. Konstantinos Peratikos, Businessman, murdered 5/28/97.

35. British Brigadier Stephen Saunders, murdered 6/8/00.

ACKNOWLEDGEMENTS

My sincere thanks go to:

My family, for your encouragement, love, and support.

Patricia Kushlis for suggesting that I write this book.

Rick and Peggy Story and Karla Ponder, for your careful and thoughtful editing. You made this book a better read.

George ("Chip") Tsantes, for providing background and opening doors to people who added immeasurably to the authenticity of *Terror Cell.* Your efforts to bring the members of the terrorist group, *17 November,* to trial would have made your father proud.

Doug Smith, Jr., for your advice and counsel regarding terrorism in Greece and Intelligence activities to counter terrorism.

Alex Kalangis, for your assistance in ensuring the accuracy of place names and in enhancing the physical "color" of Athens.

Rick Brooks, for your consultation and ideas.

All former members of the Air Defense Artillery Branch of the U.S. Army assigned to Nike Hercules missile sites, who worked in obscurity defending both the United States' and NATO's borders. I ask your forbearance of the license I took with information regarding Nike Hercules missile units in Greece.

Finally, thanks go to Jim Riordan, Betty Frovarp, Sharon Young, and Heather Buchman, for your contributions in making *Terror Cell* a reality, and to Maureen Walters, for your confidence and counsel.

PRONUNCIATION

INFORMATION

I have used Greek words in a few places. These words have been spelled phonetically in English.

In the case of *Eleeneekee Aneexee* (*Greek Spring*), the fictitious terrorist cell central to this story, the acronym for the group becomes *EA* (*Epsilon Alpha*).

Other Greek words and their meanings follow:

Afto eenay ena doro apo	This is a gift from . . ..
AsAs sto diavolo!	Go to hell!
Avrio stees octo to proee.	Tomorrow morning at 8.
Ee terroreestee xeroun.	The terrorists know.
Eteemos eesay?	Are you ready?
O dievtheendees mou xerei.	My boss knows.
Steen yia sas!	To your health!
Sto speetee konda to panapisteemeeou	At the house near the university.
Taverna	Restaurant
Thavmaseea!	Amazing!
Zeeto ee Ellas!	Praise Greece!

PROLOGUE

JULY 26, 2004

"You know, it's a beautiful day for a killing," Savvas said in an icy tone that sent a chill down Pavlos' spine.

Pavlos Manganos felt Savvas Krinon's arms tighten around his waist as he slowly drove his motorcycle past the British Embassy in Athens for the third time that morning, squeezing between the creeping automobile traffic on Ploutarhou Street. He again circled the block, driving to the quiet residential street behind the embassy and pulled his motorcycle to the curb, letting the engine idle.

"What do you think?" Pavlos asked, sliding back the dark visor on his motorcycle helmet and twisting in the seat to look at Savvas.

"It appears the English have taken no new measures with their embassy security," Savvas answered. "Just the same number of guards standing inside the vehicle gate and two more inside the building entrance." Savvas looked at his wristwatch. "Seven forty-five. He should be here in less than ten minutes. Let's get into position."

Pavlos turned around in the seat, closing his visor. He powered the cycle through the residential neighborhood, maneuvering back onto Ploutarhou Boulevard, four blocks north of the British Embassy. He drove to the curb on the embassy side of the boulevard and parked. He then pulled a cell phone from his black leather jacket pocket and rested the hand holding the phone on his jeans-clad thigh, his thumb poised over the TALK button. A wire snaked from the phone, up under his jacket and his helmet, to an ear piece. He had performed the same steps on three previous occasions; he barely had to think about them.

Three minutes after parking at the curb, the cell phone chirped. Pavlos' thumb hit the TALK button. "Go," he ordered.

"White Citroen is six blocks from your location, in the second inside lane," the Greek Spring spotter said. "Driver identified as target. Bright red hair. License is UK 747." The man paused momentarily, and then added, "There's a male passenger with him."

"Who?" Pavlos demanded.

"Unidentified," the spotter said.

Pavlos clicked off the phone and inserted it back in his pocket. "We have a complication," he told Savvas. "There's a second man in the car with the Englishman."

Savvas shrugged and said, "I have plenty of bullets."

Pavlos knew the Englishman would have to switch to the inside lane in order to enter the embassy's driveway, and with the heavy Athens morning commuter traffic, he would have to attempt negotiating the lane change well before he came to the embassy block. He looked over his shoulder and repeated to Savvas what the spotter had told him. It was Savvas' responsibility to pick out the vehicle and point it out to Pavlos.

The two men sat in silence. Pavlos kept his hands on the motorcycle's controls, feeling Savvas' left hand on his back. Pavlos knew his partner's right hand would now clutch the pistol inside his jacket. He stared intently at the flow of traffic to his right front.

Savvas suddenly rasped, "Three cars back and one lane over."

Pavlos waited until the Citroen was parallel with his motorcycle, and then slowly merged the bike into inside lane traffic. The Englishman appeared to be having trouble finding an opening to change lanes. Pavlos saw the driver's red hair. He let the Citroen pass him on the right so he could check the license plate, just to make sure. It was the one. He slipped into the middle lane behind the Englishman and waited.

Traffic moved like an army of slugs on an inexorable march on an unknown mission. Pavlos felt superior to the drones that surrounded him. At least he had a noble purpose, one that would make a difference. Could these cretins in their cars, on their daily commutes to their meaningless jobs, claim the same?

The Englishman poked the nose of the Citroen into a space that suddenly opened between two cars.

Good, Pavlos thought. He followed the Citroen back into the inside lane and crawled along behind it until they were a little more than one block from the embassy. He smiled to himself. The traffic, as thick as Turkish coffee, slogged along at five kilometers an hour. This was going to be easy.

The Citroen was now about twenty meters from the intersection this side of the Embassy. Pavlos waited for two deep breaths' time, and then swung around, just inches from the curb, to the left of the Citroen. He felt Savvas shift on the back of the motorcycle as he pulled alongside the Englishman's door. He would have loved to turn and watch what happened next, but he knew that would be foolhardy. It was his task to get them away from the scene as quickly as possible. They couldn't afford him becoming distracted.

The roar of the .45 caliber pistol sounded in Pavlos' ear and the bike shifted ever so slightly as Savvas absorbed the recoil. The pistol bucked again and then three times more, and Pavlos, out of his peripheral vision, saw red spray splatter the inside of the car's windshield.

Savvas barked, "Go, go, go," and Pavlos raced the motorcycle to the intersection, turned left, and sped away from the murder scene.

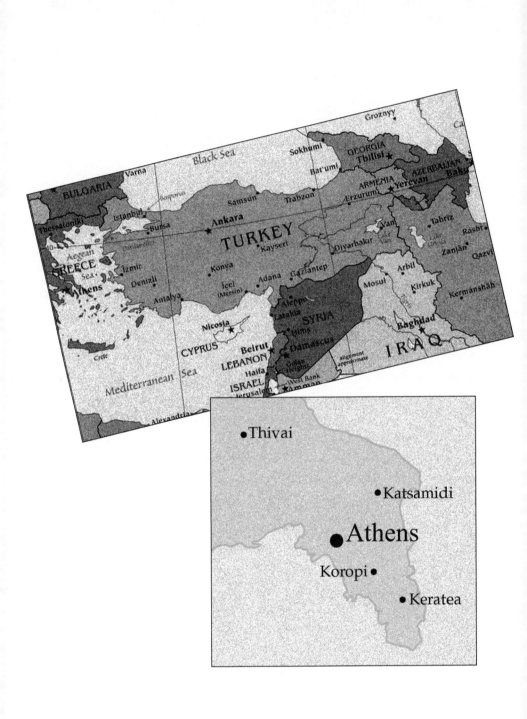

CHAPTER ONE

JULY 26, 2004

Bob Danforth knew the shit had hit the fan. He just didn't know what shit. His boss, Jack Cole, had sworn he'd leave him alone for the entire week of his vacation. Bob should have known better. Now Liz was pissed off—once again.

The drive from his home in Bethesda to Langley normally took at least an hour. At four-thirty on a Saturday morning, at eighty miles an hour, Bob figured the trip would take no more than thirty-five minutes. He rubbed his hand over his face and tried to wipe away the cobwebs of fatigue that seemed to have entangled his brain and blurred his eyesight. I'm getting too old for this crap, he thought for about the tenth time in the last month. He swiped a hand through his hair. He didn't need to look in the mirror to see how gray it had turned, or how high his forehead had become. He prided himself on being in excellent shape for a fifty-eight year old, but the daily jogs and three-day-a-week bend and grunt sessions with free weights couldn't make him young again. He and his son Michael had been jogging together for the last eighteen months, since the Army assigned Michael to the Pentagon in December 2003. Bob had noticed he was having a tough time keeping up with his son on their runs, despite them setting a slow, ten-minute-per-mile pace.

Bob smiled as he thought about his son and his daughter-in-law, Miriana. They'd left for Paris four days ago. The Army had just issued orders assigning Michael to the U.S. Army Special Warfare School as an instructor, so Michael and Miriana decided to take a trip before his reporting date at Fort Bragg. The assignment to Bragg ought to be a whole lot safer than his assignment with the 82nd Airborne in Macedonia three years ago, Bob thought. He felt his throat tighten. That assignment had nearly cost Michael his life. Bob's life, too. He forced himself to think of happier events—Michael and Miriana's wedding in 2001. It had been one heck of a party. After all the planning and emotion of seeing their son get married, layered on top of the rescue operation to free Michael from the Serb Special Forces unit that had kidnapped him in Macedonia, Bob and Liz had needed a week's vacation of doing nothing. But Jack Cole had interrupted that week off, and he was doing the same thing again.

Although he already knew the time, Bob looked at the dashboard clock: Four thirty-one. It was mid-morning in Paris. He pictured Michael and Miriana sitting at a little *cafe* in the shadow of the Eiffel Tower, eating croissants and people watching. That's what Liz and I ought to be doing, he thought, instead of my going to CIA Headquarters during my vacation, and leaving a very angry wife at home.

CHAPTER TWO

JULY 26, 2004

Bob joined the Central Intelligence Agency after leaving the U.S. Army in the early 1970s. He'd met Jack Cole, who started with the Agency in 1969, during his training. They'd worked together off and on during the past thirty-four years. Now Jack was "DDO," the Deputy Director of Operations, and Bob's boss, and Bob headed up Special Ops. To Bob, Jack was like an older brother. But, despite their relationship, Bob was about to dump on Jack for pulling him off vacation. He stopped himself when he saw the expression on his old friend's face. He could tell that something terrible had happened. Jack already looked a lot older than his sixty-two years. Long work days and tremendous stress had taken their toll. His face had become pale and slightly jowly, and his athletic body had sagged and rounded in the last few years. But he now looked sick, too. The cold, hard look in his red-veined eyes was a window to his soul. Puffy, dark bags showed under his eyes. He looked devastated—and angry.

Bob took a seat in front of the desk. "What's up, Jack?" he said.

Jack swallowed and shook his head. "They murdered Fred Grantham and Harvey Cornwell, Bob. Shot them on their way to a meeting at the British Embassy in Athens."

Bob now felt like Jack looked. "Dammit!" he exclaimed. "Who? Who did it?"

"No one's claimed responsibility yet; but it's got the signature of *Eleeneekee Aneexee—Greek Spring*." Jack slammed a hand down on his desk. "Those bastards." His face seemed older, more tired than he'd already looked when Bob entered the office. "You know how the

Greek press refers to these murderers? *EPSILON ALPHA! EA!* Like they're a fucking college fraternity."

Bob stood and paced the office, his mind awhirl with memories about Greece. His last assignment as an American Army officer had been in Greece, in 1971, the place where his son had been kidnapped the first time, when Michael was just two. He'd learned to love the country and the Greek people, despite the painful memory about Michael's abduction; but the Greek Government's execution of the investigation into terrorist groups like *Greek Spring* had left a bad taste in his mouth. Every Western Intelligence agent felt the same. Like *Theka Efta Noemvri*, the *17 November* terrorist group that assassinated Richard Welch, the CIA Station Chief in Athens in 1975, *Greek Spring* had operated with impunity for three decades. They had gained confidence and become more aggressive over those thirty years. *17 November* had murdered as many as twenty-three people, and *Greek Spring* at least another twenty-four. Fred Grantham and Harvey Cornwell could very well be the group's twenty-fifth and twenty-sixth murder victims. And not one single member of the group had been identified, let alone arrested.

"Dammit, Jack, Fred and Harvey were a couple of the best in the business. We've never had better cooperation between the agency and the Brits than we've had since Fred Grantham took over as Station Chief in Athens. And the Brits in MI-6 call Cornwell '007.' Someone, some group has pretty big balls to murder the CIA Station Chief and the British Defense Attaché."

Jack nodded. "It's time we stopped screwing around with these thugs. It's time we get payback for Richard Welch, the eight other Americans, and now Grantham," he said, referring to the Americans murdered by *17 November* and *Greek Spring*. "Plus, for all the Americans these terrorists have wounded and their families." Jack hesitated a moment, then added, "England has had a team of investigators working in Athens since *17 November* assassinated

Brigadier Stephen Saunders in Athens four years ago. The Brits are going ballistic. Cornwell's murder was *Greek Spring's* way of rubbing the Brits' noses in the dirt."

"I can pull my team together within the hour," Bob offered, "and get caught up on the data in the files by day's end. Maybe there's something we can share with the Brits which would help them find the murderers." Bob's offer sounded hollow even to his own ears. He knew that CIA analysts had gone through every bit of information the Agency had on the terrorist groups in Greece, including *Greek Spring*. They hadn't found a kernel of data that led to the identification of even one member of any of the groups. "You know, if it hadn't been for that idiot from *17 November* blowing himself up while planting a bomb in Piraeus two years ago, the Greek Government would probably never have been able to take down that organization. That guy rolled over on many of the *17 November* members."

"We could use a little luck like that every once in a while."

Jack appeared uncomfortable, anxious. His face now flushed, he stood and walked across the office, opened the door to a cabinet, and pulled out two glasses and a bottle of bourbon. He went back to his desk, splashed two fingers of booze into each glass, and lifted one of the glasses toward Bob. "Maybe you should drink this."

Oh crap, Bob thought, what now? "You'd better say whatever you've got on your mind," he said, "before you stroke out. Besides, isn't it just a tad early in the day for the hard stuff?"

Jack handed one glass to Bob anyway, then plopped back into his desk chair and lifted the other glass. "Go ahead and call your team in. You'll need all the research we can provide . . . before you go to Athens."

Bob had just sipped a bit of the bourbon and the strong amber liquid caused him to cough. It took him a half-minute to stop. "To do what?" he said.

"To head up our side of the investigation into *Greek Spring*. You'll work with the Brits. I talked to Brigadier Jeffrey Watkin-Coons this morning. They're fed up with waiting for the Greeks to catch those bastards. So am I. Whether Athens likes it or not, we're going into Greece and we're going to put an end to those psychopaths."

"That's a bit optimistic," Bob said.

Jack stopped and gave Bob a guilty look. "I'm sorry it's got to be you. I know this is going to be tough on Liz, what with Michael's abduction there years ago."

"I hate to admit it, but don't you think I'm a bit long in the tooth for field work?"

Jack's smile seemed forced. "I know this is irregular, but you know the people, the language, the culture. Plus, you're the most experienced person we've got." He paused. "Yeah, it's optimistic. But I know you can make it happen."

"I'd better call in my team. Then I'll need to go home and make arrangements, pack a bag, and smooth some feathers."

Jack's expression turned sorrowful. "You're going to need more than a bag, Bob," he said. "This is going to be a long-term assignment. You're there until *EA* is out of business."

Bob placed his glass on Jack's desk and started out of the office.

"One other thing," Jack said before Bob reached the door, "I don't care what you have to do to accomplish this mission. We want these sonsofbitches taken down."

"Pretty broad rules of engagement," Bob said. "You wouldn't want to put that in writing?"

Jack laughed. "Good luck, buddy," he said.

CHAPTER THREE
JULY 26, 2004

"Oh, Bob, this can't be happening," Liz said, wiping her hands on a dishtowel and tossing it on the kitchen counter. "You've talked about retiring in a couple of years. They're not supposed to send people in your position into the field."

Bob winced. "You mean people my age."

Liz squinted at Bob. "That, too."

"I can't think of a better way to finish my career at the Agency."

"That's bull," Liz countered, eyes flashing. "This could finish you permanently." She wanted to scream, to curse the Agency, to shout at her husband about his priorities. But she saw the determination on his face. She knew he had a burning need to set things right, to crush evil wherever it occurred. Liz waved her hands in the air as though to signal defeat. She moved against Bob and put her arms around him, burying her head into his neck. She whispered, "Whatever you've got to do, I'll live with it." Then she pulled away for a second and said, "I feel sorry for the stupid bastards you're going after."

Bob wrapped his arms around her. He'd fallen in love with Liz the very first time he'd seen her, and, if anything, his feelings for her had grown with the years. She was still as trim—maybe a bit more rounded in all the right places—as she was when he met her at a college dance in his senior year. Her long blond hair was cut in a bob now, and gray highlights had developed naturally. All in all, he still thought of her as one hot babe.

"I don't think I'll be gone more than a few months," he said.

Liz suddenly jerked away from Bob and glared at him. "What does that mean?"

Bob met his wife's gaze for a moment, but couldn't hold it. "I was just saying—"

Liz jabbed his chest with a finger. "You're telling me you're going to Greece without me; you're leaving me here?"

"This isn't a vacation, Liz. I'm—." The anger in Liz's eyes hit Bob as though daggers had struck him.

"I know it's not a damned vacation," she growled in a menacing tone. "Don't you know anything about me after all these years? Do you really believe I'd let you go halfway across the world without me? I don't like this assignment one bit; but how I feel about it has nothing to do with anything." Tears came to her eyes. "You can be one royal S.O.B., Bob Danforth."

"You're an agency wife," Bob blurted. "You know what's expected of you." He immediately knew he'd made a mistake in lecturing her and tried to gather her in his arms, but she slapped at him and stalked out of the kitchen. He watched her leave the room.

"Aw shit," Bob groaned. He realized he knew better than to pull that old "agency wife" crap on Liz. He had plenty of reasons to feel conflicted about events in his life, but the number one conflict had always been between the role of his job and his role as a husband and parent. He knew Liz and their son had suffered as a result. He shook his head and tried to rationalize his behavior: He had served his country, he had worked on projects vital to America's security, and he had made a difference. But, as true as all that might be, Bob also realized he'd let his family down. Liz wanted more children, but Bob hadn't agreed. He already felt guilty about how little time he had spent with Michael. Liz wanted stability, to live in one community, to make friends and socialize with those friends week after week, year after year. But first the Army and then the CIA had moved them all over the world—thirteen times in thirty-seven years. Most of all, Liz wanted her family to be safe. Bob couldn't even give her that. Michael had been kidnapped as a two-year-old when they were stationed in Greece. Bob nearly lost his life trying to rescue their son then. He and Michael could have been killed in the Balkans when Michael was captured by a Serb SPETSNAZ unit three years ago and Bob joined the rescue effort to bring him back. There was the assassin who nearly murdered Liz, all because of Bob's involvement in a clandestine CIA operation. And then there were all of the assignments in the intervening years where Bob had risked his own life and his wife and son's well-being.

I'll make it up to her, he told himself. This will be it. My last assignment, then I'll put in my papers. But he felt his resolve weaken almost as soon as the thought crossed his mind.

CHAPTER FOUR

JULY 26, 2004

The return trip to Langley took Bob nearly an hour. During the drive, he reflected on the compromise he and Liz had reached. He would fly to Greece without her. As soon as he got settled in and figured out the parameters of his mission, they would set a date when she could join him.

It was 11:00 A.M. when Bob entered the conference room at CIA Headquarters where his team was working. Frank Reynolds, Tanya Serkovic, and Raymond Gallegos had, in a matter of only a few hours, covered most of a eight-foot by four-foot conference table with piles of documents. Each of them was working a laptop computer and a printer was spewing paper. A projector connected to a fourth laptop sat in the center of the table atop a stack of files. Its motor ran, filling the room with a constant *whirring* sound.

"Hey, Chief," Frank said, raising one hand in an abbreviated wave, barely taking his gaze from the computer screen. "We'll be ready with a briefing in about fifteen minutes."

"Anything I can do in the meantime?" Bob asked.

"Sure," Frank said, "you can order some lunch. We haven't had anything but bad coffee since getting together at six this morning."

Bob smiled. Frank was the only guy in the Agency, including the Director, who would treat Bob like an administrative assistant. He meant no disrespect; he was just all business. Bob went to the telephone and placed an order at the cafeteria. Then he took a seat and grabbed a file folder. He'd opened it before he noticed the label: Richard Welch-23 December 1975.

Bob scanned the contents of the file. Richard Welch was the then CIA Station Chief in Athens. He was assassinated on the evening of December 23, 1975 outside his home in Old Psyhiko. According to Welch's wife, a man came up to his car and said, *"Keereeay* Welch?" Welch got out of the car, stood for a moment, and peered at the man standing in the shadows. Suddenly, the man fired three shots at Welch, one of which hit him in the heart, killing him instantly. Two other men accompanied the killer. They all got away. The file included quotes from Welch's wife, Kristina. She mentioned she had seen a suspicious gray car outside their home in the previous few days. They'd received a number of hang-up telephone calls. Concerning the killing of her husband, she was quoted as saying, "He got out of the car because he thought it was a friend. I rushed to him. But he was gone."

Bob thought again about the prudence of Liz joining him in Greece. He put the thought aside. That was a consideration he would have to deal with at another time. Besides, who was he kidding? He'd never win that battle.

The Welch file also included references to how Welch's CIA affiliation had been identified by the killers. The CIA director at the time, William Colby, espoused one hypothesis. He blamed *Counterspy Magazine*, which had published Welch's name several months before his murder. Others claimed Welch's identity had been revealed in a book by Philip Agee, a former CIA Case Officer. One note in the file caught Bob's attention: "We passed evidence to the Greek Government that would have identified Welch's murderers, but the Greeks did nothing about it."

Welch's assassination had occurred twenty-nine years ago. *17 November* claimed responsibility. Since Welch's murder, *Greek Spring* had kept pace with *17 November*. Each group had killed at least twenty-three people and committed at least one hundred violent acts of terror, and yet not one member of either group had ever been arrested or even identified until one of *17 November's* men mishandled a bomb he was placing in Piraeus in 2002.

The words " . . . the Greeks did nothing about it" stuck in Bob's mind as though they'd been laser-stamped there. He didn't want to believe it; but how could terrorist organizations operate for nearly thirty years unless the local authorities were somehow in bed with the groups? Or, at the very least, sympathetic toward them.

After replacing the file, Bob looked around the room at his team. He'd worked with these people on a number of clandestine operations over the last five years. They were as good as any the Agency had.

Forty-seven-year-old Frank Reynolds, a bookish, twenty-four-year CIA veteran, with an IQ in the stratosphere, had spent most of his career with the Agency analyzing message traffic and news reports coming out of the Balkans, Turkey, and Greece. He'd studied Serbo-Croatian, Turkish, and Greek at the Defense Language Institute, West Coast, in Monterey, California, and received his doctorate of Slavic Languages and Literature from the University of California at Berkeley. He knew more about the political systems and parties in the entire region than anyone in the free world. Frank's wiry salt and pepper hair, as usual, looked as though it had never known a comb. The man was banging at his computer keyboard as though he was trying to see how much punishment it could take.

Forty-years-old and thirty pounds overweight, Tanya Serkovic wore loose-fitting, grandmotherly dresses, but had a fire burning in her eyes that was anything but grandmotherly. She had thick, shoulder-length black hair and exotic Slavic features, with a trace of Oriental blood showing in the shape of her mesmerizing violet-colored eyes. A Bosnian expert in Eastern European Languages, and also fluent in Greek and Italian, she'd witnessed the genocide committed by the Serbs against her people, fought with the Bosnian resistance, and fled to the United States when Serb hit-squads were sent to assassinate her.

Raymond Gallegos was thirty-eight-years-old and had the dark good looks of a Latin movie star and the intelligence of a nuclear physicist. A highly decorated Army veteran, he'd earned his Bachelors and Masters degrees in Geography after a tour in the Gulf War, and spent seven years with the National Security Agency as a cartography consultant, before moving to the CIA. He was familiar with every part of Southern Europe the way most people know their own neighborhoods.

Finally, Frank huffed a loud stream of air, flung himself back against his chair, and rubbed his fingers against his scalp as though he was on a search and seizure mission for an evasive thought. "That's it," he exclaimed, "I'm ready. How about you guys?"

Tanya nodded and said, "For now."

Raymond sighed. "I've got a ton of stuff I still need to go through; but what I've read so far should give us a broad brush picture."

Bob was about to tell them to proceed, when a loud knock sounded. Raymond went to the door and let a worker from the cafeteria bring in a wheeled cart of food. The man pushed the cart to a corner, told Raymond to call when they were done, and quietly exited. It took the team a couple of minutes to create sandwiches from the cold cuts on the cart. Then, while everyone else took their seats, Frank flipped off the overhead lights, turned on the projector, returned to his chair, and picked up a remote control device.

A long list of dates, accompanied by a column of names and another column of terrorist acts popped up on the screen. At the top of the list, across the columns, were typed "23 December 1975," "Richard Welch, CIA Station Chief Athens," and "Killed by *17 November*." At the bottom of the list were Harvey Cornwell and Fred Grantham's names, along with the date "26 July 2004" beside each. The words "Killed by" with a "?" filled the last column on the line.

"You can see from this list that *17 November* and *Greek Spring* have committed four dozen murders since 1975," Frank noted.

Bob scanned the list. In addition to the nine Americans the two terrorist groups had killed, there were other foreign diplomats, Greek Parliament members, Greek prosecutors, Greek drivers of political and military figures, and innocent bystanders.

"But look what happens to the list," Frank continued, "when we add all of the incidents which involve injury, but not death, for which the groups have claimed responsibility."

Frank hit the remote again. A second list showed on the screen. The Greek terrorists had proved themselves to be world class when it came to the number of attacks they claimed as their own.

Bob shook his head. The number of incidents perpetrated by the terrorists were too many to believe that not one member of any of the groups had ever been identified by Greek authorities. If it hadn't been for a fluke, *17 November* would still be operating. He was about to express this thought, when Tanya said, "Check out the next list."

Frank again touched the remote and another list showed on the screen. There appeared to be at least fifty incidents listed there. Bombings, shootings, acts of arson, and rocket attacks directed against American business establishments: McDonalds Restaurants, Citibank offices, the Apple Computer office, Chrysler and General Motors dealerships, etc.

"Something stinks about this," Bob said.

"To high heaven," Raymond added. "You can see that *17 November* and *Greek Spring* have been the most active of the groups; but they're not the only terrorist organizations operating in Athens."

Another list came on the screen. Raymond pointed and said, "This is a summary, in chronological order, of all terrorist acts committed in Athens since 1975. You can see in the third column that *Greek Spring* has claimed responsibility for the majority of the events. But there are a bunch of other terror groups working the Athens area: *Friendship Society*—how about that for a name for a group of cold-blooded killers, *Red Line, Rigas Feraios, Revolutionary Subversive Faction, Greek Revolutionary Nuclei, Greek Fighting Guerrilla Faction, ELA, Nihilist Faction, Anti-Establishment Nuclei, Class War Group, People's Rage, People's Revolutionary Solidarity,* and *Greek Anti-Military Struggle.* At least two of the incidents are blamed on the international terrorist Carlos and ten or so of the incidents couldn't be pinned on any particular group."

"So, we've got more to deal with here than the *Greek Spring* loonies," Bob said.

"That's putting it mildly," Frank said.

"I don't know," Tanya interjected, as she left her chair, switched on the lights, and began pacing the room.

The men watched her circle the table. Bob knew that Frank and Raymond, like himself, had learned to respect Tanya's instincts. She finally came to a stop and looked at Bob.

"I think there are at least several dynamics at work here. First, notice there has never been more than one terrorist act committed on a particular day. If all of the groups that Raymond mentioned have been working independently since 1975, wouldn't you expect that, on at least one occasion, two of the groups would have pulled off something on the same day. Hell, if there were that many groups operating in Athens at any one time, they would have been stumbling all over one another."

She hesitated and stared at Bob. When he nodded, she continued. "I'll bet, at least in some of the cases, the members of *Greek Spring* called in the name of a fictitious terrorist group to confuse the authorities."

"That's a hell of an assumption, considering you don't have any evidence," Raymond said.

Tanya shrugged and returned to stand behind her chair. "The sheer number of active groups raises suspicion."

"Based on the Greek Government's performance since Richard Welch's murder, confusing the authorities wouldn't have been too difficult," Frank said. "The kindest thing you can say about the Greek terrorism investigation is it has been incompetent."

Tanya began pacing again. When she stopped this time, there was fire in her eyes. "There's got to be a whole lot more to it than incompetence," she blurted.

The hairs on the back of Bob's neck seemed electrified. He'd already considered what he thought Tanya was referring to, and that consideration made him sick. He knew there had been deep-seated anger, even hatred among many Greeks against the West ever since the CIA had orchestrated the overthrow of the Greek Government in 1967 and installed a Military Government under George Papadopoulos. The Military Government was itself overthrown in 1974 and Konstantinos Karamanlis came to power. In 1981, Andreas Papandreou, head of the PASOK Party, the Panhellenic Socialist Movement, became Prime Minister. Many in the CIA, as well as in Greece, believed that *17 November* and *Greek Spring's* memberships had come from the same anti-Military Government student organizations that also gave birth to the modern PASOK party. Bob let his suspicions ferment as he waited for Tanya to continue.

"Frank, put up the next slide," Tanya ordered, as she shut off the lights once again.

The top of the slide read:

> Article by R. Jeffrey Smith, Washington Post Foreign Service
> November 3, 1999; Page A30

The newspaper article followed.

"Look at the highlighted sections," Tanya said. "The first one makes it pretty damned clear that, despite pressure from the United States, some Greek political and security officials don't share our goal of bringing the members of groups like *Greek Spring* to justice." She then quoted from the article: " . . . *some within the Greek Government may have sought to preserve its anonymity, possibly to hide past links to the organization by top Greek officials.*

"We've got dozens of statements from U.S. officials who feel that arrests of terrorists have been blocked by the local government," Tanya said.

"Anything else?" Bob asked.

"Yeah," Raymond said. "There's plenty of evidence that the Greek police have conducted their investigations into terrorist crimes in an *interesting* fashion."

"For example," Bob said.

"A senior police officer on the scene of a shooting gave the expended shell casing to a reporter as a souvenir. Investigations are short-lived, and the police bend to political pressure and don't dig too deeply."

"Not to mention the fact that there are supposed links between the terrorists and members of the ruling left-wing PASOK party," Tanya added.

"Any of this resonate with you?" Frank asked.

Bob blew out a loud breath and rubbed his hands on his face. "It's hard to argue against the accusation that these terrorists are being protected. One of the things I observed when I was stationed in Greece in the seventies was that there didn't seem to be too many secrets. Gossip is a national sport. How these bastards could have operated in Athens for all these years without a single one of them coming under suspicion is beyond me."

Bob swiveled in his chair and faced Tanya, who had turned on the lights and retaken her seat. "Is it your theory that *17 November* and *Greek Spring* are the only active terror groups in Athens?"

"No, no," Tanya said, "that's not what I meant. I suspect there are several groups in Greece. I also suspect that some of the members of *Greek Spring,* for instance, belong to other terrorist groups. I just don't believe that all the groups claiming responsibility for terrorist acts really exist as independent organizations."

"There's another problem," Frank added. "We know that none of the *EA* group have been identified; but even if they were to be, getting them convicted is problematical. When a terrorist is captured and indicted, pressure immediately builds from leftist members of Parliament, lawyers, and journalists. The judge often yields and the accused are acquitted."

Frank searched a pile of documents in front of him and pulled out a sheet of paper. "There have been several instances where judges, prosecutors, and jurors' cars have been fire bombed. Defendants have been acquitted with no legal basis. The largest Greek newspapers belong to the Left. They often describe murders committed by terrorists as 'legal executions.'"

Bob raised his hands. "Okay, okay, I get the point."

"What now, Chief?" Tanya asked.

Bob thought a moment. "Tanya, characterize the investigations for me, in addition to the incompetence of the Greek police."

"There doesn't appear to be a central authority that has consolidated the information from each of the murders. No psychological profiling has been done. The only obvious common element associated with many of the executions for which *Greek Spring* has claimed responsibility is the same .45 caliber pistol."

"So, we've got a group of terrorists running around Athens murdering people, the Greek ruling party appears to be protecting them, and it is highly unlikely we're going to get a lot of cooperation from anyone in the Greek Government. Does that about sum it up?" Bob looked at each of the members of his team, in turn.

Tanya and Raymond nodded. Frank said, "This is going to be one nasty sonofabitch."

Tanya cleared her throat. "Well, there is one piece of good news," she said. "Now that England has lost two of its own, it'll throw the full weight of the British lion at the problem. We know the Brits won't follow the Marquis of Queensbury rules. They know how to deal with this sort of problem better than we do."

"That's because they don't have to answer to the U.S. Congress," Raymond said.

"One other thing," Frank said. "There's an FBI counter-terrorism team operating in Athens. You'll have to coordinate with them."

"The FEEBs," Tanya said, with a mischievous smile. "You know how the boys and girls at the FBI love to work with us Agency types."

Bob groaned.

CHAPTER FIVE

JULY 27, 2004

Giorgos Photos stretched his long arms over his head in an attempt to loosen the stress-knotted muscles in his back and shoulders. He was tempted to look in the mirror on the living room wall, but decided what he saw there wouldn't be good for his morale. He knew he looked older than his fifty-nine years. His posture was stooped and his unruly hair was as dry as straw and as gray as the sweater he wore. He allowed himself a moment of indulgence and wondered where all of this would lead him. When his comrades in *17 November* shot the CIA Station Chief outside the man's home in Old Psyhiko twenty-nine years ago, they'd started something he thought might bring down the Greek Government. Something that would lead to Greece becoming a Marxist state. That hadn't happened. But he hadn't given up the cause, despite the fact that he amassed a fortune from the robberies his group had pulled off and from the "grants" his benefactors from abroad had bestowed upon him. He had long ago reconciled personal wealth with trying to impose a Marxist regime on Greece. He and *Greek Spring*—he'd come up with the name because spring stood for rebirth, a new beginning—had killed their enemies at the rate of about one per year since then, and they'd engendered fear. However, he was feeling old now. Terrorism was a young man's occupation.

As he dropped his arms to his side, he turned and looked at the clock hanging on the wall above the sofa. Savvas Krinon should be here any moment now, he thought. He started to walk to the kitchen, when three knocks on the door sounded, followed by a pause, and then two knocks. He quickly went to the kitchen table and picked up the .38-caliber pistol. He padded back across the apartment to the door, removed the chain, and unlocked the deadbolt. He retreated three paces and shouted, "Come in!"

The door opened a few inches and a man called through the space, "Take it easy, it's me, Savvas."

Photos recognized Savvas' voice. But he kept the pistol leveled at the door. He hadn't survived this long by being careless.

Thirty-year-old Savvas Krinon entered the third floor apartment off Athens' Kolonaki Square. Krinon walked with a jaunty step. He moved and looked as cocky as Photos knew the man to be. His dirty-blond hair, shorn short to stand on end in a gelled butch cut, punctuated his brutish, compact build. His clothes—white Polo shirt, black slacks, and black Italian loafers—were stylish and expensive-looking. Photos met Krinon in the middle of the sitting room and embraced him.

"Two for the price of one," Photos said. "The CIA Station Chief and the top MI-6 agent in Greece. Savvas, you've made us proud. Someday you will be recognized by the entire Greek nation for your courage."

"Thank you, Giorgos. I am honored that you picked me to . . . complete this mission."

Photos released Krinon, tucked the pistol in the back of his belt, and walked toward a corner of the room. Krinon followed. Photos moved aside a heavy curtain hanging on a wooden bar suspended over the entrance to an alcove the size of a Pullman kitchen. The two men entered the tiny room. Krinon let the curtain drop behind them, while Photos switched on a radio on a small table by the right wall. He cranked up the volume on the old Sony receiver until it was loud enough to cover their voices.

A red pennant hung on the back wall. At its center, "EA" was emblazoned in red in the middle of a gold star. Faded photographs of Karl Marx and Vladimir Lenin bracketed the pennant. Below it was a picture of Che Guevara. Half-a-dozen rocket propelled grenades, a grenade launcher, ammunition for a variety of weapons, several pistols, and an AK-47 assault rifle rested in one corner.

Photos and Krinon sat in front of the radio, their straight-backed wooden chairs only inches apart.

"Any problems?" Photos asked, leaning so close to Krinon that, even with the radio blaring, he barely had to speak above a whisper.

"Nothing." Krinon snapped his fingers to indicate how easy everything went. "Pavlos brought the motorbike right up to the driverside door. A child could have offed the Englishman." Krinon laughed and added, "I was so close, I thought about tapping on the car window before shooting; you know, to see the surprise on his face."

Photos felt a sudden jolt of alarm. He knew Krinon liked killing. His bloodlust was a bigger motivator for him than the group's mission. The man also loved to take chances, a risk junky. That could become a serious liability for everyone in *Greek Spring*. He would have to keep an eye on this loose cannon.

Krinon must have noticed a change in the leader's expression. He quickly covered, saying, "Don't worry, I took care of business." He spread his hands and added, "How do the Americans say it? As easy as one-two-three." He laughed again.

"What weapon did you use?"

Krinon smiled like a kid at Christmas. He patted the bulge in his jacket. "Our most faithful friend for all these years: the .45, of course."

Photos nodded. He looked away from Krinon and stared at his Marxist-Leninist shrine for a moment. He started *Greek Spring* nearly three decades ago, espousing the Marxist-Leninism he had studied and embraced so many years earlier in Paris. That dogma had become as irrelevant as the donkey cart. It was nationalism that resonated with the Greek people, and that was how he now justified to the media and the Greek people *Greek Spring's* actions, and how he maintained his power base.

"Okay, Savvas, I want you to stay out of sight for awhile. Go back to your icon painting. Play the good citizen." Photos stood and patted him on the shoulder. "I'll be in touch."

After Krinon left, Photos moved stiffly to the kitchen table and rifled through a three-inch stack of notes and articles, putting aside information he would use to prepare the communiqué he would send to his favorite newspaper. A warm feeling went through him. *Eleeneekee Aneexee, Greek Spring,* included twenty-five members; but it had the influence of a much larger organization, thanks to its friends in the media and the government. Life was good, Photos thought, especially with the millions of dollars he had accumulated from the robberies the group had pulled off and from the "investments" his supporters in Iran, Iraq, Syria, France, and many other countries had sent him. Yes, life was good.

CHAPTER SIX

JULY 27, 2004

Jack Cole waved at Bob Danforth's secretary as he breezed by her desk and opened the door to Bob's office.

Bob was standing behind his desk, packing up the last of the files in a pouch for shipment to Greece.

"You all set?" Jack asked.

"Yeah. I'd be a lot better prepared if I had a few more days, but . . . ."

"I'm sorry about you having to be the one to go over there."

Bob shrugged. "Our's not to reason why." He pointed at a cell phone lying on the edge of his desk. "The boys and girls in TSD brought that up. It's equipped with an encryption device that will allow us to talk between here and Greece on a real-time basis, without our having to worry about someone with big ears listening in."

"The guys in Technical Service Division get more James Bond-like every day. I—"

Frank Reynolds burst into the office, cutting off Jack. Frank nodded at Jack, then walked up to Bob and handed him a file. "You should see this."

Bob plopped into his chair and began going through the file. After a minute, he tossed it in the center of his desk and glared at Frank.

Frank pointed at the file and said, "Five pages of bullshit. That's what those *Greek Spring* psychopaths sent to their buddies at the newspaper in Greece." He reached for the file and opened it. "They claim they killed Fred Grantham and Harvey Cornwell for their roles in, and I quote, 'the planning of the barbaric air strikes against Serbia and the invasion of Iraq.'" Frank looked at Bob, then at Jack, and continued, "This crap is nothing but a regurgitation of the articles and editorials that the Greek newspapers have been spouting for two years: the attack on Iraq was part of Great Britain and the United States' desire for world domination, that Saddam never committed atrocities against his own people, that the English and Americans targeted civilians in Iraq. Everything in this release has already been spewed by the Greek press, even by some of Greece's leading government officials."

"You've got your work cut out for you over there, Bob," Jack said. "You're going to have a tough time figuring out who to trust."

CHAPTER SEVEN

JULY 28, 2004

The banshee-like whine of the plane's lowering landing gear startled Bob awake. He'd preset his watch to Athens time and saw it was
8:00 A.M. Tuesday morning. The view outside invigorated him, awak-
ening a warm feeling inside. The azure, sparkling waters of the
Aegean always had that effect on him. How could such a beautiful
country, with such an inspiring history, be so screwed up as to have
terrorists running around killing people in its capital?

Bob reflected on his conversation with Liz at Dulles Airport terminal
before he boarded the plane. He'd suggested she change her mind
about coming to Greece. He'd told her he would be working day and
night and wouldn't have a lot of time to spend with her. "So, what else
is new? I'm used to your obsessive schedule," she'd responded. "I would
rather you ignore me in Greece, where I can keep an eye on you."

He'd reminded her it would be dangerous being with him. She'd
scoffed at the implication she should be afraid. Bob hadn't wanted to
get into an argument with Liz; but his instincts told him he was making
a mistake allowing her to join him in Greece. But, once again, he
reminded himself that if he told her not to come to Greece, she would
come anyway. The sweet, innocent girl he had married in the sixties had
long ago turned into one tough cookie. The thought made him smile
while he collected his carry-on and started down the aircraft aisle.

Bob claimed his luggage, went through Customs, and fast-walked
through the airport's open doors. The smell of the sea mixed with the
stink of gasoline fumes comprised his inaugural breath of Athens' air.
He suspected the stench of air pollution would get a lot worse as he

approached the center of the city. Bob spotted the white Ford Taurus he'd been told would pick him up and walked toward it.

A man perched on the front fender, wearing light-brown loafers, tan Dockers, a yellow Polo shirt, and a blue blazer, sprang forward and said in a low voice, "I'm Tony Fratangelo. Welcome to Athens, Mr. Danforth. I recognized you from your photograph."

"Good to meet you," Bob said. He shook Fratangelo's hand, then opened the car's back door and tossed in his bag and briefcase. He closed the door and slipped into the front passenger seat.

Fratangelo, a mid-thirties, olive-complected, jet-black-haired guy who appeared to be built for speed, jumped behind the wheel. He dropped the transmission into drive and pulled away from the curb.

"Thanks for picking me up," Bob said. "Anything new on Grantham and Cornwell's murders?"

"You saw the release the killers sent to the newspaper?"

Bob nodded.

"That's it, so far; except ballistics tests showed the weapon used by the killer was the same .45 pistol that *Greek Spring* has used on a number of their hits."

Bob was aware of the terrorist group's preference for using the .45 pistol for close-up murders. The weapon had become a signature of sorts. But he also suspected the repeated use of the weapon was the terrorists' way of tweaking the authorities' noses. Pure theater, he thought. "Where have you set up shop?" Bob asked.

"The office is in a station safehouse in a low-rise in Glyfada. Actually a large apartment. We wanted to get a safe distance from the embassy and other government facilities. We've got an office for you, a bullpen area for the team, a conference room, and three bedrooms for those nights when we can't get home. One of them is yours." Fratangelo snorted. "It's got a great view of the sea. It's like being a kid in a candy store; but your parents won't let you have even one little piece. I've been in the country three months and have yet to be able to take my son to the beach."

Bob looked over at Fratangelo, wondering if the Agency had assigned a whiner to him. But the man was smiling; the expression on his face showed he had merely stated a fact and wasn't bitching about it. Bob smiled back. "We catch these killers," he said, "and I'll see that you get a month on one of the islands."

Fratangelo deftly moved the Taurus into traffic outside the airport and goosed the accelerator to merge into the left lane. Bob was amazed Fratangelo was able to make the maneuver without making contact with the car behind them. Apparently the driver of that car felt the same. Bob looked back and saw the driver shoot an arm out his window, flashing Fratangelo the palm of his hand—the Greek equivalent of giving someone the finger. Some things never change, Bob thought.

"I understand Langley didn't inform the Greek Government you were coming here," Fratangelo said.

"They'll know I'm here soon enough, right after I meet with the Greek Prime Minister and the Minister of Public Order. That's one of the reasons I declined a NOC. I figured I wouldn't really need a non-official cover." Bob suspected that once the top echelons of the Greek Government learned he was in town, the word would spread throughout the government hierarchy. There were too many people in the Greek Government who were sympathetic to *Greek Spring* and other terrorist groups. He could become a target for the terrorists. His movements would more than likely be observed in and around Athens. He would have to be armed at all times. Or, in the alternative, he could talk to the CIA Office of Security at the American Embassy to see about getting a couple guys assigned to watch his back. Normally, he wouldn't move around a city like Athens with a weapon; he would let the security people do their jobs. But this assignment was different. He didn't want to feel encumbered with guards; he needed the flexibility of being able to move at a moment's notice. "But, I'd like to have a few days before I have to start looking over my shoulder," he told Tony.

"I can't figure out why any Greek would support these bastards," Fratangelo said. "Hell, they've murdered Greeks, as well as non-Greeks."

"Maybe we'll figure that out, too," Bob said.

The two men rode in silence for a minute, until Bob said, "Tell me about our team." He already knew all their names and their backgrounds; but he wanted to get a man-on-the-ground's view.

"Three of us, including me. Sam Goodwin and Stacey Frederick are attached to the embassy. Sam's been the Commercial Attaché for six years. Knows everyone and can quote chapter and verse on every damned politician and successful businessman in Greece. Stacey's been on the ambassador's staff for about eighteen months. Both speak fluent Greek and are well connected. They've been assigned to our team until *Greek Spring* is brought down."

"You've been here just a short time, right?" Bob asked, recalling that Fratangelo was working for a CIA front called Hellenic Cultural & Historical Society.

"Three months. I'm just beginning to find my way around the city."

"You studied Greek at DLI."

"Forty-seven weeks. It was a killer."

Bob empathized with Fratangelo's statement. He'd attended the Defense Language Institute's rigorous Greek language course in Monterey, California, as a U.S. Army Captain in the early seventies, before being assigned to Greece.

"How about the English team?"

"Stanton Markeson's been here for twenty years. Married a Greek gal who's quite a bit younger than he is. Everyone thinks he's a spoiled, rich Englishman who's never worked a day in his life. He's rich, all right, but there's nothing spoiled about him. Former commando with lots of medals, I hear. Hobnobs with the Greek shipping

set and throws the best damned parties around. The guy's about fifty
and looks sixty. Paunchy, aged party boy. Don't let his looks fool you,
though. Behind his boozy exterior, he's as tough as any longshoreman
is and as sharp as any Philadelphia lawyer.

"The head of their team, guy named Rodney Townsend, has been
in Greece for a couple months. Assigned to the British Embassy,
counter-terrorism type, old school, and all that," Fratangelo said,
feigning an upper-class English accent. "He's a hard case. Plenty arrogant and thinks of the U.S. as a British colony. Can't blame him for
looking down on us in one respect. The way we've handled this
whole terrorist business, at least up until 9-11. The other two Brits just
arrived yesterday. I barely met them last night. Names are Cyril
Bridewell and Marcus Swinton. They look like commando types.
Muscled up with scary eyes. We might as well put a sign on each of
them saying British Agent. They're not going to fool anybody."

"We going to be able to work with these people?" Bob asked.

Fratangelo shrugged. "They all appear to be pros; but there's no
way we're going to avoid turf battles. And don't think they give a
damn about any of the victims other than the Brits. They're here
because of the murders of the two Englishmen. As you know,
Saunders and Cornwell are the only Englishmen the terrorists have
killed." Fratangelo hesitated a moment, then added, "I've got a feeling the terrorists screwed up big time when they murdered the
Englishmen. I'm glad to have them working with us. They won't have
to operate under the same restrictions the politicians in Washington
have placed on the Agency. Those terrorist bastards have murdered
nine Americans, and, basically, all we've done is appeal to the Greek
Government to find the murderers. This isn't a diplomatic matter,
despite what the State Department thinks. This is war. It's time we
reacted accordingly."

Bob didn't respond to Fratangelo's speech, but he liked what he
said and the passion with which he said it. He agreed with him, too.

The U.S. had basically ignored the growing terrorist threat all over the globe until September 11, 2001. The way the Americans had reacted for years to terrorist attacks had only emboldened the terrorists. The only real counterstrike the U.S. had executed was the bombing of Khadafi's compound in Libya after terrorists had bombed a nightclub in Germany, killing several American servicemen. Bob had been horrified by a lot of the actions or inaction of American presidents; but the one step he'd been most concerned about was the Clinton Administration putting pressure on the Israelis to release Arab prisoners who had committed terrorist acts against Israel. The President had wanted to broker a peace accord between the Israelis and the Palestinians, and felt the only way to get the Palestinians to the bargaining table was to obtain the release of Arab prisoners. Israel had agreed to release all prisoners, except those who had committed acts of violence against Israelis. The President had pressured Israel to release all prisoners, including some who later participated in the attacks on the World Trade Center. Bob had a feeling deep in his gut that others of the most violent of these former prisoners would be heard from again.

Bob had Tony Fratangelo drive him to the American Embassy and told him to wait outside. By the time he finished meeting with the American ambassador, it was almost noon and he was feeling the effects of jet lag. His meeting had gone well. Ambassador Finch was a professional diplomat, not a political appointee who had received his position based on how much money he'd raised for a President's reelection campaign. Bob liked the man.

From the embassy, Fratangelo drove Bob to the building in Glyfada housing the CIA's special ops offices. As they pulled to the curb in front of the building, Bob looked across the street at the sparkling Aegean waters and remembered the weekends he, Liz, and Michael had spent at the Glyfada beach so many years ago. As he reflected on those days, he once again reminded himself that those weekends were too few and far between. He'd worked too damned many Saturdays and Sundays when he should have been with his family. He'd been totally committed to his Army career, and what had it gotten him? Discharged for sneaking into Bulgaria to try to rescue his son from a Communist orphanage.

"You okay, Mr. Danforth?" Fratangelo asked.

"Oh, sorry," Bob said, "just daydreaming." Bob got out of the car and followed Fratangelo inside the building.

In the office, Fratangelo made the introductions. The four then sat around the conference room table. Bob eyed the two men and one woman.

"We've got a very important job to do," he said, "and I can't do it alone. Sam, Stacey, Tony, your knowledge of the local community and its people, your contacts, and your Intelligence training and experience are going to make the difference. What I bring to the table are contacts at Langley. Anything we need, we get. Understand? This is a high priority mission. We're all here for the duration. We get the terrorists, we go home. That's it, plain and simple. Any questions?"

The three team members looked at one another. Bob could see they had questions, but there was silent jockeying going on between them to see who would go first. Finally, Sam Goodwin cleared his throat.

Goodwin was a very old-looking thirty-nine year old. His gray hair showed only tinges of its former yellow color. His deeply lined face and sallow coloring evidenced an unwell man. Bob knew the Agency could have that effect on its Case Officers. Too much stress, too much danger, too much bureaucratic bullshit, too much alcohol. Goodwin's personnel file had included nothing but glowing reports. Apparently, if he had any health problems, they hadn't affected his performance.

"You know the ruling party here looks at us as though we're the enemy, not the terrorists," Goodwin said. "The government's not going to cooperate with us in this investigation. What can we do about that?"

Sam's question seemed to break down Tony and Stacey's inertia. They followed with one question after another as quickly as Bob could offer answers. Bob could see the frustration that had built up in the three.

"Whoa, everybody," he said, raising his hands to get them to slow down. He smiled and added, "It's nice to see that passion isn't going to be a problem. I met with our ambassador before coming here. I presented him with the mission statement that Langley developed. The mission has been signed off on by the Secretary of State, the Director, the President's National Security Advisor, and the President himself." Bob paused to see their reaction. His mention of the President seemed to impress them.

"The ambassador has already scheduled a meeting for me with the Greek Prime Minister for the first thing Friday morning, August 6. Here's what's going to happen—at least what I'm pretty damned sure is going to happen—after the meeting on Friday. The Greek Government is going to turn over copies of every investigation file on every single terrorist incident of the last thirty years." He smiled again. "Your frustration over lack of cooperation from the Greeks is going to turn into frustration over being knee-deep in paper." He could see both hope and skepticism on their faces. "The next thing that's going to happen is we're going to share the information we get with the FBI Counter-Terrorism and the British teams. Once they go through the files, they'll start interrogating every victim who's still alive, family members of victims, prosecutors, and cops involved with the terrorist cases. Everyone from sponge divers to streetwalkers."

"Why turn over the interviews to the FBI and the Brits?" Stacey asked.

"Because that's not our job," Bob answered, "and that's not the best use of our time. The budget on this is unrestricted. What we're going to do is pave the streets of Athens with American dollars. We're going to build a network of informants in this city which will ultimately turn over information about some member of *Greek Spring,* or of one of the other groups. All we need is one name. As with *17 November,* one captured terrorist will bring down an entire organization."

"Unrestricted budget?" Fratangelo asked, more than a little skepticism in his tone.

Bob raised his right hand for a couple seconds, as though he was taking an oath. "Like you, I've gotten used to operating with steadily declining budgets. Congress cut our funds back for years, for decades. The politicians have degraded our ability to wage war in the Intelligence trenches. First, the Church Committee, then the Carter Administration, and nearly every Congress over the last twenty years has taken the position that it is unethical and/or illegal for the U.S. Intelligence community to put operatives in the field. Every one of us knows that the best way to gather Intelligence is to get down in the gutter with the operatives on the other side. The absence of U.S. agents and informants has, in part, allowed groups like *Greek Spring, the Red Brigade, the Bader Meinhof Gang, Al Qaeda, Abu Nidal,* and many others to terrorize the world. As far as we're concerned, that has all changed."

Bob's speech raised the eyebrows and appeared to raise the spirits of the team members. After answering their questions, Bob said, "Let's meet here tomorrow afternoon at three." Then he moved toward his office, while asking, "Tony, can you get me Rodney Townsend's telephone number?"

Bob dialed the number for the British team's offices. When he was put through to Townsend, he arranged to meet him at a restaurant in the Plaka—the old part of Athens, just below the Acropolis—at 1:00 the next afternoon. Based on the Englishman's short and unfriendly tone, Bob guessed he was in for an uphill battle in trying to get the man's cooperation.

Tony drove Bob to the Grand Bretagne Hotel at the end of the day. The drive from Glyfada took them along the beach, bracketed by sea and sand on the left and shops and high-rise residential buildings on the right. Bob commented on the amount of traffic and the wall-to-wall buildings. "If I didn't know this was Athens, I would swear I had landed in Mexico City. I can't believe what a difference three decades can make. There were about one million people in Athens when I lived here before."

Fratangelo laughed. "There's four million today, and that doesn't include the immigrants from places like Albania, which the Greeks have no way of counting."

Fratangelo turned onto a main boulevard that led slightly uphill toward the center of town. The Acropolis, wreathed in a smog cloak, sat majestically, high above the city. They drove for a minute in silence while Bob absorbed the sights.

Fratangelo's cell phone suddenly chirped. He frowned, flipped it open, and blurted a curt "Yes." He listened for a minute, a smile now showing on his face, and said, "I'll see you in twenty minutes." After closing the phone and slipping it back into his shirt pocket, he said, "That was my wife," he said. "Okay if we pick her up; it's on our way."

"No problem," Bob said. "Where is she?"

"On Vassileas Sofias Boulevard; near the Hilton. She had a doctor's appointment."

Bob laid his head against the headrest and closed his eyes. He just wanted to rest for a moment. He was surprised and a little embarrassed when Fratangelo's voice woke him. He pointed up the boulevard. "About fifty yards up the way. There they are by that tree."

Bob rubbed his face. His eyes burned from lack of sleep and pollution. Squinting against the smog-filtered brightness of the sun, he looked up the block and saw a pregnant woman seated on a two-foot-high wall, her back against thick wrought iron bars rising from the top of the wall to a height of about ten feet. As they approached the spot where the woman sat, Bob noticed that strands of her straw-berry-blond hair stuck to her forehead and her face was so red she appeared to be sunburned. A little boy of about six, wearing shorts and a T-shirt, moved in front of her, making a valiant effort to catch one of the fifty or so pigeons strutting around the sidewalk, curb, and gutter pecking at whatever it was pigeons seemed to find of interest in the dirt. The boy had braces on both legs and was on crutches. He walked in a straight, splayed-legged manner that made his pigeon hunting problematical.

Fratangelo honked the car horn, eased up to the curb, and started to get out of the car; but the woman raised her hand, as though to tell him to stay put. She flashed a radiant smile at Fratangelo, pushed off the wall with obvious difficulty, and shepherded the little boy in front of her toward the car.

When they had climbed into the backseat, Fratangelo made the introductions. "This is Mr. Danforth." He turned to Bob and said, "My wife, Michelle, and my son, Andrew."

"Achilles, Daddy," the boy shouted. "My name is Achilles."

"Oh, I forgot," Fratangelo said, winking at Bob. "This is my son Achilles."

"Good to meet you, Michelle," Bob said, as he twisted around enough to look the woman in the eye. He then looked at the little boy and said, "It's nice to meet you, too, Achilles." Bob turned back to Michelle and added, "My name's Bob."

She smiled at him. "Welcome to Athens."

Then Fratangelo asked, "Michelle, what did the doctor say?"

But before she could respond, the boy said in a high-pitched, astonishingly loud voice," Are you my daddy's new boss?"

"I guess I am," Bob answered, turning again to look at the boy. "Is that okay with you?"

Andrew held Bob's gaze for a few seconds, then nodded and said, "Only if you tell him to not work too much. Daddy works all the time."

"Oh jeez," Michelle sighed.

Bob laughed. "I don't know if I can promise that, An . . . Achilles. You know your daddy has a very important job." As soon as the words rolled off his tongue, Bob felt guilty. He knew he would work Tony Fratangelo long hours and long days, the same way he always worked himself. And, as a result, this young father would ignore his family the same way Bob had ignored Liz and Michael.

The boy was scowling now.

Finally, Bob said, "I'll see what I can do." But from the look on the boy's face, he could see the kid didn't believe a word of it.

CHAPTER EIGHT

JULY 28, 2004

Stavros Theodorakis' heart quickened. He was afraid that his face showed his excitement. It felt hot. He glanced around at the other workers and, when he was satisfied no one was watching him, ran his hands through his thick black hair. He quickly snatched his handkerchief from his back trouser pocket and mopped away the perspiration that had popped out on his forehead and on his upper lip.

Every day for the past seven years, he had performed his job as a clerk at the Ministry of Justice with a pathological attention to detail. His work ethic distinguished him from the drones in the ministry. Stavros looked around the large room, with its fourteen desks, gray-painted concrete floor, and glaring fluorescent lighting and felt only contempt for his fellow workers. Unlike them, he never left his office to go home until he had completed his daily tasks. Despite standing out among the other clerks in the office, Stavros had never been offered a promotion. His co-workers and supervisor considered him a boring, nitpicking little man who didn't have the personality or the imagination to move up.

Stavros had come to the conclusion that his co-workers' opinions of him were not too far from reality. He *was* boring; there was nothing remarkable about his appearance, his personality, or his place in the world. Only his cousin, Demetrios Mavroyianni, made Stavros feel important. Demetrios had handed him the key to the door that would allow him to periodically escape his pedestrian existence.

The Greek Government mandated that all passenger manifests for all flights entering Greece be electronically transmitted to the Greek

Ministry of Justice no later than one hour after the flight's departure for Greece. This meant that hundreds of these passenger lists arrived in Stavros Theodorakis' computer every day. Mondays were particularly onerous, because Stavros had to deal with all the manifests that had accumulated over the weekend. But Wednesdays, like today, weren't bad.

Loaded on Stavros' office computer were a myriad of reference software programs from Greek law enforcement and Intelligence agencies, Interpol, British MI-6, the CIA, the FBI, and a dozen other such organizations. It was Stavros' job to compare the names on the passenger manifests against these software programs to try to identify criminals or terrorists who might enter Greece, and to report any match to the ministry's Criminal Investigation Division. The programs not only included the real names of the criminals and terrorists, but also their known aliases. Unfortunately, most matches would be made after the criminal had already landed at the airport and melted into the Athens population. But the authorities figured it was better than nothing.

No one in Stavros' department knew he had also loaded on his computer the names of hundreds of agents and thousands of run-of-the-mill employees of Intelligence services from the United States, Britain, France, Germany, Turkey, Israel, and many other countries. These names had been provided to Stavros by his cousin, Demetrios, who had let it slip one time, after too many *ouzos*, that many of the names had come from a former CIA Case Officer. The list of names had been updated periodically from sources in France, Germany, the Middle East, and, especially, from Demetrios' many contacts inside the Greek Ministries of Justice and of Public Order.

Every so often, Stavros matched a name on a flight manifest against one of the legitimate lists in his computer. In the case of a common criminal, Stavros was diligent about immediately reporting the match to his supervisor. As far as terrorists were concerned, Stavros cleared any matches with Demetrios first. Sometimes, Demetrios told him to bury the information. But what Stavros was most interested in finding was a match between a passenger on a flight list with a name on his secret software program. That had just happened.

"Demetrios," Stavros said jauntily into his telephone, "are we still on for dinner tonight?"

There was a momentary pause on the other end of the line. Stavros guessed that Demetrios had been surprised at his use of the code words: *Are we still on for dinner tonight?* After all, it wasn't every week, or even every month that Stavros matched the name of a foreign Intelligence agent against one of his flight manifests. In fact, it had been several months since the last match: the British Defense Attaché, Harvey Cornwell.

CHAPTER NINE

JULY 28, 2004

Rodney Townsend had cultivated a reputation for being cool under pressure. An informant he had worked with in Communist East Berlin in the early eighties had wondered aloud whether Townsend had had a nerve-ectomy. Townsend had smiled back at the man, waved good-bye, and then, using false ID, driven across the border into the British Zone . . . with an East German defector hidden in a secret compartment beneath the floor of his lorry. Townsend dropped off the defector, returned to his hotel room, and spent the next thirty minutes embracing the toilet and shaking like a leaf in a windstorm.

The "cool" Rodney Townsend displayed to others was all an act, one worthy of an Academy Award. He was an emotional boiling cauldron; but had learned as a child to hide his feelings out of fear his father would use any display of emotion as one more excuse to beat him black and blue. When he went out on his first mission for MI-6 in 1981—to plant a listening device in the bedroom of a Red Chinese operative in Hong Kong—he was caught in the act by the man's Canadian mistress. He'd thought his career with British Intelligence had come to a quick and ignominious end. Instead, when the woman asked him what he was doing, there was something about her that made Townsend act rashly and, he thought at the time, stupidly. He told her exactly why he was in her boudoir. She'd reacted with wide-eyed astonishment, and, after a few seconds, devolved into hilarious laughter. "This might be fun," she'd said. Townsend wound up recruiting the woman as an undercover agent after a long night with her of slap and tickle. She'd thought that was funny, as well. He'd returned to his hotel room in the early morning and threw up until dawn.

At first, he'd thought he was a coward because of the fits of uncontrollable sweating and nausea after returning from a mission; but, as time went on, he realized that his physical reaction to dangerous situations didn't make him a coward. Running away would have. Barfing and shaking were his way of releasing stress, while others might explode in anger, get drunk, or even cry.

Townsend was at this moment seething with anger. Harvey Cornwell had been his best friend. Cornwell was an English patriot and one of the best and brightest in the British Navy and in British Intelligence. His death was a terrible loss for Cornwell's family, for England, and for Townsend.

And now the damned Americans were sending over some desk jockey to work with his team. It was bad enough that their so-called allies, the Greeks, were putting up roadblocks every time he and his team tried to gather information; now he had a sodding Yank he would have to baby-sit.

The secure telephone on his desk jarred Townsend from his thoughts. He jerked the receiver from its cradle. "Townsend here, may I help you?" he answered, ever the gentleman, despite the rage in him.

"Everything alright over there, old man?" the voice on the other end of the line asked.

Townsend recognized Brigadier Jeffrey Watkin-Coons' nasal tone. The man was upper-upper crust. Townsend knew his boss was solid. The man couldn't help it that he had been raised as a member of the British aristocracy and sounded like Prince Charles. "About the same," he said. "It's like pulling teeth getting the locals to cooperate with us. I talked with Inspector Spirothetis with the Greek Police about getting access to the information about Brigadier Cornwell's murder. He's thinking about it."

"Anything I can do?" Watkin-Coons asked.

"Thank you; but it's better that I handle it. I need the man's coop-eration. If we go over his head, he'll do nothing but obstruct my efforts going forward."

"Um, I see," Watkin-Coons mused. "Understood. Has that fellow from Langley arrived? Have you heard from him?"

Townsend sighed. "Yes, on both counts. We've arranged lunch for tomorrow."

"Let me know how it goes," Watkin-Coons said. "We should coop-erate with the Americans."

Townsend wasn't sure if his boss was just going through the motions, or if he was serious.

"Of course, sir," Townsend said. "You can be sure of my coopera-tion with the Yanks."

After Watkin-Coons hung up, Townsend smiled and thought, I'll cooperate with the Yanks, all right. I'll send them on a wild goose chase.

CHAPTER TEN
JULY 29, 2004

"*Malaka!* I don't care what the fucking Americans think. This is Greece, not Grenada. Those bastards wouldn't dare jeopardize their relationship with our country." Deputy Prime Minister Dimitris Argyropoulos smirked. "They need us more than we need them. Without Greece as a buffer against the Balkans, against Turkey, think of the chaos that could occur in the region. The Americans are scared to death."

Nicolaos Koufos, the head of the Ministry of Finance's Economic Development Department, felt hot; sweat dripped down his back, and he wiped his forehead with his handkerchief. He didn't want his nervousness to show, but he couldn't help himself. It wasn't only Argyropoulos' rhetoric that frightened him. The man had become more and more volatile over the last few years. The Deputy Prime Minister reminded Koufos of the Adolf Hitler he'd seen in old movies and newsreels. The man's right hand chopped the air the way the German madman used to. Even Argyropoulos' strutting step and dark hair and mustache resembled Hitler's.

Koufos laced his fingers over his copious belly and squirmed in his chair in an effort to find a more comfortable position. His short legs barely touched the carpet and his shirt collar was starting to feel like a garrote. He had been in complete agreement with Argyropoulos in the beginning, back in the seventies when they were students demonstrating against the Military Government. Argyropoulos was the charismatic leader of that student movement. But that was nearly thirty years ago and the environment had changed. Hell, their party was in power now. The situation had spun out of control, and he knew in his gut the longer this insanity continued, the worse the ultimate outcome would be. He suspected Argyropoulos was fooling himself about the Americans' state of mind. The man mistook American patience and attempts at diplomacy for weakness. The players on the international geopolitical chessboard were in active flux. What if the Americans decided to let Greece flap in the wind and moved their southern European operations to Bulgaria, for instance? Argyropoulos had carried the Party's original antipathy for the U.S. beyond the Party's original intent.

"I, like you, hate the Americans for what they did in 1967. The overthrow of our elected government and the imposition of a military dictatorship were terrible violations against the Greek people. It's a new century, however; the Olympic Games will be here in less than a month. We must make changes."

Argyropoulos leaped to his feet, shoving his chair back with such force that it slammed against the wall and toppled over. His face was almost purple with rage. "Don't you talk to me about change," he spat. "The American CIA overthrew our government. They took over our country. They . . ." His voice had become hoarse and he seemed to have run out of words.

"I meant no disrespect," Koufos said, trying to placate the Party's designee to be the next Prime Minister, "but Photos and his people are out of control. They've murdered Greeks, not just Americans, Englishmen, and Turks. Do we even know what these people stand for anymore? And the Olympics could be a disaster. If they follow through with their plans, Greece might never recover."

Argyropoulos stabbed his finger at Koufos. "I know what they stand for: Revenge. Payback for what our enemies did to us." He turned and righted his chair. After sitting in it, he looked at Koufos and the smirk returned. "And, remember, Koufos, you're no innocent bystander. You've been up to your neck in this since the beginning, since 1975, when *17 November* killed the CIA Station Chief. So, don't think you can walk away." The Deputy Prime Minister wagged his finger. An evil glint sparked in his eyes. "The Olympics will be like a gourmet for a pride of lions. I've waited for this for years."

Koufos felt a tremor of fear course through him. What had he gotten himself into? The fall of *17 November* had been a disaster. But at least none of the group's members could implicate him. That wasn't the case with *Greek Spring*. Giorgos Photos had been a student with him and Argyropoulos in the seventies, and he had funneled money to the terrorist cell through Photos. *Greek Spring* could ruin Greece's future and his own life. The entire world would be looking at Greece this summer because of the Olympic Games. It was the country's opportunity to pull itself up from the third world to the modern world, and this maniac, Argyropoulos, would jeopardize it all to avenge the ouster of the Greek Government thirty-five years earlier . . . and to accelerate his rise to Prime Minister.

CHAPTER ELEVEN

JULY 29, 2004

Bob left the Glyfada office in plenty of time to make his meeting with Rodney Townsend. He wanted to get off on the right foot with the man. He remembered that parking was a problem in the Plaka, so he had Tony drop him off three blocks from the restaurant. They had kept alert on the drive from the office, and hadn't detected anyone following them. But Bob didn't want to take any chances. With the directions to the restaurant Tony had provided him, Bob fast-walked up a narrow lane, while Tony blocked traffic for a couple minutes.

The Plaka dated back to antiquity. Its streets had been built for pedestrians and carts, not for automobiles. Buildings came almost to the edge of the street, separated by narrow sidewalks, or no sidewalks at all.

Bob saw the restaurant a block in the distance. After he made sure no one had followed him, he quickly moved to the restaurant entrance. He thought he spotted Townsend as soon as he entered— the only man in the place wearing a tie. His dark-blue pinstriped suit said Savile Row. Besides, the man was the only person in the place with blond hair and milk-white skin. The man looked to be in his late forties, with brilliant blue eyes, an aquiline nose, and thin lips defining a wide mouth. Bob also noticed the man's clenched jaw and fingers drumming the table—tension, impatience, or just plain anger at being here. This is probably not going to go well, he thought. I'll try to kill him with kindness.

He walked over to the man. "Rodney Townsend?" he asked in a low voice.

The man stood, nodded, and shook Bob's extended hand. "Danforth?"

Bob sat opposite Townsend at a small, round, corner table and said, "Thanks for agreeing to meet me on such short notice."

"Quite all right," Townsend said, with the warmth of a North Korean border guard. Townsend looked at his watch. "I have to be somewhere in an hour, so we should get started."

"My condolences for Harvey Cornwell," Bob said. "He was a good man."

Townsend shot Bob a sharp, narrow-eyed look. His thin lips pursed and his hands balled into fists. "You don't have a clue how good a man Harvey was. I . . .."

Townsend paused, took a breath, then apparently decided to not continue.

So much for killing him with kindness, Bob thought. He leaned forward and, in a slow and easy tone, said, "Actually, I do have a clue; I knew Harvey quite well. We worked together on three occasions—most recently on an operation in the Balkans in 2000. We got together whenever he came to the States. I counted him among my best friends." Bob let that sink in. He could tell from Townsend's round-eyed reaction that his relationship with Cornwell was a shock for the man.

"And, don't forget," Bob said, still in a quiet, easy tone, "we lost one of our best people, too. It seems to me that we have enough problems dealing with Greek recalcitrance and incompetence, without creating problems for one another." Bob checked his watch. "There's no reason for you to stay here another fifty-eight minutes if you have something better to do. I sure as hell do. I'm going to find the *Greek Spring* bastards who have now murdered five Americans and twenty or more others, including Harvey Cornwell. We can do that together, or work on the problem at odds with one another. Make up your mind right now." Bob's voice had gone from quiet and velvety to hoarse and hard.

Rodney Townsend's mouth had dropped open just enough to show his surprise. He swallowed and his face reddened, but he quickly recovered and answered. "Please forgive my rudeness; but explain to me why I should believe that anyone from the CIA would want to cooperate with us."

"All you can do is take my word on it," Bob said. "You've obviously had bad experiences working with the Agency. I apologize for that. Now that we've both apologized, why don't we start afresh."

Townsend glared at Bob for a few seconds and then a smile slowly creased his face, evolving into a belly laugh. He reached across the table and offered Bob his hand. "Sounds like a plan."

Bob shook Townsend's hand. "So, what's good here?" he asked.

Townsend laughed again. "Everything is fantastic, of course; it's a Greek restaurant. It's too bad they can't track down terrorists as well as they cook."

Bob smiled at the remark and said, "Whatever you're having is fine with me."

After ordering lunch, Bob looked around to make sure no one could eavesdrop on their conversation. Satisfied, he said, "Before leaving the U.S., I forwarded the Agency's entire file on *Greek Spring* to Brigadier Watkin-Coons, including the data on each of the investigations involving the first four Americans murdered by the group, along with our information about every murder, assault, bombing, and theft they perpetrated. I assume he will forward the entire file to you."

Townsend nodded. "We'll probably receive it tomorrow." He took a sip of water, seemed to be thinking about something, and then said, "If you will forgive me, I have to say I don't agree with the way your government has handled the investigations into *EA*."

Bob signaled Townsend with his hand to continue.

"You've allowed the Greeks to manage the entire process, and what little the U.S. has done has been handled as though the murders of your people were four separate incidents, instead of four interrelated events." Townsend had an obvious challenge in his voice and in his expression. He looked as though he dared Bob to contradict him. His expression softened when Bob not only didn't argue with him, but also agreed with him.

"That's why I'm here now," Bob said. "My government has come to the same conclusion."

CHAPTER TWELVE

JULY 29, 2004

Stavros Theodorakis loved June. It was warm, but not hot, and the annual pilgrimage of tourists was in full swing. Most visitors eventually traveled to the islands; but almost all of them spent one or two days in Athens. He especially loved the Scandinavian tourists—the girls with their pale complexions, blond hair and blue eyes. He would love to meet one of these beauties, but just the thought of approaching one made shivers run down his spine. He didn't have the nerve. Besides, he had neither the looks to attract them nor the money to entertain them.

As though the gods decided to torment him, two blond girls strolled by his sidewalk *kafeneio* table at that moment. Stavros ran his eyes over the girls, starting at their feet and moving up to their crowns of golden hair. The familiar heat crawled up the back of his neck and made his scalp tingle, while pressure built in his groin. Stavros rated the girl on the left an eight; her friend merited a nine. He twisted in his chair in order to watch them while they moved to the street corner and waited for the light to change. He sighed loudly when two young Greeks seated at the far end of the cafe, just a meter from the corner, suddenly started talking to the girls. The blonds flashed brilliant white smiles at the men, who left their table and stepped up to the girls. After a moment, all four of them were laughing. The foursome talked for another minute, then turned around and followed a serpentine path through the cafe tables to an interior table close to the one from which Stavros watched.

The heat at the back of Stavros' neck and between his legs dissipated, replaced by a familiar pain in his stomach. He knew the pain would grow quickly and he pulled a pill case from his jacket pocket and swallowed two antacids, chased down by a gulp of water. He adjusted in his chair so he wouldn't have to see the Scandinavian girls and their new Greek friends; it was bad enough that he could hear their laughter and conversation.

Suddenly a hand grabbed his shoulder and squeezed. Stavros' stomach erupted as though filled with a thousand bees; his heart seemed to stop for a second. He began to jump out of his chair, when a calming voice said, "Take it easy, cousin, it's just me."

Stavros settled back into his chair and took another drink of water while his cousin, Demetrios, moved from behind Stavros' chair and took the chair next to his.

"You startled me," Stavros said.

"No shit," Demetrios said, a smile creasing his dark, handsome features. Demetrios turned his head enough to be able to see the Scandinavian girls. He laughed, then turned back to Stravros. "You were checking out those blonds and had carnal thoughts running through that dirty little mind of yours. You like the way they look?"

Stavros felt his face go hot. He waved a dismissive hand in the air and said, "Oh, they're all right."

"All right?" Demetrios said. "They're world class. You want me to fix you up with one of them?"

Stavros felt a spark of excitement radiate throughout his being. What he wouldn't give for a night with one of those girls! Hell, what he wouldn't give for a night with any woman! He knew Demetrios could make it happen, too. He'd seen his cousin in action. His cousin had a mean streak. Stavros had seen Demetrios walk up to another man and frighten him with just a look. He also had movie star looks and his pockets were always full of cash. Women loved Demetrios. He didn't know where Demetrios got his money—he didn't have a job and his parents were poor. He suspected it had to do with Demetrios' involvement with some shadowy group he had alluded to on a couple of occasions. Stavros quickly met his cousin's gaze, then looked away. He saw the humor that had been there for just an instant depart. Demetrios' eyes had gone hard, shark-like.

"You called me," Demetrios said. "What's up?"

The tingly sensation started again; but this time it wasn't caused by the blonds. It was the excitement of being involved with something illicit, feeling a part of something dangerous. "I got a hit today," he said. "One of the passengers on a flight that came in yesterday matched up with a name on the program you gave—"

Demetrios' hand on his arm stopped Stavros. He saw the waiter approaching their table. Demetrios ordered *ouzo*, Stavros a *limonada*. When the man walked away, Demetrios skidded his chair a couple inches closer to Stavros, leaned forward, and said in no more than a whisper, "Go ahead, but keep your voice down."

Stavros took a deep breath and let it out slowly. "I got a match against the program you gave me. A man flew in on the Delta flight that landed at 8:20 A.M. yesterday. He told Customs he was here on a pleasure trip. He had one checked bag and was traveling alone. A man with the same name showed up on the computer software program you gave me."

"The man's name," Demetrios demanded.

"Robert Danforth."

"And . . .."

Stavros felt his pulse quicken. He smiled and said, "And, he's an employee of the United States Central Intelligence Agency."

Demetrios slowly moved back into his chair. "Anything else?" he said.

"He's high level in Special Operations. Been with the CIA for over thirty years."

"What about a hotel?" Demetrios said.

"Nothing yet. But it won't be hard to find him once we learn what hotel he checked in at. They'll collect his passport and put the information into the computer. I should know where he's staying within a day, two days at the latest."

Demetrios patted Stavros' arm and smiled. "You did well, cousin. Call me as soon as you know where the man is staying." He pulled an envelope from his pants pocket and placed it on Stavros' lap. "We appreciate your support," he said. Demetrios pushed his chair back, stood, and walked away, disappearing in the growing evening crowd.

Stavros peeked inside the envelope without lifting it from his lap. He fingered the cash and counted five one hundred-Euro bills.

CHAPTER THIRTEEN

JULY 29, 2004

Demetrios Mavroyianni's hands shook as he dialed the telephone number. The information his cousin, Stavros, had given him was momentous. The CIA had sent a high-level operative to Greece. He suspected that this Robert Danforth's presence was a clear sign the Americans were going to increase pressure on the Greek Government to find the members of *Greek Spring* and of other terrorist groups. Demetrios snickered. All they would accomplish, he told himself, was to add one more name to the victim list: Robert Danforth.

After he let the phone ring twice, he hung up and dialed the number again. This time the call was answered on the fourth ring.

"*Embros*," the man on the other end of the line growled.

"I have news," Demetrios said.

"*Avrio stees octo to proee*," Giorgos Photos responded. "*Sto spiti konda to panipisteemio.*"

Demetrios had been a member of *Greek Spring* since 1990. He knew instantly when and where he was to meet the leader: 8:00 A.M. tomorrow at the safehouse near the University of Athens. He was familiar with three such safehouses the group used in and around the city. He suspected there were many other meeting places about which he had not been told; but that didn't bother him. In fact, it gave him further confidence in the leader's wisdom. Never let any one member of the group know too much. He also knew that if Giorgos decided to put a hit out on Danforth, he would not be selected to do the job. Giorgos would make sure that separation was maintained between the source of the information about Danforth—Demetrios' cousin,

Stavros Theodorakis—and Danforth's assassin. It bothered Demetrios that someone else would have the honor and pleasure of murdering the American spy; but he understood why it was necessary. He would get his chance again, soon. There were plenty of targets in Athens. Brits and Americans and Turks galore. A virtual feast for *Eleeneekee Aneexee*.

CHAPTER FOURTEEN

JULY 29, 2004

So far, none of the time Tony had spent with Mikaelis Griffas had been worth Tony being away from his family. The information the man had provided him had not been of any value. But Griffas was one of only three informants he'd developed since coming to Greece, and the man seemed more excited than usual when he called Tony's cell phone number twenty minutes ago.

Tony didn't want to chance missing out on the one time Griffas came up with something valuable. Recruiting Griffas had been a real coup. The man worked in the Greek Government, on the Prime Minister's personal staff. Western Intelligence agencies had suspected for years that top officials in the Greek Government had intentionally subverted the investigations into terrorist groups. Maybe Griffas had finally come up with something concrete.

Although Griffas was a quirky sort, Tony had come to like the little guy. Griffas was nuts about the game of basketball and crazy about Michael Jordan. He always wore a Chicago Bulls warm-up jacket with Jordan's name and number on the back. At five feet, five inches and weighing no more than one hundred pounds, Griffas wasn't built for basketball. But his stature hadn't diminished his enthusiasm for the game.

Tony parked his car on a side street, two blocks from the Piraeus wharf, and walked down to the water. He strolled along the path between the water and a string of *tavernas*, playing tourist. Strands of lights decorated the *tavernas* and the murmurs of diners from a dozen different countries filled the air like the asynchronous sounds of nocturnal animals in a forest. The cooking odors drifting from the *tavernas* made Tony's stomach growl. He'd been about to sit down to a late dinner when Griffas called. He would have loved to meet the informant at one of the restaurants; but the man was paranoid to the point of desperation. He would only meet Tony in secluded, out-of-the-way places, far from his apartment in Athens, far from prying eyes and ears.

Tony didn't like meetings in dark alleys in places like Piraeus. But, if he wanted to play the spy game, he had to accept the risks. He pressed his left arm against his side and felt the comforting hardness of the 9mm pistol in the shoulder holster under his jacket.

From the path along the quay, Tony slipped down a dark lane, barely wide enough for a compact car. Warehouse-like buildings faced each other from opposite sides of the lane. The buildings on each side abutted one another, each with a closed overhead door and a recessed personnel door. Griffas had told him he'd be in the third doorway on the left. It took a minute for Tony's eyes to adjust to the narrow street's darkness. He stayed on the left side of the street, close to the wall, stopping at each doorway, his right hand now inside his jacket gripping the pistol. The hair on the back of his neck bristled; he didn't like the whole setup. After passing the second door on the left, Tony removed the 9mm and held his gunhand down at his side.

The doorways along the lane were staggered—first one on the left, then one on the right. Tony walked slowly, quietly past four doors—two left, two right, checking each one before moving farther into the lane. Just a few yards from the third doorway on the left, Tony's breath caught in his chest and his heart did a full gainer into the pit of his stomach. The noise sounded primordial—a cross between a monkey screech and a distant panther roar. Tony snapped his gunhand in front of him and rushed to a spot only six feet from the third doorway, where Griffas was supposed to be. He dropped into a crouch and growled in Greek, "Come out and show yourself. Hands up."

No response. No movement.

Tony tried again, repeating his orders.

The animal-like sound came again from the doorway.

Tony pressed hard against the wall and sidled toward the doorway. He stopped inches from the opening, took a slow, deep breath, and released it just as slowly. He took a penlight flashlight from his pocket and placed his thumb on the ON switch. He peeked around the corner of the wall, snapping on the flashlight, then jerked his head back as his mind processed what his eyes had seen—a man lying on his back in the three-foot recessed space. The door behind the prostrate man was open. Running footsteps echoed in the building, a crashing sound at the far end of the building like a door being shouldered open, and suddenly no sound at all. Tony shone the flashlight up and down the tiny street and saw no one. The same with the cavernous space in the empty building behind the open door. The only sounds he heard were his own breathing and a low moan coming from the man lying near his feet. Michael Griffas.

He knelt on the stoop. "What happened, Michael?" Tony whispered.

"They know," Griffas groaned.

"Who knows? What do they know?"

Griffas coughed, spraying Tony's face with wet droplets. When he tried to talk, a gurgling sound resonated inside his chest.

Tony moved the light and saw that blood covered the man's white shirt above his stomach. Griffas gripped a knife handle in his left hand, the blade of the weapon red with blood.

"He stabbed me." Griffas took in a rasping breath. "It hurts bad, Tony."

Tony raised Griffas' upper body and propped him against the side of the doorway. His hand came away from the man feeling wet and sticky. "Who knows? Who stabbed you?" he prodded Griffas. "What do they know?"

"*Ee terroreestee xeroun,*" Griffas gasped. "*Kai . . . O dievtheendees mou . . . xerie.*"

What the hell, Tony thought. The terrorists know; his boss knows. "Tell me what they know," Tony rasped.

Griffas' mouth opened, then closed and opened several times, like a beached fish fighting for air. Then a long venting of air escaped the man's lungs as his head flopped to his chest. Tony knew he was gone.

Tony searched Griffas' pockets, but found only the man's wallet. He backed out of the doorway and retraced his steps down the lane. He shined the flashlight on his wristwatch and saw it was nearly 10:00 P.M. He called the team office on his cell phone, hoping someone was still there. He caught Stacey Frederick on her way out. He told her what had happened and asked her to place a confidential call to the Greek police to report a dead body on the lane in Piraeus. It wouldn't do for the Greek authorities to know the CIA was involved with a murdered Greek National.

Then Tony called the Grand Bretagne Hotel and asked for Bob Danforth's room; but Bob wasn't there. He left a message to call him back on his cell phone.

Tony sagged against the wall of the building and willed himself to calm down. He could feel adrenaline surging through him and his heart rate pounding like a bass drum in his chest. He needed to compose himself. The area beyond the lane was crowded with locals and tourists. He slipped the pistol into his holster and replaced the flashlight in his pocket. He stuck his bloodstained hands in his pants pockets and strolled out the opposite end of the tiny street, keeping to the shadows, away from the moonlight. He suspected his face was dotted with blood spatters. When he reached the first cross street, he circled around the block and found his car.

Tony's stomach was in revolt over Griffas' murder. The man had been a clerk who wanted nothing more out of life than to watch as many basketball games as possible, and, perhaps, to meet Michael Jordan some day. He'd signed on with Tony as an informant for one reason only: to help stop the violence that was poisoning Greece— that violence which had now claimed him as its latest victim.

CHAPTER FIFTEEN
JULY 29, 2004

It was a relatively cool night and Bob was too wound up to sleep. It was 10:00 P.M. and he thought a walk around the Plaka might help settle him down. Bob assessed his day as he strolled through the old part of Athens, a half mile from his hotel. His meeting with Rodney Townsend had started off about as he had expected, but had finished on a high note. After they'd gotten past Townsend's initial pique, the meeting had turned out to be damned productive. He was optimistic about the working relationship that could develop between their teams. The afternoon with the CIA team had also been worthwhile. The team members were top notch and their dedication was to the point of being fanatical.

It had been a long time—over three decades—since he had been in the Plaka. This was his second visit there today. He grunted an almost silent laugh at the errant thought that attacked his brain— Wouldn't it be fun to see the Plaka as a tourist? Maybe some day, he told himself.

The walk took him into the heart of the old city; then he retraced his steps, returning to Constitution Square and the Grand Bretagne Hotel. It was just past 10:45 and he felt suddenly tired. The thought of crisp, clean sheets seemed almost sensual. He collected his key at the front desk and turned toward the elevators, when the desk clerk said, "Oh, Mr. Danforth, you have a message." Bob accepted a slip of paper from the clerk and moved to the elevators. He saw the call was from Tony Fratangelo. "Urgent" had been written across the bottom of the paper. Bob called Tony as soon as he entered his fourth floor room.

"What's up?" Bob asked.

"We need to meet," Tony said.

"I've got a meeting at ten in the morning. How about eight?"

"We need to meet tonight," Tony answered. "It's important."

Armed with Bob's room number, Tony rode the hotel elevator to the fourth floor and found room 421. After knocking and being let into the room, he dropped into a chair, removed a twice-folded 8-1/2" x 11" sheet of paper from his jacket, and placed it on a small cocktail table between Bob and him. He moved forward in the chair and said, "I lost an informant tonight. He worked on the Prime Minister's staff. I wrote down what he said on that paper."

"Lost?" Bob said.

"Murdered," Tony answered. "I wrote down on that piece of paper exactly what the man said before he died. I think I've been made."

Bob unfolded the piece of paper. When he finished reading what Tony had written, he looked up, handed the note back to Tony, and loudly cleared his throat. "*Kai O dievtheendees mou xerie.* My boss knows. What do you make of this? Who's his boss?"

Tony shrugged. "He died before saying anything else. He could have been referring to his direct supervisor . . . or"—Tony paused for a second—"he could have been referring to the Prime Minister."

CHAPTER SIXTEEN

JULY 30, 2004

George Photos paced inside his home on the Island of Evoia. He alternately stared at the floor and at Savvas Krinon. He clasped his hands behind his back and moved slowly in his usual stooped posture. Finally, he stopped and faced the window that gave him a view of the moonlit sea off the coast of Evoia. At well over six feet tall, he had to bend slightly to look out the window. Sunrise was still two hours away. He didn't like having Krinon here. This was his private retreat. He bought the property with money robbed from a Citibank branch in Athens several years earlier, and had kept it a secret from the other members of the group. But the meeting was unavoidable.

"What do you want to do, George?" Savvas asked. "Maybe we should back off for a while."

Photos sneered at the suggestion; but he didn't turn around. He didn't want Krinon to see the contempt he felt for what the man had said. He put a paternal smile on his face and then turned to look at the younger man. "No, I don't think we should back off, my friend. We have the enemy on the run. Now isn't the time to be passive."

"But they had an informant inside the Prime Minister's office. He could have exposed our supporters at the top. There could be other traitors informing on us."

"*Had* an informant, *could* have exposed. The fact that we eliminated the informant shows just how powerful, well connected we are. The question is what are we going to do about the American who recruited Mikaelis Griffas, this Tony Fratangelo?"

A gleaming smile came to Savvas' face. "That's easy, comrade; like sheep to the slaughter."

Photos smiled back and nodded. "I'll issue a proclamation about Griffas; then we'll take care of the CIA agent, Mr. Fra-tan-gel-o."

Photos took a predawn ferry from Evoia to the mainland. Krinon would catch the next ferry. Photos hired a cab to take him to a street several blocks from the apartment below the Lycavetos Monastery. He spent three hours drafting the five-page proclamation, then read the document through. He reread the last paragraph: *Our actions were courageous and in the highest tradition of the Greek Nation in combating the forces of evil corrupting the soul of the Greek people. Mikaelis Griffas was a traitor, an informant for the treacherous dogs at the United States Central Intelligence Agency, and needed to be purged. Greek Spring will see to it that all such traitors are erased from the Greek consciousness.*

He snapped a finger against the pages and sighed with satisfaction. This will raise their blood pressure, he thought. He placed the pages in an envelope and inserted them in the inside pocket of a sport jacket slung over the back of a chair. He put on a pair of sunglasses and a beret. Then he slipped on the jacket and left the apartment. After walking six blocks, he hailed a taxi and had the driver drop him off across from the United States Embassy on Vassileas Sofias.

He strolled along the sidewalk as though he was a tourist and gazed at the building that housed his sworn enemies. He laughed to himself as he noted the extreme security that had been set up to protect the embassy. His chest swelled with pride. Before Richard Welch was killed twenty-nine years earlier, you could just walk right up to the building and go inside. Now there were barricades and heavily-armed U.S. Marines all over the place. He'd learned that the Americans spent more on security at their Athens Embassy than on any of their other embassies worldwide. Because of *Greek Spring*. Because of him. "*Thavmasseea*," he said under his breath. Amazing.

Photos walked two blocks and found a residential street. The fifth house down on the right had a two-meter by two-meter recessed graveled area at the end of the driveway where trash receptacles were stored. He looked around to make sure no one was watching him, lifted the lid off one of the trash cans, drew the envelope holding the proclamation from his jacket, and dropped it in the can. He replaced the lid and walked back to Vassileas Sofias. He signaled to a cab, which pulled to the curb. Before getting in the vehicle, he showed the palm of his hand to the American Embassy and cursed under his breath, "*As sto diavolo*-go to hell."

The cab dropped him off three blocks from the Lycavetos apartment. When the cab drove away, Photos went to a pay telephone and dialed a number from memory. When his favorite reporter at the daily newspaper, *Eleftherotypia*, answered, he said, "You know who this is?"

The man responded after a few seconds. "Yes, I recognize your voice. How are you, my friend? It's good to hear your voice again."

"I'm good," Photos said. "I have another proclamation for you."

"Where is it?" the reporter asked, excitement in his voice.

Photos almost laughed aloud. After waiting a moment to ensure he was in control—it wouldn't do to leave the impression there was anything frivolous about his or *Greek Spring's* actions—he gave the man directions to the trash can where he'd left the envelope. He emphasized the fact that the address was only two blocks from the American Embassy. He knew the reporter would make a point in his article of noting the proximity of the drop site to the embassy. The reporter loved tweaking the Americans as much as Photos loved killing them.

CHAPTER SEVENTEEN
JULY 30, 2004

Bob sat at the small table in his hotel room, the remains of a late breakfast pushed to the side, a three-ring binder open before him. He knew he would have to do something about Tony Fratangelo. He couldn't be sure exactly what Griffas meant when, before he died, he told Fratangelo that "the terrorists know" and "my boss knows"; but he had to assume the worst. If the terrorists had identified Fratangelo as a CIA employee, then he could be their next target. He'd deal with the issue as soon as possible; make sure that someone was always with him. Maybe he'd have to have Langley reassign Fratangelo. For now, he needed to focus on the folio his Langley team had prepared for his meeting with the Greek Prime Minister on Friday, August 6— seven days from today. He had reviewed the contents of the briefing book a dozen times. He concentrated on the notes he'd made on the page margins in the binder.

The contents of the binder included independent research generated by the Agency, as well as excerpts from a myriad of other sources.

Bob reviewed his notes:

1. *Greece's policy in dealing with terrorists for thirty years has been schizophrenic.*

2. *Greece's location in southern Europe, close to the Middle East, and its free press make it the perfect place for international terrorist groups to get publicity.*

3. *Security forces and political leaders have appeared to back away from prosecuting investigations of the terrorists, making Greece a breeding ground for terrorist groups.*

4. *Greece's conflict with Turkey, resentment about the U.S.'s support of the military junta, and nationalism have exacerbated the situation. I've been injected into a virile petrie dish of terrorism. The Greek press—Al Jazeera West—acts like a propaganda arm of the terrorists.*

5. *Greeks are sympathetic to radical Middle East regimes (PLO, Syria, Iraq, Iran, and Libya), and Andreas Papandreou exploited this sympathy in an effort to promote Greek leadership in the Third World. It has taken a stronger stand than any other country in the European Community toward Israel.*

6. *When American and British agents in 1984 raided an apartment in Athens, captured a Jordanian member of the May 15 terrorist group, and turned him over to the Greeks, the Greek authorities released the man. They claimed the evidence wasn't strong enough and that the Americans and British violated Greek law.*

7. *Greece has become a net exporter of arms, with clients such as Libya.*

8. *Many instances of high-level Greek Government leaders' involvement with or in support of terrorists have occurred: A). Daniel Kristallis, an agent of the Greek Central Intelligence Agency, was arrested in the mid-1990s as a suspected terrorist. He had placed bombs and then taken money for providing false information about the bombs. B). Members of Parliament and certain government Ministers take public positions supporting terrorist actions. C). After terrorist Giorgos Balafas was arrested in 1992, authorities found weapons at two of his apartments, and witnesses came forward claiming Balafas murdered an attorney named Theophanopoulos. A parade of politicians visited Balafas in prison and signed letters of support for the murderer. Balafas was acquitted on appeal.*

9. *There is no legal basis in Greece for the prosecution of terror-*
    ism. The government has been debating new laws that will
    make it easier to arrest and convict terrorists; but nothing has
    been finalized.

Bob had made the notations to concentrate on the common theme throughout the briefing book: a policy of appeasement and even support for terrorists by the Greek Government. This would be his focus when he met with the Prime Minister.

He would finish the meeting with a review of the murders of Americans by the *17 November* and *Greek Spring* groups. He didn't want the Prime Minister to think for even a moment that the United States had forgotten about its murdered citizens, or that it wouldn't push for the identification and arrest of the killers. Finally, he would make it clear he was not in Greece on a diplomatic mission—whether the Greeks liked it or not.

Normally, the American ambassador would accompany him on a visit to the Greek Prime Minister; but he and Ambassador Finch had agreed it would probably not be a good idea for the ambassador to accompany him on this visit. It was important that the ambassador maintain a working relationship with the Greek Government, and Bob suspected that the Greek leader would be extremely hot under the collar after their meeting. Ambassador Finch had already set up the meeting. His secretary would call the Prime Minister's office five minutes after the scheduled meeting's start time and explain that the ambassador was tied up on a call with the Secretary of State, and that the Prime Minister meet with Mr. Danforth without him.

Bob completed his review and decided he'd crammed enough for now. The bedside clock showed it was 10:00 A.M. Tony should be waiting to pick him up out front. He stuffed the briefing book into his briefcase and draped his jacket over his shoulder. While walking to the door, he glanced out his hotel room window and saw a corner of the Parliament building across the square. It was just a short walk to the Prime Minister's office. He checked his tie in the mirror on the closet door and smiled. "Well, Bobby-boy," he said to himself, "in a week you're going to see how pissed off you can make the top guy in Greece."

CHAPTER EIGHTEEN
JULY 30, 2004

Demetrios Mavroyianni lit a Marlboro while the phone rang in his ear. He loved American cigarettes. He didn't dare smoke them in Giorgos Photos' presence—the man was pathologically opposed to everything American. So he took every opportunity to light up when he was away from the leader. He exhaled smoke from deep in his lungs. Come on Stavros, pick up the phone.

"Theodorakis, Ministry of Justice," Stavros said after the sixth ring, sounding hurried and out of breath.

"Hey, Stavros." Demetrios hesitated a moment to make sure his cousin recognized his voice.

"What is it?" Stavros asked in a whisper. "It's only been an hour since you called."

Demetrios was inclined to play off Stavros' obvious nervousness, to tease his neurotic cousin, but thought better of it. He should get off the line as quickly as possible. "Did you track down the hotel of the visitor we talked about?"

"The information isn't available yet. Perhaps by tomorrow."

"What about my earlier call?"

"The one named Tony has been in the country for a short time. He lives in Kifissia, near the corner of Kokkinara and Levidou." He supplied Demetrios with the address.

"You know my number," Demetrios said, and depressed the plunger on the telephone. He kept the receiver against his ear and pretended to continue his conversation while surreptitiously surveying the area around the phone booth. When he decided he was not being watched, he hung up the receiver and walked away from the booth.

Demetrios knew that Greek law required all hotels to take their visitors' passports when they checked in and to enter information from the passports into their computers. This information was then downloaded to the Ministry of Justice database. Ironic, he thought. The system had been put in place to track possible terrorists coming to Greece. What the government didn't know was the terrorists were using the same database to track law enforcement personnel. In another day, at the most, his cousin Stavros would pass on the name of the hotel where Robert Danforth was staying. But now he needed to scope out the house where the CIA man Fratangelo lived.

Demetrios removed the .38 caliber Colt revolver from the waistband of his trousers, hidden under his leather jacket. He stashed it in the storage compartment in the back of his Vespa, and quickly mounted the scooter and headed for Kifissia.

Giorgos Photos looked out at the huge clock mounted on an iron pole at the street corner. It was almost 2:00 P.M. "Demetrios should be here any moment," he announced. "Then we can get started."

"What's going on?" Savvas Krinon asked, looking at Pavlos Manganos who sat in an overstuffed chair in a corner of the room. It was unusual for Photos to hold meetings where more than one other member of *Greek Spring* was present.

"Patience, my friend. I believe you will find the wait worthwhile. I—" A knock on the apartment door interrupted Photos. He waited to make sure the correct number of knocks was tapped out, then stepped to the side of the door. He removed his pistol from his back pocket, unlocked the door, and shouted, "Come in."

When Demetrios Mavroyianni entered, Photos tucked away his pistol and slapped Mavroyianni on the back. "I assume you have good news," he said.

"Of course," Demetrios said, nodding at Krinon and Manganos.

"Good," Photos said, pointing to a chair at the small square wood table in the center of the room where Krinon and Manganos were seated. Mavroyianni sat down and waited for Photos to sit across from him. Then he described the location of Tony Fratangelo's house. He reported that he should have the information on Robert Danforth's location tomorrow.

"Excellent job," Photos said. He patted Demetrios on the shoulder and stood, signaling that their meeting was over. "Call me when you get the hotel information." He led Demetrios to the door and locked it after the man left. When he turned around, Krinon and Manganos were standing.

"Perhaps it's time for me to explain what I have in mind," Photos told them. "We are about to make a statement that will make all we have done before pale in comparison."

CHAPTER NINETEEN

JULY 30, 2004

Bob jumped at the sudden ringing of the telephone. He'd been so engrossed in the file he was reading that even the innocent sound of the telephone jolted him. It was nearly 3:00 in the afternoon. He watched through his open office door as Stacey Frederick answered the phone, smiled, and then told the caller to, "Come on up." She hung up the phone and announced to the rest of the team—Sam Goodwin, Tony Fratangelo, and Bob, who were seated around a large conference table—that Stanton Markeson and Cyril Bridewell from the British team were on their way up. She moved to the suite's entrance door and pressed a buzzer releasing the downstairs front door.

Two men came into the room carrying two boxes each and dropped them on the floor just inside the door. Stacey introduced them to Bob.

"I didn't sign on to be a damned day laborer," Markeson growled.

Bridewell laughed. "The climb up the stairs nearly did Stanton in."

Bob observed that Markeson was not built for physical labor. While the blond, blue-eyed, thirty-something Bridewell was medium height, powerfully built, and breathing normally, Markeson was puffing as though he'd just run a mile, uphill, with a fifty-pound pack on his back. He was short, rotund, florid-faced, and looked about sixty-five.

Bob shook the men's hands. "What's all this?" he asked as he offered chairs at the table to Markeson and Bridewell.

"Gifts from the chief," Bridewell responded. "Mr. Townsend received a copy of the files you provided London and thought he should reciprocate." He pointed at the four boxes. "These contain some of what we've been able to accumulate on terrorist activities in Greece since Jeffrey Saunders' murder four years ago. There are six more boxes down in the van. It's the sum total of what the Greek Ministry of Public Order has given us so far, plus what we've dug up ourselves."

Markeson handed Bob a floppy disk he removed from his shirt pocket. He'd gotten enough of his breath back to be able to say, "You'll find all sorts of interesting stuff on this disk. It was downloaded from the Scotland Yard computer and contains Intelligence files they've gathered since the mid-seventies on terrorist activities in Greece. The file names are fairly explanatory. You see one that seems interesting, all you have to do is access the database. The access instructions are on the disk as well."

"We have access to the entire Scotland Yard database?" Bob asked with a smile.

Markeson emitted a rolling, thunderous laugh and devolved into a hacking, smoker's cough. When he stopped coughing, he said, "I said the chief had reciprocated, not that he had lost his mind."

Bob laughed. "You had me excited there for a moment." Then he turned to Sam Goodwin and asked, "Do we have anything we can offer our guests to drink?"

"You bet," Sam said, and left the room.

"While Sam gets the drinks," Bob said to Tony, "perhaps you and Cyril could bring up the remaining files from the van."

After all the file boxes were stored in the CIA office and Sam had returned with a tray of bottles of water and *limonada,* Bob slid forward in his chair and said to the Englishmen, "Do you have a few minutes?"

"Sure," Markeson said, after he glanced at Bridewell and received a nod from the man.

Bob looked Markeson in the eye and said, "I understand you've lived in Greece for a number of years, that you are well-connected in both business and governmental circles, and that you know the Greek mentality. Tell us what you really think, your gut instincts about *Greek Spring.*"

Bob knew there was a tendency for bureaucrats to downplay the input from players in the field, especially players who had been in the field for an extended time. There was an inclination on the part of people at headquarters to look upon such operatives as though they'd "gone native," and to discount much of their input. Bob suspected the British were no different than the Americans in this regard. He still got angry when he thought about the form letters that Jimmy Carter's CIA Director, Admiral Stansfield Turner, sent out on October 31, 1977, purging the Operations Directorate of some of the most valuable people in the Agency. Termination notices were sent to agents in the field who had been in place the longest, and who knew the cultures and languages of the countries in which they were stationed. That day was still known in the Agency as the Halloween Day Massacre.

Markeson's expression turned serious. He seemed to be thinking about Bob's question and there was something about the look in his eyes, in the set of his jaw, that told Bob he wasn't used to being asked for his opinion.

It took Markeson several moments to respond, but when he did, his expression had softened a bit and there was a tone of respect in his voice. "I think we've got a very small group of thugs involved with *Greek Spring.* Maybe twenty, thirty people. The core members of the group have been at it for over two-and-a-half decades and have reached a point where they are so damned confident and arrogant they believe they can continue committing crimes with little or no fear of being caught." Markeson looked around the room, took a drink of *limonada,* and continued. "I think the group has support from well-placed persons in the Greek Government."

"How *well-placed?*" Tony Fratangelo asked.

"Very well-placed," Markeson said. "Either high-level individuals and/or people who work for those individuals and have access to information about the investigations into the terrorists' crimes."

"Any ideas about who these individuals might be?" Stacey asked.

Markeson shook his head. "I've got all kinds of ideas, but I can't think of one person who I could indict. Hard evidence is just not there. The actions taken by certain political leaders would lead one to believe they were in bed with the terrorists; but"—he shrugged—"who knows?"

"What actions, for instance?" Sam Goodwin said.

"Well, let's take the civil security forces," Markeson said. "Karamanlis broke up the security forces when he became Prime Minister in the '70s. When Andreas Papandreou took over in 1981, he further emasculated the security forces. As a result, the civil security force's performance in dealing with terrorism in Greece has been a tribute to incompetence. Karamanlis and Papandreou's actions would lead you to believe they intentionally undermined the effort to investigate terrorism.

"In the case of Papandreou, remember that he was about to take power in Greece via democratic elections when the Papadopoulos military junta took over the country on April 21, 1967, and arrested Papandreou. He would have a powerful motivation to allow a group of terrorists to take revenge on the United States and Britain for their support of the Military Government."

"Keep in mind," Bridewell interjected, "that the civil security forces played a big role in the junta. They earned a reputation for brutality against their enemies and a number of policemen were tried for torture and other human rights violations after the junta was overthrown. Government leaders have overreacted by dismantling the security forces, thereby damaging their ability to perform efficiently."

"So we don't know if Karamanlis and Papandreou were aiding and abetting the terrorists intentionally, or inadvertently," Tony said.

Markeson stretched out his hand and waved it from side to side. "Maybe both," he said. "The government's position on international terrorism has been reprehensible on more than one occasion. They have supported fundamentalist regimes in the Middle East and have actually released terrorists who were arrested after they committed atrocities here in Greece. All because they wanted the support of various Arab countries in Greece's conflict with Turkey. They also wanted those countries to make investments in Greece."

"Including the purchase of arms and munitions manufactured in Greece," Bob interjected.

"Just so," Markeson said.

Silence hung in the room. Bob guessed the others were thinking along the same line he was: How in God's name could a small group of criminals even be identified when the leaders of the country were, for one reason or another, aggressively or passively protecting them? But Bob had put a lot of thought into this question and felt the time was right for a change in the Greek attitude toward *Greek Spring* and other such groups.

"Thank you, Stanton," Bob said, rising from his chair at the head of the table, "that was very helpful. I appreciate your time and your expertise. We should probably let you and Cyril get back to your office."

The two Brits stood and shook hands with the Americans. Stacey showed them to the door and returned to her place at the table a few seconds later.

"Are we all in agreement with Markeson?" Bob asked.

Tony, Sam, and Stacey stated they were all on the same page.

"Okay, let me add a few thoughts," Bob said. "First, I think the 2004 Olympic Games are already changing the situation. The European Union is pouring millions of Euros into Greece to make it a showcase for all of Europe. For the 1992 Games in Barcelona, which coincided with the five hundredth anniversary of Columbus' discovery of the New World, the wealthier European nations made Spain a showcase for the continent. That's the plan for Athens this year. The last thing Greece or the other countries in the region want is wholesale slaughter by terrorists while they're trying to bring visitors here from all over the planet. Which means we're going to have more support from the locals in our efforts than ever before.

"Second," Bob continued, "I am certain the terrorists know this and they're going to fight like lions protecting their prides to prevent this from happening. Which means we're going to see escalation in terrorist activity. They're going to want to send a message to both their sympathizers and opponents that they mean business. And, based on the way the Greek Government has reacted to terrorist threats in the past, the terrorists probably believe the government will roll over and play dead as they ratchet up their attacks.

"Lastly, I think the essential goodness of the Greek people will prevail. There has been some sympathy among Greeks for the terrorists because the terrorists have claimed to have nationalistic motivations, and because they rose out of opposition to the military junta. The terrorists' actions of late, however, have raised some interesting questions in the minds of the average Greek. When *Greek Spring* started assassinating Greek prosecutors and businessmen, their nationalistic motivations had to have come into question."

"Sounds like we have a natural made conflict between the government and the terrorists," Sam said. "If your position is correct, we could have a serious problem. The more the government clamps down, the more the terrorists react. This thing could intensify way beyond what exists today, or what the terrorists have done in the past."

"But what makes you think the Greek leaders will change their behavior?" Stacey asked. "Remember, we've been hearing rumors for years that highly placed Greek politicians and bureaucrats have been protecting *Greek Spring.* Hell, a number of the top people have made public statements in support of terror groups. Markeson made all of that clear."

Bob rested his elbows on the table and covered his mouth with his hands, looking from one team member to the next. He thought about what Sam and Stacey had said, then sat back and said, "Both of you make good points. Sam, I think you're absolutely correct. The terrorists will more than likely become more active. But the more aggressive they become, the more likely they'll make a mistake. One of them will blow himself up in the same way the *17 November* member did, or someone will witness one of their crimes and report it to the police. And the more crimes they commit, the more they'll alienate the Greek populace." Bob turned to Stacey. "And we're going to make it very uncomfortable for anyone who defends these bastards. With or without the assistance of the Greek authorities."

CHAPTER TWENTY

JULY 30, 2004

Something was eating at Bob, but he couldn't quite put his finger on it. He'd gone back to reading case files since Markeson and Bridewell's visit. He focused on *Greek Spring's* acts of terrorism, its MO. Although they had used several different methods of violence, there seemed to be a similarity in many of the attacks. Not only was the same .45 pistol used over and over again, but the attacks usually involved more than one killer. The vehicles—vans, cars, and motorcycles—used in their attacks were often stolen. He tossed the incident file he was reading on the table and got out of his chair. *Greek Spring* had injured four Turkish diplomats in a bombing attack thirteen years ago.

Bob glanced at his watch. He expected a call from Jack Cole at Langley in five minutes, at 6:30 P.M. Athens time. Five minutes to try to dredge up what was nibbling at the fringes of his memory. Something about that attack in 1991.

Bob paced his small office. "Come on, man, think," he growled at himself. At times like this he wondered if his synapses would have sparked and given him the answer he was looking for if he were twenty years younger. He criss-crossed the office until the jangling of the telephone diverted his attention. He grabbed the receiver and plopped back down in the chair behind his desk.

"Hey, Jack, right on time," Bob said.

"You know, a phone call letting me know that you had arrived in Greece and that all was well would have been appreciated."

Bob exhaled an "Oh" into the phone and said, "Hi, Liz. I was going to call you tonight after I went back to the hotel."

"Yeah, and the moon is made of cheese."

Bob groaned. "I've been a bit busy, honey. You know how it is."

"Oh, I know how it is." She paused for a moment, and said, "Okay, here's the deal. I rented the house to a nice couple who are going to be in the area for one year while the wife finishes her doctorate at Georgetown. They're moving in next week. I have plane reservations to arrive in Athens on the sixth of August, next Friday. I've arranged to store the cars and the furniture—"

"Whoa, Liz," Bob said. He knew his voice was raised and that he had allowed anger to affect his tone; but he didn't have time to deal with this now. He was going to have a tough enough time with his mission in Greece without having to worry about Liz. "I thought we agreed to discuss the timetable for you coming over here. I haven't even got my feet on the ground yet. I don't have a place to live. You can't—"

"Hold it, buster," Liz said in a throaty voice that Bob had heard her use on their son Michael when he'd acted up. She'd rarely used the tone on him. "You need someone watching out for you. If I don't fly over there, you'll work eighteen-hour days, seven days a week, and you'll miss half your meals. Whether you like it or not, I'm coming to Athens. I'll find a place for us to live. Any questions?"

Before Bob could respond, a knock sounded on his office door, Sam Goodwin stuck his head in the office, and said, "Jack Cole on line two."

"I'll be right with him," Bob told Sam. Then he blew out an exasperated sigh and said to Liz, "Okay, I give up. E-mail me your flight information. I'll pick you up at the airport."

"Check your inbox; I sent the flight information to you yesterday."

"How'd you get my e-mail address over here?" Bob asked.

"I have my sources," Liz said with a laugh. "I miss you, Bob," she added.

"Me too, honey," Bob said, "even though you're a pushy broad."

"You're so romantic," she said.

Bob laughed. "I think I might enjoy having you over here with me."

"You think! You think!" Liz shouted playfully. "You really know how to make a girl feel wanted."

"I gotta take a call, Liz. I'll call you from my room tonight."

"You'd better," she responded and hung up.

Well, you handled that well, Bob thought as he pressed the blinking button for line two. "Sorry to keep you waiting, Jack," he said.

"No problem," Jack answered. "I assume you were talking with Liz. She should always take priority."

"How in God's name do you know that?"

"That Liz takes top priority?" Jack said.

"Godammit, you know what I meant."

"Take it easy, buddy," Jack said.

"Sorry, Jack, I guess the situation over here is getting to me." Bob hesitated a moment, then said, "You gonna tell me how you knew I was talking with Liz?"

"Because she called me yesterday and asked for your e-mail address and telephone number. I told her we had a call scheduled at six-thirty your time today and suggested she call you then. That way she would be sure to catch you. I gave her your telephone number, too."

"How long have you and my wife been conspiring against me?"

"Years, my friend. Many, many years. So, how are things?"

"Actually, better than I had hoped in some instances, and at least as bad as I anticipated in others. The team I have to work with is top notch, and the Brits appear to be willing to work with us. On the negative side, the Greek investigative process into *Greek Spring* is nothing short of a clusterfuck."

"That's why you're over there," Jack said, "to change the Greek leadership's approach. And if anyone can find the rock those bastards are hiding under, it's you."

"Thanks for the vote of confidence; but I think the upcoming Olympic Games has had as much to do with changing the Greek

Government's attitude toward terrorism as anything else. That change in attitude may be just what we need. The more pressure brought to bear on the terrorists by the Greek leadership, the more likely someone in one of the terror groups will make a mistake."

"Last I heard, there are dozens of terror cells over there. How the hell are you going to manage that situation? It will be like herding cats."

"We're going to focus on the most active group: *Greek Spring*. Our feeling is that if we take that cell down, we'll do irreparable damage to a lot of the other cells. A lot of these smaller groups may be nothing but red herrings and splinter groups. *17 November* was one of two big fish in the terrorist cesspool. Now *EA* is the only big fish left." These words had barely crossed his lips when Bob suddenly had a brain flash. He'd made the connection that had been gnawing at him before the telephone rang. Something Tanya had said back at Langley. "You have anything else for me?" Bob asked, trying to keep impatience from his voice.

"You scheduled to meet with the Prime Minister?"

"Yeah, next Friday. The sixth. The ambassador set it up."

"Remember, you've got the trump card to play if you need it."

"I know; but I don't think it will be necessary. Besides, our Olympic team is already here. Pulling the team will make the President as popular as Jimmy Carter was after he pulled our team out of the Moscow Games."

"Okay," Jack said. "Keep your eyes and ears open. If the bad guys find out you're there . . .."

"Yeah, I know. Thanks, Jack."

Bob signed off and leaped to his feet. He went from his office into the bullpen area. Files were stacked on all three of the desks there. Sam and Stacey had their noses buried in files; Tony was halfway out the door.

"Let me have your attention for a moment," Bob said, causing Tony to turn around and shut the office door behind him. Sam and Stacey pushed their chairs away from their desks. "How many terrorist organizations are operating in Athens?" he asked.

"Oh Jesus, Mr. Danforth," Stacey said, "there have got to be dozens of groups."

Bob looked at Sam and Tony and inferred from their expressions that they agreed with Stacey. "Okay, let's eliminate *Abu Nidal* and groups affiliated with Middle East groups with an anti-Israel agenda, the Kurdish PPK, anti-Turkish groups, and the like. Focus on the Greek-based organizations with objectives similar to *Greek Spring's*."

"There are still a bunch," Tony said. "*The Friendship Society, Red Line, Enraged Anarchists, Revolutionary Subversive Faction, Nihilist Faction, Anti-establishment Nuclei*, and so on."

"And what do these groups have in common, besides their stated aims?" Bob asked.

After a few seconds had passed, Tony offered an answer: "They each appear to have very few members."

"They're all violent," Sam said.

"What else?" Bob asked.

"They don't appear to have an expansion goal. They seem to care less about growing, about recruiting new members," Stacey added.

Tony and Sam were now pacing the room, as though moving helped them think. Tony said, "They have the support of people in government and in the press, and, based on their communiqués, they appear to be well-educated."

"Good," Bob said, while he moved to the window and looked out at the sea. When he turned back to the team, he looked from Sam, to Tony, to Stacey and said, "Tony, you mentioned the communiqués the various terrorist groups have issued after their assassinations and bombings. Anything strange about them?"

Tony seemed to think about the question for a moment. "Not that I can . . .." Then his face lit up. "Holy shit! Yeah, there's something real strange about their messages. Almost all of them sound the same.

I mean, the writing style, the use of certain words, even the length of the messages. It's as though the same person wrote many of the letters, as though the groups are connected with one another."

"Or, as though many of the terrorist groups were really one and the same," Sam noted.

Bob pointed a finger at Sam. "Now you've got it," he said. "What if all of the terrorist organizations—or at least many of them—which have claimed responsibility for crimes are nothing more than one group of individuals operating under a myriad of organizational titles? What if they're using different names to throw off the authorities? What if we're dealing with a cell structure, all under the leadership of one person, or of a few people?"

"That could make our job a lot easier," Sam blurted, his voice rising with excitement.

"Maybe, in one sense," Bob said. "The job does not appear as daunting if we have a small, integrated group committing these violent acts. But, if we're correct, we've still got the problem of finding a few people in a city of four million."

"Maybe we can narrow our search a bit," Sam said. "The consensus opinion of the psychological profiles the Brits have done is that the leaders of the group, or groups, are intellectuals—doctors, lawyers, educators, journalists. We should focus in on the intelligentsia."

"Here's what I want you to do," Bob said. "Go back and review every violent crime claimed by Greek terrorist organizations. Look for similarities in the crime MOs, in the style and wording of the communiqués sent after the crimes. Which newspapers did they send their communiqués to. Let's see if we can come up with something. And, two other things. I agree with Stanton Markeson. I think we are probably dealing with fewer than thirty individuals, maybe as few as twenty, in *EA*. Any more than that and I suspect someone would have made a mistake by now. No organization can operate for an extended period of time in absolute secrecy unless it's relatively small. In fact, it's staggering that not a single one of the *EA* terrorists has screwed up and gotten caught. Lastly, let's try to identify someone who was actively involved in Marxist-Leninist organizations, probably recruited as a university student, and perhaps trained in the former Soviet Union, maybe at Patrice Lumumba University, or in Cuba."

"One other thing, Mr. Danforth," Stacey said. "I think the leader has got to be an egomaniac. The tenor of the letters sent to the press has been self-righteous, egotistical. I think this guy is in the terror business for two reasons: He likes violence and he likes messing with the authorities. He especially likes tweaking the noses of the most powerful nations on earth."

"I agree," Tony said. "*Greek Spring,* like *17 November,* started with a Marxist orientation, but it smoothly transitioned into whatever doctrine was convenient—nationalism, anti-imperialism, anti-colonialism, anti-Americanism, and even anti-multinational corporations. The top guy of *Greek Spring*, and maybe of all or many of the other terrorist cells, is no longer supporting an ideology. He's in the business to feed his own ego."

"That's good thinking," Bob said. "I'm going to have Langley put together a new psychological profile on the guy. Then we'll follow that thread. We'll check with professional organizations—teachers unions, lawyers and doctors associations, and the like. Maybe someone in those groups can match up an individual against the profile."

Bob could see that his team was excited. They had long days of grunt work ahead; their eyes would become red from staring at computer screens and photocopied documents. But they now had a specific, narrower goal, instead of the almost impossible task which had confronted them.

CHAPTER TWENTY-ONE
JULY 30, 2004

July had been an unusually mild month in Athens. The temperature had stayed below ninety and a moderate wind had reduced the air pollution from a three cigarette pack per day level to about a one-pack per day level for the last few days. Friday changed all that. The temperature rose to the mid-nineties and the breeze disappeared. By 7:30 P.M., the air was gray, the pollution so bad that Pavlos Manganos' eyes burned. The traffic in Constitution Square reminded him of the bumper car concession at the amusement park he'd visited in Germany a couple years earlier. Vehicle anarchy. He would have preferred to wait in the hotel, in the air-conditioned lobby, but that wouldn't have been the smart thing to do. The hotel might have security cameras.

Pavlos' 35 millimeter Nikon camera with telephoto lens hung on a strap around his neck. He moved every fifteen minutes or so, from a spot in the shadow of the Bank of America bank branch, to a crowded place on a sidewalk behind a street vendor, to the Parliament building steps, to the front of a row of shops. He snapped pictures as though he was a tourist intent on doing a photographic study of the square. The area was so bright with street and shop lights that Pavlos knew his shots would turn out fine, even without a flash attachment.

Demetrios Mavroyianni's source at the Justice Ministry had provided them with the name of the hotel where Robert Danforth was staying: The Grand Bretagne. Giorgos Photos had sent Pavlos to watch the hotel entrance, to see if he might be able to pick out the CIA man. But Pavlos was beyond frustrated. The pollution was making him hack and he had no way of knowing what Danforth looked like. To make matters worse, he'd had to cancel his date with Lela—the third time he'd stood her up in a month. His involvement with *Greek Spring* was ruining his sex life. He was about to go to the pay phone on the far side of the square to call Lela, when a white Ford Taurus pulled up in front of the Grand Bretagne and two men got out of the vehicle. Pavlos recognized the driver: Tony Fratangelo. He'd watched the man meet with Mikaelis Griffas on two occasions. He'd seen Fratangelo walk from the small street in Piraeus to the same white Ford the night Pavlos had killed Griffas. He didn't know who the second man was, but he had a damned good idea.

Pavlos took rapid-fire pictures of the two men as the passenger started up the front steps of the hotel and the driver said something to him over the top of the car. The other man turned and looked at Fratangelo, saying something in return. Pavlos snapped a full frontal shot of the man standing in the hotel entrance, highlighted by the hotel's lights.

The heat and smog forgotten, Pavlos felt exhilarated, as though jet fuel pumped through his veins. If his instincts were correct, he had just photographed Robert Danforth, a high-level CIA man, a target to rival *17 November's* first target: Richard Welch.

CHAPTER TWENTY-TWO

JULY 31, 2004

Dimitris Argyropoulos wanted two things out of life. He wanted to bring down his enemies: The United States, Britain, and Turkey. And he wanted to capture the imagination of the Greek people in a way that would imprint his name in the minds of every citizen and catapult him into the position of Prime Minister. As Deputy Prime Minister, the odds were in his favor that he would succeed the present Prime Minister in the next round of elections, four years from now. But Argyropoulos didn't want to wait. He stared out at the top edge of the rising sun as it broke above the sparkling Aegean waters and felt his chest swell with the promise of a glorious future for him and his country.

He turned his wrist so that the sun lit up his watch face: 6:30. The ferry would dock in another fifteen minutes. He checked around the boat deck to make sure none of the other passengers were too close to him. It wouldn't do for one of them to recognize him. He pulled his black knit fisherman's hat lower on his head and snapped his windbreaker over his neck, partially covering his face. This would have to be his last trip to Evoia. But it would be the most important one.

Giorgos Photos picked up Argyropoulos at the Evoia ferry dock. The ride to Photos' home took ten minutes. The Deputy Prime Minister sensed the other man's anxiety. It matched his own. It wasn't that he was frightened. In actuality, he was excited. They were meeting to finalize a series of actions that would prove to be the seminal events of Greece's modern history and of its future. They rode in silence until Photos pulled into the driveway of his home.

"*Eteemos eesay?*" Argyropoulos asked.

"Yes, I'm ready," Photos answered.

Argyropoulos came around to the driver-side of the car and hooked his arm inside Photos' arm. "Good, my friend. Let's go inside. Our country awaits its destiny."

The windows of Photos' house were shuttered; the doors now locked. The only light came from a table lamp in a corner of the living room. Photos turned on a projector connected to a laptop computer on a small round table in the middle of the room. The light beam from the projector lit up one white wall. Photos then tapped on the computer keyboard and a list showed on the wall.

"I made some entries last night based on information I received from one of my people in Athens." He laughed. "Our luck is getting better with each day."

Argyropoulos stared at the projected image and noted with satisfaction that Photos had added several names to the list since he had seen it last. "Who is this Robert Danforth?"

"A highly placed CIA Special Operations officer. He's been with the Agency since the seventies. He was with the United States Army before that. And you're going to love this; he was stationed here in Greece during the time of the junta. Danforth helped keep the Colonels in power. He was part of the bastard Americans' plot to deny our people an elected government."

"All very interesting," the Deputy Prime Minister said, "but why is he on the list?"

Photos laughed again. "Because he's in Athens as we speak. The CIA sent him here to stop us."

Argyropoulos shook his head in wonder. "Isn't that ironic?" he said.

Photos ran down the list, briefing Argyropoulos on the proposed chronology of events, beginning with an attack on the British, then the killings of CIA agents Danforth and Fratangelo, and ending with the *coup de grace*.

Argyropoulos questioned Photos on every detail of every detail of the plan. When he had asked every question he could think of, he walked over to the wall by the front door and flipped on the lights. Photos switched off the projector.

"You can make all of this happen?" Argyropoulos asked.

"And more," Photos said. "The actions we just went through are the high points. We will fill in the gaps between the major events with a hundred attacks that will demoralize our enemies. We will bring them to their knees."

"This will ruin the attendance at the Olympic Games."

"Exactly," Photos said. "The business community will be up in arms. The Prime Minister will lose his supporters there. There will be a crisis of confidence in our leader."

Argyropoulos nodded a half-dozen times as he thought about the sequence of attacks Photos had just described and the consequences. If the man and his terror cell performed, Argyropoulos knew the Prime Minister would be forced to resign and he would replace him. He would govern a new Greece, a Greece of his own design. A country that would attain a level of influence and respect it had not enjoyed for over two millennia, a country divorced from the suffocating influence of The United States, England, and Turkey. He smiled at Photos and said, "You will hold a place of honor in our government and will become a national hero."

Photos stood and approached the Deputy Prime Minister. They clasped one another's arms and simultaneously said, "*Zeeto ee Ellas*," cheering their country.

"I need to sleep," Argyropoulos said. "I was up all last night. I'll catch the ferry back to the mainland after dark tonight."

Photos led Argyropoulos to a bedroom. "I'll have something prepared to eat when you wake. The ferry leaves at nine P.M."

"Thank you, my friend."

Argyropoulos undressed and slipped into bed. He turned off the table lamp by the bed and stared into the blackness of the room. I'll have to find a way to get rid of Photos and his people, he thought. I can't afford to have anyone around who could tie me to the terrorists. That goes for the head of the Economic Development Department in the Ministry of Finance, Nicolaos Koufos. The man is losing his nerve.

CHAPTER TWENTY-THREE
JULY 31, 2004

Nicolaos Koufos felt like a man in the darkest jungle who knew someone was hunting him, but couldn't see or hear anything. The fluttering feeling in his gut seemed to be occurring more frequently. *Greek Spring* was out of control. Koufos couldn't connect present actions taken by the group with what he considered its noble creation.

But there was nothing he could do to change things. He was in too deep. If he reported what he knew about *Greek Spring* to the Ministry of Public Order, he would incriminate himself. He could kill Photos. *Eleeneekee Aneexee* would wither away without Photos' leadership. But Koufos knew he didn't have the nerve to be a killer.

Perspiration broke out on Koufos' forehead and ran down his spine. He wanted to pray for forgiveness, for deliverance; but he didn't believe God would listen to someone who had fallen as far as he had. He started to rise from his desk chair when his cell phone rang. He pulled the phone from his suit jacket pocket and snapped it open. "Hello," he said, trying to steel his voice to hide the despair he felt.

"You sound tired, Nicky."

"No, no, I'm fine," he lied. "What are you up to, Vassa? How was your trip to Paris?"

"Glorious," Koufos' sister said. "The food, the shopping, the men. I suffered from sensory overload."

Koufos didn't approve of his sister's lifestyle. She spent too much money and had the morals of an alley cat. If he were her husband, he would straighten her out or dump her. "You keep taking these trips and you'll ruin your husband."

Vassa laughed. "I couldn't go through his money if I shopped twenty-four hours a day, seven days a week. Hell, the interest income alone is staggering."

"Okay, Vassa, what's on your mind?"

"I can't call my only brother to say hello after being away for two weeks?"

Koufos was already tired; Vassa was making him feel exhausted. "Okay, sister, you've said hello. I've got work to do. I'll see you tomorrow when the family gets together for dinner."

Before he could hang up, Vassa shouted, "I've got tickets to a football match."

Koufos' stomach erupted. His sister's use of the private code they had established surprised him. She'd been away for two weeks. She hadn't been back in the country long enough to have any new information to pass on.

"Ye-e-s?" he said. "Which game?"

"Panathenaikos against AEK. Tonight at seven."

CHAPTER TWENTY-FOUR
JULY 31, 2004

The Fratangelos had invited Bob to their home for dinner. He'd come close to begging off, but decided to accept their invitation. He didn't want to offend Tony, and he admitted to himself that a home-cooked dinner with a real family might be a wonderful change. He'd rented an Audi A6 sedan and told Tony he would be at the Fratangelo home in Kifissia at 7:30. It was 6:00 now and he had to make two phone calls, one to Langley and the second to Liz.

The call to Jack Cole was fairly routine, other than the part of the conversation about Fred Grantham and Harvey Cornwell's murders. Bob rehashed the conversation after he hung up. He picked up the Grantham/Cornwell file, randomly reviewing papers. Much of the attack was similar to other *Greek Spring* attacks. The same weapon. Two men on a motorcycle. Cornwell on his way to work. Heavy, slow-moving traffic—making the Englishman a sitting duck. It had been a fluke that Fred Grantham had been along. On any other day, the CIA Station Chief would have driven to the meeting at the British Embassy in his own vehicle. But it had been in the shop and Grantham had called Cornwell and asked for a ride. They lived a few blocks from one another.

But comments made to an MI-6 investigator by Cornwell's widow had been tormenting Bob. He looked for the transcript of the taped interview and dug it out of the middle of the file. He found the section he was looking for.

"Did the Brigadier have a routine regarding the time he went to work, the route he followed?" the investigator had asked.

"Absolutely not," Mrs. Cornwell had responded. "Even before Stephen Saunders' murder, all government employees were ordered to avoid a routine, the time they left home, the route they followed."

"Could anyone have known your husband's route and schedule that morning?"

"Of course. He always called the office before leaving the house, to tell them he was on the way in. He could have mentioned which street he was going to take. He did that once in a while."

"Did he call in that morning?" the investigator asked.

"I don't know. I was busy getting the girls ready for school."

"When he would call in, do you know who he talked to?"

"It varied from day to day. Whoever was in the office and happened to take the call."

Bob realized the assassins could have been waiting for a target of opportunity. Maybe they hadn't selected Cornwell in advance that morning. Perhaps he just happened to be the unfortunate Brit who drove into the gun sights of killers that morning. But that wasn't *Greek Spring's* M.O. They were careful planners. If the killers knew where and when to find Cornwell, that could mean there was a traitor in the British Embassy.

Bob shook his head as though to clear it of the unwanted thought. It was inconceivable; but something in his gut told him he needed to pursue this line of thinking, no matter how abhorrent it seemed.

He put the file away and called Liz.

"Hey, babe," he said after she picked up the phone.

"Well, that's a little better start than the last time we talked."

"You're not going to bust my chops right off the bat, are you?"

"You deserve worse than that," she said, but Bob could hear the humor in her tone as the butterflies in his stomach took flight. The same butterflies that always seemed to be present when he thought about how much he loved this woman.

"You know I want you with me," he said. "I can't help it if I worry about you."

She relented and said, "I know that, Bob. But I married you for better or for worse." She laughed and added, "There's been a lot of worse; but think how boring our lives would have been otherwise."

"Boring sounds good," he said. "Boring sounds real good."

"Uh-huh. I suppose you want me to believe that."

Bob laughed. "I'd better sign off," he said. "Tony and Michelle Fratangelo asked me to their house for dinner tonight."

"Good," Liz said. "I'm glad someone is looking out for you. Love you."

"I love you too, honey. See you next Friday."

CHAPTER TWENTY-FIVE

AUGUST 1, 2004

Giorgos Photos dropped Dimitris Argyropoulos off at the Evoia ferry dock late Saturday night and watched the massive blue and white boat carry the Deputy Prime Minister toward Athens. Then he returned to his place, slept for eight hours, and drove back to the ferry dock just after dawn on Sunday morning.

Photos felt charged with electricity. All he had worked on for almost three decades was approaching fruition. The movement had been grounded in Marxism in the beginning, but that message no longer resonated with the Greek people. Nationalism grounded in anti-Americanism and an independent Cyprus—free of Turkish occupation, had become more popular themes. So, *Greek Spring* had adapted. Now, they were less than two weeks away from having their man in the Prime Minister's seat. When that happened, on the heels of more assassinations and a devastating attack on the Olympic venue, the Greek people would embrace the cause. They would embrace Argyropoulos as their new leader when he assured the nation there would be no more terrorist attacks, when his hand-picked enforcers raided the safehouses of the terror groups in Greece and wiped out their members. Photos smiled. He would personally see to it that the members of *Greek Spring* were eliminated.

It was 10:20 Sunday morning when Photos pulled his car off the ferry and wound his way through the Athenian streets. He decided to stop at a *taverna* along the water. He hadn't eaten since the night before and he knew he wouldn't have time to stop for food until later that night. His meeting with Pavlos Manganos would take several hours. Planning was the essence of *Greek Spring's* success.

He stopped at *Taverna Marathonos* and selected a table in the back, under the shade of a blue canvas cover. After the waiter took his order, Photos stretched his long legs in front of him and stared out at the sea. A stiff wind was whipping at the water, making it choppy. Whitecaps danced across the surface. Photos thought that the situation in Greece, like the sea before him, was about to get unsettled. He blurted a slight laugh. His cell phone chirped as the waiter served him coffee and a croissant.

"Yes," he answered.

"Can you talk?"

Photos recognized Demetrios Mavroyianni's voice. He looked around. Only one other table was occupied, and that was at least ten meters away.

"Go ahead," he said.

"I tried to call you last night."

"I was in a meeting; my phone was switched off. What's going on?"

"My contact at the Ministry of Justice called last night. He ran through visa applications on his computer. He thought there might be something interesting there after he discovered that the American, Danforth, had arrived in Greece."

"I assume he found something."

"He thought the Americans would probably send more than one person over here."

"That was very industrious of him," Photos said, getting impatient with Mavroyianni. "Did he find another match?"

"Hah, that wasn't even necessary. The name of the woman on the visa request has the same last name as Danforth's." Demetrios paused for a moment, as though he was building up the suspense, then added, "And according to her visa application, she's due to arrive in Athens—"

Photos cut him off. "I'll be at the same place we met last time," Photos declared. "Be there at 3:00." He hung up and considered what he had just been told. If Danforth's wife was coming to Athens, then there was a strong possibility he would be at the airport to greet her. He would have preferred to watch Danforth's movements for several weeks before setting up an attack. But an opportunity seemed to be about to present itself. And killing the CIA agent *and* his wife would send a message that would be like a spike in the heart of the American spy organization.

He picked up the croissant and devoured it.

CHAPTER TWENTY-SIX

August 1, 2004

Nicolaos Koufos hadn't slept at all. His meeting with his sister, Vassa, had been brief but poignant. Vassa said she had gone to bed with her fat husband that afternoon, explaining how disgusted she felt fucking him.

"Please spare me the details," Koufos had complained. "The last thing any brother wants to hear is the particulars of his sister's sex life."

"Nicky, you're such a prude," Vassa said. "You should open your mind, you might learn something. I suspect your wife, Sofia, would appreciate a little variety in her bed. I could teach you—"

"Enough!" Koufos growled. "Do you have something to tell me, or not."

Vassa laughed, put her arms around her brother, and whispered in his ear.

It was now Sunday morning. Koufos sat on his back patio, a copy of *Eleftherotypia* propped up before him. He didn't have a clue what was written on the newspaper pages. But he didn't want to get into a conversation with Sofia while he thought about what he would do next. He thought about his alternatives: call his contact with *Greek Spring*, call the authorities, or do nothing. He recognized that his conscience was driving him crazy. It took him an hour to come to the conclusion that he had no choice.

"I need to run an errand," he told his wife, standing and walking toward the house.

"Don't forget the family will be here at 5:00," she said. She didn't bother to ask where he was going. Her husband's position with the government was always taking him away.

Koufos nodded and entered the house through the back door. How the hell can I continue to look my brother-in-law in the eye, he thought as he stepped to the telephone.

"Hello," the man said.

"Do you know who this is?" Koufos asked.

"Of course, sir. Can I be of assistance?"

Koufos checked his watch: 11:00. "Be at the drop site in one hour." He hung up and walked to the refrigerator. He took out a plastic water bottle and dumped the contents in the sink, placing the bottle upside down on the kitchen counter, ensuring there was no moisture left in it. Then he moved to his office and scribbled the names Rodney Townsend, Cyril Bridewell, and Marcus Swinton on a scrap of paper. He added the words: Secret Brit. Intelligence team and an address. After rolling the paper into a small tube shape, he returned to the kitchen with his briefcase under his arm, shook the bottle several times, saw that it was dry inside, and inserted the rolled up piece of paper into the bottle. He capped the bottle and put it inside his briefcase.

The ride along the wooded narrow two-lane road toward Katsamidi took thirty minutes. Five hundred meters from the entrance to what used to be the former Greek King's summer palace, he stopped his car and executed a U-turn. He left the car and moved to a guardrail, the plastic bottle in one hand and a screwdriver in the other. Railroad ties supported the steel guardrail. Koufos went to the third railroad tie on the left and slipped the edge of the flathead screwdriver in a slot five centimeters from the top of the tie. He popped the top off the tie, dropped the bottle into a hollowed out space, and replaced the cap. He scurried back to his car and drove away. He was still shaking when he arrived home.

CHAPTER TWENTY-SEVEN

August 1, 2004

Bob had enjoyed his visit with the Fratangelos even more than he had thought he might. Tony's wife, Michelle, had been an exceptional hostess and cook, and Andrew had been a joy to be around. Bob learned that Andrew had spina bifida, a defect in the arch of the vertebrae that results in a failure of the vertebrae to fuse. The boy had already suffered through a half-dozen operations and, according to Tony, was about as mobile as he was ever going to be.

Tony had explained Andrew's condition in a matter-of-fact way. It was just something they had all come to accept, including the little boy, who didn't appear to know he had a problem, despite the braces on his legs and the crutches he used to get around.

The boy seemed to have gotten past the point of blaming Bob for Tony's long workdays and suckered Bob into a game of chess. Trying to be the good guest, Bob intentionally moved some of his key pieces into positions that made them vulnerable to Andrew's attacks. After all, he was playing against a six-year-old. They were five minutes into the first game, when the boy looked at Bob and said, "You're either the worst chess player in the world, or you're throwing the game."

Bob heard Tony snort a laugh behind him. "You'd better play your best game against this little hustler," Tony said.

They started a new game, and Bob discovered that Andrew Fratangelo was not only a chess prodigy, but ruthless when he was on the attack. They split the first two games; then Bob lost the third game in a blitzkrieg that lasted less than ten minutes.

After Michael put Andrew to bed, Bob asked, "Where did he learn to play like that?"

"I'm sorry about that, Mr. Danforth," Tony said. "He loves to hustle our guests. Michelle's father is a Grand Master. He spent a lot of time with Andrew when we lived in Virginia. Andrew apparently inherited the chess gene from his grandfather."

"First of all, it's about time you and the rest of the team called me Bob. Second, don't apologize for Andrew beating me. Twenty years from now I'm going to be able to tell people I took one game from Grand Master Andrew Fratangelo. Of course, I won't mention he was only six-years-old at the time!"

It was Sunday, just after noon, and Bob had slept late and just finished breakfast in the hotel dining room. He signed the check, went to the front desk and asked for his car to be brought up. He needed to go to the office and was feeling guilty about getting such a late start.

Athens' streets were crowded with families driving to wherever Greek families go on Sundays—church, relatives' houses, the beach, parks, historical sites, and restaurants. It took Bob an hour to get to the Glyfada office. He anticipated he would have the office to himself, since he had told the rest of the team to take the day off. They had all worked fourteen-hour days during the past week, and he didn't want his people burning out. But he found Tony, Stacey, and Sam had all beat him in.

"Happy Sunday, folks," Bob announced by way of greeting.

Sam and Tony waved at Bob; Stacey picked up a file and followed him into his office.

"You know that idea about tying one of the terrorist leaders to the Communists?" she said.

"Tell me you found something," Bob said.

"Not yet; but I think we may have a chance of making a connection."

"How so?"

"I had breakfast this morning with a friend of mine with the Czechoslovakian Embassy. She's in their Intelligence Section and was recently assigned to Greece from D.C. We got to know each other in the States."

"All in the spirit of détente," Bob said.

Stacey smiled. "That and the fact we go bar hopping together. We seem to like the same kind of men. Anyway, I brought up the subject of the terrorists and the thought that one or more of the leaders might have been trained in a Communist school or terrorist training camp supported by the former Soviet Union. She told me she'd do some research and see if she could find something."

"That's good work, Stacey. Keep me informed if anything comes of it."

The young woman blushed from Bob's praise and left the office.

Bob thought about Stacey's information. It was amazing what a difference a few years could make. He would have just as soon shot any Iron Curtain Czechoslovakian Intelligence Officer as look at one just a few years ago. Now CIA and Czech agents spent evenings together meeting men in the nation's capital.

But Stacey had given him an idea he should have thought about himself. He booted up his computer and sent an encrypted message to Frank Reynolds at Langley: *Contact former Soviet bloc sources for information about all Greeks who attended Communist training schools and/or terrorist training camps sponsored by Soviets.* Bob had taken Stacey's idea a giant step forward. If this request bore fruit, he would see to it that Stacey Frederick's personnel file included a letter of commendation.

CHAPTER TWENTY-EIGHT

August 1, 2004

Giorgos Photos watched Pavlos Manganos pour two inches of retsina wine into each of three glasses. Manganos handed one glass to Photos, a second one to Demetrios Mavroyianni, and then picked up the third glass. The three men lifted their glasses. *"Steen yia sas,"* Photos toasted.

"Yia sas," Manganos and Mavroyianni repeated.

While they each sipped from their glasses, Photos wondered about the embarrassment of information riches that had fallen into his hands. It normally wasn't this easy. He might be the recipient of one bit of information that could lead to the identification of one target. Suddenly, it was as though he had received a cornucopia of leads and potential targets. Again, he was a bit uncomfortable with the time sequences involved with these potential opportunities; but he had to take the chance. This was the beginning of the final campaign, the campaign that would lead to the climactic event.

The slip of paper that had been passed to him by one of his cell members had identified three British Intelligence Officers operating in Athens, along with an address he assumed was their headquarters. two out of three of *Greek Spring's* last assassinations had been Englishmen. Three more would send a message to the bastards that they were messing around with the wrong people in the wrong location. They'd planned an attack against the English, against the British Tourist Bureau. An attack against British Intelligence was a whole other matter.

The information about the English was a bounty in and of itself; but the information from Elizabeth Danforth's visa application and about her flight number, arrival date and time into the Athens airport really excited Photos. *Greek Spring* had principally targeted political enemies, both foreign and domestic. The next phase of the campaign he and Dimitris Argyropoulos had devised not only included attacking political targets more frequently, but also involved hitting their family members and civilians at random. They were going to create an atmosphere in which no one felt safe, in which the citizens of Greece would cry out desperately for a leader who would make them secure. The assassinations of Robert Danforth and his wife and of the Brits would be big steps in that process.

Photos took a seat at a table. The other two men followed suit.

"Demetrios, I want you to surveil the address we were provided. See if you can identify the people who go in and out of the building. Follow one of them at the end of the day. Find out where they go, who they meet with." He passed a sheet of paper to Mavroyianni with the names of the three Englishmen printed on it. "These are the ones we're interested in."

Photos turned to Manganos. "Pavlos," he said, "you will follow the American. You know what he looks like. I want to know his habits, where he goes each morning, and so on."

Manganos nodded his understanding.

"We must assume that Danforth will meet his wife when her plane arrives. But, of course, that isn't a certainty. So, in addition to following the man starting tomorrow morning, I want you to be like a hair on his ass on Friday morning. If he moves toward the airport, our team will be ready."

"Do you plan on hitting them as they leave the airport?" Mavroyianni asked.

Photos slowly rubbed the fingers of one hand over his chin and inhaled a long, deep breath. After loudly exhaling, he looked first at Manganos and then at Mavroyianni. "I've thought about that a lot. It would probably be easier that way; but I think we could do it with a great deal more impact in Constitution Square."

Photos wasn't surprised at the other two men's reactions. They each placed their glasses on the table and stared at him. Round-eyed shock showed on their faces.

"You're assuming Danforth will bring his wife to the Grand Bretagne Hotel?" Manganos asked.

Photos met the man's gaze and said, "Yes."

"There are *Evzones* guards right across the street in front of Parliament, not to mention a dozen policemen wandering around the square," Mavroyianni said. "The American woman's plane gets in around ten A.M. That would put Danforth and his wife in the square around noon. The sidewalks around Constitution Square will be crowded. Mostly Greeks."

"All the better," Photos said. He carefully noted each man's surprise. Mavroyianni and Manganos looked at one another. They didn't appear happy.

"Now isn't the time to get queasy about what we're doing. It's time to put pressure on the government. It must learn that the more it cooperates with our enemies, the more we will retaliate. The Americans and the English wouldn't have investigative and Intelligence people here without the agreement of the Prime Minister. We must teach the Greek Government a lesson. Are you ready to do your duty?"

First Mavroyianni, then Manganos nodded his head, albeit reluctantly.

"I asked you if you are ready," Photos shouted.

"Yes," Manganos replied.

"I'm ready," Mavroyianni said.

CHAPTER TWENTY-NINE

AUGUST 2, 2004

Monday morning turned out to be more of the same for Bob. Lots of research, a meeting with Rodney Townsend at the British team's offices off Kolonaki Square, and a long telephone conversation with Jack Cole at Langley. Bob knew that Intelligence work was mostly sweat, eye strain, and frustration. But it was those things that solved cases. He was disappointed to learn that nothing had come back from the Agency's contacts with the former Soviet bloc. He realized he was being impractical to assume they would have any news for him this quickly; but he had an almost primal feeling that something would come from that source.

Bob wasn't especially looking forward to the afternoon. He had scheduled an appointment with Ambassador Finch for 2:00 today to go over the agenda for Bob's meeting with the Greek Prime Minister on Friday. When he'd called the ambassador to confirm the meeting, Finch informed him he was going to invite Grady McMasters, the Chief of the FBI's Counter-Terrorism unit stationed in Athens, to join them. Bob had objected, but the ambassador had threatened to pull his support if Bob didn't agree. Bob knew he would have to meet with the FBI man sooner or later, but he would have preferred later.

"I'm not going to have two different U.S. agencies running around Athens without each other's knowledge," the ambassador had said.

The CIA and the FBI didn't have the warmest of relationships. McMasters would surely get his back up when he learned a CIA covert team was operating in Greece without his knowledge. The President of the United States had personally authorized the formation of the

CIA team in Greece, and, for whatever reason, had not informed the FBI Director of his decision.

Bob wanted to spend his time productively—not get into a pissing match over turf or jurisdiction. He didn't know McMasters, but his experience in working with the FBI didn't leave him feeling optimistic about the meeting that afternoon.

The ambassador's secretary showed Bob into the ambassador's office at 2:00. The ambassador was seated behind his desk. A second man stood by the bank of windows.

"Bob Danforth, meet Grady McMasters," the ambassador said.

McMasters looked like Goliath in a light-blue Sears Roebuck suit. He stood at least six feet five inches tall and weighed around three hundred pounds—much of it muscle. The guy was a monster and seemed to relish the effect he had on most people. He crossed the thick blue carpeted floor and shook Bob's hand while staring into Bob's eyes with an obvious challenge. He turned the simple greeting into a competition. When Bob thought the giant might crush the bones in his hand, he reached up with his left hand and pressed his thumb into the inside of the big man's wrist, causing McMasters to yelp. The FBI agent's face went red as he released his hold on Bob's hand.

"Well, gentlemen, I see you've introduced yourselves," Ambassador Finch said with a smile. "Shall we get started?"

McMasters shot Bob an evil look before turning around to face the ambassador. He moved toward one of the chairs facing Finch's desk, but did not sit. He pointed a sausage-sized forefinger at Bob, who was seated in a chair three feet away, and barked, "What the hell's going on? Since when is it the Agency's business to be—"

Finch stopped the FBI man. "I would appreciate it if you would sit down, Mr. McMasters." He waited until McMasters had done as asked, then continued. "You both work, through your respective chains of command, for the President of the United States." Finch made a point of meeting first McMasters', then Bob's eyes. "The President personally made it clear to me he expected both of you and all your people to cooperate over here." Again, Finch paused for effect. "Do we understand one another?" he asked.

"I'm happy to cooperate," Bob said.

McMasters grunted.

"What was that, Mr. McMasters?"

The FBI man's face turned red once again. "Of course we'll cooperate with our friends at the Agency."

"Excellent," Finch said, a smile again creasing his mouth. "Let's go over the agenda for the meeting this coming Friday with the Prime Minister."

CHAPTER THIRTY
AUGUST 2, 2004

Demetrios Mavroyianni took a seat at a sidewalk cafe table across the street from the building in Kolonaki Square housing the British offices. After arriving at 7:00 A.M. and eyeballing the men who went in and out of the six-story office building for the next hour, Demetrios chatted up the waitress who had been serving him coffee. He asked her if she knew of any Englishmen named Rodney, Cyril, or Marcus who worked in the building across the street. The Greek girl was tripping all over herself trying to please the good-looking Demetrios.

"Sure, there's an Englishman named Marcus who comes in here all the time."

Demetrios lied to the waitress, telling her he was a newspaper reporter writing about foreign investors buying Greek real estate. That he had information the men he'd asked her about were working for a British realty company. "Would you be willing to point out this man when he leaves the building?" he asked her.

The girl smiled and said, "The one called Marcus comes in every morning about this time for coffee and a pastry." She looked at her wristwatch. "He should be here at any moment."

Once the girl ID'ed Marcus for Demetrios, he knew he'd already spotted the guy when he entered the building earlier. He thanked the girl, got her phone number, and left. The girl was a little young; but she had a killer body and a look about her that told him she would be eager to please. Besides, if they hit the Englishmen, the girl might put two and two together and tell the police that a man had been asking about them.

She could describe him to the police. He would have his fun and then dispose of her. Just one more sacrifice for the motherland.

Giorgos Photos hung up the telephone in the house in Keratea, a small town south of Athens. He threw open the shutters, rolled his shoulders, and sucked in a deep breath. The clean air filled his lungs. He knew in a couple of months the odor of grapes being processed into wine would be heavy in the air. Now the sea air wafted over the village and gave Photos a peaceful feeling.

Demetrios had come through. He'd identified one of the British agents. And Pavlos Manganos had called earlier and briefed Photos on what Danforth had done that day. He was intrigued by the Glyfada address Manganos had given him, where Danforth had spent the better part of the morning. He would have to get pictures taken of everyone entering and exiting that place. The Glyfada building could be the American version of the British offices in Kolonaki Square. All in all, it had been a very productive day.

Photos closed the shutters and thought about how he would respond to the information he'd received. He wanted to make a grand statement, and would prefer to take plenty of time in planning something. But time was of the essence. In an instant, he decided he would need the Libyan for this assignment. He'd used Musa Sulaiman before. *Al Qaeda* hired the man out for special assignments to groups around the world that didn't have the skills needed to execute certain special projects.

An errant thought crossed his mind. He would need to warn Koufos and his sister, Vassa, about his plans. No point in eliminating a valuable source. Vassa's husband had been an unwitting and important source of information for *Greek Spring*. He didn't wanted to kill him . . . just yet.

CHAPTER THIRTY-ONE

AUGUST 3, 2004

Jack Cole, like Bob Danforth, knew in every cell of his being that Stacey Frederick had developed an interesting, and possibly investigation-changing idea. If there was a training connection between the leaders of *Greek Spring* and Soviet bloc schools or Soviet-sponsored terrorist training camps, the Agency might be able to identify one or more of the terrorist organization's people through contacts with former members of Soviet bloc Intelligence services. Jack's instincts told him that, because the *EA* had started out as a Marxist group, there was a damned good chance some of the *EA* members would have a Soviet connection.

The biggest problems the CIA had, however, when dealing with sources from former Communist countries, was getting those sources to cooperate with them, and how much credence they could place on whatever information they did get. The paranoia of the Russians and the Intelligence people from their former satellites, like Bulgaria, Czechoslovakia, and Yugoslavia, hadn't diminished with the fall of the Iron Curtain. And, of course, sharing Intelligence with the CIA wasn't these peoples' top priority. Half of them were now involved with criminal organizations that seemed to be running the region.

In addition to Frank Reynolds, Tanya Serkovic, and Raymond Gallegos, Jack had assigned a dozen agents to ferret out whatever information they could about Greek nationals who had contacts with the Communist Governments of the Soviet bloc, or who had been trained in their schools and terrorist camps. He had also called a friend at the Federal Bureau of Investigation and asked for his help. Now he had to suffer through the difficult period of waiting.

Jack sat across the conference room table from Frank Reynolds and watched the man organize the papers he'd brought with him.

Frank looked up and said, "We don't have much to report."

"Just give me what you've got."

Frank hunched his shoulders, as though to say, Fine with me if you want to waste your time. "Raymond Gallegos has a contact in a Maryland security company—you know, alarms, listening devices, hidden cameras. That sort of thing. The guy who owns the place is Bulgarian. He was fairly high up in the Bulgarian Intelligence Service before defecting here. We believe he was the mastermind behind the assassination attempt against the Pope."

Jack's mouth opened, then closed. He decided to hold his tongue for the moment. The Intelligence business truly made for strange bedfellows.

"The guy has given us some pretty good info in the past. He told Raymond to come back in a week. Everybody you assigned to this project is digging under every possible rock, but . . .."

"What's on your mind?" Jack asked.

"Oh, hell, we're pushing on a string. Because Congress changed the laws governing Intelligence gathering, I'm not optimistic. We should have hundreds of contacts we could go to for information. Instead, we have a dozen or so people who were behind the Iron Curtain, and almost every one of them was a low level functionary who didn't have access to anything more important than petty criminals."

"So, what's your point?" Jack asked, smiling.

Frank threw up his hands. "No point, just venting. But if Sergei the Bulgarian at the security company doesn't come through, I don't have a lot of hope any of our other contacts will come up with anything."

"What else?" Jack said.

"We're seeing an increase in message traffic coming out of Greece to several places in the Middle East. I have to tell you, I'm worried. This heightened chatter usually happens right before a terrorist attack.

I passed this on to Bob Danforth in Athens. He and his crew need to keep a low profile for a while."

"I don't recall message traffic increasing before previous terrorist attacks in Greece," Jack said.

"That's right. This usually happens before something momentous involving Middle Eastern terrorists. Like the attacks on the World Trade Center. Past attacks in Greece have probably been pulled off by the local members of the Greek terrorist cells. If this message traffic is indicative of Middle Eastern terrorist involvement in something big, then perhaps one or more of the Greek groups is enlisting help from their Arab big brothers. Or maybe the Greeks aren't involved at all."

"Jesus," Jack exclaimed. "How long has this been going on?"

"It started this morning. The NSA intercepted a call coming from some little town south of Athens to Mosul, Iraq. Message traffic then branched out from Mosul to Shiraz, Beirut, and Tripoli. From what they were able to decipher in the conversations—of course, they were brief and cryptic—the caller in Greece was trying to contact someone named 'the Priest.' These calls set off a veritable daisy chain of subsequent calls to numbers we are certain are being used by members of *Al Qaeda*. We were able to trace several of the calls and passed on their locations to Covert Ops. The calls emanating from Mosul basically passed on the Greek caller's request. Then we picked up a call from Peshawar placed this afternoon to a public telephone in a drugstore in Athens. Neither the caller nor the recipient identified themselves. They spoke French. The Linguistics Section listened to the tape and determined that the caller was an Arab who had learned his French in Libya. They couldn't tell us anything about the recipient of the call, other than that his French was impeccable, possibly a native Frenchman."

Jack rehashed what he had just heard. He stood and walked to the far side of the conference room. After a moment, he turned and said, "Maybe the linguistics guys *did* tell us something."

Frank looked at Jack expectantly. "How so?"

"Bear with me for a moment. Let's make a few assumptions. First, the man who started the calling chain is part of one of the Greek terrorist groups. If he isn't, then we're wasting our time. But, at this moment, we have nothing else but time."

Frank nodded as though to show Jack he was following his line of thinking.

"The second assumption is that the original call from south of Athens was placed by a Greek."

Frank held up a hand and said, "Whoa, we have no way of knowing that."

"I'm making that assumption based on the fact that all of the *17 November* members identified by the police are Greek. I know it's a stretch, but I believe, like *17 November, Greek Spring* is one hundred percent Greek. And I think the communiqués that the terrorists send out after their attacks show they're Greek. They refer to Greece as 'our country.' They say things like, 'our heritage,' 'our history,' and so forth."

"Okay," Frank said. "But you're building one assumption on top of another assumption. That's a weak foundation."

"I'll give you that; but let me continue. The Linguistics Section said the recipient of the call spoke fluent French. So, if we have a Greek who was born and raised in France, maybe we can narrow down the target list for our Bulgarian friend."

Jack could see that Frank was skeptical; but unless the man could come up with something better, this was at least something that gave their assignment some purpose.

Jack started for the door, but stopped and said, "Frank, I want you to call Bob and tell him my half-assed theory. And remind him to keep his head down."

CHAPTER THIRTY-TWO

AUGUST 4, 2004

Musa Sulaiman stared at his image in the mirror. He adjusted his robes and straightened the heavy gold chain around his neck. The Greek Orthodox cross on the chain was slightly akimbo; he fixed that as well. As always, the headdress felt uncomfortable; but it completed the disguise.

The flight from Cairo to Istanbul had been uneventful. It was the next and last leg of his trip that could prove problematical. Despite the apathy of the Greek authorities toward combating terrorism, Musa knew it would only take one conscientious or inquisitive cop to expose him. His travel documents were excellent, but they weren't foolproof.

Satisfied with his appearance, he left the Istanbul Airport bathroom and walked purposefully to the gate. He avoided making eye contact with other passengers; he didn't want to encourage conversation.

Musa boarded the plane last, watching each passenger go from the waiting area to the Jetway. He looked for anomalies—a bulge under a man's jacket that might indicate an armed air marshal; a man who carried himself like a soldier or cop; a man or woman who was particularly alert. He took his assigned window seat in the fourteenth row and turned toward the window. He stared out at the tarmac and pretended to be interested in the baggage handlers loading luggage into the plane's cargo compartment. Anything to avoid conversation with his seat mate— a blond woman who looked English. At least she didn't appear to be Greek. And thank *Allah* the middle seat was empty.

Musa continued looking out as the aircraft took off and quickly attained cruising altitude. His neck was beginning to ache from holding his head in the same position. He quickly stretched his neck and rolled his shoulders, glancing to his right, just as the blond woman looked his way and smiled.

"Hello, Father," she said in Greek. "Have you been in Turkey long?"

The woman's Greek surprised Musa. He forced himself to concentrate on his answer. To drive away any trace of an Arabic accent from his voice, to adopt the correct tone. "Yes," he answered. "Six months. I've missed Greece."

"What have you been doing?" she asked.

"Studying Byzantine records. It's my specialty."

"That's amazing," she said. "I did my doctoral work on the Byzantine period's influence on literature and music. Where have you been studying?"

Musa was stumped. But he was the best killer in the world and had survived in a very dangerous business because he could handle pressure. "Erzurum, in far eastern Turkey," he said. "At an old monastery." He figured that Erzurum was so remote there was no way the woman would be familiar with it.

The woman's forehead knitted and her eyebrows arched. Musa could tell she was thinking about his answer—and she didn't seem to like it. And he didn't like the way the conversation was going.

"Where in Erzurum?" she asked him.

Musa swallowed and forced himself to breathe slowly. "You are familiar with the area?" he said.

"Oh, yes," she said. "Where was this monastery in Erzurum?"

Her tone had changed. There was nothing friendly about the way she'd asked the question. Musa pulled the airline magazine from the seat pocket in front of him and opened it to the back page, where there was a map of the region showing the airline's flight coverage of Greece, Turkey, and several Arab countries. He held the magazine on his lap and tapped the page with his finger. "You see where Turkey and Iran touch here," he said, making the woman lean over to see where he pointed. He looked past her at the passengers on the other side of the aisle—a German-speaking couple who appeared to be sleeping. When her face was a foot away from his arm, Musa shot his fist at the woman's head, striking her left temple a tremendous blow. Her head snapped to the right, but Musa grabbed the sleeve of her jacket and jerked her back. He quickly set her back in her seat and turned her head toward him. He didn't want anyone noticing the lump that would soon show.

When he had the woman in a position that made her appear to be asleep, Musa looked around again, then opened the woman's purse which she had placed on the middle seat between them. He started to reach for her wallet, when he noticed a leather folio in the purse. On one side of the folio was a silver badge that had the words Defense Intelligence Agency imprinted on it. On the other side was an ID card with the woman's photograph and her name: Special Agent Margaret Ryan.

Musa knew he couldn't depend on being able to keep the woman unconscious for the rest of the flight. And what would happen when the plane landed in Athens? He couldn't allow her to regain consciousness. He reached through a slit in the side of his robe and into his pants pocket. He found the tiny pill and extracted it. Again, he glanced around. The flight attendants were serving refreshments to the passengers. They were at the tenth row, their backs to him. He quickly looked at the woman. His heart seemed to stop. She moaned and moved her head from side to side. Musa took her chin in his right hand, turning her head towards him. He shoved the pill into the back of her throat.

The woman's complexion suddenly turned red. Her body went rigid, her arms flailed, and then her hands went to her throat. She convulsed as her breathing became louder. Froth bubbled from between her lips. People all around her reacted. Some stood and approached the woman, others rang their call buttons, and still others shouted for help.

Musa released his seat belt and stepped over the woman. "Please help," he called out in Greek, "this woman needs assistance. Is there a doctor on board?" All the while, he kept an eye on the woman. He watched with satisfaction as the poison he had fed her shut down her nervous system and caused her lungs to go rigid, strangling her.

The passengers were unusually quiet for the remainder of the flight. An emergency medical crew met the flight when it landed in Athens. They rushed on board through the Jetway, while the passengers were offloaded through the plane's back door. The one hundred seventy-eight men, women, and children were herded into the terminal and began processing through Customs.

After clearing Customs, Musa slipped into a restroom stall and shed the priest's garb. He had on black slacks and a black shirt under the robe. He removed his false beard and mustache and waited until the restroom was empty. Then he exited the stall and moved to a trashcan. He dumped the lot into the can, including the woman's ID and badge, combed his hair with his fingers, and left the bathroom. He walked to the airport exit, smiling as he heard one Greek policeman shout to another, "Where's the priest? We need to question the priest."

Giorgos Photos was in a high state of anxiety. *EA* had a reputation for executing highly organized, well-planned attacks. It was one of the reasons the group had survived for so long without a single member of the group being identified. He was about to violate his policy of extensive planning and extensive practice. He sat in a Mercedes sedan across from the avenue into the Athens Airport. He could see the woman he'd sent to pick up the Libyan standing next to her car opposite the main entrance to the terminal building. So much depended on the man making it through airport security. Musa Sulaiman would be a key to the plan he had designed.

CHAPTER THIRTY-THREE
AUGUST 4, 2004

It had been a long, tough day and Bob felt it in every bone of his body. His eyes burned and he had trouble getting them to focus on the words in front of him. He adjusted his reading glasses on his nose, trying to improve his vision. It didn't work. He and his team had reviewed almost every damn file that even mentioned France. They had culled one hundred and twenty-three files from the morass of files loaded on the computers—six hundred and fifty-three incident reports, four hundred and sixteen terrorist suspect profiles, a couple hundred Intelligence reports on subjects ranging from the psychopathy of terrorists to the social and economic reasons for suicide bombers, and fifty-seven files on Greek citizens with some connection to France. The French tie ranged from Greeks who had studied in France to those who had arrest records there for a variety of crimes, predominantly associated with illegal street demonstrations. Over half of the fifty-seven Greeks with French connections had been associated with the French Communist Party.

Bob wasn't any further along than he'd been when the other members of his team left the office at 8:00 P.M. It was now 11:00. Over the last three hours, he had concentrated on the fifty-seven files. They intrigued him for several reasons. The Greek Ministry of Public Order very recently constructed them. Bob had asked the head of the ministry, Constantine Angelou, to target intellectuals, university professors, and political figures. He had been skeptical the Greeks would do a thorough job, considering their past performance, but Angelou surprised him. The reports were comprehensive and, in some cases, startling. The subjects of the files included highly placed members of recent Greek administrations, numerous university professors, writers, and journalists who had been schooled in France during the sixties and seventies, many who had been members of the French Communist Party. A few were involved with violent street protests in Paris, including demonstrations against the United States and Israel and in support of governments that backed terrorists, like Libya and Syria.

It wasn't possible to identify a person as a member of *Greek Spring* or of any other group from the information in any of the files; but Bob prayed one or more of the people mentioned in the files had at least a connection of some sort to someone in one of the terrorist organizations. These people had all the credentials to be members of one or another terrorist cell or, at the very least, to support terrorists with money, information, and/or influence. Maybe one of this group of fifty-seven would open the door to the terrorists.

Bob closed his eyes and buried his face in his hands. He knew in his gut something was about to happen. The "chatter" between Greece and the Middle East was ominous. He and his team had to come up with a tie to *Greek Spring*—the big gun among all of the terrorist groups—before something big went down. And he didn't like acknowledging to himself that they couldn't do it without help. He placed calls to Rodney Townsend with MI-6 and Grady McMasters at the FBI. Both men were still at their offices and agreed to meet Bob at 8:00 the next morning.

CHAPTER THIRTY-FOUR

AUGUST 5, 2004

Giorgos Photos paced the floor of the Keratea safehouse, while looking over the list Musa Sulaiman had given him. "You're sure this will be enough?" he asked.

Musa, lounging on a sofa, stroked his chin and gave Photos a paternalistic look, as though he was dealing with a disappointing child. "Photos, are you now questioning my judgement?"

Photos tried to meet Musa's gaze, but he had to look away after a few seconds. The man's large hooked nose, bloated dark lips, wide mouth, and beady black eyes made for a frightening sight. Like the features of a prehistoric avian. "No, no, Musa, of course not. I just like to be careful."

"Tsk, tsk, my friend, you need to have more confidence."

"But will you be able to do it all in such a short time? I am—"

"Enough!" Musa blurted. "If you're going to continue to sound like a frightened little girl, I will leave. I have no interest in working with weaklings."

Photos moved to a worn, plush armchair and dropped into it. "This is a big step for us," he said, trying to control the anger that boiled within him over the Arab's insult. "If something goes wrong now, all our plans could be ruined."

Musa laughed disdainfully. He stood and walked to the living room window and closed the shade against the rising sun. He returned to the sofa and said, "Are you crazy? What we will do two days from now will change everything." He jabbed a finger at Photos and growled, "You and your puny band of gangsters have done less damage in thirty years than my Arab brothers did against the Great Satan in September of 2001. It's time for *Eleeneekee Aneexee* to grow up. I'm about to make that happen."

Photos nodded; he didn't trust his voice. He was concerned . . . and frightened . . . and pissed off. He had never taken any action against his enemies that would match the enormity of this event. Just the thought of it made his stomach ache. They were so close to the final stroke, the act that would catapult him and his benefactors to the top of the Greek Government, and would turn the minds of the Greek populace inward. He would finally realize his life's dream of making Greece a Marxist-Leninist state.

"Did you hear me, man?" Musa shouted.

"Yes, I heard you," Photos said. "I'm ready."

"Excellent. It's set, then. On Friday, I will deal with the British and you will take care of the Americans."

CHAPTER THIRTY-FIVE

AUGUST 5, 2004

Bob met Grady McMasters and Rodney Townsend at the FBI's offices in what used to be the Joint United States Military Advisory Group Greece's (JUSMAGG) offices at 8:00 A.M. He shared the CIA's information about the intercepted telephone call between Greece and Iraq with the two men. He also talked about the theory that one of the Greek terrorists had a connection to France because of the man's fluency in French. He'd allowed the information to sink in for a moment and then answered their questions. They both expressed reservations about the weakness of the link to France, but they also acknowledged that it was just this sort of link that often caused Intelligence breakthroughs. Besides, they had nothing better to offer.

"Our people think something is about to go down. I need your help. We've identified fifty-seven Greek nationals with some tie to France. I suggest we split up these files among our three agencies. Working together could speed up the possibility of finding one of these bastards, and bring down the whole organization."

"I say again," McMasters said, "we're probably wasting our time."

Townsend stood and looked first at McMasters, then at Bob. "We're sure not working on anything that sounds as promising as what Bob just laid out for us," he said.

"Oh, what the fuck," McMasters barked. "When can we see the files?"

"I'll have them delivered to your offices today," Bob said.

Pavlos Manganos stood by the front window of a bookstore across the street from the office building. He had followed Danforth from his hotel and waited in the store for the American to emerge. When Danforth finally did, an hour later, Manganos followed him. He trailed fifty meters behind as the CIA man walked to a car, where another man waited behind the wheel. Danforth entered the vehicle, which immediately pulled away from the curb. Manganos raced back to his motorcycle and sped to catch up with the car. He tracked the two men to the building in Glyfada.

Manganos parked down the block and used his cell phone to call Photos. "The American is at the Glyfada place," he said.

"Leave him for now," Photos ordered. "I have something more important for you to do. Come to Piraeus."

After Photos ended the call from Manganos, he dialed Demetrios Mavroyianni's cell phone number. "Where are you?" he said.

"In Kolonaki, outside the Englishmen's offices."

"Are they all there?" Photos asked.

"I guess," Mavroyianni answered, his tone betraying his boredom.

"I want you to come in," Photos said.

"What's happening?" Mavroyianni said, an edge of excitement now in his voice.

"Just come in," Photos snapped. "Piraeus."

CHAPTER THIRTY-SIX

AUGUST 5, 2004

"Is everything in order?" Dimitris Argyropoulos asked, his hands balled into fists and buried in his pants pockets to hide their trembling. His future, his place in history rode on the events of the next eight days.

"As much in order as they can be," Photos answered.

Argyropoulos didn't like Photos' answer. "What are you telling me?"

"Nothing . . . it's just that everything is happening so quickly. I—"

"Quickly, my ass. We've waited twenty-nine years for this. I've thrown all my support behind you for nearly three decades; I've risked everything to suppress investigations into your activities. Are you telling me it has all been for nothing?"

"No, no, that's not it. I just don't like being rushed."

"*Malaka!* You listen to me. You *will* make this happen. This is our time. If you blow this opportunity, I'll have your balls. Everything is in place for this summer. The Kurds are on board; our man at the missile site will do whatever he is told; and the Greek people are ready for greatness. You can set the tone with your actions in the next two days. CAN YOU DO IT?"

Photos paused before answering. "Yes, I can do it," he finally said.

"Good, Giorgos, good. I much prefer congratulating you on success, than cutting off your balls."

Photos tried to get his breathing and heart rate back to normal after Dimitris Argyropoulos terminated their telephone conversation. It took fifteen minutes before he had calmed down enough to place a call to Musa Sulaiman. He asked the Libyan in French, "Are you ready?"

"You shouldn't call me," Sulaiman barked. "I already told you that everything is set."

"I know, I know. It's just that—"

Sulaiman spat out a lengthy chain of Arabic, cutting off Photos.

Photos didn't understand the words; but he understood the Libyan's tone. He opened his mouth to respond just as he heard Musa slam down the receiver.

Photos felt as though steel bands were wrapped around his chest; he could barely breathe. He had run *Greek Spring* for three decades and had taken incredible risks. Now that egomaniacal politician, Argyropoulos, and this psychopath, Sulaiman, were treating him like some unruly teenager. Even with the tightness in his chest, Photos paced the room in the safehouse, clenching and unclenching his hands, cursing under his breath. Finally, he threw on a windbreaker and walked out the back door. Despite a steady drizzle, he had to get some air. He was fearful that if he didn't, he might explode.

"Sonofabitch! Sonofabitch! We got it," the Greek Ministry of Public Order agent shouted. "We got it."

The man's supervisor, sitting next to him in the van parked two blocks from the small house in Piraeus, put down his coffee cup and snatched up an extra pair of headphones. "What is it?"

"A conversation between two men. They spoke French. Then one man said something about everything being set. Then he got angry and cursed at the other man in Arabic." The communications expert rewound the tape and played it back for his supervisor.

"Arabic?"

"Yes."

"Maybe this isn't about drugs, after all. Get the tape over to head-quarters; I want it translated as soon as possible."

The supervisor then got on the telephone and called his boss. "You know that house in Piraeus we received a tip about? The one where the old man called in and said he thought there was drug dealing going on?"

"Sure, what about it?"

"I don't think it's drugs. We heard a conversation in French, then Arabic. We should consider raiding the place."

"On what evidence?" his boss asked. "Because some old bastard sees a bunch of people coming and going at odd hours and thinks there's drug dealing going on, and because you hear Arabic and French spoken? What! Frenchmen and Arabs don't use drugs?"

"We taped a conversation—"

"That's it? You've got to be kidding me."

"You need to trust me on this," the supervisor said. "I know it's weak, but I've got a feeling."

"Oh, wonderful. And I've got a pension that's supposed to start in two years. You better get me more to work on than that. Call me when you've got more than a feeling. And get someone at headquarters to approve a raid . . . if you get more information. I'm not sticking my neck out."

Giorgos Photos wanted to flee and leave it all behind. He had millions of dollars tucked away as his "runaway" money—his sponsors in the Greek Government and from other countries had been very generous over the years. He was nervous about what was going to happen over the next few days; he was pissed off about the way he'd been treated by Argyropoulos and Sulaiman; but now he was just plain scared to death. While walking in the rain, he'd spotted a gray van with an antenna on its roof. The truck was two blocks from the safehouse but had a line of sight to it. Had the police tracked him down?

But Photos couldn't run. He'd left his address book in the house, along with a detailed description of the attacks planned for this week.

God forbid the police found these things. It would ruin everything. He circled the block and entered the safehouse through a basement door at the rear. All the while, his heart beat like a jackhammer and sweat cascaded from his already rain-wet body. He recycled in his mind the conversation with Musa Sulaiman. No names had been mentioned. He was sure nothing incriminating had been said. He breathed a bit easier as he crept up the backstairs to the second floor. After gathering up his address book, the attack plans, and some cash stashed there, he fled the house. The weapons would be forfeited, but there was nothing he could do about that. Although they were clean of fingerprints, the police would easily trace them. After all, they had belonged to the police before *Greek Spring* stole them.

The translation of the phone conversation was telephoned back to the supervisor in the van. He held his breath as the linguist related the meaning of the Arabic words.

"The man speaking Arabic called the other man 'a cowardly son of a leprous whore.'"

"That's it?" the supervisor said.

"Let me finish," the linguist retorted. "He went on to say, 'This is the last time I do anything for this cowardly professor. I ought to blow up his fucking pink island house, rape his daughters, and castrate his sons and grandsons.'"

CHAPTER THIRTY-SEVEN

AUGUST 6, 2004

Bob thought he was dreaming. It took several seconds before he realized the ringing telephone by his hotel room bed was real. He fumbled with the receiver and finally got it right side up and pressed against his ear. The digital clock on the bedside table showed 2:15 A.M. His heart lurched. Calls in the middle of the night usually meant bad news.

"Hello," he said in a gravelly voice.

"Bob, it's Tony Fratangelo."

"What's up, Tony? Is everything all right?"

"No one's hurt, if that's what you mean. There's good and bad news."

Bob heard Tony exhale loudly into the phone. "Give me the bad news first," he said.

"The damn Greek bureaucracy struck again," Tony said. "I got a call from an investigator with the Ministry of Public Order. He'd set up a listening post outside a house in Athens. Apparently, some citizen thought something was going on because strangers kept going in and out of the place at odd hours. My contact heard something suspicious—someone talking in Arabic after having a conversation with another man in French—and called his boss. His boss decided that covering his ass was more important than swinging into action. By the time the tape of the conversation was translated and the assault team called in, the place had been cleaned of everything other than a cache of weapons."

"They didn't catch anyone?" Bob asked.

"Nope. But get this; most of the weapons in the house were identified as having been stolen from a police armory six years ago. *Greek Spring* claimed responsibility for the crime at the time."

"That's good news," Bob said. "Any fingerprints?"

"Not a thing."

"What about the translation of the conversation?"

"That's worrisome. The conversation in French sounded as though there was something going down. But the words in Arabic were a completely different story. One of the men on the call was obviously frustrated with the other man and was cursing him out. The really interesting part of what he said involved the mention of a professor with a pink house on some island."

"A professor, huh," Bob said. "That *is* interesting."

"Yeah, and my informant was damned excited about the mention of a pink house," Tony said. "You see, nearly every island in Greece has very strict zoning codes. It's the law on most of the islands that the outside color of structures must be white. Even the shutters and doors have to be painted according to zoning laws."

"Sonofagun," Bob exclaimed. "Of course. Every house I've ever seen on any of the islands has been stuccoed white. But how do the Greeks propose finding one pink house on one island out of a thousand islands?"

Tony shrugged. "Hell, I don't have a clue. I guess they could try to identify the islands which don't have strict zoning codes."

"Well, at least we have something. I want you to find out all you can from your contact about what the Greeks are going to do with this information. Then I'm going to take it to the Prime Minister. I'm meeting with him later this morning. I'm going to put him on notice that if someone leaks this information to the bad guys, or if they do nothing to investigate this lead, we will have proof the Greek Government is aiding and abetting these terrorists. The President has lost all patience with the way they've handled the investigation over the years. It will mean the end of all aid to Greece. Several EU leaders have also agreed to pull the plug on Greece if the U.S. takes the first step over this terrorism issue."

"Jesus, boss, that'll shut down the Greek economy and undermine the current government. Without financial support from the U.S. and other European countries, they won't even be able to pull off the Olympics."

"It's put up or shut up time," Bob said. "The Greeks either prove they're serious about bringing down these terrorist cells, or they suffer the consequences. And, speaking of the Olympics, the President is prepared to tell the Prime Minister that the U.S. will withdraw its team from the Games. We announce we're pulling out, and there will be a chain reaction, with dozens of other countries following suit. It's all been arranged. The Russians, Chinese, English, Canadians, and many more are already on board."

"How about the Germans and French?" Tony asked.

"Nothing's changed there," Bob answered. "They're still sulking about us toppling Saddam Hussein last year without their permission."

After fleeing the safehouse on Thursday, Giorgos Photos called Demetrios Mavroyianni and Pavlos Manganos to call off the meeting scheduled at the safehouse. He ordered Demetrios to assist Musa Sulaiman; Pavlos would contact Savvas Krinon and the two of them would deal with the Americans. Photos could tell from the men's voices that their blood was up.

Photos then hid out in another one of his safehouses until early Friday morning. He made his way to the docks and paid a fishing boat captain twice what he would have made on that day's catch to take him to Evoia. He was shaken about the authorities finding one of his safehouses, and he didn't want to be anywhere near Athens when Musa went into action—he checked his wristwatch—in about two hours. About an hour after the boat would drop him on Evoia.

Evoia was the place where Photos went to physically and spiritually replenish his energy. He loved his island home and dreamed of retiring there some day. He would be able to do that if things occurred as he had planned. Only another week.

After the boat docked at the island, Photos walked to his home. He keep looking at his watch for the next hour. He knew that news of the attacks would be all over the media just minutes after Musa, Demetrios, Pavlos, and Savvas did what they'd been told to do.

CHAPTER THIRTY-EIGHT
AUGUST 6, 2004

Musa Sulaiman had worked frenetically during the night. Despite what he'd told Giorgos Photos, he too didn't like working under a tight schedule. It meant inadequate planning. And he didn't like working with people he didn't know. Photos had assigned Demetrios Mavroyianni to assist him because Demetrios was the only *Greek Spring* member who could identify one of the Englishmen. He would know when at least one of the British agents was inside the building. The man seemed to Musa to be enthusiastic about working with him and very committed to the *Greek Spring* cause; but Musa had survived in a very dangerous business for a very long time by being suspicious and cautious. But he was being paid a quarter of a million dollars for this job. For that amount, he could accept more risk.

The van that Mavroyianni provided had Greek and English lettering on both sides, reading *Anna's Plants & Flowers*. He'd stolen the vehicle from in front of the Hilton Hotel while the driver was inside making a delivery. Mavroyianni painted over the side panels, while Musa finished constructing the bomb.

Made from lawn fertilizer, black powder extracted from two cases of shotgun shells and stuffed into two glass jars around battery-powered detonators, and ammonium nitrate, the explosive device was the terrorist's favorite concoction. All of the materials that went into it were easily acquired without raising suspicion. Photos had stored the materials in three separate storage units, waiting for a day just like this one. Musa filled the bottom third of two wheeled, fifty-five gallon drums with the fertilizer, and then placed a jar with the black powder and detonator on top of the fertilizer in each drum. He then poured two pounds of crystallized ammonium nitrate over each jar. He added more fertilizer until the drums were full. Ball bearings and nails were then strapped with masking tape to the outsides of the drums.

Musa used a hydraulic lift to raise the drums to the level of the van's cargo area and gently pushed them into the back of the van. He bracketed the drum bottoms into place so they wouldn't slide. It was now 7:00 A.M.

"Are you ready?" Musa asked. "You understand what you must do?"

Demetrios smiled. "What's there to understand? I go to the restaurant across the street from the building at seven-thirty and order coffee and a roll. When I see any of the Englishmen enter the building, I call you on your cell phone. It will take you seven minutes to reach the site. I finish my coffee and roll, pay the tab, and walk away five minutes after I make the call."

Musa grunted. "Good. Don't be tempted to stop and watch what happens." He picked up a ball bearing off the floor and tossed it to Demetrios. "One of these innocent looking little things will punch a hole right through you if you're standing in the wrong place."

"Don't worry, I'll be as far from that place as possible when the bomb goes off."

Demetrios Mavroyianni felt like a teenager on his first date. His legs bounced up and down and he had to hold his coffee cup in two hands to prevent his shaking hands from spilling the liquid. He wasn't scared; he was excited. This is about as good as it gets, he thought. The little waitress who had given him her telephone number the last time he was in the cafe couldn't seem to do enough for him. Demetrios hadn't had time to call her to set up a date. This operation was going down more quickly than he had anticipated. He had to do something about the girl. She'd now seen him twice. He couldn't take the chance she would identify him to the authorities.

He checked his watch. He was feeling nervous and a little scared. He glanced around like a junkie looking for his connection, when an idea came to him. He saw the waitress was serving two men on the far side of the cafe. A fiftyish-looking man stood behind a cash register not far from where the two men sat. Demetrios looked at the menu on the table in front of him and saw the telephone number printed on the bottom of the front page. He pulled his cell phone from his jacket and dialed the cafe's number. When the man behind the cash register answered, Demetrios gave him a false name and said he needed ten croissants brought to the travel agency across the street.

"That will be ten Euros," the man said. "Give me fifteen minutes."

Demetrios' stomach did a flip-flop. "Listen," he said, "I screwed up. I was supposed to pick up the croissants before I came in this morning. My boss is going to have my ass. If you can get them here in less than five minutes, I'll pay double."

The man behind the cash register blurted a laugh. "Now you're talking my language. Twenty Euros and a tip for the girl."

"Deal," Demetrios said, relief washing through him. He finished his coffee after taking another bite from the breakfast roll. He dropped a bill on the table, waved the waitress over, and said, "I'll call you tonight, I promise. I've been really busy."

She smiled and blushed. "I'll be at home after six."

No you won't, Demetrios thought. He brushed his fingers against her arm before she walked away. He heard the man behind the register call out, "Soula, I need you to run across the street."

Demetrios spied the Englishman the waitress had pointed out to him the other day entering the office building across the street. He quickly punched in Sulaiman's cell number and said, "It's a go."

Musa drove the van toward the target. He was a block away when he noticed two moving vans pull up to the front of the building, parking half on the sidewalk. The large vehicles had effectively blocked his ability to park by the curb. He could stop the van on the street-side of the bigger vehicles, but they would absorb the blast, protecting the building. To make matters worse, an Athens cop was watching the moving vans as though he couldn't decide whether he should make them move on or let them park there.

The traffic moved at sloth-like speed, which gave Musa time to amend his plan. For a moment, he had an impulse to drive by the building, to call off the attack. But the money he would be paid made up his mind for him.

The policeman moved to a spot halfway between the moving vans and the building entrance. He confronted the two truck drivers and all three men were involved in an animated discussion.

Musa pulled his baseball cap down tight on his head and drifted to the right, away from the main flow of traffic, toward the corner of the sidewalk, just behind the first moving truck. He was ten feet from the curb when he floored the accelerator. The van jumped the curb, sped past the rear of the moving truck, and crashed into the cop and two drivers. Two of the men's bodies flew backward, smashing into the building's glass door entry. Musa felt and heard the wheels of the van thud over the third man. He let the van careen through the glass windows of a travel agency, crushing a woman in a suit against a wooden desk. As though everything moved in slow motion, Musa saw the green eyes of a young woman wearing a waitress uniform staring at him. Her eyes grew large; her mouth dropped open. She stood at the rear of the shop, trapped by the van. Her arms were raised as though she was surrendering, a large white paper bag suspended in one of her hands.

Musa leaped from the van and landed in the debris of broken glass, wood shards, and a melee of paper. Shouts and screams echoed around him, but none of that worried him. He knew from experience that people would be running for their lives, not standing around watching. He counted on people reacting in that way. He slipped the detonator-triggering device from his tan coveralls pocket and calmly walked out of the storefront and into the building's main entryway. He moved through the corridor to the rear of the building, to the door he knew, from reconnoitering the building the day before, accessed an alley. He ran down the alley. Where it terminated at a two lane cross street, he stopped and pointed the television-like remote control box back in the direction of the van. He pressed the detonator and then ran to the left as fast as he could. He felt the concussion from the blast and then heat rolled over him. Knocked to his knees, he had to struggle to regain his feet. Running again, he moved farther from ground zero. He knew he was now far enough away from the blast; he didn't want to be anywhere near the area when the police started to react. He tossed his baseball cap into a Dumpster, then unbuttoned his coveralls on the run. He stopped after another hundred meters and stepped out of the coveralls, balling them up and throwing them onto a garage roof. Musa looked back over his shoulder in the direction of the blast. A massive white smoke cloud rose above the Kolonaki Square area and moved with the wind in Musa's direction. The eerie sound of screams and sirens drifted on the wind.

Musa stuck his hands in his pants pockets as he slowed to a walk. He wanted to shout the joy he felt. His reputation would rise even more around the world. And the fee he would receive for this job would swell his Swiss bank account to eight figures for the first time. He smiled with an inner peace that warmed his flesh and thrilled him to his core.

CHAPTER THIRTY-NINE
AUGUST 6, 2004

Bob had accepted Tony and Michelle Fratangelo's offers to accompany him to the Athens airport to pick up Liz. Because Bob was scheduled to meet the Greek Prime Minister at 10:00 A.M., they would all meet Liz at the airport. Bob would then drive her to the Grand Bretagne Hotel, while the Fratangelos would follow in their car. Bob would drop Liz at the hotel, and then leave with Tony for his appointment. Michelle would do whatever she could to get Liz settled in and answer whatever questions she might have about living in Athens. He hoped Andrew Fratangelo would be on his best behavior. Tony had explained that their babysitter had cancelled at the last minute and they had no one else with whom to leave the boy. Bob knew Liz would be beat after her flight. As much as she loved kids, a little boy—especially one as precocious as Andrew—could be trying under the best of circumstances.

Tony parked near a shade tree two blocks from the airport entrance, where he had a good view of traffic leaving the airport. He would see Bob's rented gray Audi when it pulled away. Bob found a parking spot in the airport lot and entered the terminal building.

"Hey, good looking," Bob whispered as he came up behind Liz at the baggage carousel.

"I hope you're a young, tall, dark-haired Greek; otherwise, I'm going to be very disappointed," she said.

Bob laughed. "You'd better turn around and give me a big kiss."

Liz laughed in answer—the laugh that always reminded Bob of windchimes, turned, and wrapped her arms around his neck. "Promise me you won't ever leave me alone again," she said. "I can't stand being away from you."

Bob hugged her, lifting her off the floor. "That's a promise I'd love to make," he said, lowering her to her feet.

She gave him a skeptical look, then smiled and said, "That didn't sound like a commitment; but we can discuss that later. Right now I want to get to the hotel, take a shower, and spend the rest of the day in bed with you." Her smile turned lascivious and she kissed his cheek. Her smile disappeared when Bob's expression suddenly changed. "What?" she asked.

Bob looked at his watch and then back at her. "I've got an appointment with the Prime Minister at ten, about two hours from now. I'll drop you off at the hotel, run to my meeting, and return as soon as possible."

She turned back to the luggage carousel, as though she was trying to hide her reaction to Bob's announcement. But she quickly turned again and said, "Better late than never; just don't make me wait too long, or I'll find that young, good-looking Greek."

"If you weren't so damned beautiful and sexy, I'd take that as an idle threat," Bob said.

Liz kissed him on the lips and said, "Now, that's the kind of talk a girl likes to hear."

Pavlos Manganos felt the usual rush of adrenaline as he punched the TALK button on his cell phone.

"Man and woman in a gray Audi just left the airport."

"No one else with them?" Manganos asked the spotter, a tone of incredulity in his voice. Danforth had always been in the company of another man—at least for the last few days.

"No one that I saw," the spotter said.

Well, I'll be damned, Manganos thought. "Okay, you know what to do. Call when you're ready to hand them off."

Manganos flipped the cell phone closed and briefed Savvas Krinon on what the spotter had told him. Krinon just shrugged.

Tony saw Bob drive out of the airport. He couldn't pull in behind the Audi until five other vehicles had passed. He finally drove away from the curb, not in any great hurry to catch up with the Audi. As long as he kept the Danforths in sight, and as long as he got to the hotel at the same time Bob arrived there. It wouldn't do for Bob to be late for his appointment with the Prime Minister. And it wasn't a good idea for Bob to be anywhere in Athens without someone watching his back.

"My God," Liz said, "traffic is terrible. What happened to the Athens of the seventies?"

"Thirty years, that's what happened. And three million more people."

He reached over and touched her arm. "You sure it's all right turning you over to Michelle Fratangelo and her son?"

"Actually, I'm looking forward to meeting her and having the chance to ask about housing." She looked at Bob and grinned. "Not to mention shopping."

Bob breathed a quiet sigh of relief. He searched in his rearview mirror for the Fratangelos' white Taurus. A large panel truck directly behind him obscured his view.

Thirty minutes after the first call from the spotter, Pavlos Manganos' cell phone rang. "Go!" he barked.

"Ten blocks from the square; two blocks from your location," the man said.

Manganos turned on the motorcycle seat and stared back over Savvas Krinon's shoulder. He craned his neck until the awkward position and the tension in his body made his neck ache. He looked to the front for a second and rubbed his neck; then he quickly turned again toward the direction from which the Danforth vehicle would come. Almost as soon as he looked back, he spotted the gray Audi and the motorcycle driven by the spotter. When the spotter was fifty meters away, he peeled off the boulevard onto a side street and disappeared.

CHAPTER FORTY

AUGUST 6, 2004

Exhilarated was the word for the way Giorgos Photos felt. He couldn't sit. He wanted to shout his joy but was afraid the nosey old biddy in the house up the road might hear him and think someone was in trouble. He moved around the living room of his Evoia home like a tiger in a cage, never taking his eyes off the television screen. The television news announcer's voice had a frantic quality about it as she described the devastation in Kolonaki Square.

The bomb had done more damage than Photos had imagined. The upper floors of the six-story building had collapsed, leaving only twisted metal girders showing above the third floor. Rubble had mounded from the building's lobby, over the sidewalk, and on the street. Two large moving vans by the curb had been torn apart as though they were tin cans. Men in hard hats and protective clothing crawled over and around the ruins like ants on a damaged anthill. People wandered around the scene as though in a daze, their faces and clothes covered with ash and concrete dust. Ambulances clogged the street in the distance and emergency vehicle strobe lights flashed. Sirens provided an aural background that would normally have been irritating to Photos. This morning, the noise sounded like music.

The announcer kept repeating that hundreds of people worked in the building, including a large number of foreign nationals. "The vast majority of the occupants of the building," she said, "are Greek citizens. This explosion could prove to be one of the worst disasters of modern times. No one has claimed responsibility for this savage act."

Photos was confident there would be an uprising of emotion—anger, fear, and sorrow—over the loss of so many Greek lives; but there would also be a demand by the people for action from the government. There would no longer be sympathy for *Greek Spring*, or for other terrorist groups. And that would be just fine with Photos. The plan was for *Greek Spring* to disband, disappear. There would no longer be a need for the group. Its original goal of establishing a Marxist-Leninist state would soon be a *fait accompli*. Photos would have been instrumental in changing the course of Greek history.

The TV screen again showed survivors stumbling around the building's wreckage, their eyes wide with panic. Rescue workers assisted a few away from the scene. But the survivors appeared to be few and far between. The anchorwoman's pretty, but concerned face came back to the screen.

"Christo Loutsos is now on the scene. What do you have to report, Christo?" the woman asked.

"Katerina, I've just talked with Inspector Socrates Yiatrakis. His team of investigators has found traces of ingredients from an explosive device. There is now no question about this terrible incident in Kolonaki Square being an accidental explosion. It appears someone planted an explosive device in a van that was driven into the Lambrakis Building and then detonated. Witnesses have come forward to claim they saw a van run down three men standing on the sidewalk outside the building just seconds before the explosion occurred. One witness says she saw a man jump down from the van and race through the building right before the explosion. We have no information about this man or whether he escaped the blast and perished when the building collapsed."

"Thank you, Christo," the announcer said. "We'll get back—"

Photos used the remote control to mute the television. His heart was now beating so fast, he thought there might be something wrong.

He stepped outside, took a seat on a bench in his backyard, and stared out at the water a half-kilometer in the distance. He felt his heart rate slow. He laughed out loud. "You're getting too old for all this excitement," he told himself, and laughed again. There would be more excitement soon, he thought.

CHAPTER FORTY-ONE

AUGUST 6, 2004

Bob immediately knew a large explosion had occurred. The concussion was a familiar sensation. He had experienced similar sensations in Vietnam, the Balkans, the Sudan, and Afghanistan. He immediately scanned the horizon for the telltale smoke that usually accompanied explosions. Nothing showed.

"Did you feel that?" Liz asked.

"Yeah, I did," Bob said, while punching the car radio's ON dial. His cell phone suddenly rang.

"Danforth," he answered.

"It's Tony. I just got a call from a friend at the FBI office here. There's been an explosion somewhere near their building."

"I felt it just a moment ago," Bob said. "It must have been a big one to detect it this far away from the FBI building. Did your friend say where exac—hold on a minute, there's a bulletin coming over the radio."

A man on the radio started speaking in frenzied, rapid-fire Greek. Bob was only able to pick up part of what the man said; but it was enough to divine the substance of the announcement. An explosion had occurred at the Lambrakis Building in Kolonaki Square and had leveled the building. The authorities feared the casualty count would be very high.

"Turn on your radio," Bob told Tony. "Channel 87.7. There's been an explosion in Kolonaki Square. The Lambrakis Building. Do you know it?"

"Shit, Bob, the MI-6 team is housed in that building."

Bob let that information sink in as he took advantage of a sudden opening in traffic and sped into the left lane. "We need to get Liz and your family to the hotel as quickly as possible. I want them off the streets. Call the office and have whoever is there contact Langley and let them know what's going on. I'll call McMasters at the FBI offices and tell him I want to meet at the embassy. This could be the beginning of what we've been expecting from the terrorists."

"What about your meeting with the Prime Minister?" Tony asked.

"Oh, I'm going to meet with him," Bob said. "But first I want to gather as much information about what happened in Kolonaki. If this was another terrorist incident . . . .." He left the thought hanging.

Pavlos Manganos saw the gray Audi speed by his position. For once, traffic wasn't working in his favor. Vehicles were moving fast. He shouted at Savvas Krinon and pointed after the Audi. Then he put the motorcycle into gear and raced after the car. He moved from lane to lane, quickly gaining on Danforth's vehicle. He didn't need to be on top of the car yet; but he didn't want to lose sight of it. He knew traffic would come to almost a standstill when the Audi entered the Constitution Square area. That's where he and Savvas would do the job.

Tony pulled around the panel truck that had screened his view of Bob's car. He hit the accelerator when he saw the gray Audi speed ahead, putting ten car lengths between them. He wanted to arrive at the hotel with Bob, so the offloading of his family occurred simultaneously with Liz Danforth exiting the Audi. Tony would give his car keys to the hotel valet and leave the hotel with Bob. He explained all this to Michelle. She had been through this type of exercise before. She didn't ask any questions; she would do what was expected of her.

Bob told Liz what he had heard about the explosion and what he needed her to do at the hotel. This was old hat to her. Like all wives of professional soldiers, career diplomats, and CIA lifers, Liz would act according to the demands of the situation.

"I'll come back to the hotel as soon as I can," Bob said.

Liz reached over and touched Bob's right arm, as though telling him that whatever he needed to do was all right by her, and that he should be careful.

He smiled at her, then jerked his head back to the front.

Savvas Krinon's assassination plan was slightly different this time. He adjusted the net bag suspended around his neck, making sure the opening in the top of the bag was in the best possible position for him to reach inside and extract the grenade. He touched the hammer in the inside pocket of his leather jacket with a gloved hand. Instead of the one-step process of firing a pistol, this would involve two steps: smash the window glass with the hammer—letting it drop to the ground—then toss the grenade through the broken window. They were just three blocks from where the hit would go down.

"That man is crazy," Andrew Fratangelo declared from his seat in the middle of the Taurus' backseat.

Tony ignored his son's high-pitched words. He had other things on his mind. He saw Michelle shift in her seat and look back at their son. "Who's crazy?" she asked in a placating tone.

"The one on the motorcycle," Andrew said, pointing. "He's not supposed to drive like that, is he, Daddy? You always say you should-n't go from lane to lane like that. Isn't that right?"

"That's right," Michelle said. "That's what Daddy always says." She turned back to look out the windshield. "He's right, you know," she told Tony, "look at that maniac." She jabbed a finger to the front of their location.

Tony picked out the motorcycle about six car lengths ahead, in the middle lane. Two men rode the bike; each wore motorcycle helmets and black leather jackets. The jockeying motorcycle didn't hold much interest for Tony. Athens was notorious for its demented, reckless drivers. But he kept an eye on the motorcycle because, like watching a bullfight or a NASCAR race, he wondered when something awful might happen. The two guys on the bike were risking their lives.

Tony saw Bob move from the center lane to the left lane. The cycle mirrored Bob's maneuver. Bob passed a couple vehicles, then pulled back into the center lane. The motorcycle again copied Bob's maneuver, remaining two cars back now. It surprised Tony that the motorcycle driver pulled back in Bob's lane, because the left lane suddenly opened up, offering a freer path. He concentrated a bit more on the bike. When Bob again pulled into the left lane and the motorcycle almost immediately followed suit, Tony's antennae quivered.

"You have your seatbelt on?" he asked Michelle.

"Of course," she said. "Why?"

"Check on Andrew's belt; then tighten yours."

Tony picked up his cell phone and dialed Bob's cell number. "Shit!" he exclaimed when the phone rang busy.

"Daddy said a bad word," Andrew said.

"What's going on?" Michelle asked.

"I think that motorcycle is following the Danforths. I called to warn them, but their phone is busy."

"What are you going to do?" she asked, her voice suddenly tremulous. She looked at Tony, then back at her son.

Tony slowly shook his head. He gave Michelle an apologetic look. "I don't have time to drop you two off and still be able to catch up to the Danforths. I want you to crawl over the seat. You and Andrew need to get down on the floor. Don't even think about raising your head until I tell you it's safe."

"Tony, what—"

"Just do it, Michelle. It'll be okay; I promise."

After Michelle laboriously climbed into the back, unbuckled Andrew, and got down on the floor, Tony flipped on his bright lights and his emergency flashers. He jammed his foot on the accelerator and pressed down on the horn until the car in front of the Taurus moved into the next lane. Tony careened from one lane to the next, gaining on the motorcycle, but worried sick he wouldn't get there in time. And worried he was endangering his family if he did get to the motorcycle in time. And then there was a ghost of a thought pecking at a corner of his brain: What if I'm over-reacting? Andrew was correct; the man was driving the bike like a maniac. But what if that was all there was to it?

Tony decided he needed to get close enough to the motorcycle to be in the position of being able to herd it away from the Danforths. But all three lanes of traffic were now blocked in front of him. His heart hammered in his chest and perspiration ran down his face, chest, and back. His hands were wet on the steering wheel.

He wanted to try Bob's cell phone again, but he didn't dare take his eyes off the road or try to drive with one hand. But Michelle could do it. He slipped his cell phone from his shirt pocket and dropped it over the seat.

"Ouch! What was that?" Michelle said.

"It's my cell phone," he shouted. "Hit the REDIAL button. Keep calling until you get through."

Tony was now three car lengths behind the motorcycle; but there was a solid block of vehicles between him and the Audi. There was no way he could get close to them. Traffic was slowing and bunching up now that they were two blocks from Constitution Square. Then he saw the motorcycle change tactics. No longer satisfied with remaining two car lengths behind the Audi, the cycle driver moved between the center and outside lane. The passenger on the back of the bike reached inside his jacket. Tony saw he now held something in his right hand, which hung down by his right leg. He couldn't be sure, but he thought it might be a pistol.

Pavlos moved the bike up one car length. He was about to pull alongside the Danforths' car, when a Fiat jerked right, switching lanes, cutting off Pavlos' approach. By the time the lane was clear before him again, Danforth had put fifty meters distance between them.

Tony was frantic. He was blocked. He looked to the right. There was no way he could move over two lanes to the sidewalk. A landscaped median separated the lane he was in from oncoming traffic. He had only one option. He drove the Taurus' leftside tires onto the four-inch median, the rightside tires resting in the street. He gunned the engine, picking up speed as the sound of bushes and flowers scraped the Taurus' undercarriage. Car horns blasted in his wake as he passed the barely moving traffic. He grimaced and ground his teeth when the Taurus side-swiped one of the cars in the inside lane, the screech of metal sounding like giant fingernails scratching a blackboard.

"What was that?" Michelle screamed.

Tony ignored her and kept driving. He was gaining on the motorcycle. But he could see it had again caught up with the Audi. The man on the back now had his right hand extended as the bike approached the driver-side rear door. The man retracted his hand as the bike moved inches from the car door.

Tony heard a crash of metal come from under his car. There goes the muffler, he thought. He laid a hand on the horn again. But this time he didn't let up. Maybe Bob would hear the noise and look around him. Maybe he would spot the men on the cycle.

"Mr. Danforth, oh my God!" came from the back of the Taurus. "I got him, Tony, he's on the phone."

Tony shouted at Michelle. "Tell him to brake NOW! Just tell him to hit his brakes."

Michelle screamed Tony's instructions. He saw the Audi's brake lights burn red at the same moment the motorcycle passenger's hand slashed out. Tony saw the man was armed with a hammer, not a pistol. What the hell! he thought as Bob's car's tires screeched and the bike shot past the Audi.

There was something in Michelle's voice that made Bob do exactly what she had yelled. He'd hit the brakes as soon as she'd screamed at him. He saw the motorcycle in his sideview mirror as it went past him, just after the glass in the door behind him shattered and shards blew all over the vehicle's interior. He knew what was going on without really thinking about it.

"Get out!" he shouted at Liz, as he released his seatbelt. He reached over to open the glove box and started to again tell Liz to get out, when he noticed blood covering her blouse. Blood poured from her nose and mouth. He stuck his hand into the glove box and fished for the 9 mm pistol he kept there. But before he could grip the weapon, his door was jerked open. He sat back in his seat and looked to his left. A helmeted man stood by the open door. The visor on his helmet was open and he smiled down at Bob. The man had a grenade in his right hand.

"Afto eenay ena doro apo Eleeneekee Aneexee," the man said. The man's fingers flexed and the spoon from the grenade tumbled away in a series of somersaulting arcs.

Bob moved to leap at the man, who suddenly disappeared as a giant flash of white sped by, ripping off the Audi's driver-side door. Bob couldn't quite process what had just happened; not until the flash of white metamorphosed into a Ford Taurus and slammed into the motorcycle and its driver which sat ten yards away. Then Bob remembered the grenade and dove on top of Liz, dragging her down below the dashboard as an explosion blew out the Audi's windows.

CHAPTER FORTY-TWO
AUGUST 6, 2004

Liz moaned, then Bob felt her shift beneath him. He moved off her and helped her sit up.

"You okay, honey?" he asked.

"Wha . . . what happened?" She touched her fingers to her nose and groaned. She looked at her fingers. "I'm bleeding."

"You hit the dashboard when I slammed on the brakes. Your lip is cut and you have a bloody nose. I'm going to get out of the car and look around. I'll be right back. Okay?"

She nodded, then said in a trembly voice, "Heck of a welcome to Athens."

Bob tried to respond, but his voice cracked. He leaned over and kissed the side of her head, then left the car and ran toward the Taurus. The normal confusion of Athens traffic had turned into pure bedlam. Screams and shouts filled the air; a few bloodied people wandered aimlessly around the scene. Several of the vehicles in the area were pockmarked with shrapnel. Two cars separated the Audi from a blue truck. Flames licked the truck's now-scorched roll up back door. Bob guessed the man with the grenade had been hurled over the two cars and landed beneath the back of the truck. It amazed him that the man must have held onto the grenade as he flew through the air.

Bob saw Tony slumped against the Taurus' steering wheel. He ran to the driver-side front door and threw it open. He pulled Tony back against the seat. Tony's eyes fluttered open; then he attempted to get out of the car, but yelled and grabbed his leg.

"It's my knee," he said. "Michelle and Andrew?"

Bob looked through the rear window glass and saw Tony's wife and son lying on the floor. Michelle looked up at him and gave him a relieved smile. "They're fine," Bob told Tony while he opened the back door and helped them out.

"You okay?" he asked.

"We're—" Michelle stopped when she saw Tony. "Oh my Lord," she cried.

"I think he's going to be fine," Bob said. "I need you to do me a favor. I'll get Tony out of the car. Go over and help Liz out of the Audi. I want all three of you to go over to the sidewalk. Get away from the cars."

"But—"

"NOW, Michelle," Bob said.

He watched Michelle take Andrew over to the Audi. When she opened the door to help Liz, Bob turned back to Tony. "I want to get you out of the car. There may be others around. I doubt it, but I don't want to take any chances."

Tony grinned. "I did a hell of a job on my car, didn't I?"

Bob smiled and said, "You did one hell of a job on that motorcycle, too."

Tony leaned on the top of the open door and hopped on one leg around the car. He looked at the wrecked motorcycle and a man pinned beneath it.

Bob walked over to the motorcycle and lifted it off the man. He put his fingers against the man's neck and felt for a pulse. He was alive. He searched him for weapons and found a .38 caliber pistol in a shoulder holster under the man's jacket. Bob's hand shook as he stuck the pistol in the waistband of his slacks. He recognized the feeling of coming down from an adrenaline high. But, just as his shaking abated, anger overcame him and the shaking started all over again. These bastards had nearly killed Liz. Tony Fratangelo had risked the lives of his family members to save them. As soon as he made sure

Liz and the Fratangelos had been taken care of, he was going to keep his meeting with the Greek Prime Minister. The tenor of his meeting with the man would be altogether different than he had planned. It would no longer just be tense.

CHAPTER FORTY-THREE

AUGUST 6, 2004

The Greek Minister of Public Order, Constantine Angelou, personally placed a call to the Prime Minister's office. He demanded to speak to the PM, but was told by the Prime Minister's secretary that the Greek leader would not be in the office for another hour.

"Dammit," he shouted, "I need to talk with him now."

"I'm sorry, Mr. Minister," the secretary said, "but I have no way of getting in touch with him. He gave me orders to—"

"Then put me through to the Deputy Prime Minister," Angelou demanded.

After being transferred to the Deputy Prime Minister's office and going through his secretary, Angelou was finally put through to Dimitris Argyropoulos.

"What can I do for you, Constantine?" Argyropoulos said.

Angelou tried to control his excitement, but he found it difficult to do so. "We finally got one of the bastards," he blurted.

Argyropoulos said, "What bastards are you referring to?"

Angelou picked up on the Deputy Prime Minister's condescending tone. He'd never liked the arrogant son-of-a-bitch, but he wasn't about to let the man's attitude affect the high he felt.

"*Greek Spring*," Angelou said. "*Epsilon Alpha*. We got one of their killers. He's on his way to Hellenikon Hospital right now. The idiot tried to assassinate an American. Botched the job; nearly killed himself in the process. His partner blew himself up. Can you believe it? After all these years, we have one of them in our hands."

Angelou paused for a moment; Argyropoulos didn't say a word.

"I've got to run," Angelou said. "Let the Prime Minister know, will you?"

Angelou hung up and ran from his office, gathering up his body-guards as he hurried down the hall to the elevator that would carry him to the parking garage under the building. He cracked his knuckles, crossed his arms, uncrossed his arms, and then stuck his hands in his pockets. His body fairly vibrated with tension and excitement. This was the seminal moment of his life. He said a silent prayer, asking God to keep the terrorist alive, at least until his men had the chance to interrogate him. Angelou knew the man would talk. His agents had unparalleled skills at convincing suspects to divulge whatever information they had.

Dimitris Argyropoulos felt as though there was a little man inside his stomach, poking at it with a red-hot fork. This can't be happening, he thought. Not now. Not after all he had worked for. He needed to stay calm, to come up with a way out of the situation. He needed to improvise.

Argyropoulos moved to his desk and opened a drawer. He extracted a bottle of *ouzo* and, not bothering to use a glass, swigged the clear liquid straight from the bottle. He felt the liquor hit his stomach and send calming fingers of warmth throughout his body. After a minute, he decided on a course of action. He snatched his cell phone off the desk and rushed from the office. Ignoring his secretary asking if he wanted his car brought up, he took the stairs to the first floor and walked to the back of the building, to the alley. He checked to make sure there was no one else around, then called Giorgos Photos' cell telephone number.

Before Photos could even say hello, Argyropoulos yelled, "You fucked up, Photos. You have potentially ruined everything."

"What are you—"

"The police have one of your men. The attack on the Americans failed. One of your men is dead; the other is in custody at Hellenikon Hospital."

"Oh, my God," Photos moaned. "God help us."

"Strange thing for a Marxist to say," Argyropoulos said in a calm voice. "I suspect the last place you can count on for help is from heaven." Argyropoulos' voice suddenly went loud and angry. "You pay attention, Photos. Either solve this problem, or tell your wife to start planning your funeral. You won't be able to hide anywhere on the face of the earth. Your man in the hospital must not talk to the police." The Deputy Prime Minister's throat was dry and his pulse pounded in his head. He swallowed, then added, "And tell that cow you're married to that she'll have to bury your three sons at the same time she buries you."

He closed the cell phone, cutting the connection.

Argyropoulos paced the alley. He couldn't take the chance Photos might fail. He needed a backup plan. If Photos failed, Vassa would not. He'd recruited Nicolaos Koufos' sister ten years ago, after a three-year, torrid affair with the woman. Vassa lived on the edge. That was the way she liked it.

CHAPTER FORTY-FOUR

AUGUST 6, 2004

Stanton Markeson's blue blazer was white with the concrete dust hovering like a London fog over Kolonaki Square. He felt violently ill, but not just because his lungs were congested with dust, or because of the sight of torn and broken bodies strewn about the Square. It was because he should have been inside the Lambrakis Building when the bomb detonated, inside with his mates. And he would have been there if the explosion had happened on any other morning. But he was late getting in this morning because his wife decided she wanted to fool around.

She had shocked Stanton when she came to his room that morning and climbed into his bed. They hadn't made love in a year . . . maybe it had been longer than that. And now she had come on to him twice in one week. Stanton had figured out a long time ago that his marriage was based on something other than love and sex. Vassa was in it for his money; he was in it because he loved having her on his arm. No matter where they went together, men stared at her, their faces full of envy. He thought she no longer desired him—he was years older than she was, and his body was undesirable. He was short, fat, and plain looking.

Sex this morning had rejuvenated his spirit and given him hope that maybe there was a future for them. But those feelings were long forgotten as he watched rescue workers dig into the rubble and emergency vehicles cart bodies away. Somewhere in the remains of the building were the bodies of his fellow agents, Rodney Townsend, Cyril Bridewell, and Marcus Swinton. And another twelve secretaries, clerks, and analysts. All gone, because of some asshole terrorist group.

Vassa Markeson lay in her tub, surrounded by bubbles. She wanted the hot water to wash away the disgust she felt. Screwing Stanton was like fucking a walrus. But her orders were to protect him until *Greek Spring* had no further use for him. As long as she could funnel the information she pulled out of Stanton to her contacts with the terrorist group, her husband was more valuable to the group alive than dead. But a dead Stanton Markeson, Vassa knew, would make her one of the wealthiest women in Greece. That was her ultimate goal.

The telephone rang. Vassa picked up the wireless handset from the edge of the tub. She listened to her old lover tell her what he wanted her to do.

"You don't want much, do you?" she said, butterflies fluttering in her stomach. It had been a long time since she'd killed anyone. She'd missed it.

"I understand your concern, Vassa, but this is important. If you don't succeed, it could be our ruin."

Idiot, she thought. I'm not concerned; I'm so damned excited I could piss myself. "I want something in return," she said.

Argyropoulos didn't respond.

"Did you hear me?" Vassa asked.

"I heard you. What do you want?"

"I want to be rid of my husband. I'll do what you want; but only if you take care of my problem."

Argyropoulos was quiet for a long moment. When he finally spoke, he sounded angry. "All right, my dear; but you must perform first. You take care of my problem, and I will take care of yours."

CHAPTER FORTY-FIVE

AUGUST 6, 2004

Bob left Liz, Michelle Fratangelo, and her son Andrew at the hospital after Sam Goodwin and Stacey Frederick arrived to stand guard. Bob had called them and ordered them to come armed to the hospital. He wasn't going to take any chances. He would have preferred to leave Tony at the hospital, too; but Tony had borrowed a pair of crutches from the emergency room and insisted on joining him.

"There's no way I'm going to let you go anywhere in this city without backup," Tony had argued.

After what Tony had done to save his and Liz's lives, Bob didn't have the heart to argue with him. Bob drove to the Prime Minister's office. American Ambassador James Finch was waiting outside the building. Although the original plan had been to exclude the ambassador, events of that day had changed things.

Finch, accompanied by Grady McMasters and two uniformed Greek guards armed with automatic weapons, looked worried as he came over to Bob and Tony as soon as they exited their automobile.

"You guys all right?" the Ambassador asked, while the guards led them into the building, moving slowly in deference to Tony's walking with crutches.

"Yeah, thanks, we're fine," Bob said. He pointed at Tony and added, "Tony's a bit worse for wear."

Finch shook his head. "And Mrs. Danforth?" he asked.

"She'll be okay," Bob answered. "She's at the hospital now getting patched up." He met Finch's gaze and said, "You sure you want to be here? This could get tense to the point that you may never be welcome here again."

Finch's jaw clenched and his eyes narrowed. "I want the Greek Government to know we're taking this terrorism business seriously. Today's attacks escalated things to another level. No more screwing around, no more willingness to put up with the Greek Government's ambivalence and incompetence when it comes to these terrorists. I'm going to tell the Prime Minister that as soon as we're through here this morning, I will call the President and ask him to beef up our presence here, including ATF, more FBI, DEA, and, of course, the Agency."

Bob looked over at McMasters, then back at Finch. He realized that Finch was right. "Sounds good to me. How do you want to do this?"

"I'll run the meeting," Finch said. "I know the Prime Minister. I know just how hard to push him. I'm going to tell him I want you and Grady McMasters in the loop on everything Greek law enforcement is doing regarding the terrorists. And, I'm going to tell him I personally want a daily report on the investigation into this *professor* mentioned in the wiretap on that Piraeus apartment."

"What about the threat of pulling our team from the Olympics?" Bob asked.

"I'll use it *if* I feel it's necessary. But I suspect you'll agree that it won't do us any good in the world of public opinion. I think Jimmy Carter did the U.S. more harm than good when he pulled our team from the Olympic Games in Russia after the Soviets invaded Afghanistan."

Bob nodded. "Yeah, I agree, up to a point. But Greece isn't Russia. This country is barely surviving from an economic basis. If we pull our team, and a dozen other large countries follow suit, Greece could suffer in a big way. It's one hell of an axe to hold over their heads."

"We'll see," Finch said. "I suspect we won't need to use the threat."

"It's your call," Bob said, as they entered the reception area to the Prime Minister's office.

At that moment, a handsome, dark-haired, olive-complected man dressed in a blue pinstriped suit entered the reception area and approached Finch.

"Mr. Ambassador, I am so pleased to see you. Please accept my regrets for the terrible incident that occurred this morning. Thank God none of your people were killed. How are they?"

Finch shook the man's hand, and then pointed at Bob. "Prime Minister Ierides, this is Mr. Robert Danforth. He and his wife were the targets of the terrorist attack this morning." He then pointed at Tony and mentioned that the Fratangelo family was on the scene at the time of the attack and that Tony had been injured.

The Prime Minister walked over to Bob, then Tony, shook their hands, and expressed his condolences. "Please let me know if there is anything I can do for your families," he said.

Bob nodded. Tony gave no response. Bob noticed that Ambassador Finch did not mention that Tony and he were with the CIA.

"Please come into my office," Prime Minister Ierides said, turning and proceeding the group of men into a spacious, richly appointed room. A twenty foot by twenty foot Persian carpet covered the floor. The chairs and a sofa were plush. A massive mahogany desk sat at one end of the room. Dark blue velvet drapes were open, revealing three banks of windows and a spectacular view of the Acropolis. The sun's rays streamed into the room, backlighting a man standing in front of the middle set of windows.

"Ambassador Finch, you have met Deputy Prime Minister Argyropoulos," the Prime Minister said.

"Of course, it's good to see you again," Finch said. He then introduced Bob and Tony to the Greek Deputy Prime Minister.

The Prime Minister asked everyone to sit down. "It was Dimitris who informed me of the attack this morning," the Prime Minister said. "We are both very upset about what happened and will do all in our power to bring the criminals who were behind this to justice."

Bob looked at Argyropoulos while the Prime Minister spoke. Unlike the Prime Minister, Argyropoulos didn't appear to be particularly upset. In fact, he looked downright bored.

"We thank you for your concern," Finch said in a flat, unemotional tone, "but with all due respect, that isn't enough, Mr. Prime Minister. Since 1975, your government's expressions of concern are all that have been forthcoming as a result of a long string of attacks against Americans." He paused, then said in a hard voice, "Including nine murders." Finch's expression was menacing. He looked directly into the Prime Minister's eyes, his gaze never wavering. Bob enjoyed watching the Prime Minister become more and more uncomfortable by the second as Finch spoke with the full force and effect of the United States Government behind him. The ambassador paused for several seconds, then began speaking again.

"These gentlemen with me today are only the beginning of a contingent of law enforcement personnel from the United States who are going to be in Greece until *Greek Spring*, and every other terrorist organization, is eradicated. We will accept no more excuses."

"I understand your country's frustration over our inability to identify these terrorists," the Prime Minister said, "but Greece is a sovereign country. You have no right to infiltrate my country with American agents."

"Infiltrate?" Finch said. "We're not infiltrating anyone into your country. We're going to openly flood Greece with agents of every federal law enforcement organization. If you object to the United States assisting your country in its investigation of these terrorist groups, then my government must come to the conclusion that you, your administration, and your country are not serious about stopping these murderous attacks. If that is the case, Mr. Prime Minister, I will be forced to recommend to the President that he immediately declare Greece a terrorist state and ban all Americans from traveling to your country." Again Finch paused for a few seconds. He then added, "And

I assure you there are another dozen or so countries prepared to do the same."

The Prime Minister had remained remarkably calm during Finch's speech. His complexion had reddened slightly. But Bob noticed that Deputy Prime Minister Argyropoulos appeared to be extremely agitated. His face had gone scarlet and his mouth was set in a grim, lipless line. The man fidgeted in his chair and the look in his eyes was hateful. Bob would loved to have placed a bet on how long it would take Argyropoulos to blow. He guessed no more than thirty seconds.

The Prime Minister slowly rose to his feet. The others in the room stood as well. "You have made your position quite clear, Mr. Ambassador. I will take your comments under advisement and get back to you by no later than this afternoon with our reaction. I appreciate your candor and your concern. Hopefully, we will be able to resolve this situation to our mutual satisfaction."

"I look forward to hearing from you, Mr. Prime Minister," Finch answered.

The Americans began to leave the room, when Argyropoulos suddenly shouted, "How dare you threaten this government!"

The Americans turned to face Argyropoulos.

Right on schedule, Bob thought. Just about thirty seconds.

"You come in here and insult the leader of my country. You treat us as though Greece is some petty principality which has to kneel before your country—"

"That's enough, Dimitris," Ierides said, his face now at least as red as Argyropoulos' face.

"No, this must be said," Argyropoulos growled. "These Americans come in here with their CIA spies"—he pointed first at Bob, and then at Tony—"and pretend they want to stop the terrorists. But what they really want is to once again take over our country, just like they did in 1967. I will never—"

"I said that's enough," the Prime Minister said, his voice vibrating with anger. He turned to Finch and said, "My apologies, Mr. Ambassador, to you and your associates."

"Apology accepted, Mr. Prime Minister," Finch said as he turned back to the door and led the American contingent from the office.

Like a squad leader, Finch walked down the hall to the elevators, Bob and Tony in line behind him. Tony did his best to keep up on his crutches. No one said a word until they left the building and the ambassador's car pulled up to the front. Finch looked at each man in turn. "I think that was a particularly productive meeting," he said. He smiled and added, "I'll get back to you gentlemen after the Prime Minister contacts me later today. I will ask him what they're going to do about finding this professor character and his pink house." He looked at Bob and said, "And I sure as hell want to know what they're going to do with the guy the police carted away after the attack on you this morning."

The ambassador entered the back of his limo and was whisked away. Bob watched the car pull away, then told Tony, "It looks as though the first round of our counterattack was just fired."

Tony smiled. "Sure looks that way. I'm beginning to like the ambassador."

"You agree with Finch?" Bob asked. "About the meeting upstairs being productive?"

"Absolutely," Tony answered, "don't you?"

"Of course," Bob said with a smile. "I suspect that was the first time any American has talked to any high level Greek politician the way Finch just did. I'll bet you a bottle of retsina that the Prime Minister's call to Finch this afternoon will be very constructive. But our meeting was worthwhile in a completely different way."

Tony shot Bob a quizzical look. "How so?"

"How did Argyropoulos know we're CIA?"

"Sonofabitch," Tony said

"Yeah, sonofabitch," Bob said.

"How would he know?"

Bob hunched his shoulders.

"You don't suspect that the Deputy Prime Minister is in cahoots with the terrorists?"

"I suspect everyone," Bob said. "Remember what your informant, Michael Griffas, said: 'He knows . . . my boss knows.' He could have been referring to the Prime Minister, or some supervisor within the Prime Minister's office. Or he very well could have been speaking of Argyropoulos."

"It's my understanding that the Prime Minister and the Deputy Prime Minister share much of the same staff," Tony said.

"And, as Deputy Prime Minister," Bob added, "Argyropoulos probably has access to every bit of information the Greeks have about the terrorists, and about every step the Greek authorities are about to take against them."

"Sounds like we need to dig into Argyropoulos' background," Tony said.

"Sounds like one hell of an idea," Bob said.

As they walked to their car, Bob had another thought. He would call Ambassador Finch and share his suspicions with him.

CHAPTER FORTY-SIX

AUGUST 6, 2004

The call from Prime Minister Ierides went as well as Ambassador Finch could have anticipated. Ierides started off by again expressing his regrets over the attack on the Danforths and the injuries to Mrs. Danforth and Mr. Fratangelo, and he apologized for the Deputy Prime Minister's outburst. Then he told Finch that he and his country would welcome all the assistance the Americans could provide. They discussed what the government was doing to try to identify the professor in the pink house and also the interrogation of the terrorist who was under guard in the hospital.

"What's the man's condition?" Finch asked.

"He's barely conscious and in a lot of pain. The doctors have him so pumped up with painkillers that he's not lucid enough to answer any questions yet. It's going to be a few days before we can get anything out of him. I've put Deputy Prime Minister Argyropoulos in charge of the investigation into the attack on the Danforths. You should have no concerns going forward about my administration's commitment to identify and capture these killers."

Finch's stomach cramped. Bob Danforth's telephone call had been on Finch's mind all afternoon. Argyropoulos' comment about Danforth and Fratangelo being with the CIA could have been nothing more than guesswork, but something about the man's comments during the meeting in the Prime Minister's office told him there was something more than a lucky guess at work here.

After he finished talking with the Prime Minister, Finch called Bob and told him what the Prime Minister had said.

"If my instincts are correct, Mr. Ambassador, I think the Prime Minister just put the fox in charge of the chicken coop."

"Be careful, Mr. Danforth," Finch said. "Despite my tone in the meeting at the Prime Minister's office, we're still dealing with the popularly elected government of a country that is important to our geopolitical strategy. How long do you think our relationship with Greece would last if we falsely accused the number two man in the Greek Government?"

Bob assigned Stacey Frederick and Sam Goodwin the job of checking into Dimitris Argyropoulos' background. They had a tough job ahead of them. There was no way they could use their contacts inside the Greek Government out of fear that word would get back to Argyropoulos. Stacey came up with the idea of using one of the Agency-friendly reporters working for the French News Agency, Renee Deschamps, to get the information they needed. Deschamps agreed to call Argyropoulos' office to get his permission to do a story on his rise in the Greek political hierarchy. Argyropoulos was so excited about the prospect of his story being distributed to the international press that he agreed to meet with the reporter the next morning.

Bob, Stacey, and Sam briefed Deschamps about the questions the reporter was to ask Argyropoulos.

"Remember," Bob said, "ask him if he was involved with politics when he was a student, who his associates were back then. We need to get him to divulge these associates' names and their contact information. Also, ask if he ever spent time overseas."

"Overseas?" Deschamps asked.

Bob nodded. "Do your best to find out if he spent any time in either France and/or in any of the former Soviet bloc nations."

"*Tres bien,*" Deschamps said, but the look on his face said he was confused.

CHAPTER FORTY-SEVEN

AUGUST 7, 2004

Giorgos Photos was desperate. Savvas was dead. That was fine. But Pavlos Manganos was lying in a hospital. The man had been with *Greek Spring* for years. He was a gold mine of information for their enemies. Photos had to make sure Manganos didn't talk. Loyal follower or not, Photos knew the Greek police had ways to make Manganos talk.

He could send one of his men to take care of Manganos; but what if the man botched the job? That could put two of the group's members in the hands of the authorities. What he needed was Musa Sulaiman. It would cost him a lot of money; but what good was money if Manganos talked, gave the police Photos' name, and he wound up in prison?

He wanted to focus on the main event, the *coup de grace*. But first he had to take care of this Manganos mess. The opening ceremony of the Olympic Games was one week away. Photos sighed. I'll get this one problem solved today, then work on the final details for August 13.

He walked outside his island home and called a number on his cell phone. His wife had returned from visiting her brother and sister in Boston and he didn't want her to overhear the conversation. She knew about his involvement with *EA*; she didn't know that he was the group's leader. He didn't want her to overhear any of his plans. He would have to get her off the island, as Evoia would be his base of operations for the next few days. She'd be happy to be back home near Sounion, anyway.

The phone call was routed through a series of exchanges that ultimately connected Photos to a cell phone in the Turkish-controlled section of Cyprus, where Sulaiman was spending a week at the beach.

Musa Sulaiman jerked awake at the sound of his cell phone. He slowly sat up on the lounge chair and drank from the bottle of mineral water on the table beside him. Then he reached for his phone.

"Yes," he said.

"It's me, I need your assistance."

Musa glanced at the woman lying on the lounge chair next to him. Her ripe, voluptuous body made his groin ache. He loved German women. They were pliant and demanding, all at the same time. She was an architect from Landstuhl. She thought he was a rich Egyptian ship owner. He was going to charge that fucker, Giorgos Photos, a lot of money to walk away from this golden piece of ass.

CHAPTER FORTY-EIGHT

AUGUST 7, 2004

Bob was scheduled to meet Stanton Markeson at noon at a small *taverna* in the Pangratis neighborhood of Athens. First he made sure Liz was comfortable in their room at the Grand Bretagne Hotel. She'd slept late and Bob ordered in room service for her. After eating, she dozed off—the medication the doctor gave her was helping her get through the pain of her injuries. Bob left her with a Marine guard stationed outside the room—compliments of Ambassador Finch.

Tony Fratangelo waited on the street in front of the hotel. He now drove an Agency-issued dark-blue Chevrolet Tahoe. At Bob's request, he drove to the Fratangelo home in Kifissia. Bob wanted to see how Michelle and Andrew were doing since their "venture," as Andrew described the terrorist attack. Bob was especially concerned about Michelle's health considering her pregnancy. Mother and son seemed no worse for wear, and after spending a half-hour with them, Bob and Tony left for their meeting with Stanton Markeson.

This wasn't really a business meeting with Markeson. Bob wanted to express his condolences. The news hit that morning—the remains of Markeson's co-workers' bodies had been found in the debris of the Lambrakis Building. No one on the British team survived the blast. Markeson was at the *taverna* when Bob and Tony arrived. They joined Markeson at an inside table.

"You know, the Olympic Stadium where the first modern games were held back in the late eighteen hundreds is right behind that building," Markeson said in a detached way, pointing across the street.

The man had a faraway look in his eyes and his color was some-where between gray and white, his posture hunched. He looked as though he'd slept in his clothes.

Bob nodded. He leaned forward and tried to catch Markeson's gaze; but the man's eyes were cast down at the tabletop. Bob looked at Tony, then back at Markeson. "I'm terribly sorry, Stanton. I know this must be very difficult for you."

Markeson raised his head and looked at Bob. "I should have been there."

Bob scooted his chair closer to the table. "That doesn't make any sense," he said. "If you were dead, you wouldn't have the chance to find the bastards who did this to your friends, to avenge their deaths."

The waiter came to their table at that moment and took their orders. After he walked away, Bob said, "I was rereading some of the files you gave us. There was something that bothered me about the dialogue between Harvey Cornwell's widow, Marjorie, and the agent who investigated his murder."

"How's that?" Markeson asked, his voice still sounding dispirited, disinterested.

"She mentioned that her husband would call the office each morn-ing before driving in, to advise of the route he would take."

Markeson now looked bored. "That's correct. So what? We all did that. Except we don't call in to the *office.* We specifically call the duty officer. We rotate through all the officers, each of us taking our turn as duty officer. We all used to be headquartered on the embassy com-pound. Our group, as well as the members of the diplomatic contingent, were on the duty roster. If too many people called in on the same day and said they were planning to use the same route, or if the duty officer was aware of a traffic tie-up along a certain route, he might suggest an alternative."

Bob rubbed the back of his neck. "I'm just trying to discover if there are common elements evident on the days of the murders of

Harvey Cornwell and Stephen Saunders, as well as on the days of the attacks on other British personnel."

Markeson hunched his shoulders. "I guess I could look into it," he said, without much enthusiasm.

CHAPTER FORTY-NINE

AUGUST 7, 2004

Jack Cole had a 2:00 P.M. tee time. This would be the first time in three months that he'd even thought about taking a Saturday afternoon off. He had just finished stuffing some files into his briefcase, when his office telephone rang.

"Cole here," he said.

"Mr. Cole, it's Raymond Gallegos. We got a hit."

"What do you mean?" Jack asked.

"The Bulgarian guy, the former agent who's running a security firm in—"

"Yeah, I remember. What do you have?"

"We showed him the list of names compiled in Athens, the one with names of Greeks who had some connection to France. The Bulgarian recognized three of the names. Two of them went through training in Eastern Europe—one in Bulgaria and the other in Russia. The third one was in Cuba."

"What do you have on these people?" Jack said.

"Not a lot; but what we do have are their names, their addresses, what they do for a living, stuff like that."

Jack held his breath for a few seconds. "Is any of the three a teacher or professor?"

"Sorry, boss. All three of the names the Bulgarian recognized are government bureaucrats or officeholders."

Jack was momentarily disappointed. But he knew they were further along than they were just moments earlier. "Good job, Ray," he said. "How quickly can your team get down here to the office?"

"We're already here."

"I'll be right down; give me five minutes. By the way, did you show the photographs in the files to the Bulgarian?"

"No," Raymond said. "All we had were the names and some background information. The photographs hadn't downloaded yet."

"But that wouldn't have picked up someone who was using an alias before, or who has changed his name since coming back to Greece."

"You're right," Raymond said. "After we have all the photographs, we'll go back out and meet with the Bulgarian."

"Okay."

Jack hung up, called to cancel his tee time, and left his office to make his way down to where Bob Danforth's Langley team was busting its ass on what could be one more wild-goose chase.

CHAPTER FIFTY
AUGUST 7, 2004

After Bob Danforth, Tony Fratangelo, and he left the restaurant in Pangratis, Stanton Markeson stopped at Rodney Townsend's house. He'd intended to call on Townsend's widow, Meg, but there were a dozen cars parked outside her place. She appeared to have all the support she needed. He'd started to drive to his home on several occasions, but changed his mind each time. He needed action; he wanted to do something, to avenge the deaths of his friends and co-workers. The problem was that he didn't know what to do. Markeson drove aimlessly around Athens like a leaf blown in the wind. As the sun was setting, he found himself parked along the water in Vouliagmeni.

He had never felt so low and useless. Thoughts scattered through his mind in a disorganized, disconnected manner, as though someone was channel surfing through his brain. Then one thought suddenly gained purchase in his memory banks when he remembered what Danforth had said to him. Something about common elements associated with all of the attacks on British citizens. It hadn't seemed like much at the time Danforth mentioned it; but now it at least gave him an idea about something he could do. He pulled away from the curb and headed to the British Embassy. Even though the MI-6 office was destroyed in the blast, along with all the hard copies and computer files stored there, at least the computer files could still be accessed through the embassy computer system. They backed up their records at MI-6 Headquarters in London. He could access that database from the embassy.

Markeson drove at well over the speed limit. He now had a purpose. It took him forty minutes to reach the embassy and another thirty minutes to get set up in an office with access to a computer terminal. He accessed the MI-6 database and pulled up the list of attacks against British citizens in Athens. There had been eleven of them— two fatal; six with serious, but non-fatal injuries; and three with minor injuries. The eleven incidents did not include yesterday's attack on the Lambrakis Building.

He copied the list to a new Word file. Then he opened the incident files one at a time, looking for commonalties. He spent three hours poring over the files, but came up with nothing. He was starting to feel exhausted, and had come to the conclusion he was wasting his time, when he remembered what he'd told Danforth about the duty officer system used by the embassy.

Markeson opened the computer file that showed the daily duty officer's name. He scrolled down to the first terrorist incident, dating back six years. The duty officer that day was Victor Bergeson, a career Intelligence officer who had retired shortly after the attack that had seriously wounded a British Army officer.

Markeson scrolled down to the next incident date: two years after the first attack. He was the duty officer on that day. He typed his name across from the date. Markeson found he was also the duty officer on the date of the third incident. This didn't really surprise him. Statistically, this could have been just the luck of the draw. *Bad* luck. His turn at duty officer came up about every twenty days. The counterterrorism team and certain embassy officers were on the duty roster. Even after moving to the Lambrakis Building from the embassy compound two months ago, Markeson and the other agents on the counterterrorism team took their turns on the duty roster.

But when Markeson saw his name listed as duty officer on the date of the fourth attack, a shiver ran up his spine. He was downright sick to his stomach when he discovered he'd been duty officer on the days of all but the first attack against British citizens. He didn't need to consult the computer to see who was on duty the day the terrorists from

Eleeneekee Aneexee murdered Harvey Cornwell. He was. He'd never forget that date.

It made no sense. Markeson paced around the small embassy office, trying to reason things out. Ten attacks against Englishmen and women on ten days when he was duty officer. It was statistically improbable. But what was the connection?

Markeson called down to the embassy's resident security officer, Reginald McHugh. "Regge, you have a minute?"

"Sure, Stanton. What do you need?"

"I'm upstairs in the—"

"I know where you are, Stanton. Remember, I'm the security officer."

Markeson forced a laugh. "Right you are," he said. "Would you mind coming up here?"

"On my way."

While he waited for McHugh, Markeson studied the list again. He typed his name next to the incident dates on which he was the duty officer. He felt as though a block of ice had been stuffed inside his abdomen. "This makes absolutely no sense at all," he said.

"What's that, Stanton?" McHugh asked from the doorway. He was a small, compactly-built Irishman, with brown hair and hazel eyes. Markeson had worked with McHugh for three years and had a profound respect for the man's intelligence and courage. He trusted McHugh, but he didn't want to tell him too much just yet. He didn't know where this conversation might lead.

Markeson pointed at the two chairs in front of the desk and moved around the desk to sit in one of them. McHugh took the other chair.

"I want you to help me with something. Could someone gain access to our communications system?"

"Sure," McHugh said, "but it wouldn't be for very long. We sweep our offices at least once per week, and we don't do it on any set schedule. Once in a while we find a bug, but that's rare."

Markeson thought about McHugh's answer for a moment. He shook his head.

"What's going on, Stanton?"

Markeson wanted to think about what he'd discovered, to take time to reason it all out. But something told him this was a problem beyond his experience. He stood and told McHugh to come around the desk with him. "Look at this list," he said, pointing at the screen.

"What is it?" McHugh asked. "I'm not familiar—" McHugh stopped in mid-sentence and said, "Oh."

"Yeah, you see the problem?"

McHugh gave Markeson a sympathetic look. "Bloody hell," he said, "this isn't possible."

"It's not only possible, it happened."

Now Markeson watched McHugh pace the office. They were silent for well over a minute. Finally, the security officer said, "What made you even look into this?"

"I had lunch today with the American CIA Chief, Bob Danforth. He mentioned reading something in the Cornwell investigation file about how we call the duty officer before leaving our homes. I didn't think much about it, until I matched the dates of attacks with the names of the duty officers on those same days." He pointed at the computer screen. "I have to tell you, Regge, this scares me to death."

"I can understand that. But let's stay cool and think about this. Let's go over the days when you were on duty. Did you follow a routine on those days?"

Markeson shook his head. "The only routine I followed was arriving at the embassy an hour earlier than usual. I typically got in about seven A.M. I took different routes. I usually stopped and picked up rolls and coffee, but alternated where I bought the stuff. I can't think of anything I did that could be considered routine."

"Which telephone did you take calls from? Your office?"

Markeson considered the question, then said, "Sometimes; but once I get into the embassy, I usually move around the building. I check with the night duty officer to find out if there were any incidents during his shift. I meet with the communications officer in the crypto vault and get the current one-time pad information and find out if there is any classified message traffic. You know, there's a lot to do before the rest of the staff arrives."

"So, how did you take the calls if you were moving around the building?"

"I have the receptionist transfer the calls to my cell phone." Markeson pulled the phone from the breast pocket of his sport jacket. "I always have it with me."

McHugh and Markeson stared at each other, as though the same thought had hit them.

McHugh said, "The receptionist is always a Greek National. She could have kept the line open when she transferred the calls to you. She could have listened in on every damn conversation."

Markeson felt high voltage electricity course through him. But the charge lasted only a few seconds. "Probably, but not likely. We've had four different women in the receptionist position since the first attack. I can't believe the terrorists could have co-opted all four women. Besides, why did the attacks only occur on the days when I was the duty officer?"

McHugh nodded as though to indicate his agreement. He was silent for a while, then said, "Have you recently had your cell phone swept for bugs?"

Markeson laughed, then blushed. It was policy that all electronic devices had to be checked for bugs every month; but it was a policy rarely adhered to, unless a phone, or laptop computer, or PDA was in for repair with one of the local contractors that worked for the embassy. The security staff would always inspect the device when it returned from the contractor. Markeson had never had a problem with his cell phone, and didn't want to be without the phone while the security people inspected it. So he'd never handed it over for a security check.

"I never thought it was necessary, as I always have it in my possession. I never lend it to anyone."

"You're sure about that?"

"Of course."

"Let's take it downstairs and give it a once over," McHugh said.

Markeson handed over his cell phone and followed McHugh to the security office. He watched the man slowly wave a handheld wand over the phone. The wand beeped each time McHugh passed it over the phone.

"Strange," McHugh said.

"What?" Markeson said.

"Give me a minute." He removed the back of the cell phone and inspected the inside. Then he took out the battery. "I don't get it," he said. "The wand indicated something was transmitting from the phone; but I don't see anything." He slowly rolled the phone over in his hand, holding it close to his face.

McHugh moved to a workbench and searched in a drawer for something. Finally, he removed a tiny screwdriver from the drawer and worked on four screws securing the back and front of the phone together. He separated the two halves and laid them side-by-side. He adjusted an eight-inch diameter magnifying glass on a flexible neck to just over the top of the workbench. The twenty-power glass enlarged the inner workings of the telephone. "Well, I'll be damned," McHugh said. "You've been bugged, my friend."

"What are you talking about?"

"Someone put a very advanced listening device inside your cell phone. Every word you or a caller speaks into this telephone is being transmitted to another location. How long have you had this phone?"

"About four years."

"In other words, since about the time of the second attack. The one on Victoria Bryson."

Markeson nodded.

"I assume the phone was issued to you by the embassy."

Markeson swallowed. "No, actually, it was a gift from my wife."

CHAPTER FIFTY-ONE
AUGUST 8, 2004

Giorgos Photos was scared to the point of paranoia of meeting Musa Sulaiman at one of *Greek Spring's* safehouses in Athens. The phone tap and raid on one of the group's safehouses had shaken his confidence. He was even more frightened about meeting Sulaiman on the Island of Evoia since he received the most recent call from Dimitris Argyropoulos. The Deputy Prime Minister informed him that the Americans suspected *some professor who owned a pink house on a Greek island had a telephone conversation with an Arab believed to have links to Al Qaeda.*

As soon as Argyropoulos ended their conversation, Photos called a local painting contractor and hired him to paint his island home white. Then he called his wife at their home near Sounion and ordered her to vacate the house there and travel to the Island of Samos, where her parents lived. She wasn't happy about having to move again, having just left Evoia, but she did as she was told.

Despite his plans to make the house on Evoia his operations base for the next week, Photos knew he would have to change that. After terminating the call to his wife, he grabbed a flashlight, went outside, used a key to unlock a padlock securing the cellar door, and entered the cool, dark space. He dragged a rusted metal cabinet away from the stuccoed wall, exposing a two-foot by three-foot hole. He pulled a wooden box from the cavity. After replacing the cabinet, he hefted the box off the floor, and, grunting with effort, carried it outside to a fifty-five gallon drum. He turned the box over, dumping its contents of documents into the drum. After retrieving a can of gasoline from the cellar and carrying it to the drum, he poured gasoline on the papers and dropped a lit match into the drum. The papers ignited with a *whoosh* and Photos jumped back. He watched the fire burn for a minute and, when he was confident the flames would consume the documents, he returned to the house. He packed a bag with clothes and seventy-five thousand Euros, drove down to the ferry dock, and, after a forty minute wait, took the ferry to the mainland.

Photos drove south into the Peleponnesos, to the Corinth Canal, where he'd arranged to meet Sulaiman. The area would be heavy with traffic, between tourists and Greeks on Sunday drives, so Photos allowed plenty of time for the drive. He made it to the Corinth Museum an hour earlier than his 3:00 P.M. appointment. He played tourist while waiting for Sulaiman to show, slowly walking through the museum, viewing the exhibits of ancient Greek sculptures, pottery, statuary, and weaponry. It is this legacy that I am trying to preserve, he told himself. This greatness that must be restored to Greece.

"Enjoying yourself?"

Photos jumped at the voice behind him. He jerked around and saw Sulaiman standing three feet away.

"Sorry, I didn't mean to startle you," Sulaiman said, although the grin on his face told Photos that's exactly what the killer intended.

"You didn't startle me," Photos said. "I . . . .." Photos stopped himself. He realized he was just giving Sulaiman more satisfaction. The grin on the man's face had grown into a full-blown smile. "Let's go outside," he said.

The museum grounds were strewn with chunks of marble of all sizes and broken pieces of statuary and pottery shards. Photos led Sulaiman to a spot where the remains of ancient stone columns lay haphazardly at the top edge of a hillside that looked down on the canal. They were well away from other sightseers They circled the pile of broken columns and looked out at the sea.

"I need you to take care of a problem for me," Photos said in French.

"What kind of problem?"

"One of my men, Pavlos Manganos, was seriously injured and is now in the hospital. He is heavily sedated and has not spoken to the police, yet. But I can't take the chance he'll talk."

"What are you worried about?" Sulaiman said. "Why would he say anything about your organization? No one will connect him to *Greek Spring*."

"They've already done that," Photos said.

Sulaiman whipped around and stared at Photos, who continued to look out at the water. The Libyan's voice turned gravelly and threatening. "What do you mean?"

"My man was injured while trying to kill an American CIA official. The pistol he carried will soon be tied to us. We stole it from a Greek police station and later took credit for the robbery. Once they check the serial number on the weapon, they will know for sure that Manganos is one of us."

"And you're sure your man hasn't talked to the police?"

"Take my word for it. My source is very highly placed."

"You've put me in a very dangerous position," Sulaiman growled. "If the authorities have already identified you as an associate of this Manganos, being here with you could be my end."

"No, no, they haven't got a thing out of Manganos. I swear it. I want to keep it that way. That's why I called you."

"You want me to kill your man, is that it?"

"Yes." Photos could feel Sulaiman's gaze on him and felt sweat pour off him. "I think—"

"I don't give a shit what you think. Why don't you have one of your own people do the job?"

Photos swallowed. His throat was parched and his heart beat a mile a minute. "The police already have one of my people; I didn't want to take the chance of another member of my group being captured."

"In other words, you consider this a very risky assignment."

"Well, yes," Photos answered.

Sulaiman seemed to think for a long moment about what Photos had just said. When he finally spoke, he gripped Photos' arm and pulled him to him. "This is the last time I will work for you, do you understand?"

Photos couldn't make his voice work. He nodded.

"And this will cost you another two hundred and fifty thousand dollars. If the fee hasn't been transferred to the same account as last time by five P.M. today, the deal is off."

Photos nodded again.

"Now, give me the location of the hospital and Manganos' room number."

CHAPTER FIFTY-TWO

AUGUST 8, 2004

Stanton Markeson had now gone without sleep for over forty-eight hours. He'd suffered from survivor's guilt on Friday night, having been away from the Lambrakis Building when the bomb went off, and stayed up all night Saturday agonizing over an evil worm of a thought that had been boring into his brain since meeting with Reginald McHugh at the British Embassy.

At first, he ran scenarios through his head about how a terrorist group had slipped a bugged cell phone to an unsuspecting Vassa, who then gave it to him as a gift. But the more he thought about it, the sicker he became. He couldn't ignore the possibility that Vassa had intentionally passed him a "hot" phone. And, when he thought about her sudden passion for him on Friday morning, he felt absolutely nauseous.

Markeson stayed in the embassy on Saturday night and tried to come up with a resolution to his nightmarish thoughts. But the evil worm just kept burrowing through his brain. He was sick at heart. If Vassa had betrayed him, then he was responsible for eleven terrorist attacks, including Fred Grantham and Harvey Cornwell's murders and the murders of his co-workers and all the innocent people who worked in the Lambrakis Building.

Markeson felt anger seep through every cell in his body. But, despite the anger, he prayed he was jumping to the wrong conclusion. He left the embassy when the sun was halfway to the western horizon on a beautiful Sunday, and drove to his home. He needed to confront Vassa. He turned onto his street, stopped, and pulled over to the curb while still fifty meters away. A black limousine with tinted windows was parked in front of the house; his wife, Vassa, was stepping into the vehicle. She had a small suitcase in her hand.

"Hello, my dear," Dimitris Argyropoulos said. He kissed Vassa's cheek while wrapping an arm around her shoulders and pulling her to him.

Vassa turned her face toward Argyropoulos. "A kiss on the cheek, Dimi. Is that the best you can do?"

Argyropoulos laughed. "Of course not." He pressed her to him and kissed her lips. She responded immediately, stabbing her tongue into his mouth.

When they pulled apart, Argyropouols said, "Ah, I've missed you. The things we do for our country."

Vassa squinted at Argyropoulos. "What's our country got to do with you dumping me?"

Argyropoulos wagged a finger at her. "You know better than that. We couldn't very well continue to see one another while you were married to a British agent and I was Deputy Prime Minister."

Vassa seemed to consider that for a moment, then said, "So, how is this going to work?"

Argyropoulos looked toward the glass divider between them and the driver. Satisfied that the glass was tightly closed, he reached into a leather, soft-sided briefcase between his feet, extracted a pistol, and handed it to Vassa. Argyropoulos laughed. "Ierides put me in charge of the investigation into Friday's attack on the American CIA agent. One of the assassins is now in the hospital in critical condition. As of fifteen minutes ago, he had not regained consciousness. I've called the hospital to let them know I'm going to stop there at seven P.M."—he looked at his wristwatch—"an hour from now. I've instructed my advance man to notify the police detail and the medical staff that I want a briefing from them at seven-thirty, after I look in on the captured terrorist. My man will clear the floor by seven-fifteen. That will give you time to enter the hospital, find Pavlos Manganos' room three-twenty-four, put a bullet in his brain, and make your escape."

"What are you going to do, drop me off at the front door?" she asked sarcastically.

"No, my dear, I told my driver to drop you off at the Celestine Palace Hotel. You will check in, drop off your bag in the room." He smiled at her and brushed the back of his hand over her breasts. "We will meet there after our business at the hospital is complete."

"How do I get to the hospital?" she asked.

"After you go to your room, you will leave the hotel by a back exit, cross the lawn behind the hotel, where my assistant, Ari Stokolos, will pick you up. He'll take you to the side of the hospital where you'll enter the building via an emergency exit door that has been disabled and propped open."

"And how do I get back to the hotel?"

"Ari will be waiting at the emergency exit."

"Where I'll wait for you to join me?"

"Exactly right," Argyropoulos said.

"And you *will* join me at the Celestine Palace?"

"Of course, my dear."

"Don't delay," she said. "I'm already wet with anticipation."

"Did you miss me that much all these years?" he asked with a leer.

"Of course, Dimi," she said. "But there's nothing like putting a bullet into a man's head to make a girl really excited."

Argyropoulos shuddered. Her words were sobering enough, but it was the look in her eyes that sent shivers up his spine.

CHAPTER FIFTY-THREE
AUGUST 8, 2004

Jack Cole rubbed his right eye, trying to stop the twitch. The twitching always seemed to begin when he was under extreme stress. Frank Reynolds' call five minutes ago had raised his stress level to 6.8 on the Richter Scale. Frank had informed him that Raymond Gallegos hadn't been able to connect with his Bulgarian contact. The man had literally gone fishing. There was a sign hanging on the front door of the Bulgarian's security company saying that he had gone fishing and wouldn't return until Tuesday, August 10. Raymond had tried to call the man on his cell phone, but received no answer.

Jack knew there was no guarantee the Bulgarian would be able to shed any more light on any of the people in their files, but there was always hope.

What had really elevated Jack's anxiety level was the fact that the opening ceremony of the 2004 Olympic Games was just five days away. Although the CIA had no hard evidence that international or Greek-based terrorist groups had targeted the Games, there was little doubt in his mind that some terrorist act would occur, especially after the train bombings in Madrid last March. The Olympic Games were too lush a target of opportunity for the psychopaths running terror organizations. And the thing that made the Athens Games so vulnerable was the proliferation of terrorist groups based right there in Greece.

The terrorists wouldn't even have to pass through passport control to enter Greece. Members of *Greek Spring* and other Greek groups were already in the country, as were thousands of Muslim immigrants. There could easily be *Al Qaeda* members hiding among these immigrants. Like jackals, they could lie in wait.

CHAPTER FIFTY-FOUR

AUGUST 8, 2004

As a senior U.S. official in Greece, Bob was expected to attend the memorial ceremony at the British Embassy for the Englishmen and women murdered in the Lambrakis Building bombing. He made it clear to the other members of his team that he wanted them there as well.

Security at the British Embassy was even more intense than usual. General traffic in the area had been diverted away from the embassy compound. Traffic going to the compound had to go through a checkpoint, where every driver and passenger's ID was checked against a list of names. Vehicles were inspected inside and out. Security personnel with bomb-sniffing dogs circled every vehicle. It took Bob and Tony an hour to pass through the checkpoint, and another fifteen minutes to park the Tahoe. Although Tony was still on crutches, he was able to match Bob's brisk pace from the parking lot to a massive white tent erected on the grounds for the occasion. There were no seats available, so they found space to stand at the right rear of the tent just as the English Ambassador began speaking.

The final British death count in the bombing was seven men and five women. In addition, four Greek nationals who had worked for the Brits died in the blast. The ambassador talked about each of the victims, giving information about their time with the government, their educational background, and their family situation.

An hour passed, and the ambassador had turned the podium over to an Anglican priest, when Bob nudged Tony and whispered, "Do you see Stanton Markeson?"

Tony shook his head. "I was wondering the same thing. I don't think he's here. Strange, isn't it?"

Bob nodded.

Tony pointed at Stacey Frederick who was seated five rows from the back and said, "Stacey knows Markeson quite well. She may know something."

The priest spoke for fifteen minutes, led the audience in a prayer, and then thanked everyone for coming to honor the memories of the deceased.

Bob and Tony made their way to the other side of the tent and got Stacey's attention before the audience began leaving. Stacey hustled out of her seat and came over to them.

"Have you seen Markeson?" Tony asked.

"No, sir. I assumed he was pretty torn up about the whole thing, but Reginald McHugh, the Embassy Security Chief, told me Stanton took off this afternoon. Said he burned rubber when he left the embassy, like he was in one hell of a hurry to get somewhere."

"Huh," Bob said. "McHugh say anything else?"

"Not really. But something seemed to be bothering him. I tried to find out what it was; but he wasn't talking. He appeared to be concerned about Stanton, though."

"Introduce me to McHugh," Bob said. "Tony and I will be outside by the parking area."

While Stacey went to locate McHugh, Bob led Tony outside to their vehicle.

"What's on your mind, boss?" Tony asked.

"The results of three decades in this business. For Markeson to miss the memorial ceremony for his buddies, something very important must have come up. Something very, very important."

While waiting for Stacey and McHugh, Bob called the hotel to check on Liz. He was pleasantly surprised when she answered the phone with a strong "Hello."

"Hey, babe, how are you feeling? Where's the guard?"

"My babysitter is outside in the hall. He won't let me leave the room and, according to him, that's on *your* orders. Is that correct?"

"Jeez, Liz, when I left there this morning, you looked like you'd gone ten rounds with Mike Tyson. You've got two black eyes, a swollen nose, a cut lip, and who knows what else. This is no time to be gallivanting around town. I'll be back in an hour or so. We can grab a bite to eat in the hotel dining room and—"

"First of all," Liz said, her voice tinged with anger, "I am not interested in *gallivanting* around town. But I'm not going to let some pissant Greek assholes turn me into a prisoner. So, you tell Moose McGurk out in the hall, or whatever his name is, to let me out of here."

Bob saw Stacey coming toward him with a short, squat, brown-haired man in tow. He sighed and thought how nice it would be to have back again the shy, retiring girl he'd married so many years ago, instead of the tougher-than-nails woman that girl had turned into. "Put Stein on the line," he told Liz. "But if you leave the room, he's going with you. I don't want an argument about that."

"Why would I argue about having a handsome young man escort me around Athens? Besides, I already figured that would be part of the deal."

Bob gave Liz's guard new instructions and closed his cell phone as Stacey walked up. She introduced Reginald McHugh to Bob and Tony.

"Nice to meet you," Bob said. He waved his arm in the direction of the tent and said, "Unfortunate circumstances."

"Bloody right," McHugh said.

"I was surprised that Stanton Markeson wasn't in attendance today," Bob said.

McHugh shrugged. "The man's got a lot on his mind."

Bob gave McHugh a narrow-eyed look. "Besides the death of his comrades?"

Again McHugh shrugged.

"Something tells me you've got something on *your* mind," Bob said. "Why don't you share it with us. We're on your side, remember."

McHugh half-turned, as though he was going to walk away; but then he turned back and said, "I shouldn't be telling you anything; I haven't shared this information with my superiors yet." He sighed and, after looking down at his shoes for a moment, looked back at Bob. "I found a bug in Markeson's cell phone. He told me the phone was a gift from his wife. He hung around here through Saturday night. I couldn't get him to share his thoughts with me; but I could tell he was upset. Then he took off this afternoon like he was on a life or death mission."

"Do you know how to contact him?"

McHugh gave Bob an embarrassed smile. "I have his cell phone number." He paused a moment and said, "The one with the bug inside."

Bob ordered Stacey to join him and Tony after leaving McHugh. They took off in the Tahoe, with Stacey driving and Tony in the backseat. Bob told him to try to raise Markeson on his cell phone, reminding him to be careful what he said to him. *Greek Spring* could be listening. Tony dialed the number McHugh gave them, but no one answered.

Bob turned to look back at Tony. "I'm going to have Stacey drop me off at the hotel, then I want you both to pick up Sam and try to figure out where Markeson is. I've got a feeling he knows something about the attack on the Lambrakis Building."

Stacey looked incredulous. "You can't believe he's in bed with *Greek Spring*," she said.

"I didn't say that," Bob answered. "I just find it very suspicious that a man who is usually at his office at the crack of dawn picks the day when terrorists blow up his office to come in late." Stacey opened her mouth as though she was going to object, but Bob held up a finger to cut her off. "I'm not necessarily saying he had anything to do with the blast; I'm only saying it's suspicious that Markeson wasn't there when the building was destroyed. I just want to know why he wasn't in early last Friday and why he missed the memorial ceremony."

Bob let his comments sink in, then added, "And I want you to dig up everything you can on Mrs. Markeson. She gave the cell phone to her husband. It may not have been bugged when she gave it to him, and even if it was, she may not have known anything about it; but let's assume the worst. That Markeson's wife is somehow associated with *Greek Spring.*"

"Jeez," Stacey said.

"Right," Bob said.

Stanton Markeson trailed the limo. After getting close enough to read the license plate number—he'd hoped the vehicle had diplomatic plates so he could tie it to an embassy; but it had commercial plates, which told him nothing—he dropped back so the limo occupants didn't get suspicious. He followed the car to the Celestine Palace Hotel, watched Vassa get out with her suitcase and enter the hotel, and then followed the car as it circled the block and came to a stop in front of the Hellenikon Hospital. Markeson's anger had brewed just below the surface for hours. Combined with a lack of sleep, his emotional state had exhausted him. But he suddenly felt recharged with energy when he recalled that the terrorist Pavlos Manganos, who had been involved in the attack on the Danforths on the same day as the Lambrakis Building bombing, was in this hospital.

He pulled his car into the parking lot in front of the hospital and watched a man exit the rear of the limo. The man looked familiar, but in the waning light he couldn't identify him.

What the hell is going on? he thought.

Markeson decided he would watch the ten-story hospital building for a while. If nothing interesting transpired, he would drive back to the Celestine Palace Hotel and confront Vassa. God please don't let her be mixed up with *Greek Spring,* he silently prayed.

Markeson sat in the car for fifteen minutes, hoping the man he saw get out of the limo would return. Maybe he'd recognize him when he came out of the building, under the security lights, facing toward him. But sitting in one place was fatiguing. The renewed energy he'd felt a few minutes earlier had dissipated and he felt himself nodding off. He rubbed his face with his hands and then slapped his cheeks. Stay awake, he told himself. He realized he couldn't sit here for too much longer. He was so damned tired. He had just about made up his mind to go back to the hotel and try to find Vassa, when he detected movement out of the corner of his right eye. He looked in that direction and saw a dark colored sedan pass through the parking lot, bypass the front of the hospital and stop at the far end of the building. It was a strange place for a car to stop—away from the hospital's front entrance and at the side of the building. There was no parking spot there.

He watched a figure move from the front passenger seat, under the canopy of several large shade trees, and toward the side of the building. The figure paused for a moment and looked toward the front of the hospital. The limo was still parked there, one hundred meters to the right of where the figure stood. Markeson was more curious than suspicious—until the sun's last rays peeked below the tree branches and highlighted the figure: Vassa. He was confused. What was she doing here? Then, like being hit with a lightning bolt, the thought struck that if Vassa was involved with *Greek Spring,* her presence here must have something to do with the terrorist in this hospital. He had a sinking feeling. His prayer had gone unanswered.

Markeson reached under the front seat and felt around until his fingers touched the Walther PPK he kept there. He gripped the weapon, leaped from his car, and ran toward the hospital's front door. He slipped the pistol under his jacket, into the back of his slacks. He was quickly winded and drenched with perspiration. The limo driver, leaning against the driver-side door of his vehicle and smoking a cigarette, stared at Markeson, but didn't move.

Markeson found the reception desk and flashed his credentials. He didn't give the young female receptionist time to absorb the information on his ID card. Between the official looking card and his fluent Greek, he hoped she would assume he was somehow associated with the Greek Government. When she shot to her feet, almost coming to attention, he knew his ruse had worked.

"Yes, sir," she said, "what can I do for you?"

"Pavlos Manganos. What floor is he on?"

"He is on Floor Three," she said. "Room three-twenty-four. You will need to check in with the policeman there."

Markeson hurried to the elevator and paced back and forth until the door finally opened. He punched the "3" button, rode the elevator to the third floor, and rushed from the elevator car, ready to deal with the police guard on duty. He was shocked to find no policeman outside the elevator.

The corridor led off in two directions from the lobby. To the left, the corridor was empty; to the right, about halfway down, a chair rested against a wall. Not a person was in sight in either hallway. Markeson's heart rate sped up. There should be at least one guard in the lobby and another one outside Manganos' room. Suspecting that the chair was where a guard should be sitting, Markeson moved in that direction. He reached under his jacket and extracted the pistol, letting his hand hang by the side of his leg. Still ten yards from the empty chair, movement suddenly sounded behind him, sending his heart into his throat.

Markeson spun around. He brought his gun hand up, ready to squeeze the trigger.

"Ochi, ochi, min—"

Markeson kept his pistol trained on the white-clad nurse and put his finger to his lips, telling her to keep quiet. As he moved over to her, she backed against the hallway wall, covering her face with her hands.

In Greek, he said, "I'm not going to hurt you."

She didn't move, her hands still covering her face.

Markeson softened his voice. "I'm not going to hurt you. Where are the guards?"

The woman lowered her hands, clutching them against her breast. "The . . . the . . . his Excellency, Minister Argyropoulos ordered them to the conference room on the second floor for a briefing. The medical staff, too. I am the only one here."

Argyropoulos, Markeson thought. Dimitris Argyropoulos, the Deputy Prime Minister. He thought the man who got out of the limousine had looked familiar. Argyropoulos was the one who picked up Vassa at their home and dropped her at the hotel. "Where's Manganos?"

She hesitantly pointed to her left and said, "There. Room three-twenty-four."

"He's alone?" Markeson asked.

The nurse nodded.

Markeson considered sending her downstairs to fetch the policemen with Argyropoulos; but he figured if the Deputy Prime Minister was up to something, he would delay the police. "I want you to find a room at the other end of the hall, one with a telephone. Lock the door and call the police emergency number. Tell them there's a madman on this floor who is threatening to kill the Deputy Prime Minister." The woman started to run down the corridor, when Markeson growled, "Don't come out of the room until I tell you to."

He stuck the pistol back in his trousers waistband and pulled his wallet from his jacket. He took Stacey Frederick's business card from the wallet and read her office number. He used his cell phone to call the number—screw it if *EA* was listening in—and recognized Sam Goodwin's voice. "I have a situation here at Hellenikon Hospital.

Possible assassination of Pavlos Manganos in process. I can't be sure; but I don't like what's going on around here."

"Jesus, Stanton, what do you need?" Goodwin said.

"Shit, I don't really know what I'm facing here. I'd appreciate it if you could send a couple of your chums up here to cover my back. I'll be in Manganos' room, number three-twenty-four."

"You got it. Bob Danforth is at his hotel. That makes him the closest to your location. I'll call him now."

He wasn't certain the Greek police would respond to the nurse's call, or, if they did, if they would come to the hospital in time. But he was sure the Americans would come. Now that his own team had been eliminated, he would have to depend on Danforth and his crew.

Markeson moved quickly to room three-twenty-four and looked around. A door to the right of the entry opened onto a bathroom. The light was on. A man lay in the single bed in the room. Beeping monitors were mounted on a shelf above the bed. Tubes snaked from medical drips and the monitors into the man's nose, arms, and under the cover into who knew where. The patient looked more dead than alive. A white curtain attached to a circular track in the ceiling was drawn from headboard to footboard on the far side of the bed. A chair sat outside the curtain at the foot of the bed. Markeson moved toward Manganos and lightly shook his arm. The terrorist didn't even groan. Markeson skirted the bottom of the bed and looked behind the closed part of the curtain. There was a recessed window there that had been covered with a two-centimeter-thick piece of steel, obviously to discourage an attack from outside the building into the terrorist's room.

Markeson adjusted the curtain, closing off the bed from view from the room entry. He walked to the bathroom and tested the door, opening and closing it several times. He was relieved to find that it swung silently. He pushed the light switch to the left of the bathroom door, plunging the room into darkness, entered the bathroom, leaving the door slightly ajar, sat on the toilet, and waited.

Vassa climbed three flights of the emergency staircase and checked her watch. It was 7:25. She coolly took a cigarette case from her left jacket pocket, while touching the right pocket with her fingers to feel the reassuring outline of the pistol that Dimitris had given her. She lit the cigarette and drew the smoke deep into her lungs, feeling the nicotine calm her. Vassa thought about meeting Dimitris in the hotel room after she took care of business here at the hospital. It had been years since they had been in bed together. She couldn't help herself; she felt charged. Dimitris had always been an excellent lover—rough, the way she liked it, and attentive to her needs. And she had to admit, fucking the next Prime Minister of Greece made her thighs tremble and her insides heat up.

The unmistakable throbbing beat of helicopter rotors penetrated the hospital room walls. Markeson was shocked that the Greek authorities had responded so quickly. Then an idea came to him that he was about to look like an idiot. What if he had overreacted? What if there was no plot against Manganos? But where was Vassa?

Vassa first heard the helicopter, then felt the thrumming of its rotors. She hardly gave it a thought. It was now 7:30. The floor should be clear. Dimitris would have gathered the guards and the medical staff for the briefing. She opened the door to the third floor and briskly moved to 324, looked left, then right, quietly opened the door, and moved into the pitch darkness.

Musa Sulaiman straightened his white medical smock with the Caduceus embroidered on its breast pocket and instructed the helicopter pilot to keep the aircraft's engine running on the helipad atop the hospital building. He reminded the pilot he would need to make the return flight to the Athens heliport after he dropped off the cooler with what he had told the man contained whole blood. Sulaiman stepped from the helicopter with the cooler, crossed the helipad, and opened the access door at the far end of the roof. He descended the emergency staircase through seven floors and stopped in the stairwell on the third floor. The smell of cigarette smoke hung in the air. A crushed butt lay at his feet. He opened the cooler and took out a Smith & Wesson .22 caliber pistol and a silencer. He screwed the silencer to the pistol muzzle and then removed two grenades from the cooler. He assumed there would be guards outside Manganos' room, as well as others guarding the elevator lobbies on the third floor and on the main level. He wasn't worried about the ones on the first floor; but he needed to dispense with the guards on the third floor.

He looked at his watch and saw it was 7:32. He held his breath and opened the door, peeking down the hall. There was no one there. Musa blinked and surveyed the hall again. He couldn't believe it. He stuck the grenades in his smock pockets and stepped into the corridor, the pistol at his side. Room number 330 was on his right. He walked down the hall toward 324, ever alert to someone entering the hallway, still wondering what had happened to the guards.

Markeson heard the *shushing* sound of the room door opening. He held his breath and tightened his grip on his pistol. The click-click-click of heels reverberated in the room. Silence for a few seconds. Then the sound of the metal rings of the curtain scraping against the metal curtain track in the ceiling. The snicking noise of a pistol hammer being operated. He opened the bathroom door enough to slip inside the hospital room, raised his pistol, and flipped on the light switch.

In the instant that Markeson turned on the lights, he saw Vassa standing next to the comatose Manganos, a pistol in her hand pointed at the man's head. She jerked around and loudly sucked in a breath. Her eyes were round and her mouth was gaping.

"Hello, wife," Markeson said. "Fancy meeting you here."

"I . . . I . . . was just—"

"Just what, dear? Making a quick stop at the hospital to murder one of your cronies so he can't talk with the authorities."

"No, that's not—"

"Shut up!" Markeson barked. "You've made a fool of me; you've used me in the worst way." He paused, then said, "Drop your pistol."

Vassa did as ordered, the pistol in her hand clattering to the tile floor. Markeson stepped around her and kicked the pistol under the hospital bed. He grabbed Vassa by the arm and turned her, placing her between him and the door. "How long have you been mixed up in this?" he demanded.

Her face was red, but the fear in her eyes was beginning to subside. "Years," she said. Then she smirked and said, "You've been a big help, Stanton, so willing to share your thoughts with your loving wife. Every damned thing you ever told me was passed on to my friends at *Greek Spring*. How does that make you feel?"

Markeson felt sick. He'd been more than a fool. He was responsible for the deaths of his friends and co-workers. "What does Argyropoulos have to do with this?" he demanded.

Vassa gave him a smile that seemed to be formed from sinister darkness within her. He couldn't believe he hadn't seen this part of her before. Or, perhaps he had and just ignored it. This thought only served to make him feel more wretched.

"What do you want to know, Stanton? About Dimi Argyropoulos, my lover, or the man who is going to be the next leader of Greece?"

Markeson didn't think she could shock him any worse than she already had, but he found he was wrong. It took a moment to catch his breath before he said, "Everyone knows Argyropoulos is going to be the next Prime Minister."

She smiled her thin, evil smile again. "Oh, he'll be much more than that. He'll be the Supreme Leader of the first Marxist government of Greece. And I will be there at his side."

Markeson shook his head and began to tell his wife she was an even bigger fool than he was, when the door opened and a man in a white smock entered. The man's clothes caused Markeson to drop his guard for a split second. In that moment, the man raised his arm and fired a pistol. The first round hit Vassa in the back of the head, spraying Markeson with blood and brain matter that exited the front of her skull. Vassa slumped to the floor without making a sound. Markeson fired his pistol at the same instant the man in the white smock fired again. Markeson heard the man grunt as he felt the man's second shot rip into his chest.

Sulaiman cursed as he fired two more rounds at the man who had shot him and watched the man fall backwards against the bed and slide to the floor. Musa then stepped forward and fired two shots into Manganos' brain. His right shoulder burned as though a hot poker was pressed against it. Each time he had pulled the trigger, his shoulder felt as though it was smashed with a sledgehammer. He looked at the source of the pain and saw blood already soaked the right side of his smock. He cursed again, while looking around the room. Satisfied he had accomplished his mission, he turned and looked into the hall. Still empty. He ran from the room, back to the staircase, up to the roof, and over to the helicopter. He anticipated the pilot would balk when he saw the blood on his coat; but the pistol would convince the man to fly back to the airport.

CHAPTER FIFTY-FIVE

AUGUST 8, 2004

When Bob received the telephone call from Sam and learned about Stanton Markeson's call to the CIA office, he instructed Sam to contact Tony and have him go to the hospital.

Bob took a taxi from the Grand Bretagne Hotel to Hellenikon Hospital. He quickly entered the building, ran straight to the elevator, and pushed the UP button. At the third floor, he drew his pistol from a shoulder holster under his suit jacket, cautiously exited the elevator, and found the corridors empty. He moved as quietly as possible to Manganos' room, his attention momentarily diverted by the sound of what sounded like a helicopter flying over the top of the building.

The door to 324 was wide open. A bloody scene greeted him. Red pools swamped most of the floor from the inside of the door to the hospital bed. A woman lay three feet into the room. Her eyes were wide open in a death stare. A gaping, gruesome wound occupied most of what had been her forehead. Bob recognized Stanton Markeson lying between the woman and the bed. He stepped around the woman and the blood encircling her body, and moved beyond the curtain, making sure the rest of the room was clear. He reholstered his pistol and held his breath while he looked at the terrorist in the bed. Someone had shot the man in the head. Bob walked to Markeson and squatted next to him. He checked for a pulse and was rewarded with a faint, fluttering beat.

"Hang in there, Stanton," Bob said, standing and moving to the door. "I'll get help."

Markeson weakly shook his head. His lips moved, but no sound came from him.

Bob hesitated a moment, then the clatter of running footsteps sounded behind him, from out in the hall. He looked over his shoulder as two uniformed police officers appeared, their weapons drawn. The bodies and the pools of blood seemed to stop them at the entry. Then the policemen moved aside and a man in a suit took their place in the entryway: Argyropoulos.

"Ah, Mr. Danforth," Dimitris Argyropoulos said, "we meet again." Argyropouplos stared at the female body and seemed momentarily unsettled. Then he pointed at the bed, at Markeson, and then at the female. "You've been busy, I see," he said.

"You think I did . . ." Bob said, but stopped. This wasn't the time to get into a discussion with the Deputy Prime Minister about who shot the woman, Markeson, and Manganos. He needed to get help for Markeson. Bob turned and moved to Markeson. "He's still alive," he said, stabbing a finger at one of the cops. "Get a doctor."

The policeman ran off. Argyropoulos glared at Bob. Markeson coughed, causing Bob to look at him. The Englishman reached up and grabbed the lapel of Bob's jacket. His lips moved again, but still no sound came from his mouth. Markeson somehow kept a grip on Bob's jacket. Bob leaned closer.

"What is it, Stanton?"

Markeson coughed again, spraying a fine mist against Bob's face and his white shirt. Bob reflexively brushed a hand against his cheek and saw it was smeared with blood. He leaned even closer to Markeson. While the man spoke in a hoarse whisper into Bob's ear, Bob saw out of the corner of his eye that Argyropoulos' face was rigid and flushed.

"What are you doing?" Argyropoulos demanded.

Bob ignored him and listened to Markeson's words. But the Englishman suddenly stopped speaking; his eyes fluttered and closed.

"Get him away from that man," Argyropoulos screamed, grabbing the arm of a uniformed policeman and shoving him into the room. The officer stepped into the blood framing the dead woman, slipped, and fell onto her body. The policeman cursed and awkwardly got to his feet, snatched hold of Bob's jacket, and tried to pull him from the room.

Bob twisted the cop's wrist until the man released his jacket, then he propelled the officer toward the doorway where he ran into Argyropoulos, knocking the Deputy Prime Minister to the hallway floor.

Two female nurses rushed into the room at that moment.

"He's lost a lot of blood," Bob told the nurses in Greek, while pointing at Markeson. "The other two are dead. Take care of him."

In the hall, Argyropoulos' face had turned apoplectic, while he struggled to his feet. "What did he say to you?" he shouted at Bob. Before Bob could answer, Argyropoulos screamed at the police officer who had fetched the nurses, "Arrest that man."

The cop seemed confused. His hand went to his hip holster. He couldn't seem to make up his mind as to whether or not he should draw his weapon.

Argyropoulos' voice raised another pitch while he shouted, "I said arrest that man."

Bob raised his hands and looked at the cop. Again in Greek, he said, "It's okay, officer, I'll go with you willingly."

This seemed to placate the young officer, who visibly relaxed and removed his hand from his pistol butt.

"Oh, by the way," Bob said, "I'm armed; would you like to take my pistol?"

The officer turned crimson red and looked from Bob to Argyropoulos—who was fuming by this point—and back to Bob.

Bob took pity on the officer and drew his pistol, handing it over to the young man by the barrel.

Bob clenched his jaw and moved toward the doorway, avoiding the pools of blood. He stopped and got in the Deputy Prime Minister's face. "You asked what Mr. Markeson said to me." He paused. Argyropoulos swallowed. Bob waited a few seconds more. Markeson had been incoherent. Whatever he had been trying to tell Bob had come across garbled. But, for some reason, he didn't want to tell that to the Deputy Prime Minister. Finally, he smiled at the politician and walked past him into the corridor.

"I believe his Excellency ordered you to arrest me," Bob said to the policeman.

CHAPTER FIFTY-SIX

Sam Goodwin joined Bob at the police station and explained about Markeson's call to the office, requesting assistance. The police appeared to be confused about the call from the nurse, the one where she said someone was trying to assassinate the Deputy Prime Minister. They seemed inclined to keep Bob and Sam at the station until they ironed out what had happened at the hospital, but a call from the American Ambassador to the Greek Prime Minister, and a call, in turn, from the Prime Minister to the Minister of Public Order changed everything. The cops' attitudes toward Bob altered immediately and he was turned loose. The sun was just coming up as he left the central police station.

Bob found Liz in a high state of anxiety when he returned to the hotel. His story about what had happened at Hellenikon Hospital did nothing to assuage her fears. They held each other for a long time. He was glad to have her there. It had been a rough seventy-two hours and having his best friend with him made things seem better.

"I didn't think it was this bad," Liz said. "I thought you were exaggerating when you said I shouldn't come over here."

"At the time, I probably was exaggerating," Bob said. "Things have escalated in the last week." He pulled away from Liz and loosened his tie as he dropped heavily on the bed. He brushed his hair back with his fingers and stretched out on the bed. "But what's got me worried is what's coming up. I think the terrorists' increased activity is a preamble to their trying to disrupt the Olympic Games." Bob closed his eyes and groaned. "I've got to figure this out."

"Maybe if you get a little sleep, your mind will work better."

"Yeah, maybe I'll grab a short nap," he said. "Wake me in an hour." He rolled over and was out in a matter of seconds.

Liz watched over Bob from a chair in the corner of the bedroom. He looked very pale, she thought. Every time she looked at him, her heart swelled with love and pride. This was the only man she had ever loved. The prospect of life without him left her feeling hollow and lost. She pressed a finger against an eye and obliterated a tear. He had experienced too many years of danger and stress, too many injuries. He needed to retire; but her nagging him about it would do no good. It had to be his decision, arrived at independent of outside pressure. He has to get out of this business, she thought, or he'll never see his grandchildren.

Bob's cell phone jarred her from her thoughts. She ran to the table next to the bed and picked it up before the second ring. It surprised her that the phone hadn't awakened Bob. One more bit of evidence that he was exhausted. Even the slightest noise would usually wake him.

"Hello," she whispered, walking from the bedroom into the suite's sitting room.

"Mom, it's Michael."

"Hello, Michael. How are you and Miriana doing? How's Paris?"

"We're fine. But what about you? It's all over the news up here about the terrorist attacks. At first, they just reported that an American couple had been targeted; a moment ago they mentioned your names. How's Dad?"

"We're fine, son. It was a couple of incompetent hoodlums who couldn't get out of their own way."

"Uh huh," Michael said, sounding as though he didn't believe a word his mother had said. "Where's Dad?"

"Fast asleep. I'll have him call you when he wakes up. You have your cell phone?"

"Yeah. Listen, Mom, maybe I should fly down there."

Liz laughed. "Don't think your dad and I can take care of our-selves?"

"Come off it, Mom. I'm just worried about you guys."

Liz's throat felt tight. She swallowed and said, "I know, son, and I appreciate it. Don't worry, we'll be fine."

"I love you," Michael said.

"I love you, too, son. Give Miriana a hug for us."

Liz pushed the END button on the cell phone and sagged into a plush chair.

CHAPTER FIFTY-SEVEN

AUGUST 9, 2004

"Holy cow!" Sam Goodwin said.

Stacey Frederick felt her pulse accelerate. Sam was known among his co-workers as unemotional, tea-totaling, and sort of boring. 'Holy cow!' from Sam was akin to someone else releasing a loud, violent stream of profanity.

"What?" Stacey asked, her voice a bit louder than she intended.

"You've got to see this."

Stacey moved from her desk to Sam's. She looked at the sentence in the document in front of him, where his finger tapped the page. She read to the bottom of the page and then pulled a chair over to Sam's desk.

"Where did this come from?"

"It was in the stuff sent over by the Ministry of Public Order. Apparently, the leaders of the junta weren't the only Greek leaders who spied on their fellow countrymen. Argyropoulos was under surveillance that was ordered by his own party as far back as twenty years ago. The man must have had the party leaders concerned."

"How so?" Stacey said.

Sam blushed. "He couldn't keep his pants on. He made Slick Willy look like an amateur. I guess the party leaders were afraid Argyropoulos might wind up in bed with the wrong person. Like the Profumo scandal in England or JFK *shtupping* Judith Exner while she was Sam Giancana's mistress."

"*The wrong person*, such as the wife of one of the party leaders," Stacey added.

Sam nodded. "Yeah, that too," he said. "So, this report shows Argyropoulos had a long-term affair with Nicolaos Koufos' sister, Vassa. Koufos is now in charge of Economic Development in the Ministry of Finance and one of Argyropoulos' allies."

"And we now know that Vassa Koufos married Stanton Markeson in 1996."

Sam stood and moved around the room. He shook his head. "This gets curiouser and curiouser. Stanton is wounded, Vassa Markeson and Pavlos Manganos die in the same hospital room, and Dimitris Argyropoulos just happens to be getting a briefing in the same hospital, at the same time."

"You need to call Bob," Stacey said.

CHAPTER FIFTY-EIGHT
AUGUST 9, 2004

When Dimitris Argyropoulos left the hospital on Sunday night, August 8, the night of Manganos and Vassa's murders, he felt conflicted. Vassa had obviously killed Manganos. That was good. Apparently, her husband had interfered and they'd shot each other. That also was good. The trail back to him had been obliterated. Neither Manganos nor Vassa could give the police any information, and Vassa had gotten her wish: Her husband would probably die from his wounds. He'd laughed about that. The one thing bothering him was what Markeson might have said to Danforth.

Now, on Monday afternoon, August 9, Argyropoulos felt more than conflicted; he was downright confused. Things didn't make sense. The ballistics tests on the pistols found in the hospital room showed that neither of the two weapons had fired any of the shots that hit the Markesons or Manganos. Markeson's Walther PPK had been fired; but no bullet had been found. The police had found a pistol on Danforth, but that weapon hadn't been fired. Neither had the pistol he'd given Vassa.

And now this. He had just learned the police were investigating the death of a helicopter pilot. The man's body had been found in his aircraft yesterday evening. His throat had been slashed. An employee at the heliport told the police that a dark-skinned man in a white medical coat had hired the chopper. Argyropoulos remembered the sounds of a helicopter over the hospital last night. Could it have been the same helicopter?

Argyropoulos couldn't make sense of any of it. And there was still his worry about what Markeson might have said to Danforth. He needed to get with Giorgos Photos, to make sure the man was on top of things. There were only four days until history would be made.

Giorgos Photos had waited to board the airplane until television news reported Manganos' death. He couldn't make sense of the news about Vassa Markeson's death or her badly-wounded English husband. Vassa had been a valuable information resource for *EA* for a long time. Her presence at the murder scene confused him. He knew about the woman's relationship years ago with Argyropoulos, and that caused him to wonder if Argyropoulos had sent her to kill Manganos. That worried Photos. It would mean Argyropoulos didn't have confidence that Photos would get the job done.

He had hoped he would hear from Musa Sulaiman, but he wasn't particularly surprised the assassin hadn't contacted him. Sulaiman was an independent bastard. He'd killed Manganos; his fee had been deposited in his account in Switzerland; and he'd said he wouldn't work for *EA* again. So there was no reason for him to call.

Now, high above the Aegean, Photos checked his watch. The plane was on schedule. The private landing strip's lights were visible below. He would be on the ground by 8:00 P.M.

Photos smiled. Aren't détente and globalization wonderful? Just a few years ago, he couldn't have flown into Communist Bulgaria without all sorts of red tape. Now he could go almost anywhere he wanted with nothing but a passport. His university position gave him all the reason he needed to travel to other countries, all in the name of research. It would be different for the Kurds, especially with heightened security surrounding the Olympics.

The plane's tires screeched and the small aircraft bounced, floated up for a few seconds, then settled on the runway. The pilot taxied to a small metal building at the north end of the small terminal. When the aircraft stopped, the co-pilot opened the door and dropped the stairs.

Photos stepped to the ground and used a hand to shield his eyes from the glare of the car headlights pointing at him. Valise in hand, he walked to the car and opened the right rear door.

"Welcome to Bulgaria," the man in the backseat said.

Photos climbed inside the vehicle. "Welcome to the future, Mahmoud," he answered.

Mahmoud Abdalan patted the valise that Photos had placed on the seat between them. "And a great future it is." Mahmoud started laughing, and soon Photos joined in. Thirty seconds passed, and then Mahmoud shouted something in Kurdish at the driver, who pulled the car away from the metal building and drove several kilometers to a house overlooking the Black Sea.

It was too dark to see the water, but Photos looked out at the lights of houses scattered along the shore and imagined what the sea must look like. He cleared his throat and said, "I assume your men are in place."

"Of course," Mahmoud said. "All fourteen of them will arrive by boat before light tomorrow morning. The tour bus will pick them up at eight A.M., and will cross the Greek border well before noon."

"How about the border guards?"

"No problem," Mahmoud said. "The credentials you provided are unchallengeable. Just a bunch of Turkish football fans from a club in Ankara on a tour of the region on its way to the Olympics, to watch their national team."

"Good," Photos said. "And you have directions to the place in Koropi?"

Mahmoud chuckled and said, "Don't worry, my friend, everything is in order. We will succeed, and your people will own Greece, and my people will finally have a chance to have their own homeland."

Photos wished he didn't have to worry, but that was his job and his nature. So much was riding on Mahmoud and his Kurdish fighters. They were an integral part of Photos' plan to take control of Greece. He would accomplish his mission to turn his country into a Marxist-Leninist state. And Turkey would be in such turmoil, there was no way the government there would be able to deal with a Kurdish uprising at the same time it was trying to avoid war with Greece. Mahmoud and his Kurdistan Liberty and Democracy Party would finally achieve an independent nation.

"The opening ceremony will be in full swing by ten A.M. on Friday. Your men should be in place well before that time."

"I understand," Mahmoud said. "That's why we're going in two nights before. Make sure your man is there."

"It's all done. The base commander, Major Petroangelos, is with us. He'll get you inside the base. You'll take out the gate guards. At that time of night, most of his men will be asleep in their barracks. They should be easy to deal with."

"You know we don't have to kill the airmen. We can subdue them. They won't be a danger to us once they're bound and gagged."

"I want all but one of them eliminated," Photos said. "The Greek people must become enraged about the attack. Kill Petroangelos as well. No one should be left who can compromise us. All we need is one wounded airman who can tell the world that a group of Turks was responsible for the attack."

"Okay, okay, that's the way it will be done."

"Good," Photos said. "The Chinook will be in place to evacuate you and your men from the base on Friday. The base commander has taken care of arrangements. You have to get out of Greece as soon as possible."

Mahmoud gave Photos an impatient look. "I know, my friend, I know."

Musa Sulaiman alternated between cursing and praying. The pain was stunning. He wanted to slit the throat of the hack digging at the bullet in his right shoulder. He almost regretted declining anesthesia; but he couldn't take the chance of being sedated. Trying to take his mind off the pain, he thought about the money in his bank account. *Allah* had been good to him. He had faith that a thousand virgins awaited him in heaven some day for the attacks he had executed against the infidels; but the money in Zurich would buy hundreds of long-legged Brazilian women before he went to the afterlife.

He would use one of his false IDs and hide in Rio de Janeiro, where the idiots running *Al Qaeda* couldn't find him. It was only a matter of time before one of those maniacs in the mountains of Pakistan decided he should make the ultimate sacrifice and blow himself up for the cause in some suicide bombing.

CHAPTER FIFTY-NINE

AUGUST 9, 2004

Despite having slept for only four hours, Bob felt rested. Sam Goodwin's news had given him a surge of energy. Bob telephoned Tony and asked him to come by and drive him to the office. Then Bob showered, dressed, and, while waiting for Tony to show, called Jack Cole at Langley. They discussed Sam's information about Argyropoulos, as well as the list of Greeks with some connection to France.

While waiting for Bob and Tony, Sam and Stacey pulled up information about the Deputy Prime Minister from both the Greek Ministry of Public Order and the British files. Argyropoulos had taken part in the 1973 student demonstrations against the junta. This was neither surprising nor uncommon. Many of the individuals in the current Greek administration traced their political careers back to student activism against the junta. Vassa Markeson, however, was too young to have played a role in the riots and demonstrations of the seventies. When Bob and Tony arrived at the office, they joined in the conversation.

"Do you have any idea how Argyropoulos and Vassa Markeson met?" Bob asked.

"Nothing yet," Stacey said, "although it could have been through social ties. Both their families, the Argyropouloses and Koufoses, are well-to-do and have been big-time players in Greek politics."

"I could call some of my contacts at the Ministry of Culture," Sam offered. "I play tennis with a guy who's like the Vanderbilt of Greece. He knows all of the heavy hitters on the Athens social register."

"Good," Bob said. "Find out all you can about the two families and ask if he knows anything about the affair between the Deputy Prime Minister and Mrs. Markeson."

Bob pointed at Tony. "Don't you have a couple of informants who could help us?"

"There's one who might be of some help. His daddy owns the second largest shipping company in Greece. He probably runs in the same circles as the Argyropoulos and Koufos families."

Bob nodded. "Good; follow up on that lead. There's something that still bothers me. What was Stanton Markeson's wife doing in that hospital room?"

"And just to confuse the matter even more," Stacey said, "we received a call from the detective working the shootings at the hospital. He told us the ballistics tests had come in on the two pistols found on the hospital room floor. Stanton Markeson's pistol, which was identified by the British Embassy as the weapon assigned to him, had been fired. Despite scouring the room and the hallway outside the room, they couldn't find the bullet. The shell casing was there, but they couldn't find the bullet."

"Which might mean Stanton hit someone."

"That's right," Stacey said. "In fact, the police found a trail of blood that started at the end of the corridor, went up the stairs to the roof, and then stopped there."

"I heard a helicopter last night," Bob said, "just as I approached Manganos' room."

"And remember the body of the helicopter pilot the police found," Sam added. "There's got to be a connection."

"What about the ballistics test on the second pistol? How about fingerprints?" Bob asked.

"Whichever of the Greek cops picked up the pistol, he destroyed whatever fingerprints were there," Stacey said. "Another example of state of the art police work. But the ballistics side of the story is intriguing," Stacey said. "That weapon had not been fired; but when the police traced the serial number, they found it was taken from a Greek Army outpost in a raid in 1997." Stacey consulted a legal pad in front of her and said, "On March 4, 1997, *Greek Spring* issued a communiqué which listed the weapons they had 'legally appropriated' from the Greek Army. The serial number on the second pistol matched one of the weapons listed in that communiqué."

"Which means someone with connections to the terrorist organization carried that weapon into the room," Tony said.

"Correct," Bob said, "and I'll bet it wasn't Stanton. If Stanton was going to murder Manganos, he wouldn't have called our office to ask for assistance. So, it had to be either Stanton's wife or the person we have to presume Stanton shot, and who shot Stanton and his wife and Manganos. But, if I had to guess, I would pick Mrs. Markeson."

"Why?" Sam asked.

"The wounds I observed showed none of the typical powder burns usually evident in execution style slayings. The assassin, especially in the case of Manganos, shot his victim up close and personal. The absence of gunpowder residue indicates the killer used a weapon with a silencer. Sure, he might have carried a second weapon, but I doubt it. Besides, if the killer had brought in another pistol, there was no need for him to use it. He shot all three people in the room with the silenced pistol. Ballistics has already proved that. Why pull the second gun? And, if he did pull it, why wasn't it fired? Vassa Markeson carried the second pistol into that room."

Bob's words seemed to have stunned the others.

"Holy cow!" Sam said. "That means she was connected to *EA*." Sam looked around at the others as though he was waiting for someone to argue the point. Then he added, "Markeson's wife slipped him the bugged cell phone on orders from EA."

"And if Vassa Markeson was literally sharing Dimitris Argyropoulos' bed, as the Greeks' own investigative report shows, where does that put the Deputy Prime Minister?" Sam said.

CHAPTER SIXTY

AUGUST 10, 2004

For the first time in his life, Dimitris Argyropoulos couldn't decide what to do. He was beside himself with fear about what Markeson might have whispered to Danforth after Markeson was shot. Now the Englishman was in the Intensive Care Unit at Saint Mathias Hospital, and trauma surgeons and other doctors had been brought in from England to care for him. Additionally, British Special Operations personnel had taken over security outside the ICU and augmented security outside the hospital building. There was no way a team of terrorists could infiltrate the hospital. Argyropoulos tried to get the Prime Minister to order the British soldiers from Greece, but Yiannis Ierides would have none of it.

The only hope Argyropoulos had was that Markeson would die or would be too weak to say anything more. Three days, that's all he needed. Ierides and most of the members of Parliament would be dead by then. He would accede to the top position in the country at a time when Greeks would be clamoring for revenge. The Englishmen and the Americans would be ordered from his country. He would see to that. And he would arrange to have Markeson silenced permanently. The thought warmed him.

He stopped pacing and looked across his office at his assistant, Ari Stokolos. "We're almost there, Ari."

"It's been a long time coming, Dimitris." Ari stretched his arms over his head and groaned. "This old body of mine can't handle much more of this. You remember when we were in school together? We'd study, play, drink, and get no more than four hours sleep, and still be ready to go the next morning."

"Fifty-five isn't old, Ari."

"Tell that to my bones. I feel ancient."

"Hah, that's just your imagination." Argyropoulos began pacing again. "That bastard Photos better do his part."

"You worry too much, my old friend. Photos has kept that group of psychopaths and hoodlums together for a long time. He's been on the front-lines forever. He'll make it happen. Don't forget it was him who came up with the idea of involving the Kurds and the Iranians. Without his connections with the Kurds, the Mullahs, and *Al Qaeda*, none of this would be happening."

Argyropoulos sucked in a long breath and waved a hand, as though to tell Stokolos he understood. "What time is it?" he asked.

"You've got fifteen minutes to make the meeting. I'll have your driver come around."

After Stokolos left the office, Argyropoulos returned to the chair behind his desk. He thought again about Vassa and felt a wave of relief. She had been a potential liability. He rubbed his crotch and admitted to himself he had looked forward to returning to the Celestine Palace the other night. Vassa had been one of the best. He had been curious to see whether the years had made a difference. But on the value scale, no piece of ass outweighed what he had to gain.

He thought about telephoning Photos, to make sure everything was in place; but he didn't want to take the chance the call might be monitored. Ever since the police had wiretapped one of Photos' safe-houses, Argyropoulos had been reticent to contact the man unless it was absolutely necessary.

On the flight back from Bulgaria, Photos felt as though he had thousands of electrodes attached to his body. He fairly vibrated with nervousness. Over three decades had gone into the effort. The years in France, working with the Communist Party, stirring up the student groups and the trade unions. The years before that studying in Bulgaria and Cuba. The months in the Libyan training center. The time he'd spent cultivating contacts in Iran and the Kurdish areas of Iraq and Iran. All for this. Three days and it would all have been worthwhile.

He hadn't slept well for a week; but he suspected he wasn't going to sleep well until this week was over. After the airplane landed at the private airstrip in Athens, he drove to a nearby gas station to use the pay phone. He called Demetrios Mavroyianni and told him he wanted to see him. He gave Demetrios the location and time for the meeting, then quickly terminated the call. Now that Savvas and Pavlos were out of the picture, Demetrios and his crew would have to take up the slack. He'd deal with that tonight, and then cut off further communications with any of the members of *EA*. They were all good men and women, who would do what was expected of them. They had never numbered more than twenty-five, including Photos—it had been important to keep the group small and controllable. Now there were only twenty-three of them left. Demetrios and his three-man team would assist the Kurds. The other eighteen, excluding Photos, had tickets to the opening ceremony of the Olympic Games. It was a reward for their loyalty. The Kurds would take care of Demetrios and his people while flying over the Aegean in the Chinook helicopter that would evacuate them from the Koropi base. The others would die along with most of the senior members of the Greek Government. No one would be left who might become a liability to Photos and his allies in the new government.

He looked at his dashboard clock after pulling out of the gas station: almost noon. He drove to the restaurant in Koropi. He didn't want to be late for his 1:00 meeting with Major Lambros Petroangelos, the missile site's commanding officer.

CHAPTER SIXTY-ONE
AUGUST 10, 2004

Frank Reynolds and Raymond Gallegos were parked outside Grigor Madanowski's security service business when the former Bulgarian Intelligence Officer drove up in his British racing-green-colored van. Painted on the side of the vehicle in eight-inch white letters were the words,

Madison Security Services
Alarms, Surveillance & Investigations

The company's address and telephone number were painted below in smaller print.

"How was the fishing, Grigor?" Frank said, intercepting the man before he reached the shop's front door.

Madanowski looked up and down the sidewalk, and then at Frank. He muttered something in Bulgarian and then said in English, "What is it with you guys? You can't remember my new name." He pointed at the van and said, "See, it's Gregory Madison now."

Frank smiled. "To us you'll always be Grigor the Bulgarian, Intelligence agent extraordinaire, the poison tipped umbrella assassin. It helps us recall that you were our enemy for so many years."

"You know damned well I never used that umbrella device."

"I'll bet you worked with those KGB assholes in arranging the hit on Markhov in London," Frank said. "That umbrella trick was pretty slick. A little ricin in an iridium pellet at the tip of an umbrella. A poke in the back of Markhov's leg. One dead Bulgarian defector."

"What can I do for you guys?" Madanowski said.

"Now that you're a citizen of the Free World, we'd like you to look at some pictures for us," Raymond said.

The Bulgarian unlocked the shop door and waved the two CIA men inside. He followed them and locked the door behind him. "Is this more of that Greek shit?" He effected a childlike voice and sing-songed, "Did you know of any Greeks with a French connection?" He laughed. "That's funny. French connection. Like that movie with Gene Hackman." He laughed again.

"Yeah, Grigor, you're a fuckin' riot," Frank said. "Ray, show the comedian the photographs."

The photographs from the individual files had been enlarged at the CIA lab and placed in a folio. Ray dropped the folio on a counter and flipped it open to the first picture.

"Before you get started," Ray said, "here's what we're looking for. If you recognize the faces of any of these people, just say so. Then we want to know why you recognize the individual and what name you knew him by."

Madanowski tipped his head in agreement, but before he looked at the first photograph, he said, "The names may not be of much use. Most trainees who went through our programs used aliases. Just like in your CIA. The instructors never knew their real names. In fact, they usually called the trainees by a first name only."

"Okay, so forget the names," Frank interjected. "Let's just see if you recognize any of them."

Madanowski paged through the folio in a slow, deliberate fashion. He established a sort of cadence in turning the pages. He spent a bit more time with the twenty-seventh photo, but finally shook his head and moved on. He didn't say a word until he came to the forty-first picture.

"Sonofabitch!" he exclaimed, "it's the Professor. He loved Marx the way the Pope loves Jesus Christ."

Frank looked over Madanowski's left shoulder, while Ray peered over his right shoulder.

"The Professor?" Frank said. He had memorized the names of every person in the folio. Madanowski had just identified Giorgos Photos as a dyed-in-the-wool Marxist.

"Brainy bastard," Madanowski said. "Arrogant, too. Thought he was better than everyone else. But he was a diehard disciple of the cause. Spent time at our Intelligence Academy in Sofia, then went to Patrice Lumumba University in the Soviet Union. Worked with the Party in Paris, then . . . yeah, that's it; he went to Cuba where he trained with Che Guevara. Last I heard he played with the Arabs in a terrorist camp in Libya before returning to Greece."

Frank's breath caught in his chest, his throat felt tight. "When would that have been?" he asked. "When he returned to Greece."

Madanowski rubbed his chin and seemed to think about Frank's question. "I'd guess it was around the early seventies."

Ray stabbed a finger at the folio. "Check out the remaining pictures."

The Bulgarian finished going through the folio, but didn't recognize any of the other faces. "Sorry, boys," he said, "that's the best I can do for today."

"That's alright, Mr. Madison," Frank said, which earned him a smile from the Bulgarian.

Ray picked up the folio and followed Frank to the door. "We owe you one, Grigor," he said.

"It's Gregory. And, you're goddam right you owe me one," Madanowski said with a laugh. "But you know what surprises me is you don't have the Greek in your folio who was the real star."

Frank abruptly stopped, causing Ray to run into his back. Both Americans turned and stared at the Bulgarian.

"The one we thought would one day lead a Marxist-Leninist Greece was a guy we called Casanova. The guy could hardly keep his cock under control. He must have screwed half the women in the program, and one of the female instructors, too. Good looking guy. Normally, we would have washed a guy like that out of the program out of fear that his sexual inclinations might one day compromise him. But he was so damned smart and . . . how do you say it? . . . gung ho, we felt he might be worth the risk."

"What else can you tell us about this guy?" Ray asked.

"Not much. I know he was involved with the ruling political party in Greece after the junta was deposed, but"—Madanowski hunched his shoulders—"I haven't kept up with events over in Greece, or much of anywhere else since coming to America twelve years ago."

Frank and Ray briefed Tanya Serkovic when they returned to Langley. Jack Cole was in a meeting with the Director and couldn't join them. Tanya got damned excited about what Frank and Ray had learned.

"Bob's still convinced the terrorists are planning something to coincide with the Olympics. This could be the break we've been waiting for."

"I wish Madanowski could have come up with more about this Casanova character," Ray said.

Frank said, "Yeah, but maybe what we did get will tie in with something the Athens team has."

"Let's keep our fingers crossed," Tanya said.

CHAPTER SIXTY-TWO
AUGUST 10, 2004

When the telephone rang in the Athens team's office at 6:15 P.M., Bob and Stacey were the only two there. Tony and Sam were out working their contacts about the Vassa Markeson/Dimitris Argyropoulos connection. Stacey snatched the receiver out of its cradle and barked a loud, "Yes!"

"Having a bad day, Frederick?" Frank said. He didn't wait for her to respond. "Well, I'm about to turn your shitty day around. Get Bob on the line."

"Hold on," Stacey said.

Bob came on the line a few seconds later. "What do you have, Frank?" he asked.

"Our Bulgarian friend ID'ed one of the photographs. You were right. The photographs were the key, not the names. He didn't know any of these people by their real names. He singled out one guy, name of Giorgos Photos."

"Wait a second," Bob said. "I'm going to pull up his file." It took half-a-minute to access Photos' file, and for Bob to peruse it. After doing so, he said, "Looks like a strong possibility of being, at the very least, sympathetic to the terrorists. We'll get right on it. Anything else?"

"Yeah," Frank said. "Our friend talked about a trainee they called Casanova. Apparently, the guy was a real cocksman. He said the guy was good looking, smart, and got involved with politics on his return to Greece. They thought he was going to be a real superstar. Ring any bells?"

Bob didn't respond and, for a moment, Frank thought the connection had been cut. "You still there?"

"Yes, I'm here."

"We hit on something?" Frank asked.

"Yeah, maybe. I want you to download several photographs of the Greek Deputy Prime Minister, Dimitris Argyropoulos, and run them by your Bulgarian friend. Call me right back with his reaction."

"You're serious?" Frank said. "The number two guy in the country."

"Just get those photographs in front of your man, Frank. I want an answer yesterday."

"You got it."

Ray was already on the telephone, dialing the Madison Security Services number. The ringing telephone filled the room from the speakerphone. Then the answering machine kicked in. A female voice with a soft Southern accent said: "You've reached Madison Security Services. We are out on a call at the moment. Please leave your name, number, and the time, and we will call you back at our earliest opportunity."

"Wonderful," Frank groaned, "fuckin' wonderful. Call the guy's cell phone."

Ray punched in Madanowski's cell number. After three rings and a few clicks, a recording kicked in saying that the cell phone subscriber was out of the service area.

Tanya pulled her cell phone from a jacket pocket and dialed a number. After a few seconds, she said, "Detective Wilburn, please."

"What are you doing?" Ray asked.

She held up a finger, telling him to hold on. A few seconds passed, then she said, "Hello, Burt, it's Tanya."

She listened for a while, then said, "I did too; we should do it again some time. Listen, I've got a problem and I need your help. I'm trying to locate a guy. Do you think you could put out an APB on a vehicle?"

She was quiet for another moment and said, "Yeah, Burt, it's vital. But I don't want any of your boys shooting this guy on sight. He hasn't done anything wrong. I just need to talk with him as quickly as possible." She put Frank on the line and had him describe the Bulgarian and his van.

The detective must have said, yes, because Tanya thanked him and hung up.

"Good thinking, Tanya," Frank said. "But what was that business about doing something again? You stepping out on us at night."

Tanya told Frank to go to hell, but she did it while blushing.

CHAPTER SIXTY-THREE

AUGUST 11, 2004

Giorgos Photos was having a pretty good day, despite the tension he felt. The meeting with Major Lambros Petroangelos had gone as he'd expected. Petroangelos was the good soldier. He would do as he had been ordered. The fact that the junta had murdered his father made him the perfect *Greek Spring* supporter; the fact that he had twice been passed over for promotion made him the perfect disgruntled Air Force officer . . . and traitor. Photos thought he would miss Petroangelos' enthusiasm and sense of humor. Photos was confident the Kurds would succeed in every aspect of their mission, including killing Petroangelos.

The call from the Iranian had made his day even better. The Iranian Mullah was a duplicitous bastard, Photos thought; but the Mullah had so much to gain, and really nothing to lose. He had recruited Iraqi pilots who were members of Saddam Hussein's extended family and who had come from Saddam's home town of Tikrit. They were not only Baathist Party members, but were all closet fundamentalist Muslims. They were willing to risk their lives to strike a blow against the West. The Iranian had provided Mirage fighter jets from the inventory Saddam Hussein had "parked" across the border in Iran after the first Gulf War.

Now Photos needed to disengage from the action. He wouldn't be anywhere near the Olympic Stadium or the Koropi missile site on Friday. He would have loved to return to his place on Evoia, but that wasn't an option since Argyropoulos warned him the authorities were looking for a professor who owned a pink house on an island. At least the house wasn't painted pink anymore. He wouldn't return to Evoia until Argyropoulos was in power. He had a brief moment of panic over the thought the police might somehow find the island house and tie it to him. Then Photos laughed aloud. Argyropoulos would suppress any evidence the police might find. And Photos was confident the police weren't that motivated to find anything anyway.

CHAPTER SIXTY-FOUR
AUGUST 11, 2004

Mahmoud Abdalan and his fourteen-man crew cruised south on the National Highway in the rented tour bus. The fifteen Kurds were decked out in blue and yellow warm-up suits with Turkish flag patches sewn on the left breast of the jacket and *TURKIYE* emblazoned across the backs. The Kurds knew what was expected of them. They sang Turkish songs and cheered loudly for the Turkish national soccer team. Abdalan, seated in the front seat right across from the Greek bus driver, had to stifle a laugh as he watched the driver's face. Knowing how the Greeks felt about Turks, Abdalan guessed the driver's insides were churning stomach acid by the quart.

"How many hours to Koropi?" Abdalan asked the driver.

The driver wouldn't look at Abdalan. He answered in a flat voice, "Two hours."

"Where am I supposed to take you in that piece-of-shit town?" the driver asked. "Why stay so far from Athens?"

"I'll tell you where you're to take us when we get to Koropi." Abdalan rubbed his thumb and forefinger together. "Money, my friend, is the reason we're staying there. Athens hotels are too expensive."

This time, the driver glanced at Abdalan. From the look on the man's face, Abdalan guessed the Greek understood his point about saving money.

The two hours turned out to be three-and-a-half hours, but Abdalan had allowed for plenty of time in his schedule. Besides, he wasn't supposed to arrive at the Greek Air Force site near Koropi until after midnight. He ordered the driver to stop at a *taverna* ten miles north of Koropi at 10:30 P.M. The place was doing a decent business—Greeks tended to eat late—but was far enough off the beaten path to not be crammed with customers. The patrons all appeared to be locals, not tourists.

Abdalan ordered one of his men to stay with the bus. The team's baggage was in the storage compartment under the vehicle. He didn't want to take the chance the driver might try to steal something from them. If the man opened up one of their bags and discovered the weapons there, the whole plan would go up in smoke.

The team's entry into the *taverna* caused the place to go dead quiet. A man near the front who Abdalan guessed was the owner didn't look happy. He opened his mouth, but before he could say anything, Abdalan slipped him a twenty Euro bill. The owner's expression didn't change, but he grabbed a handful of menus and led what he thought was a group of Turks to a large dining room at the rear of the building. Abdalan smiled at the occupants of the tables they passed. There were a lot of people in this place who would remember the group of men with Turkish flags on their clothes, especially when the news got out that Turks had taken over a Greek Air Force missile site and killed the airmen there.

The owner barked orders to a couple of waiters who pulled several tables together, and the Kurds took seats around the tables. Abdalan checked his wristwatch. They had an hour-and-a-half to kill until midnight.

CHAPTER SIXTY-FIVE

AUGUST 11, 2004

Tanya Serkovic's mind had been whirling with the different possibilities available to terrorists in Athens. The Olympic Games offered terrorist organizations a plethora of opportunities. She pored over the map of the Olympic venue, trying to come up with the most likely location for an attack. She was fairly certain any attack would be relatively unsophisticated, but bloody. The terrorists would be unlikely to attack from the air. The Greek Air Force would have fighter jets patrolling the country's borders, and air-to-air missile sites formed a ring around Athens that would hopefully bring down any planes that evaded the fighter jets. Thousands of police and soldiers would be pressed into duty in and around the Games. Dozens of foreign Intelligence agencies were operating in Greece, working on trying to identify suspects. She had pretty well come to the conclusion that any attack would be on some peripheral Olympic site, or against a facility that had absolutely nothing to do with the Olympics.

The telephone rang, interrupting her thoughts.

"Hello," she said, feeling groggy and exhausted.

"Tanya, it's Burt."

Burt Wilburn's voice brought Tanya alert. "What's up?" she asked.

"We got your boy," he said.

"Where?"

"A Maryland State Trooper stopped him on the interstate on his way back to the District. The trooper called me and escorted him to D.C. police headquarters." Wilburn chuckled. "He's really pissed off.

Keeps screaming that this is supposed to be a free country. What do you want us to do with him?"

"I need to get him out here to Langley. I'll send someone down and—"

Wilburn interrupted her. "Why don't I drive him out to you?" he said, "it's on my way home."

Tanya knew Langley was way out of Wilburn's way. She also knew the man was using driving Madanowski to Langley as an excuse to see her. She'd never found time for a relationship with a man, but Wilburn was breaking down her usual level of resistance.

"That would be great, Burt. How soon can you be here?"

"Give me a half hour."

"You got it."

Tanya hung up the phone and called Frank Reynolds, who was down in the cryptology lab. She gave him the news, asked him to call Raymond. She would inform Jack Cole. They would all meet at 5:00 P.M., when Burt Wilburn and Grigor Madanowski were due to arrive at Langley.

CHAPTER SIXTY-SIX
AUGUST 12, 2004

Mahmoud Abdalan paid the restaurant tab in cash and stood. His men followed his lead and exited the *taverna*. It was now fifteen past midnight.

The men congregated outside the bus, which was parked at the far side of the dirt parking lot. Mahmoud surveyed the lot. Other than his men, there were no other people around. Only three cars were parked in the lot, and those were on the other side of the parking area, close to the *taverna* entrance.

"It's time," Abdalan told one of his men, who immediately turned and walked to the bus door. While his man climbed into the bus, Mahmoud watched the *taverna*'s front entrance. He heard the sounds of struggle coming from inside the bus, but he didn't turn to look until the sounds stopped.

"Help Abdul move the body," Mahmoud told another one of his men. "Let's go," he growled at the rest of his team.

The driver's body lay on the bench seat in the back of the bus. The man named Abdul, the only member of the team besides Abdalan who was fluent in Greek, got behind the wheel, while the remainder of the crew took seats. Abdalan took his seat opposite the driver's seat.

"Take the road south for five point two kilometers," Abdalan said, reading from the instructions Photos had given him in Bulgaria. "There's a church on the right side of the road. Pull in there, behind the building."

Abdul started the bus and did as he'd been told. After he drove into the church lot, Abdalan shouted, "Everyone out. Get your bags and bring them back in here. We'll change on the go. Check your weapons."

Screened from the road and any passing vehicles, the men raced from the bus and pulled their bags from the storage compartment. They hustled back inside and, without saying a word, shed their warm-up suits and replaced them with all-black outfits—black knit caps, black long-sleeved shirts, and black slacks—to match their black cross trainers. After Abdul had changed, he pulled the bus back onto the road, The only sounds inside the vehicle were the metallic noises coming from bolt mechanisms being tested and magazines being inserted into assault rifles.

After five miles, Abdalan directed Abdul to take a right on an unmarked narrow road that formed a forty-five degree angle with the main road. This road climbed away from the main road on an ever-steepening grade. There were no houses or other buildings in sight. The only lights came from what appeared to be antennae and several buildings on top of a mountain approximately four thousand feet above the floor of the Koropi valley. There were still about five hundred feet of elevation to the top of the mountain when Abdalan shouted, "On the floor; don't get up until I tell you."

His orders weren't really necessary; his men had been well trained. But Abdalan was a careful man.

Abdalan remained in his seat while Abdul drove the vehicle closer to the top of the mountain. After five minutes, Mahmoud stood and tapped Abdul on the shoulder. "Take that left turn up ahead. The road from here to the base is one kilometer. It curves twice before you'll see the fence and the guard shack. Turn on the emergency blinkers and take it slow. Stay in first gear."

Abdul switched on the blinkers and turned left, following the road until the guard shack was visible. He stopped and waited for Abdalan's instructions.

Abdalan saw three men outside the shack, which was positioned on the left side of the road, just inside an eight-foot-high chain-link fence topped with concertina wire. It was now 12:44 A.M. He told Abdul to get out and talk to the guards.

Abdul opened the door, stepped to the ground, and walked toward the perimeter fence. He'd intentionally left the bus lights on. They would hinder the guards' vision.

"What are you doing here?" a young airman demanded. "This is a military installation. You shouldn't be here."

"I'm sorry, but I'm having transmission problems," Abdul shouted above the noise of the bus motor. "Can you call a mechanic?"

"It's the middle of the night," the airman said. "You'll need to stay with the bus until the morning. But you have to move it back down the access road."

"What's going on?" a second man from the guard shack demanded as he joined the first airman. He appeared to be in his late thirties and spoke with authority.

"Just some bus driver, Major," the airman said. "He's having some kind of mechanical problems." Then the airman lowered his rifle at Abdul and, in a nervous voice, said to the other man. "At least that's what he said; but he made it all the way up the access road. And what's he doing up here, anyway?" He glanced briefly at the officer. "Something's wrong, Major. We're twenty kilometers off the main road."

"Go outside and check out the vehicle," the Major said, "and be careful."

"But, Major, that's not—"

"Do as I say," the Major shouted. "We can't have a bus sitting outside the gate, blocking the entrance." The officer waved at the second guard who was now standing outside the shack. "Go with Corporal Patrakos."

The second guard unslung his weapon and followed the first guard outside the gate.

Abdul said, "I'll go inside the bus and work the gears so you can hear the noise the damn thing makes."

The first guard waved the muzzle of his rifle at Abdul. "Stay right here," he growled. He looked at the second guard and said, "Watch him; I'm going to check out the bus."

Abdalan knew that if the guard came aboard, he would have to open fire on the man. He had no doubt the second guard and the officer would eventually be killed, as well; but probably not before the guard shot Abdul. Abdalan thought something had gone wrong. Giorgos Photos had told him he had a man inside the missile site. This wasn't going down as he expected. He moved his hand under his leg and touched his pistol, when the Greek officer suddenly moved through the gate to within a few feet of the two airmen, reached inside his tunic, withdrew a pistol, and shot the two guards in the backs of their heads. Abdalan heard the telltale *pfft, pfft* sounds of pistol rounds going through a silencer.

"Now," Abdalan shouted.

The rest of the Kurds leaped to their feet and retook their seats. Abdalan ordered two of them to follow him as he left the bus. He told them to assist Abdul in throwing the guards' bodies into the bus' luggage compartment. He approached the Greek officer and saw the man's nametag: PETROANGELOS. "How's it going to go down from this point?" Abdalan asked.

"I'll ride with you up to the command and control building. There are three men on duty inside. The rest of the airmen are in bed in the barracks."

"Are the men in the command and control building armed?" Abdalan asked.

"They are issued pistols, but their weapons are kept inside a vault." The Major laughed. "After all, the only time they would need to get their weapons would be when the guards at the front gate called to warn them there was a problem." He laughed again and Abdalan couldn't help but feel a visceral disgust and hatred for the man. Ally in this operation or not, the man was a traitor to his own men and to his country. He would take pleasure in executing him after he was no longer useful.

"Where are Photos' men?" Abdalan said.

"The one named Demetrios called an hour ago. He said he and his three men would be in position outside the perimeter fence around the missile storage area down near Koropi by 3:00 A.M. tomorrow. Don't worry, they'll make sure no one interferes with the missiles once the attack begins."

Abdalan nodded and grunted. The heart of the Nike Hercules Missile Base was the command and control center here on the top of the mountain. Along with the radar equipment, it was on high ground where radar could get long-range line of sight. The weapons—the missiles and the warheads—however, were positioned down in the valley. The command and control center used the radar to see targets and control the firing of the missiles.

A problem, Abdalan knew, would be with the American contingent outside the missile storage area. The Greeks manned the command and control center at the top of the mountain. There were no Americans stationed there. But there were about twenty-five U.S. Army soldiers assigned to that part of the base near Koropi. Their job was to maintain two-man control of the exclusion area, within the outside perimeter fence. Although the Nike Hercules missiles belonged to the Greek Air Force, the arm plugs that turned the nuclear warheads mated to the missiles into lethal weapons were under U.S. Army control. Two American soldiers were on duty outside the missile storage area at all times. It took two men to open the safe holding the arm plugs, and it took a TOP SECRET/CRYPTO message from higher command to authorize the mating of an arm plug to one of the missiles.

Abdalan looked at his watch. They were supposed to sanitize the command and control site and wait. The real action was supposed to start at 3:00 A.M. on the 13th, a little more than twenty-six hours from now. How in *Allah*'s name Photos was going to get the Americans to arm a nuclear weapon was beyond him. But Photos had told him he had it covered.

CHAPTER SIXTY-SEVEN

AUGUST 12, 2004

Bob had tried to get some rest, but he was too wired to sleep. He got out of bed at 1:00 A.M. and padded across the room to the sitting area, closing the bedroom door behind him so as not to disturb Liz.

He booted up his laptop and scanned some of the files loaded there. Acid seemed to be running through his system. He was downright scared to death. The 2004 Olympic Games opened tomorrow and, because it was such a potential stage for the terrorists to get global attention, he just knew something was going to happen. But what?

He pulled up another file as his cell phone chirped. He picked up the phone from its charger. "Hello."

"Bob, it's Jack; we've got news."

"Good or bad?" Bob asked.

"Both," Jack answered. "We just sat down with our Bulgarian friend. You know who I mean?"

"Yeah, sure."

"We showed him photographs of the Deputy Prime Minister. The guy recognized him immediately as the man they called Casanova. He was the superstar for the Communists; the one they thought would finally give the Communist Bloc a warm water port by turning Greece into a Marxist state. Argyropoulos graduated from every damned top Communist training academy. And he had ties to *Bader Meinhof, Brigade Rosse,* and *Abu Nidal.* The bastard was a sleeper for the Soviets."

"Jesus," Bob exhaled, "this guy's the next Prime Minister."

"Maybe not, once this information gets out," Jack answered.

"I'm not that confident," Bob said. "The political atmosphere in Greece is so anti-American, anti-NATO, that I wouldn't be surprised if the man was hailed as a hero." Bob paused, then said, "It would be a different story if we could prove he was in bed with *Greek Spring*. Even the die-hard fanatics would have difficulty defending Argyropoulos if it was proved he was associated with a terrorist group that has been responsible for murdering Greeks."

"It makes you wonder what he was doing in the hospital when that terrorist, Manganos, was killed, doesn't it?" Jack said.

"And, remember," Bob added, "Argyropoulos had an affair with Stanton Markeson's wife years ago. The fact that she was in the hospital room makes me think she and Argyropoulos still had a relationship of some sort."

"How's Markeson doing?" Jack asked.

"He's still critical. Hasn't said a word yet."

"I'll bet he's got a hell of a story to tell," Jack said.

"Let's hope he gets the chance to tell it."

"The Games start tomorrow," Jack said, worry etching his voice.

"Yeah, and, despite the assurances from the government here that everything is secure, I'm not feeling confident. They've had the Olympic venue sealed for the last month-and-a-half. The security network will include 10,000 military personnel working with 40,000 police and a 200-member team trained by us and the Brits to handle CBN attacks. But these *Greek Spring* assholes are committed and determined. The entire contingent of chemical, biological, and nuclear experts in the world won't stop these guys if they've made up their minds to act. One woman pretending to be pregnant, with a stomach pouch full of explosives, could do a lot of damage."

"And what if high-level people in the Greek Government are aiding and abetting these assholes?" Jack said. "Like our friend Argyropoulos."

"You got that right," Bob said. The line went silent for a moment, then Bob said, "You know, now that I reflect on it, I don't think it's going to be a traditional suicide bomber attack. The terrorists can do that sort of thing at any time or place. My gut tells me they're going for a bigger statement than a suicide bombing. This is their moment in the sun, and I don't think they're going to let it pass."

"What kind of bigger statement?" Jack asked. "Don't tell me you're thinking chemical or biological."

"Hell, I don't know, Jack. It could even be nuclear. We know Pakistan, Iran, and North Korea have the technology. They could supply *Greek Spring* with the stuff. It's not as if they've been shy about sharing technology with rogue nations. Especially nations which have supported terrorism. Think about what we learned about Libya after Khaddafi decided to get on the side of the good guys this past January. The guy's WMD program was a whole lot more advanced than any of us thought. And, I think the Greeks, despite their reactive approach to dealing with terrorism, are pretty well prepared for a standard type of terrorist event. One of their spokespersons was quoted as saying, 'Aside from any fantastic scenarios, there is only one reality: Greece is preparing very hard to organize an absolutely safe Olympic Games.' I think it's one of those *fantastic scenarios* he referred to that we need to worry about. Some sort of dramatic attack against the Olympic venue, with lots of dead and wounded. Right there on television, broadcast to the world."

"What do you recommend we do about Argyropoulos?" Jack asked.

"Well, *we* can't arrest him, and I don't know who we can trust in the Greek Government to share this information with. So, I suggest we put a tail on him. See if he meets with any suspicious characters."

"You know," Jack said, "if he's in with the terrorists, he's not likely to attend the Olympics. His avoiding the Games could be an indication that something's about to happen there."

"I had the same thought," Bob said. "But there are a lot of events that go on simultaneously, so he could be at a soccer game outside the city, when an attack occurs at some other venue. Or he could be innocent and, just by the luck of the draw, not be planning on attending an event the terrorists have targeted. The only event I am aware of that he is going to be at is the opening ceremony. He and the Prime Minister will be together in a box with the rest of the Greek cabinet and some of the leaders of the Greek Parliament. Most of the members of Parliament will be in the stadium as well."

"Well, that ought to be one time when it's safe," Jack said.

"You'd think," Bob said. "I hope—"

The hotel room telephone interrupted Bob. "Hold on a second," Bob told Jack. He walked to a table and lifted the telephone receiver. "Yes," he said.

"Mr. Danforth, it's the front desk. There are a gentleman and a lady down here who want to see you."

"At this hour! Who are they?" Bob asked.

"The man says he's your son."

CHAPTER SIXTY-EIGHT

AUGUST 12, 2004

Bob hugged Miriana. He then held Michael at arms length and looked him over. "Paris must be agreeing with you."

"It's been great. The only thing wrong with it is all the Frenchmen running around the place."

Bob laughed, then he turned serious and said, "What are you two doing here?"

Michael's face reddened. "Come on, Dad. Two terrorist assassins try to blow you and Mom up, Mom winds up in the hospital, and you want me to play tourist in Paris?"

Bob held his hands up, palms out, and said, "Okay, okay, I get it. But I'm up to my neck in alligators. I don't have time to spend with you and Miriana."

Michael smiled. "We didn't come down here for you anyway. It's Mom we're here to see."

"I figured that out already," Bob said, smiling back at his son.

"Where is she?" Miriana asked.

Bob pointed at the closed bedroom door. "She's sleeping and—"

The bedroom door opened and Liz stepped through into the sitting room. "What's all the noise?" she said, rubbing her eyes. When she dropped her hands, she shouted, "Oh my, what a surprise!" She rushed to Michael and Miriana and gathered both of them into a hug.

It took an hour for Michael and Miriana to bring Liz up-to-date on their vacation, while Bob showered, shaved, and dressed. He'd decided any hope he had of getting any more sleep that night was shot.

When Bob returned to the sitting room, he asked Michael if they'd arranged for a room at the hotel.

"Right down the hall," Michael said. "They already took the bags to the room."

"I think I'd like to change my clothes," Miriana said.

"And I need to get cleaned up," Liz said. She returned to the bedroom.

"Why don't I meet you in our room in a minute," Michael told Miriana, who came over to him, kissed his cheek, and took the room key he held out to her.

After Miriana left, Michael joined his father who had taken a seat at the suite's small dining table. "What's going on, Dad?" he said.

Bob's first instinct was to gloss over the situation in Greece. Despite Michael's position as a U.S. Army officer, and the fact he had a Top Secret security clearance, Michael did not have a "need to know" about the situation in Greece. But Michael had just flown across Europe because he was worried about his parents and Bob was not about to insult his son by feeding him a bunch of pabulum.

"I can tell you a lot," Bob said, "but I can't tell you everything."

Michael nodded.

Bob briefed Michael about the terrorist groups in Greece and the Agency's theories about Greek Government involvement with some of the groups. He explained to Michael the sympathies some of the Greek press and many Greeks had for the terrorists who had grown out of opposition to the junta. He finished with a recent history of terrorist attacks.

"So these groups have been targeting Americans, Englishmen, Turks, and even Greeks, and have been operating for decades."

"Right, and now that *17 November* has been taken down, the worst of the lot is this *Greek Spring* cell."

Michael looked at Bob and scrunched his eyes. "So, what's changed all of a sudden?" he asked. "Why send you over here?"

Bob smiled. *Good question,* he thought. "Two things." He held up one finger. "Enough was enough. The Brits came to the same conclusion at about the same time we did." Now showing two fingers, Bob added, "And the 2004 Olympic Games."

"You sound and look really worried, Dad."

"It shows, huh? Every four years, we gird for a terrorist event at the Olympics, ever since Munich in 1972, and, thank God, nothing much happens."

"Except that crazy guy Rudolf in Atlanta."

"Yeah," Bob said. "That was the last thing the FBI expected, some domestic wild man. But this year I think things are different. The Greeks have allowed these terror groups to gain confidence and strength for thirty years. And they're not operating alone. Every nutcase in the Middle East, especially since we destroyed Saddam Hussein, is looking for a platform from which to make his point. We've got plenty of Intelligence showing groups like *Hamas* and *Al Qaeda* have been financing Greek cells as surrogates. The Olympics will be a great opportunity for these groups, through organizations like *Greek Spring,* to hurt their enemies."

"So, you think there will be a repeat of Munich?" Michael said.

Bob spread his arms in a "who knows" gesture. "At least," he said. "But I've got a burning feeling inside that says Munich was benign compared to what we might see this year."

"You're serious, Dad?"

"Yeah, I'm serious. And I believe the Greek terrorists, with their big brothers to the East, are about to graduate to a higher level."

"What do you mean, like chemical or biological?"

Bob just nodded.

CHAPTER SIXTY-NINE

AUGUST 12, 2004

Maroula Stephanopoulos had had enough. First that arrogant professor had bought the place down the road from her home, where she had lived her entire life, where her parents and grandparents lived before her. Where she raised three sons and a daughter. She had nothing against university types, as long as they didn't impact her life. But, when the arrogant, no-good man painted his place pink, she couldn't sleep for weeks. The house looked like a watermelon every time the sun went down. Then people started coming and going at all hours, disturbing what little sleep she was able to get. They would arrive after dark and leave before the sun came up. Their motorcars would drive her crazy, the engines roaring in the nighttime quiet, the tires spraying gravel at all hours.

And then there was the disrespect this Dr. Giorgos Photos showed her and the people on the island. He hadn't invited her or any of her neighbors to his home, he turned down invitations that had been offered him, he didn't support the local church, he didn't even shop on the island.

And now there were workmen crawling all over the place, making noise with their tools, shouting at each other, and playing radios all day long. They were painting the professor's house. She thought about going over to the house and giving the man a piece of her mind. But after thinking about it for two days, she came up with a much better idea.

"Anna," Maroula shouted into the telephone, "it's your sister."

"Maroula, you don't have to yell, I can hear you."

"Oh, sorry. How are you?"

"Oh, all right. The arthritis gets me down sometimes. And you?"

"The same. The pills help. How is your son?"

Anna's tone brightened. "Wonderful. Pericles is truly a gift from God. Did you know he was promoted to Detective with the Athens Police Department?"

"Yes, Anna, you told me the last time we talked. How's that girlfriend of his?"

"*Po, po, po*, I don't know what he sees in that woman," Anna said, lowering her voice. "She talks too much, wears clothes that show off her body, and, can you believe it, lives by herself in an apartment. What sort of woman leaves her parents' home before she marries?"

Maroula sympathized with her sister, letting her moan and groan about the injustices of the modern world. After listening for several minutes, she said, "So, Pericles is still living at home?"

"Of course," Anna said with pride. "He's a good boy. He's outside now fixing a shutter, before he goes to work."

"I wish I had a son who was a policeman," Maroula said. Then she began to cry, and when Anna asked her what was wrong, she told her about the awful man who lived nearby who was making her life a living hell.

Anna listened to her sister and said, "Let me get Pericles on the telephone. He'll know what to do."

Maroula waited for her nephew to come on the line, then, when she heard him say hello, she started crying again.

"What is it, Aunt Maroula?" Pericles said. "Are you all right?"

She continued crying and, between sobs, told Pericles about the terrible man who lived down the road. She mentioned the man's visitors and the noise and his lack of respect for the people of the island.

"But, Aunt Maroula, there's nothing I can do about this. It's not a police matter. Besides, I have no jurisdiction outside Athens."

"But you could call the local police, couldn't you, and ask them to talk to the man? He's awful; I mean, what kind of person comes as a stranger to an island and paints his house pink? Every other house on Evoia is white; but not Mr. Photos' place. It's against thousands of years of tradition, it's an insult to our history, it's—"

"What did you say?" Pericles demanded.

"It's against our tradition, it's—"

"No, no, about the house being painted pink."

"That's right. He moved here two years ago and the first thing he did was paint the house a god-awful color. Can you imagine? It's the only house on the whole island that isn't white."

"What's does this man do for a living?" Pericles asked, his voice strained and loud.

"He's some sort of professor, why?"

CHAPTER SEVENTY

AUGUST 12, 2004

While Miriana accompanied Liz on a tour of Constitution Square and the Plaka, Bob took Michael to the CIA office in Glyfada. He played the proud father, introducing Michael to his team members. They were talking with Tony, when the telephone rang on Tony's desk.

"Hello," Tony said into the receiver. He listened for a moment, then punched the speaker button and replaced the receiver in its cradle. "Lieutenant, you're now on speaker."

"Okay," the caller said.

"This is Lieutenant Zavitelos with the Ministry of Public Order," Tony said. "He has some information for us. Start all over again, please," Tony told the caller.

In heavily accented English, Zavitelos said, "We received a call an hour ago from a detective with the Athens Police Department. One of his aunts had just called him about a neighbor of hers on Evoia. Apparently, the old lady was upset about noise coming from the neighbor's house and mentioned the neighbor's house was painted pink."

Bingo, Bob thought. Maybe we finally got a break.

"The detective got the neighbor's name and then called the hotline number we'd put out to law enforcement offices throughout the country. I took the call and put the name into our database. The neighbor, Giorgos Photos, is Professor Emeritus at the university. We're checking him out, but haven't been able to get anything on him yet, except for information about his educational credentials and his family. The local constable on Evoia went to the man's house, but found only a painting crew. They couldn't tell him where Photos was."

"Did they find anything in the house?" Bob asked, trying to control the excitement he felt. Giorgos Photos. The man who Grigor Madanowski had identified as having been trained by the Communists and terrorist cells around the world.

"Nothing important," Zavitelos said. "There was a fifty-five gallon drum with two feet of ash in it behind the house. Someone must have been burning paper."

"Any other information on Photos?" Sam asked.

"We have an address from his university employment records," Zavitelos said. "His primary residence is listed as being near Sounion. We sent a squad to see if Photos is there."

"Where can we reach you, Lieutenant Zavitelos?" Bob asked.

The officer gave them his cell and office phone numbers and promised to keep them informed of any progress.

After the Greek officer terminated the call, Bob asked Tony, "How well do you know this guy Zavitelos?"

"Pretty well," Tony said. "I think he's pretty straight up. He's been forthcoming with information, and seems to be embarrassed about the way his government has executed the investigation into the terrorists."

"You think he'd let you tag along with him?"

Tony shrugged. "You want me to call him back and ask?"

"Yeah. I want you to be on him like white on rice. The second you learn something, call my cell."

"Right," Tony said.

"Sam, I want you to fly over to Evoia. Get the local police to take you to Photos' house. Go over every inch of the place." Bob then turned to Stacey. "Go through our computer files and get everything on Photos."

After Bob and Michael went into Bob's office, Michael asked, "Could this guy be important?"

"Big time," Bob said. "We taped a phone conversation someone had with a man we suspect is an Arab, a Middle Eastern-based terrorist. The

Arab mentioned a pink-colored house owned by a professor on an island. You may not know this, Mike, but there aren't a lot of pink houses on the Greek islands."

Michael nodded. "You know, I was thinking about what you said about some sort of major terrorist attack."

"Uh-huh," Bob said.

"When I was at the Pentagon, I was assigned to a special project that modeled potential terrorist attacks on the United States. We looked at hundreds of possible points of vulnerability and hundreds of possible vehicles for introduction of chemical, biological, or nuclear agents. Our conclusion was that most of the alternatives we investigated were impractical. Chemical and biological agents are extremely unstable, difficult to process, and even more difficult to transport. Nuclear materials aren't that easy to come by, despite all the hype we read in the newspapers. And they're unstable and expensive. Maybe thirty million dollars for a suitcase dirty bomb."

"Of course, this isn't the United States," Bob said. "Greece has more porous borders than we do with Mexico, and that's saying something. And the Greeks haven't been especially aggressive about trying to prevent terrorists from entering their country."

"I'll give you that," Michael said, "but I think terrorist organizations are becoming more sophisticated. It doesn't matter where the target is located; their methods are being elevated to a more high-tech level. Sure, there are still suicide bombers with explosives wrapped around their chests who kill a small number of victims; but if you're correct about the terrorists wanting to make a big statement, a suicide bomb attack isn't going to get the job done."

"What are you getting at?" Bob asked, finding Michael's reasoning interesting. He'd already told Jack Cole that he believed the same thing: If anything was going to happen, it wasn't going to be the garden variety suicide bomber attack.

"At the Pentagon, we came to the conclusion the 9-11 attacks taught the terrorists an important lesson: that an airborne assault is preferable to a ground assault. Even the best air traffic control system in the world can't ensure that a renegade or hijacked aircraft won't get through."

"So, are you telling me you believe an attack might come from a hijacked airplane?"

Michael shook his head. "I don't know, Dad. Sure it might be an aircraft. All I'm saying is I would be surprised if they tried ramming a truck loaded with explosives into one of the Olympic venues. We've learned how to deal with that sort of attack. Remember the suicide attacker last year who went after the Turks' building in Baghdad. All he did was ram into a concrete blockade, blow himself up, and shatter a lot of windows. Their methods are changing as we learn to counter them."

Bob began pacing. Michael made sense, and he also had elevated his concern. It was as though a small voice inside his head was telling him he had to get his act together, that something big was about to go down. The voice had been there for weeks now, but it was becoming louder and more frequent.

"Since we're playing hypotheticals here, what type of weapon would you guess the bad guys would use?"

Michael rested his chin in one hand and said, "That's where I'm stumped. As I said before, chemical and biological weapons are problematical, and nuclear weapons aren't easy to acquire."

"What if you were a terrorist; what would you do?" Bob asked.

Michael laughed. "There's a question." He hesitated for a moment, then said, "And I want to make the ultimate statement."

Bob nodded.

"I'd go nuclear."

"I thought you said—"

"Yeah, I said nuclear weapons are hard to acquire; but I'd still go nuclear."

Bob was enjoying the discussion. He was impressed with Michael's thinking. "Where would you find the weapons? How would you bring them into the country."

Again, Michael paused to think about Bob's question. Finally, he said, "How have the Greek terrorists acquired their weapons up to this point?"

Bob gave his son a querulous look. "We're talking apples and oranges here. You're talking about nuclear weapons. These guys have been using pistols, and rifles, and basic explosives. Maybe a rocket launcher here and there. But nothing close to a nuclear payload, or a delivery vehicle sophisticated enough to carry a nuclear device."

"I understand," Michael said, "but tell me how these terrorists have acquired their weapons to this point."

"They've stolen them," Bob said. "Primarily from military and police installations."

Michael spread his arms. "Well, then I guess they'd do the same thing to get nuclear weapons. I don't think they'd import weapons into the country. There would be too many obstacles to getting them into Greece. I'd guess they'd follow the same M.O. they've used up to now: Steal nuclear weapons from someplace inside Greece."

Bob wanted to blow off what Michael had just told him, but he didn't dare do so. As incredible as what his son had said, now that he'd heard Michael's theory, he couldn't ignore it. He didn't view the theory as his top priority; but he would have to assign one of his people to look into the possibility.

CHAPTER SEVENTY-ONE

AUGUST 12, 2004

Sam Goodwin took a helicopter over to Evoia and instructed the pilot to land in the parking lot next to the ferry dock. The local constable, a twenty-something, six-foot-tall local boy named Yiannis Portokallis, met Sam in the lot and drove him to Photos' property. The constable led Sam through and around the house, showing him how he had searched the property. The smell of fresh paint burned Sam's sinuses.

"What about the cellar?" Sam asked when they were outside, pointing at the padlocked cellar door.

"It was locked," Portokallis said. "I didn't think I should break the padlock."

Sam held his breath for a while, not wanting to show his frustration, then looked around for something to pry the hasp off the door. He found a hammer inside the house and brought it back outside. After ripping the hasp and padlock off the door, Sam opened it and stepped inside. He asked the constable for his flashlight and shined it around the room. Nothing seemed out of place. An odd assortment of dilapidated furniture, a metal cabinet, and empty wooden boxes were arrayed against the room's walls. Then Sam noticed footprints in the dirt floor, near the front of the cabinet. He and Portokallis pulled the cabinet away from the wall, exposing an opening. The outline of a rectangle was evident in the dirt inside the opening.

Sam returned the flashlight to Portokallis and left the cellar. He circled the house and returned to the fifty-five gallon drum he'd noticed before. Lying a few feet away was an empty wooden box that could have made the impression in the dirt behind the metal cabinet.

"Give me a hand," he said to the constable.

"Excuse me?" Portokallis said. "Give you a hand?"

"I need your help," Sam explained. "Let's turn over this drum."

The two men tipped over the drum and upended it. A torrent of ash and what appeared to be burned fragments of paper poured onto the ground. Sam crouched down as a car horn blared. The constable excused himself and went around the house. Sam used the hammer to stir the debris, spreading it out over an area the size of a child's rubber wading pool. He kept moving the ashes around until he came upon a piece of singed paper. He carefully picked up the fragment— about half the size of an 8-1/2" x 11" piece of paper. The top half of the paper had been burned. The side that was up was blank. Sam turned it over. Typewritten in Greek on the reverse side was a short numbered list of items. The list started with the number 5 and ended with the number 7:

5. $250,000 Mahmoud Abdalan # 125900765-0090.
6. $350,000 Parviz Mirzadeh # 328507753-8930.
7. $2,760,000 Maria's account # 70931074-7612.

He took a Ziplock plastic bag from a jacket pocket, inserted the slip of paper into the bag, sealed it, and put it back in his suit jacket. The constable returned at that moment.

"Who was that in the car?" Sam asked.

Portokallis blushed. "My wife," he said. "She wanted to know when I would be home for dinner."

God save me, Sam thought. He stirred the ashes again, but found no more intact pieces of paper. He pulled his cell phone from his pants pocket and called the Glyfada office.

"The place has been cleaned out," he told Bob. "It looks as though there was a box of documents in a hidden space in a locked basement. Whoever was here must have burned them before taking off."

"Damn," Bob said. "You got nothing?"

"I found a scrap of paper with three names on it, along with dollar amounts and what looks like bank account numbers."

"Give me the information from the paper, then wait for the Greek investigative team, which I understand is flying over there right now. They're going to look for fingerprints and the like."

"Okay," Sam said.

"Oh, and Sam, has anyone else seen this information?"

"No, no one."

"Good. Let's keep it that way. I don't want anything getting back to the terrorists."

CHAPTER SEVENTY-TWO

AUGUST 12, 2004

Bob had just hung up the telephone after Sam's call, when the phone rang again.

"Bob, it's Tony. There's no one here at the Sounion house. We did find a neighbor who said she saw Photos' wife Maria leave in a car yesterday."

"No sign of Giorgos Photos, I suppose."

"You got that right."

"Did it look like the house was being abandoned?" Bob asked.

"No," Tony said. "The closets and dressers are full of clothes and we found a half-dozen photograph albums. It appears they're planning to return. But we didn't find a damned thing on Giorgos Photos. He doesn't even show up in any of the photographs."

"Come on back to the office," Bob said. "I want you to find out where every nuclear weapon in Greece is located."

"Nuclear weapons? Do you know something I should know?"

"Just being careful, Tony. As far as I know, the only nukes in and around Greece are under U.S. control. I'm primarily concerned about weapons inside the Greek borders. Don't worry about weapons on our ships."

Stacey Frederick had a phone glued to her ear the entire time that Bob was on the other line with Sam and then Tony. When she finally hung up, she told Bob, "That was Frank Reynolds on the line. I was checking to see if he had any more information on Photos." She looked dejected. "Just the same stuff they passed on before from the

Bulgarian. That Photos went through training in Bulgaria and that he was a leader of the student demonstrations in Paris years ago."

"When was Photos in Paris?" Bob asked. Before she could respond, he added, "Was he there at the same time our friend, Casanova, was there?"

"Frank told me that Madanowski made a point of saying that Casanova and the Professor were friends while in Paris. He also knew they were students together at the University here in Athens before going through Intelligence training."

Bob's heart was pumping a mile a minute. "Anything else?"

"Oh yeah, boss. The Bulgarian said the Professor spent time in Northern Iraq and Western Turkey working with the Kurds. He also spent two months in Iran after the fall of the Shah."

Bob took the legal pad on which he'd written the information Sam had given him and placed it in front of Stacey. "See what you can find on the first two names."

Stacey eyed the pad. "The second name looks Iranian," she said.

Bob nodded. "And I think the first one is Kurdish."

"You know Photos' wife's name is Maria," Stacey said.

Bob patted Stacey on the shoulder. "Yep, I know. See if you can find out where Maria Photos was raised, if she has family anywhere else in Greece."

"You think she's gone underground?"

"That's exactly what I think."

"Maybe she's ignorant about her husband's activities," Stacey said.

"Yeah, maybe."

CHAPTER SEVENTY-THREE

AUGUST 12, 2004

Giorgos Photos sat on a chair on the deck of a thirty-eight foot sailboat, located in a cove east of the Attican Peninsula. He'd gathered the sails and anchored the boat. The orangey-red sun was melting into the sea, spreading red fingers of brilliance across the water's surface. He stared in the direction of Koropi and wondered what was happening at the missile site's command and control area. As bad as he wanted to phone Abdalan on his cell phone, he didn't dare. The Kurd would either pull it off or he wouldn't. The man was a professional; the odds of success were in his favor.

He looked at his wristwatch and saw he had two minutes before calling Mullah Parviz Mirzadeh. The Mullah had been a radical fighting the Pahlavi Shah, before becoming a senior Muslim cleric. The Ayatollah Khomeini had elevated him from an obscure part of Azerbaijan, in northwestern Iran, to the heady environment of Tehran. The radical Mirzadeh, who Photos had known in Paris so many years ago, was now akin to the Beria of Iran, with tentacles spreading throughout the Middle East. He was very quietly the *Al Qaeda* connection in Iran.

Photos poured himself an *ouzo* and splashed in an inch of water. After downing the cloudy drink in one gulp, he dialed the Mullah's number.

"Right on time, my friend," Mirzadeh said with obvious joy. "Are you ready for tomorrow?"

"I've been ready for tomorrow all my life," Photos answered. "I assume all is set."

"Of course. We will strike a mighty blow tomorrow."

Photos had always appreciated the man's talent for understatement. "And your Kurdish problem should go away."

"Ah, yes," Mirzadeh said. "Our army will drive the Kurds in Iran across the border into Turkey to join their brethren there." The Mullah paused, then said, "They're a contentious lot, you know, always crying about independence and wanting their own nation. Once they're all across the border, it will be Turkey's problem. And the lands they occupy in Iran will be occupied by real Persians."

"There are many other minorities in the area, are there not?" Photos asked.

"Oh, yes, many. Assyrians, Chaldeans, Turks, and more. But they too will be relocated." He laughed at his choice of words. "Relocated. How do you like that?"

"Whatever makes you happy, my friend."

The Mullah belly-laughed. "This makes me very happy."

"And the planes?" Photos said.

"Everything is ready."

"We should have an absinthe together, like in the old days in Paris."

"Alcohol is abhorrent to Islam," Mirzadeh said.

"Right," Photos said. "I'll have to drink two, yours and mine."

Mirzadeh laughed again, but there was less humor in it this time. "We really are very different, my Greek friend."

Now it was Photos' turn to laugh. "We're not different at all, Parviz. Maybe our religions are different—Islam versus Marxism; but we each want the same thing. Power. And we're willing to do anything to get it."

Photos ended the call to the sounds of his and Mirzadeh's boisterous laughter.

The sea was now red wine-dark. Photos had one light burning at the top of the mast and lights at the bow and the stern. Hundreds of lights blinked on the shore in the distance. Close, he thought. I'm as close to the realization of all my dreams as I have ever been.

CHAPTER SEVENTY-FOUR

AUGUST 12, 2004

Mahmoud Abdalan walked inside the perimeter fence of the missile site's command and control area. His men were now posted at the front gate and at fifty-meter intervals around the site. The Greek major was handling communications with the missile storage area down near the town of Koropi. Abdalan prayed that no enterprising Greek officer from higher command decided to pull a surprise inspection at the missile site. With the Olympics starting tomorrow, he suspected that all Greeks had only one thing on their minds: the Games.

He passed the Greek barracks building and quickly covered his mouth and nose with his handkerchief. *Allah protect us*, he thought. He moved away from the building and ordered two of his men to seal it, closing the doors and windows. The heat was already causing the bodies inside the barracks to putrefy.

Abdalan moved to a storage building, threw open the door, and switched on the lights. The only surviving Greek airman of the massacre inside the barracks sat blindfolded and gagged in a corner. The man's face was bruised and bloodied; he shook as though he was freezing. Abdalan knew it was fear and shock that caused the man's trembling.

"You Greeks will be sorry you ever threatened my country," Abdalan said in Turkish, playing his role. "Turkey will once again conquer you Greeks and make you the slaves you were meant to be. Not only will Cyprus be ours again, but so will the mainland." It didn't matter that the airman couldn't understand a word of Turkish, as long as he understood that Abdalan was speaking Turkish.

The airman's shaking intensified.

Abdalan left the building, slamming the door behind him. If the airman didn't die from a heart attack, he would have plenty to say about the Turks who took over the base and killed his comrades.

CHAPTER SEVENTY-FIVE

AUGUST 12, 2004

The drive to the hospital where Stanton Markeson was being cared for was an adrenaline rush. Bob had relinquished the car keys to Michael while he made one telephone call after another. He discovered that his son approached Athens traffic as a challenge.

"Who taught you to drive?" Bob asked while he dialed a number on his cell phone.

Michael smiled and said, "Mom. You were always too busy to do it."

"Oh, Jesus," Bob said. Then a woman who said her name was Inspector Sonya Crane answered his call.

"Inspector Crane, this is Robert Danforth. Do you know who I am?"

"Yes, sir," she said, "what can I do for you?"

"I understand Stanton Markeson has regained consciousness and—"

"With all due respect, sir, how did you—"

"Let's not waste our time, Inspector. I'm on my way to the hospital. I want to talk with Stanton and I want to make sure I can get past your guards out in front of the building and outside his room. I would appreciate it if you would see that I am not delayed."

"I'm not sure I can do that, Mr. Danforth," Crane said. "My orders—"

Bob cut her off. "I'm going to give you a telephone number for Brigadier Jeffrey Watkin-Coons' private number in London. I was hoping I wouldn't have to bother him; but I see now that it's going to be necessary. Call the Brigadier and tell him Robert Danforth is requesting immediate access to Stanton Markeson. I'll be at the hospital in fifteen minutes." He disconnected the call and reflexively stomped his foot into the car's floorboards as Michael raced up behind a slow-moving car, jerked the steering wheel to the right, and zipped around the car. Bob pointed to the intersection ahead and, in as calm a voice as he could muster, said, "Take a right at the light."

Bob wasn't sure if Inspector Crane had called London, or decided that bothering Brigadier Jeffrey Watkin-Coons was not a particularly good idea. Whatever the reason, the skids were greased for his entry to the hospital. One of the English Special Operations people outside the building opened the car door for Bob even before Michael had brought the vehicle to a screeching stop.

"Wait here," Bob instructed Michael. "I'll be back down as soon as I can." Then he hurried inside the hospital, following the Special Ops guy to an elevator, which took them to the fifth floor where three armed men stood guard. As Bob trailed the Englishman down the hall, he noticed two more armed men stationed at intervals along the hallway. And an additional two stood outside a room in the middle of the corridor.

Inside Markeson's room, Bob immediately questioned the accuracy of the information he had received by telephone from a cooperative member of the nursing staff. Markeson did not look as though he was recovering. He looked like death warmed over. He was gray in color. His eyes were closed; the only sounds in the room were the steady beep-beep-beep of a heart monitor and a sonorous, labored breathing. A gray-haired, thin, diminutive man, wearing a white smock and looking down at a clipboard, stood at the foot of the bed. A young woman in slacks, a white blouse, and a blue blazer stood on the far side of Markeson's bed, her eyes boring into Bob's from the moment he entered the room.

"Inspector Crane?" Bob guessed.

"Yes, sir. You must be Mr. Danforth. Sorry about—"

"You've got nothing to be sorry about. Besides, I got what I needed." He shot her a self-deprecatory smile.

She nodded back. "This is Dr. William Maybury, Mr. Markeson's physician," she said.

The man with the clipboard looked up at Bob. "He's very weak and is in and out of consciousness." The man hunched his shoulders. "I can't tell you when he might be able to talk again."

Bob turned back to Crane. "Has he said anything?"

She shook her head. "Not much, and nothing we've been able to understand. He's said something that sounds like '*dimi*' several times, but none of us can figure out what he's talking about."

Bob moved to the side of the bed and lightly gripped Markeson's forearm. "Stanton," he said, "it's Bob Danforth; can you hear me?" Bob watched Markeson's face, but saw no reaction at all. He tried again. "Stanton, it's Bob Danforth; can you—"

Markeson's eyelids fluttered and then stopped moving, remaining only half-open.

Bob leaned over the bed, hoping Markeson would see his face and recognize him. "It's Bob Danforth," he said again.

Markeson's eyelids did another dance, but when they stopped this time, his eyes were fully open. Bob felt Markeson's arm move.

"Vassa . . . Dimi . . . terror . . .."

"Dimi?" Bob asked. He waited a moment, then moved his hand and grasped Markeson's hand. "Squeeze my hand if you can, Stanton. If your answer is yes, squeeze my hand. Okay?"

Bob's chest swelled with relief when Markeson's hand flexed.

"What is this dimi?" Bob asked. "A place?"

Markeson's hand remained still.

"A person?" Bob said.

Bob felt Markeson's hand lightly squeeze his own. "Dimi is a person?" Another squeeze.

"He's a terrorist?"

No reaction.

"Is he associated with the terrorists?"

Squeeze. Markeson's lips moved, but no sound came out.

"Is dimi a man?"

Squeeze.

"Is this the man's name?"

Squeeze.

"Do you know the man's last name?"

Squeeze.

Bob thought for a second. "I'm going to go through the alphabet. When I say the first letter of the man's last name, squeeze my hand." Bob looked at the doctor and saw the worried look on the man's face. He was afraid the physician was about to cut him off. He turned back to Markeson and said, "A."

Markeson squeezed his hand with more force than he had before.

"The man's last name starts with an A?" Bob asked, just to make sure.

Squeeze.

"Was your wife involved with this man?" Bob asked.

Markeson's eyelids rolled shut. He seemed to have lapsed back into unconsciousness; but then Bob felt Markeson's hand squeeze his.

Then a thought struck Bob that made the hairs on the back of his neck tingle. Were his suspicions about to be proved correct? "Dimi is short for Dimitris, isn't it, Stanton?"

Markeson squeezed Bob's hand three times in succession.

Bob took in a long, slow breath. He turned to the physician and said, "Doctor, would you mind leaving the room for a minute?"

The doctor's expression and body language told Bob the man was going to argue with him; but Inspector Crane came around the bed and took the doctor's arm.

"Let's make this as easy as possible," she said.

The doctor looked angry, then unsure of what to do. By the time he opened his mouth to object, Crane had moved him to the hall and shut the door behind him.

"You're telling us that Dimitris Argyropoulos is part of *Greek Spring*, aren't you?" Bob said.

Squeeze.

"How do you know this?" Bob asked, realizing too late he'd asked a question that couldn't be answered with a yes or no. He was about to rephrase the question when Markeson made a low moaning sound. Markeson's eyes blinked, then closed again. He sighed. Then he squeezed Bob's hand with more strength than Bob would have thought possible and rasped, "Vassa said . . .."

The effort to say these words seemed to have been too much for Markeson. His hand relaxed in Bob's. Bob thought the worst for a moment, but was relieved to hear the steady beep of the heart monitor.

He squeezed Markeson's hand and then patted the man's arm with his other hand. "Don't worry, Stanton, we'll take care of him."

CHAPTER SEVENTY-SIX

AUGUST 12, 2004

Stacey Frederick had labored for hours, going through files. The names *Abdalan* and *Mirzadeh* had popped up in a few instances; but there was nothing that would tie the names to terrorism or Greece. The Abdalan in the database was a Kurdish poet, and the Mirzadeh was a professor in Chicago who had emigrated from Iran in 1979.

It was already dark outside and she was feeling dead tired. The wall clock said it was 2:00 P.M. on the East Coast of the United States. She looked over at Tony Fratangelo who had his head buried in notes and files. He was working on something Bob had assigned him. She started to suggest they go out and grab dinner, when she decided instead to call Tanya Serkovic's number at Langley.

"You've reached extension 5369," the recorded voice said. "Leave a message."

After a beep sounded, Stacey said her name and was beginning to leave a message, when Tanya suddenly came on the line.

"Sorry about that," Tanya said, "I'm working on something and didn't want to be disturbed, unless it was important. How are things over there?"

"We're busting our ass chasing ghosts. Bob Danforth is paranoid about something happening during the Olympic Games; but no one has even a clue about what it might be."

"I hear your frustration," Tanya said, "but I'd trust Bob's instincts."

"I do, I do," Stacey said. "I'd just like to come up with something."

There was a pause on the other end of the line, then Tanya said, "You called me."

"Yeah, I thought I might run something by you. I've been trying to get a hit in the terrorist database on a couple names, without any luck. I thought I'd see if you have any bright ideas."

"Give me the names and whatever you know about them."

"I don't know a thing about them, except one of the names sounds Iranian and the other Kurdish. The first one is Parviz Mirzadeh and the other one is Mahmoud Abdalan." She spelled the names for Tanya.

"Give me thirty minutes," Tanya said. "I'll walk downstairs to the Iran and Turkey desks. Maybe someone down there will recognize the names."

"Thanks, Tanya. I'll be here at the office."

After hanging up with Tanya, Stacey tried to find a match on the names in the database by changing the spelling. She even tried making an anagram out of the names, but it was futile. She had just stopped for a cup of coffee when Tanya called back.

"Where did you come up with the names you gave me?" Tanya asked.

"Sam Goodwin found a half-burned piece of paper at Giorgos Photos' island home. The names were on the paper, along with what appeared to be bank account numbers and large sums of money."

"Well, you hit a home run," Tanya said. "The boys on the country desks didn't even have to look in their files. The reason you didn't make a connection with these two names in the terrorist database is because neither of them is categorized that way. Parviz Mirzadeh was an advocate of Marxist causes decades ago while an exchange student in France; but he returned to Iran and found religion. The guy on the Iran desk knew Mirzadeh right off the bat because he's a member of the Iranian Ruling Council. He's from Azerbaijan and has a base of political and religious support from that region. He lives in Teheran most of the time, but his ancestral home is located about fifty miles south of the Russian border and thirty miles east of Turkey."

"That's Kurd country, isn't it?" Stacey asked.

"Well, there are a lot of Kurds there; but there are dozens of other ethnic groups in Azerbaijan, too."

"What about Abdalan?" Stacey said.

"The man on the Turkey desk knew all about Mahmoud Abdalan. He's a real hero to the Kurdish people, but is known to be more of a diplomat than a warrior. He lives in a village almost right on the Turkey/Iraq border, no more than a mile from Iran. There's no evidence Abdalan has ever been involved in any sort of terrorist activity. The same goes for Mirzadeh."

Stacey thanked Tanya and tried to make sense out of what she'd just learned. She walked to the wall in the conference area and looked at the world map hanging there. She tapped a finger on the northwest part of Iran, on Azerbaijan. She then moved her finger westward, across Azerbaijan and into Turkey, to the Turkey/Iraq border. "What's the connection?" she wondered aloud. Why would a slip of paper found in Giorgos Photos' backyard have the names of an Iranian cleric and a Kurdish politician on it? She felt a tremor of something—excitement or fear, she wasn't quite sure. Maybe both.

She grabbed her desk phone and dialed Bob's cell number, settling back into her chair while the telephone rang.

"Hello," Bob said.

"It's Stacey. I've got something here; the problem is I don't know what I've got."

"In our business, that's not unusual. Tell me about it."

Stacey related what she had learned and then waited. After several seconds, Bob told her he would be in the office in thirty minutes. After he hung up, she had a long period of uncertainty. What if I'm causing one of the top people in the CIA to come down here late at night for no good reason?

Bob and Michael were on their way back to the Grand Bretagne Hotel when Bob received Stacey's call. He shut his cell phone and said, "I need to go to the office. We'll go to the hotel first and drop you off. I'll take the car from there."

"I don't know Athens very well at all," Michael said, "but isn't the hotel out of our way? If you don't mind, why don't I tag along? I'm having a great time."

Bob laughed. "You're supposed to be on leave, not gumshoeing around Athens."

"If the truth be known, Dad, I was bored silly in Paris. This is the best time I've had since going on vacation. I trust you won't tell Miriana that."

Bob made an "X" on his chest with his finger. "Cross my heart," he said.

At the Glyfada office, Bob made Stacey go over again everything she had gathered on Mirzadeh and Abdalan. Tony sat down with them. When Stacey finished, Bob asked, "Does it seem strange to you that Mirzadeh and Abdalan come from the same part of the world; that their home towns are no more than fifty miles apart?"

Stacey winced. "The whole area is a hotbed of violence and ethnic strife. It's probably just a coincidence. Besides, the last I heard, there is no love lost between the Iranians and the Kurds."

Bob nodded. "It could be that Mirzadeh and Abdalan don't know one another. Maybe our boy, Photos, is in league with the two of them for two completely different reasons; but I find the geography intriguing."

Stacey shrugged. "Remember what Madanowski said. That Photos had contact with both Iran and the Kurds. I don't know, though. It's probably just coincidental."

"There are no coincidences in this business," Bob said. "Let's decide what the hell we're going to do with this information."

"By the way," Tony said, "I got that information you wanted."

Bob had dumped so many demands for information on his people, he couldn't remember what Tony was referring to. Tony must have noticed the confusion showing on his face.

"The location of nuclear weapons in Greece. The Defense Nuclear Agency had the information down to the serial numbers on the weapons. Most of the American weapons in Greece were shipped out years ago, after the junta was overthrown. The only reason governments since then have agreed to keep nukes in the country was because they saw them as a deterrent against an attack from Turkey, particularly with the Cyprus situation." He smiled and said, "We've got nukes mated to missiles in Turkey for the exact same reason. It's like a mini Cold War."

"Where are these weapons?" Bob asked.

"There's a U.S. Army Artillery Detachment headquartered in Katsamidi, not too far from Athens. There are Nike Hercules missiles there, some with nuclear weapons. The detachment commander also has three other teams: one each in Thivai, Koropi, and Keratea. Thivai is about sixty miles north of Athens. The other two sites are south. All four American teams control the arm plugs that go into the nuclear weapons to make them go hot. The weapons are already mated to missiles, which are the property of the Greek Air Force."

"These are the only nukes in Greece?" Bob said.

"That's it," Tony said.

Bob walked around the room for a minute, then said, "I'm going to think about this Abdalan/Mirzadeh/Photos connection for a minute. I want you to call Langley and get Jack Cole to call the Pentagon. They need to contact the commander of this artillery detachment and get him to personally check out each of his sites. He needs to inventory his nuclear arming plugs and nuclear weapons."

CHAPTER SEVENTY-SEVEN

AUGUST 12, 2004

Mullah Parviz Mirzadeh made his nightly obeisance to *Allah*, thanking his God for all that had been granted him in the temporal world and for the great honors that would accrue to him in the afterlife. He knew *Allah* would bestow all of the riches of heaven upon him for what he was about to inflict on the infidels.

He put his prayer rug in the closet and walked outside his home near Urmia in northwestern Iran. He ordered his driver to take him in the Land Rover to the secret airfield in a small valley ten miles from the Turkey/Iran border. There were no fences, berms, or revetments that would indicate this location was a military installation. A half-dozen armed Iranian soldiers dressed as tribesmen patrolled the area. The only buildings were seven huts replicating a tiny Kurdish settlement.

Mirzadeh told his driver to take him past the huts, to a flat area that was dense with juniper bushes. At one end of the area, the Land Rover stopped and Mirzadeh stepped from the vehicle. He lifted the corner of a camouflage net and stepped under it. Two armed guards came to attention. There, looking sinister to Mirzadeh, were the instruments he would use to wreak havoc on the infidels. The six French Mirage jets with Iraqi markings sat like prehistoric predators. The sight of them made Mirzadeh's heart speed up.

"Where are the pilots?" he asked.

One of the guards pointed in the direction of the huts. "Getting some rest," he said.

Mirzadeh nodded, walked around the airplanes, enjoying their beautiful symmetry and immense power. After circling all six aircraft,

Mirzadeh moved to a table in a corner of the camouflaged, open-air hangar that covered an area the size of a soccer field and removed a large white cloth covering a half-inch stack of maps. He ran a finger across the top map, along the route the planes would take, moving his hand until his finger stopped on the city of Athens. He flicked his forefinger against that spot on the map and said, "Boom."

Mirzadeh left the hangar by the same way he'd entered it. He marched quickly to one of the huts and used a key to unlock a padlock on the door. He entered and closed the door behind him. After flipping on the light switch, flooding the little one-room building in light powered by a 200 KW gasoline generator, he changed from his civilian clothes to his robes. Up to now, he had donned paramilitary clothing, dark glasses, and a long-billed cap when meeting with the pilots. He didn't want them to be able to identify him should one or more of them have a change of heart and leave. But now, things were different. The mission would begin in the early morning hours and Mirzadeh's guards had orders to shoot anyone who tried to leave the site. It didn't matter that the pilots knew his name, not after the aircraft were airborne. The planes had been rigged to prevent the pilots from bailing out or from landing.

The Iraqi pilots—rabid Iraqi nationalists, fellow tribesmen of Saddam Hussein's, Islamic fundamentalists, and *Al Qaeda* supporters—had been told, up to now, that Mirzadeh was a Saudi connected with *Al Qaeda*. That they were going to fly a mission that would give them the opportunity to avenge the overthrow of the Iraqi leader by the Americans in 2003. That's all they knew up to this point. Mirzadeh would fill in the blanks now and tomorrow morning.

The Mullah left the hut and paid a visit on the Iraqis. Three of them were asleep; one pilot lay in bed, reading; and the other two were playing backgammon. The hut was divided into multiple sections— six private sleeping areas, each surrounded by a curtain, a sitting area for playing games and eating, and a bathroom. When Mirzadeh entered the hut, one of the men playing backgammon seemed confused for a moment, then stood and shouted at his sleeping comrades to wake up. When all were awake and standing, Mirzadeh embraced each man in turn.

"I can see you are surprised by my dress," Mirzadeh said, smiling at the men. "It is time you know who I am, and that you are about to take part in something even bigger than you might have imagined. Your moment of revenge is upon you." He told them his name and his position in the Iranian Government. When he was confident the men were duly impressed, even awed, he asked, "Are you ready to punish the Americans for the humiliation they heaped upon Saddam, Iraq, and the entire Muslim world?"

The senior pilot spoke for his comrades. "We are ready, *Arbob*," using a title of profound respect.

"Good," Mirzadeh said. He gave a fatherly smile to each of the men and said, "Your rewards in this life shall be great, but as nothing compared to the rewards you will receive in heaven." He smiled again. "I have arranged for your rewards to begin this very night. And after you complete your mission tomorrow, you will each receive two million Euros. Life will be good for you."

Mirzadeh clapped his hands and the hut door swung open. Several guards dragged six girls into the hut. They were dressed in tribal garb, with long colorful dresses and scarves covering their heads and faces, and gold and silver necklaces. The girls huddled together. One was crying. These were the most beautiful girls in their Assyrian village on the west side of Lake Urmia. Mirzadeh had arranged for their kidnappings. He knew the oldest of the six Christian girls was barely thirteen years old, the youngest was ten. After the Iraqis were done with them, Mirzadeh would let his soldiers have their way with the girls. Then they would be disposed of. The only fate for all infidels.

He waved at the pilots as he walked from the hut. "Enjoy yourselves," he said. "And get some rest. You have long flights to make tomorrow."

CHAPTER SEVENTY-EIGHT

AUGUST 13, 2004

Sam Goodwin had returned from Evoia. The whole team was in the Glyfada office, poring over files, waiting for updates on inquiries they had made about Dimitris Argyropoulos, Giorgos Photos, Parviz Mirzadeh, Mahmoud Abdalan, and a myriad of others. Michael Danforth was pitching in wherever he could.

Jack Cole's call from Langley came in a few minutes past midnight.

"Bob," Jack Cole said, "the Pentagon is on board. They'll have the commander of the 37th Detachment contact you there. He'll be told to take orders from you."

"Thanks, Jack."

"Are you sure about this?" Jack asked.

"Hah," Bob blurted. "I'm not sure about anything. I'm operating on a whole lot of hunches. But the sum of all my hunches adds up to a bad feeling. We've got the number two guy in Greece playing footsy with the worst terrorist group in the country. Argyropoulos has a Marxist resume that would rival some of the former members of the Soviet Politburo. And there's not much I can do about it without more than what I got from a half-conscious British agent. And, of course, there's the good professor, Giorgos Photos, who has disappeared, along with his wife and children."

Bob took a deep breath, trying to keep his growing frustration from showing in his voice. When he continued, his frustration wasn't any less, but at least his tone was calmer.

"Don't forget the names on the slip of paper found at Photos' home on Evoia. What's with the names Mirzadeh and Abdalan? There's no love lost between the Iranians and the Kurds, so why do their names show up on Photos' list?"

"You have a gut feeling about that, too?" Jack said.

"The only feelings I have are pain and frustration," Bob said, staring up at the world map on the wall in front of him. Something had been bothering him about the connection between Mirzadeh and Abdalan since the men's names had surfaced. He zeroed his gaze in on the areas in Iran, Iraq, and Turkey that the Kurds occupied.

"Walk me through something," he said. "The Iranians, like the Iraqis, have had a running feud with the Kurds for generations, right?"

"Right," Jack said. "The Kurds are an independent, warlike group who have been fighting on the ground as well as lobbying at the U.N. for decades for their own homeland."

"Which covers parts of eastern Turkey, northern Iraq, and western Iran," Bob added.

"If the Iranians could do one thing with the Kurds, what do you think that would be?"

"If they thought they could get away with it, they'd nuke the whole bunch. They have a long history of viciously suppressing their ethnic minorities, and that goes a lot further back than just the Pahlavis who ruled Iran up to Khomeini's takeover."

"Hum," Bob said. "What sort of conditions would have to exist for the Iranians to take decisive action against the Kurds?"

"That's a difficult question." After a long moment, Jack said, "I guess the answer is that they would be able to do just about anything they wanted to do if the geopolitical situation was in such upheaval that the superpowers would have other priorities that were more important than protecting some ethnic group in the boonies of Azerbaijan."

"Like a war?" Bob said. Before Jack could answer, Bob added, "That pain in my gut just spiked."

"What do you mean?" Jack asked.

"We've been focusing on our concerns about some pissant terrorist group pulling off an ambitious attack during the Olympic Games. What if it's bigger than that?"

"Like what?"

"Hell, I don't know," Bob said, "but I think we'd better take some unusual steps. Jack, do you think you could get the National Reconnaissance Office to point one of its satellites at the spot where Turkey, Iran, and Iraq meet?"

"I'll check," Jack said. "Anything else?"

"Yeah," Bob said, "let's get an Airborne Warning and Control System aircraft over that area, too."

"An AWACS?"

"Yep. In fact, make it two AWACS. We should also have one hovering over western Turkey."

"Anything else?" Jack asked, sarcasm in his tone.

"Now that you mention it, I could use an SF or Delta Force team in my hip pocket, just in case."

"Jesus," Jack said.

"Oh, and one other thing, Jack."

"You've got to be kidding me," Jack said. "What more could you possibly want?"

"Michael's here in Athens and—"

"I thought he was in Paris."

"He was, but after the terrorists went after Liz and me, he decided he needed to come down here to check on his parents. He's been hanging around with me since he and Miriana arrived."

"Nice boy," Jack said.

"Yeah," Bob agreed, "but I'm starting to get worried about him being down here without orders. Even though he's on vacation, the Pentagon authorized overseas travel to France alone. He could get into trouble just being in Greece."

"Not to mention getting involved with the CIA and international terrorists," Jack said.

"You understand my concern?"

"Of course. What do you want me to do?"

"I'd say nothing if I thought I could order Mike to return to Paris; but that isn't going to happen. He's obviously made up his mind to mother hen his mother and me until his leave is over, which isn't for another week. Maybe you could pull some strings and get your buddies at the Pentagon to add Greece to his travel authorization."

"I'll take care of it," Jack said, "and I'll call you about your other requests as soon as I put it together. Forget the Delta Force unit, though."

"I appreciate it; I know you're going out on a limb, considering we don't have more to go on. And I was just kidding about the Delta Force."

"Bullshit!" Jack said. "If this turns out to be a fiasco, at least I'll be able to take comfort in the fact that you will be forced to retire along with me."

CHAPTER SEVENTY-NINE
AUGUST 13, 2004

Captain Simon Barrows fingered the slip of paper on which he'd written the telephone number his commander had called to give him. He didn't know what was up, but he sure as hell didn't like it. First, Colonel Swetland had awakened him at 1:00 A.M. This usually meant one of two things: a surprise inspection team had just arrived to check on his unit's state of readiness, or one of his men had been thrown in a Greek jail for fighting, DWI, or some such thing. But, in this case, it was something altogether different. The Colonel just gave him this telephone number, told him to ask for a man named Danforth, say Jack Cole told him to call, and to do whatever Danforth told him to do. When he asked Colonel Swetland for clarification, the Colonel had barked at him, telling him to do what he was told to do. His commander's reaction had surprised Barrows. Barking wasn't the Colonel's style. Then the Colonel told him to get rid of whatever Scandinavian or German or English girl he had in his bed and to call the number.

He assumed the Colonel had guessed that he had a guest in his bed—Helga somebody from Dortmund, Germany. He couldn't possibly have known for sure . . . he hoped. It took him a minute to wake up Helga and another thirty seconds to push her into the living room, onto the sofa, where she dropped off to sleep again. He then returned to his bedroom, shut the door, and was now wondering what he was about to get into. Barrows turned on the bedside lamp and set the slip of paper down on the lamp table. He dialed the number.

"Who's calling?" a female voice said.

"Mr. Danforth, please. I was told—"

"Just a minute. I asked you who was calling."

"Oh, sorry. Captain Simon Barrows, Commander of the 37th United States Army Artillery Detachment."

The woman told him to hold. Ten seconds passed, and then a man came on the line.

"This is Bob Danforth."

"Mr. Danforth, this is Captain Simon Barrows. I'm commander of the 37th Detachment. I was ordered to call you and to say that Jack Cole told me to call."

"Yes, I've been expecting your call, Captain Barrows."

Danforth gave Barrows directions to a building in Glyfada and, after telling him to get his ass to the building in less than thirty minutes, abruptly hung up.

"Michael, an Army captain by the name of Simon Barrows is on his way down here," Bob said. "His orders will be to do whatever it takes to inspect each of his four team locations before mid-morning. That's going to be a tall order, considering his teams are spread out all over Greece." Bob waved two sheets of paper in front of Michael. "These just came in over the fax. Barrows is about your age and has an outstanding record. But he's Air Defense Artillery, with no combat experience and minimal weapons training. I want you to go with him. You're Ranger trained and have been in combat. You'll see things that Barrows might miss."

"Trying to get rid of me?" Michael said.

"This will help, Mike. There's not much you can do around here, anyway."

"Okay, Dad, if it's what you want."

Barrows, dressed in a summer weight, Class "A" uniform, showed up in less than the thirty minutes Bob had given him. Bob explained what he wanted him to do and said Michael would accompany him. Barrows seemed relieved to learn that Michael was U.S. Army. The two took off in Barrow's burgundy-red Camaro.

More out of nervousness than real need, Bob called his team together in the conference room. He made them go over their individual assignments, repeating what they had learned about Photos, Argyropoulos, the Kurd, and the Iranian Mullah. He'd had them digging into the backgrounds of Photos and Argyropoulos' family members and associates. But, other than Photos' fellow workers at the university and Argyropoulos' fellow political party members, they found nothing.

When they all finished their briefings, Bob asked Tony about the tail he had asked the Greek Ministry of Public Order to put on the Deputy Prime Minister.

"They're still following the guy. He went to some pre-Olympic Games opening shindig, and then his driver took him home. He's been there ever since. The bastard hasn't done anything that could be considered suspicious. What I can't believe is how easy it was to get the Ministry of Public Order to put a tail on Argyropoulos."

Bob smiled. He didn't want to tell them just yet that he'd had a heart-to-heart telephone conversation with Prime Minister Ierides, who had promised to call Constantine Angelou, the Minister of Public Order. Ierides didn't like the whole idea. He'd told Bob he expected an apology when his administration proved Argyropoulos' innocence.

CHAPTER EIGHTY
AUGUST 13, 2004

"You superstitious?" Simon Barrows asked Michael as he pushed the Camaro to over one hundred miles per hour going north on the National Highway out of Athens.

"No, not particularly," Michael said. "Why do you ask?"

"It's Friday the thirteenth."

"Oh," Michael said. "I didn't even know it was Friday. Been on the road for a couple weeks."

"What's this all about?" Barrows asked.

"What did my father tell you?"

"Nothing," Barrows said.

"Then I guess that's all I can tell you. Nothing."

Barrows went silent for a minute, gunning the engine even faster. "Well, at least tell me this. Why is a U.S. Army Captain hanging out with a bunch of spooks?"

Michael couldn't help himself. He jerked his head and stared at Barrows. "How the hell do you know they're spooks?"

"Oh, come on. They've got Agency written all over them."

Michael's opinion of Barrows went up a notch. He laughed and said, "I'm on leave. My wife and I were in Paris and came down here to visit my folks. My father told me to take a ride with you. That's all I can tell you."

Barrows snatched a quick look at Michael. He smiled and said, "Bullshit!"

Michael looked back at the highway and smiled.

"So, tell me what we're looking for?"

"Anything unusual. Strange people or vehicles around one of your sites, missing missiles or warheads, that kind of thing."

Barrows again jerked his gaze toward Michael. "Missing missiles and warheads. Do you have any idea how big the Nike Hercules missile is? It's forty-one feet long and weighs over ten thousand pounds. They don't just go missing."

Changing the subject, Michael asked Barrows to describe the layout at each missile site. Barrows obliged, including listing the number of Greek and American personnel that manned each of the four sites. He explained that each site included a missile storage area, where an American team was stationed. The Americans maintained two-man control of the nuclear arming plugs in a safe outside the storage area. The Greeks had sole responsibility for the command and control area, which was separated by some distance from the missile storage area.

"So we dictate when the nuclear weapons are armed. If we don't insert the arming plugs in the warheads, the missiles are just several tons of metal and high-explosive accelerant."

"That's right," Barrows said, "although some of the missiles are not nuclear capable. About half of them have HE warheads."

"Why aren't all the missiles mated to nukes?" Michael asked.

"It only takes a few to provide a deterrent, I guess. But, practically, the HE armed warheads can take down one plane, or a close formation of planes, pretty damned well."

"So, these are surface-to-air missiles?"

"That's their primary mission, to knock down enemy aircraft before they can drop their payloads on friendly territory. But they can also be used in surface-to-surface mode. The commanding officer in the command and control trailer can put any of the missiles into a surface-to-surface mission."

Barrows pulled up to the missile site perimeter gate where his "D" Team was located, outside Thivai. The drive had taken forty-five minutes. It was now 2:30 A.M. Barrows was surprised to find the Greek site commander at the entry gate guard shack. Apparently, he had received a phone call from his commander similar to the one Barrows had received from Colonel Swetland.

It took them, along with a team of Greek and American security personnel, thirty minutes to search the area inside the perimeter fence. Then it took another twenty minutes for them to walk the outside of the perimeter fence. When they were satisfied that nothing was amiss, Michael and Barrows ran back to the Camaro and sped south toward the Charlie Team site, near Katsamidi.

Barrows roared south down the highway. It was after 4:00 A.M. when they turned off the highway and entered a winding, two-lane road that meandered through lush forest. The Camaro was not made to take the curving road at speed, forcing Barrows to keep the speedometer below forty miles per hour for most of the way. It was 4:30 in the morning when he pulled up to the "C" Team gate. They performed the same routine inside the perimeter fence at this location, and, again, found everything in order. No missing missiles, no missing warheads, no strangers.

The terrain around the site was steeper and rockier than at Delta Team, which made the exterior search problematical and more time-consuming. Barrows checked his watch when they were done and then looked at his gas gauge. "It's after 5:30. I've got just enough gas to get to a station. It'll be nearly 7:00 before we get to the next site. Are we on some kind of deadline?"

Michael shrugged. "Mid-morning."

Barrows looked shocked. "What's that mean? Nine, ten, what?"

"I'd say ten," Michael answered. "What site is next?"

"Bravo Team," Barrows said. "It's near a little town called Koropi."

CHAPTER EIGHTY-ONE
AUGUST 13, 2004

Grady McMasters met Bob at 7:00 A.M. for breakfast in an out-of-the-way coffee shop near the beach in Glyfada. Over croissants and coffee, Bob briefed the FBI man on the information his team had gathered and the hunches he had formulated.

"Not much to go on," McMasters said, frustration in his voice.

"That's an understatement," Bob said. "The thing that keeps gnawing at my insides is that I could have this whole Olympic Games terrorist thing blown way out of proportion."

"Better safe than sorry," McMasters said. "You do have a lot of capital on the line with the Prime Minister, though. If things don't go the way you think they might, he's going to be pissed, and Washington will probably send you a return airplane ticket and a pink slip."

McMasters' words troubled Bob for an instant, then he smiled and said, "You know my wife has been wanting me to retire for five years now."

McMasters laughed. "Yeah, but I suspect she would have liked to see you take a pension into retirement."

Bob groaned. "That's not even funny, Grady."

"No, I guess it isn't," McMasters said. He seemed to go inside himself for a few seconds, then added, "For what it's worth, I think you're onto something. My men and I will be there if things go down the way you think they might. You can count on our support. I'm sorry we got off to a bad start. I forgot for a while we were both working for the same boss and on the same cause."

Bob reached over and slapped McMasters on the arm. "I'm glad you're covering my back."

McMasters' face reddened. He seemed embarrassed. "I heard your son and his wife arrived in Greece," he said, quickly changing the subject.

Bob nodded. "My wife is fit to be tied. When I called her this morning, she asked where Michael was. I told her I sent him out on a little reconnaissance mission. She didn't seem to appreciate the fact I had involved our son in CIA business."

McMasters raised an eyebrow. "She might have a point."

"Not you too," Bob said. He laughed and explained that Michael had been hanging around playing Bob's bodyguard and he didn't want him around if the shit hit the fan.

"So, like the little fat kid in a street football game, you sent him long, with no intent to ever throw him the football."

"Sort of," Bob said. "Michael had a theory that if the terrorists were to use a nuclear weapon in an attack against the Olympics, they would acquire the weapon from inside the country, versus sneaking it into Greece from another country."

"Where in God's name would they find a nuclear device in Greece?" McMasters asked. "That's a bit farfetched."

"That's what I thought, too. But I figured it was worth checking out anyway."

McMasters nodded to show his agreement, then said, "You're sure Argyropoulos is going to be at the opening ceremony today?"

"Absolutely. He was already planning on attending the opening. His schedule calls for him to make an appearance there. After the Prime Minister officially opens the Games, some of the top people in the government are going to disperse to a variety of parties and other functions. Argyropoulos is supposed to drive to a heliport near the stadium and take a helicopter to Delphi, where there's going to be a ceremony honoring the ancient games that took place on the plain below where the Delphic Oracle sat."

"So, the Olympic Stadium could be the terrorists' target, and Argyropoulos would conveniently be on his way out of town."

CHAPTER EIGHTY-TWO

AUGUST 13, 2004

Mullah Mirzadeh's men carted away the six Christian girls at 7:00 A.M., while the captain of the guard woke the Iraqi pilots. After waking them, the captain and two of his men stood guard outside the pilots' hut while the men washed and dressed. Then they led the pilots to a table set up in the hangar, off to the side of the parked jets. A breakfast of melon, berries, pastries, tea, and coffee was served while patriotic Iraqi music played through speakers arrayed in all four corners of the hangar. After eating, the men were given time to pray.

"Good morning, gentlemen," Mirzadeh said as he entered the hangar.

The pilots greeted the Mullah by standing and bowing.

"Let's perform the preflight check on the airplanes, then we can go over your flight plans."

The pilots followed Mirzadeh to the airplanes, where the six Iraqis separated, each man walking to his assigned jet. Though they were experienced pilots who had performed hundreds of preflight checks, there was no way for them to detect the sabotage that had been done to the electronics that governed the canopy ejection systems and the landing gear. They finished their inspections in twenty minutes, and then congregated at the map table at the back of the hangar.

Mirzadeh uncovered the maps and, using his hand, showed the men their present location.

"This mission is the most important one of your lives," Mirzadeh announced. "It has been imperative that no one outside of you and my men here know that you and the jets are in this location. I hope you understand that I couldn't even divulge our exact location to you before, in case one of you should change your mind about taking part in the mission and . . .." Mirzadeh didn't finish his comment and tipped his head as though to say, I'm sure you understand.

Mirzadeh tapped a finger on the map at a point where two jagged red lines started, near the city of Orumiyeh in western Iran. "We are near here," Mirzadeh said, tapping the spot three times. "You will notice that the lines drawn on the map converge at one location—Athens. The Olympic Games. Where the Vice President of The United States and many other leaders from Christian countries will be in attendance."

Mirzadeh looked at the pilots as they reacted to this news. "You will take different paths to the target, to reduce the risk of radar picking up the planes. If you follow instructions and fly low, you will minimize the chance of being spotted. It is not important that you arrive on target at exactly the same time. In fact, the shock of sequential attacks will be even greater than if all six planes drop their bombs only seconds apart.

"This is a risky mission," he continued. "The odds of all of you returning safely are low. The rewards to those of you who succeed and return will be great. If you accomplish your mission and have the misfortune of not returning safely, I will see that your name lives forever with those of other great Islamic martyrs. You will have places of honor by the side of *Allah*. And your families will live out their days with riches and honor."

Mirzadeh looked for fear in the pilots' eyes; but he was pleased to see they showed only excitement. He let them think about the glory that would accompany their names, whether they lived or died on this mission, and then said to the senior pilot, "Ali, you will fly northwest to the Black Sea, where you will skirt the Turkish coast until you approach the Bulgarian border. From there, you will fly south over the Aegean. Remember, you must fly below radar."

The pilot came to attention and said, "As you command, *Arbob*."

Mirzadeh pointed at two other pilots and explained their parts in the mission. They would fly above Ali's plane, like a three-layer pastry. "I pray that you are not detected by radar," Mirzadeh said; "but if you are, the radar operators will see only one image, one aircraft."

Mirzadeh then traced the routes on the map for the other three pilots. They would follow the border between Turkey and Iraq, to the Turkish border with Syria. They would stay over the common border with Turkey and Syria until they came to the Mediterranean. Their route would then take them between Crete and the Turkish coast, into the Aegean, and northwest to Athens. Like the other three pilots, they would fly in a stacked formation.

"It is time to suit up," Mirzadeh said. He embraced each man in turn, kissing them on each cheek. The Mullah watched the men go to equipment lockers at the opposite side of the hangar. While they dressed in their flight gear, he growled at the captain of the guard, "Have the ground crews remove the camouflage netting and clear the runway of the fake trees and bushes. Then have them tow the planes to the runway. It is time."

CHAPTER EIGHTY-THREE

AUGUST 13, 2004

Michael's eyes burned from lack of sleep. The brightness of the early morning sun only made him feel worse. "You doing okay?" he asked Simon Barrows.

"I sure hope all of this is worth the effort. I'm exhausted and, more importantly, my men and the Greeks we work with probably think I'm nuts."

"You're an officer; your men already think you're nuts. I can't speak for the Greeks, but I suspect they think all Americans are a little weird anyway."

Barrows looked over at Michael and grimaced. "Are you trying to make me feel better?"

"It's not working?" Michael said.

"Not one bit." Barrows pointed down the road. "The road to the Bravo Team site is up ahead." Barrows turned right after a couple hundred yards and drove for a mile until they came to the missile site's entry gate. As with the previous two sites, a Greek Air Force officer stood inside the perimeter fence, waiting for them. But, in this case, he wasn't the base commander. It was a young lieutenant named Alexandros Kantelos.

Michael and Barrows stepped from the Camaro and Barrows introduced Michael. "Where's Major Petroangelos?" Barrows asked the Greek officer.

Kantelos turned to look up at the mountain that separated Koropi from Athens. "He's up at the command and control center."

Barrows nodded, as though he found nothing unusual about what Kantelos had told him. "You got your instructions from higher command?"

Kantelos shrugged. "Yes, but I'm confused. They want us to inventory the missiles and warheads." He smirked and said, "Has someone lost his mind? Where in God's name would one of our missiles go?"

Barrows smiled. "I asked the same question; but it isn't the first time I've been asked to do something that makes no sense at all."

"Well, I suggest we get it over with. Today is supposed to be my day off, and"—he smiled, his face glowing with anticipation—"I have tickets to the opening ceremonies at Olympic Stadium."

Kantelos took the lead and walked Michael, Barrows, and the American duty officer, a Lieutenant Chris Schroeder, through the site. They met up with another Greek officer and two American guards at the entrance to the exclusion area. Michael decided to remain with the American guards while Barrows accompanied the Greek officers inside. He watched them disappear underground, then stared at the row of missile launchers on the other side of the exclusion area fence. All six of the launchers had white missiles mounted to them. The missiles were as long as semitrailers, with four fins at the rear. Strips of red ribbon stuck out from 12-inch by 12-inch doors affixed with screws to each missile, about five feet back from the tips of the noses. Michael guessed this was where the plug would be inserted to arm the warhead.

He looked at the metal door which Barrows and the others had entered and temporarily zoned out, thinking about how nice the king-size bed in his room at the Grand Bretagne Hotel would feel. At first, he didn't pay particular attention to the flash of light that struck his eye. He turned away, closed his eyes, and rubbed them. When he opened his eyes, there was the flash again. It lasted no more than a half-second. This time he tried to pinpoint the source of the light. It seemed to have come from the far side of the exclusion area, from beyond the perimeter fence. Michael moved to his right, to get an unobstructed view of the area there. As with the two other sites, this missile facility was built on a series of plateaus, with the exclusion area on the highest plateau. The headquarters buildings and barracks were on the lowest level, down near the road. Maintenance and storage buildings and a soccer field occupied a plateau in between. From where he stood, Michael had a clear view of the two lower plateaus and the entrance gate to the site.

He moved his gaze slowly from left to right, trying to identify the source of the light flashes. The ground outside the site's perimeter fence, as with the sites at Katsamidi and Thivai, had been cleared out to twenty yards from the fence. Beyond this open space, the site was surrounded by rocky, boulder-strewn ground dotted with scrub oak and juniper bushes.

Barrows and the Greek officers exited the underground storage facility and Michael was about to walk back to join the others, when the bright light shined once again. And this time, Michael saw movement among a grouping of boulders about fifty yards above the exclusion area plateau. He'd originally tried to find the light source out of curiosity—he'd come to the conclusion he was wasting his time on these missile site inspections and was getting bored; but now his senses were on alert. The flash of light could have come from some metal object worn by a shepherd tending his flock. But something made him doubt it.

He met Barrows as he left the exclusion area and waited while the Greek officers locked the gate behind them.

"Anything else?" Kantelos asked Barrows.

Barrows shook his head. "Enjoy the Olympics."

The Greek officer smiled and said, "I intend to."

The Greeks walked away. Barrows and Schroeder went over to the two American guards and chatted with them for a minute, doing what good officers should do, checking on their men's welfare. When

Barrows and Schroeder rejoined Michael, they walked back toward the headquarters area.

"You have access to weapons here?" Michael asked Barrows.

Barrows gave him an incredulous look, as though to say, What additional nonsense are you up to now? He shook his head a few times, then stopped and said, "Of course we have weapons; this *is* a military post. What do you want to do, go hunting for goats?"

Michael stepped closer to Barrows. "That's right, I want to go hunting. But not for goats. I'm more interested in the guy who's up in the rocks above the exclusion area."

Barrows and Schroeder jerked toward the hills and started to stare at the hill above the base; but Michael hissed, "Don't look up there."

Barrows face had gone nearly crimson; Schroeder's face looked pale. "What do you want to do?" Barrows asked.

"Do you have M-16s?"

Barrows nodded. "And .45 caliber pistols."

"We're going to take a nice leisurely walk to wherever your arms room is located. We're going to draw out a couple weapons, and we need to borrow boots and fatigues. These deck shoes and Dockers I'm wearing and your dress uniform ain't going to cut it up in those hills. Can you pull together five of your men?"

"Sure. What are you planning?"

"We're going to try to find out who's spying on this place."

Michael and Barrows used the headquarters building to change into clothes Schroeder supplied. They were nearly dressed when a non-commissioned officer, a Sergeant E-6 named Jackson, and four other enlisted men arrived.

Barrows introduced Michael to his men. "We have a possible problem," Barrows said. "The reason I'm here this morning is to follow up on Intelligence that terrorists might be targeting one of our sites. Captain Danforth here saw at least one man in the hills above the exclusion area. We need to find out who he is. You will take orders from Captain Danforth, do you understand?"

"Yes, sir," Jackson said.

"Thanks," Michael told Barrows. He looked at Schroeder and asked if he could get his hands on a few radios. "I want to be able to keep in touch with you here in the headquarters building."

Schroeder looked crestfallen. "I thought I'd go with—"

"Sorry, Lieutenant, but I need you here. You're going to be responsible for making this work." He waited to get a reaction from Schroeder. When the man nodded, Michael continued. "We need a diversion. I'll bet those missile launchers up there can put on quite a show."

"Yes, sir," Schroeder said. "They make a hell of a lot of noise when they are elevated into firing position."

"I want you to talk with the Greek lieutenant who gave us the tour, what was his name?"

"Kantelos," Barrows said. "But he was about to leave for Athens."

"Call the front gate and tell the guards we need him back here. Lieutenant Kantelos needs to take his men up to the exclusion area and have them raise some of those launchers."

"What can I tell Lieutenant Kantelos?" Schroeder asked.

"Good question," Michael said, smiling at the man. "Tell him just what we know. That we saw someone up in the hills and that we're going to check it out. Raising the launchers will act as a diversion."

"He's going to want to send a squad of his people with us," Barrows said. "He's not going to want to miss out on any action. Besides, the Greeks are responsible for base security."

"I don't want a bunch of armed Greek airmen, who I can't communicate with, up in those rocks. Tell Kantelos to have a squad of his men ready to come to our assistance if we call for help."

Michael turned to Sergeant Jackson. "The sun's pointed at the hillside, directly in the eyes of whoever is up there. I noticed there are

several personal vehicles parked here, screened by the barracks building. Can you and your men get into one of those cars, with your
weapons, without being seen?"

Jackson said they could. "They'll see us leave the base, though," he
said.

"That's exactly what I want them to see. When you get down the
road far enough so it will appear you've left for town, take the access
road up toward the command and control center. When you get
halfway up the mountain, pull over and work your way into the hills.
I want you to come in from above whoever's up there. Captain
Barrows and I are going to come in from the other side. If there are
bad guys in the rocks behind the exclusion area, I suspect they'll be
looking down over the site, not up toward the mountain. We'll take
one of the radios; your team and Lieutenant Schroeder will each have
one. Unless we're fired upon, I want everyone to maintain radio
silence. I'll key the radio mike—two clicks—when we're in position,
and *if* we've sighted any bad guys. Jackson, three clicks on your radio
will indicate you're in position."

"Shouldn't we alert headquarters in Elefsis?" Schroeder asked.

"Let's wait and see what we find," Barrows said. "I don't want to
give the desk jockeys there heart attacks over some goat herder who
accidentally wandered into the area." Barrows waited for Schroeder to
respond. When the lieutenant nodded his understanding, Barrows
added, "Schroeder, your job is to monitor the radios. You call headquarters if you hear shots fired."

"Okay, guys, let's do it," Michael said.

CHAPTER EIGHTY-FOUR

AUGUST 13, 2004

A ground crew bulldozed the hundreds of trees and shrubs that had been scattered around the runway to camouflage the brown-colored tarmac. A second crew used a half-ton truck to tow the first of the six Mirage jets onto the runway. After unhooking the hitch from the jet, the crew raced back to the hangar and brought out the second aircraft. When all the planes were lined up, one behind the other on the tarmac, the pilots harnessed into their seats, the canopies latched, Mirzadeh radioed to Ali, the senior pilot, to start his engine.

"*Hammurabi's Hammer* begins," Mirzadeh said into the microphone, using the mission's code name. "*Allah* will watch over you. The infidels will learn to never violate Islamic soil again."

"*Inshallah*," Ali said.

"Yes, God willing," Mirzadeh said.

The roar of six jet engines filled the air, reverberating off the hills forming the sides of Mirzadeh's secret valley airfield. The ground trembled as though an earthquake had begun.

The Mullah said a silent prayer for the success of the mission, while he watched the planes shoot skyward, their afterburners glowing red-hot. When they banked away from the valley and Mirzadeh could no longer see or hear them, he turned to his captain of the guard and growled, "Dismantle the place, and blow the charges in the hills. I want the airfield covered with enough debris that no one will ever be able to find any evidence the planes took off from Iran."

"Yes, *Arbob*, it will be done."

Mirzadeh noticed a hint of doubt showing on the captain's face. "Is something bothering you, Homayoun?"

"No, *Arbob* . . . it's just that I can't figure out how the pilots will be able to penetrate all the way into Greece without being seen. Even flying low in a stacked formation won't protect them all the way into Athens."

Mirzadeh felt his face tighten and go hot. He almost blurted an angry retort, but then decided it was a logical question from an intelligent man. Homayoun had been a valuable supporter. He deserved respect.

"You must have faith, Homayoun. In *Allah* and in me. Do you have that faith?"

"Of course, *Arbob.*"

"Good," Mirzadeh said.

While Homayoun directed his men in the destruction of the secret airfield, Mirzadeh told his driver to bring around his Land Rover. It was time to get away from here. Homayoun would take care of everything. He would order his men to transport the supplies, generators, and other equipment out of the valley, and he would detonate the explosives planted in the hills, swamping the huts and the airfield in rock and dirt.

Mirzadeh pictured the Mirage jets flying to their destination. He suppressed a smile. It wouldn't do for his driver to think he was anything but serious and severe. He turned to look out the passenger side window and again prayed that the plan would work. The planes were nothing but sacrificial goats. The pilots were as good as dead the instant they took off.

CHAPTER EIGHTY-FIVE

AUGUST 13, 2004

Ever since the American-led invasion of Iraq, U.S. AWACS planes had flown regularly scheduled flights over the area encompassing Iraq and its borders with Kuwait, Saudi Arabia, Turkey, Iran, and Syria. Usually these aircraft were accompanied by fighter planes, such as F-16 Fighting Falcons, to "cover their backs." But there were no planes available to provide cover at this time, so the surveillance planes took off solo. The American military tried to have at least one plane in the air at all times; however, this was not always possible. Two of the AWACS aircraft were down for maintenance when Jack Cole's request arrived at the Pentagon. The third plane assigned to this theatre of operation was being refueled in mid-air.

The planes, through an agreement with the countries, flew across the borders of Kuwait, Saudi Arabia, and Turkey. In the cases of Iran and Syria, the planes only approached the borders.

But there was no agreement needed for the National Reconnaissance Office to direct satellites in outer space to look down on Iran and Syria. Although the NRO had many satellites, and some of those satellites criss-crossed the same areas of the Earth, it wasn't possible for the NRO's "eyes in the sky" to watch every part of the planet twenty-four hours a day.

So, none of the NRO's satellites picked up the six Mirage jets as they took off from the secret airfield in western Iran. Nor did they spy the men moving supplies and equipment from the airfield. But one of the satellites did pick up the image of a massive explosion near the Iraqi and Turkish borders with Iran. The images the satellite captured were electronically transmitted to NRO headquarters. This served to bring the area to the attention of analysts who went to work on the photographs. When they decided the images were of man-made explosions, they conveyed this information through channels to CIA headquarters, which, in turn, contacted the Pentagon to see if any of the military units in northern Iraq had detected any sort of explosion in the general area.

The upshot of this burst of activity that started with the NRO and ended with the Central Command in Iraq was that the satellite photos were written off as nothing more than an anomaly. Some mining excavation work, perhaps.

Just as the excitement of all those involved with trying to decipher the strange satellite images had subsided, another stimulus caused a tidal wave of adrenaline to burst upon several military commands. It started with a calm, but concise message transmitted from the now-refueled AWACS plane flying thirty thousand feet above western Turkey.

"This is AWACS 1402. We've got a fast moving bird flying due west along the border between Syria and Turkey. He's flying low and is twenty miles from the Aegean."

"You have an ID?" Air Force Command answered.

The AWACS Intelligence Officer swallowed hard and wondered if this was the sort of incident that ruined careers. "I hit it with an IFF command." He paused a moment and said, "It came back as Iraqi Air Force."

"The Identification Friend or Foe System told you the plane was Iraqi? That's impossible. We destroyed the whole Iraqi Air Force. They don't have any planes or pilots left."

"That's what I thought, too," the Intel Officer said.

"Keep an eye on the plane," headquarters ordered. "I'll get back to you; I've got another alert coming in."

The Communications Officer at Air Force Command took the second call, which was coming in from AWACS 1435—one of the planes that had been down for maintenance and had just been released for duty—flying along the Turkish Black Sea coast. By the time he had finished with the Intel Officer on the second AWACS flight, the Commo Officer knew he had a serious problem. He bumped the information he had gathered from the two AWACS flights up to higher command. The Colonel he talked with there already seemed to be a little excited. The news the Communications Officer passed on to the Colonel seemed to shock the man.

"I want you to tell your pilots to patch directly into here. Do you understand?"

"Yes, sir," the Communications Officer said. "What's going on?"

"Just do as I ordered. NOW!"

The Commander in Chief of 7th Army, United States Army in Europe, headquartered in Heidelberg, Germany, had authority over all U.S. military operations in Europe and the Middle East. The good thing about the way the U.S. military was constituted was that lower level commands had been empowered to make tactical decisions without having to wait for the Commander in Chief to approve every action. But when it came to authorizing the use of nuclear weapons, not even the Commander in Chief of USAREUR and 7th Army had that kind of authority. While the Commander waited for the White House to authorize the use of tactical nukes, he contacted his counterpart at the U.S. Navy and told him he needed intercept aircraft off a carrier in the Mediterranean. He ordered the Southern Command to go from DEFCON 5—the normal peacetime readiness condition—to DEFCON 4—the normal increased Intelligence and strengthened security measures condition. Changes in DEFCON status occurred in sequence. He already knew that they would have to quickly move to DEFCON 1, unless the situation very quickly changed for the better. He contacted NATO Headquarters and had them put their units on alert, including the Nike Hercules missile sites in Turkey and Greece.

Thirty minutes after taking this action, he raised the defense condition from DEFCON 4 to DEFCON 3, putting the units on above-normal force readiness. Minutes later he ordered all units in Greece and Turkey to go to DEFCON 2, and then to DEFCON 1— maximum force readiness.

CHAPTER EIGHTY-SIX

AUGUST 13, 2004

Lieutenant Chris Schroeder's left leg jackhammered the floor while his right hand tapped a pencil against his desktop. He hadn't been this nervous since the night he'd lost his virginity. The radio sat in front of him. He knew that neither Danforth and Barrows, nor Jackson and his team could have gotten into place yet, but he wanted to know what was going on out behind the base. Jesus, he thought, what if there *are* terrorists up in the hills.

"Lieutenant, you're driving me crazy with that tapping," Sergeant James Jefferson, the unit's Crypto Clerk, said.

Schroeder gave Jefferson an apologetic look and stood. He began pacing the room, hoping what Danforth had seen in the hills was nothing more than a goat herder.

"Lieutenant, do you have to keep pacing?"

Schroeder sighed and plopped back down in a chair. He willed himself to calm down and had just about done so, when the teletype machine behind him exploded with activity, sending Schroeder to his feet and his stomach into his throat. He moved to the machine and felt as though his heart had stopped. He turned to Jefferson. "Get the cards out of the vault," he said, "we've got a TOP SECRET/CRYPTO message coming in."

"Probably another damned exercise," Jefferson said. "Those jerks at headquarters are always coming up with ways to ruin a perfectly good day."

Schroeder and Jefferson went through the coded cards and verified that the identification code used in the message coming from Missile

Command Headquarters in Frankfurt, Germany, was valid. The message text was also coded. Jefferson took the appropriate one-time pad from the vault and used it to decode the message. By the time he was three-quarters of the way through it, his hands were shaking. He slid the message and the one-time pad to Lieutenant Schroeder, who decrypted the message. They compared their work and found they had identical results:

> All units of 37th USAAD to immediately go from DEF-
> CON 5 to DEFCON 4.

They had barely finished decoding the message, when a second coded message came through. This ordered them to go to DEFCON 3. Within thirty minutes, they had gone to DEFCON 1. All warheads were to be armed. Foreign national units were being directed to elevate missiles to firing position. Firing authorization and target information would be provided by separate message. All leaves and passes were cancelled. Acknowledgement of the messages and confirmation of actions taken were requested.

Jefferson stared wide-eyed at Schroeder. "What the hell is going on, Lieutenant? We've gone from DEFCON 5 to DEFCON 1 in less than an hour."

Schroeder pointed a finger at Jefferson. "Prepare a response to the message. Tell them we'll comply. I'm going to call Lieutenant Kantelos to see if he has received orders from his people or from NATO."

"What about Captain Barrows and the other men?" Jefferson asked.

"Shit!" Schroeder rushed to the table where he'd left the radio. He reached for it as two squawks burst from it. Captains Danforth and Barrows were already in place . . . and they'd seen intruders among the rocks.

Schroeder snatched the landline receiver from its cradle and called Elefsis. Normally, if there was a problem, he would call the 37th

USAAD headquarters, but since Barrows, the 37th's Commanding Officer was here, he figured Elefsis was the appropriate alternative.

"Sergeant Brewster speaking, sir; what can I—"

"Brewster, it's Lieutenant Schroeder at B team. We've got intruders in the hills behind the site. Captain Barrows and some of our men are up there trying to find out what they're up to."

"My God, on top of everything else," Brewster said. "We got people running around here like chickens with their heads cut off. What the hell is going on, Lieutenant?"

"Go find the Colonel, Brewster," Schroeder ordered. "I—"

An explosion stopped Schroeder in mid-sentence. Then a second explosion sounded, followed by the unmistakable staccato bursts of automatic weapons fire.

CHAPTER EIGHTY-SEVEN

AUGUST 13, 2004

The AWACS planes repositioned themselves to better track the two jets they had spied earlier. The AWACS personnel were now communicating directly with USAREUR Headquarters, which had come to the conclusion the two jets were vectoring in on the Aegean. One Mirage had pretty much followed the southern border of Turkey, while the second plane flew along Turkey's northern border. In the last ten minutes, as the jets reached the Aegean, they'd started to narrow the distance between themselves.

The USAREUR Commander in Chief paced the OPS Center floor, a telephone earpiece over one ear, the telephone cord tethering him to a connection under a long table supporting a dozen color monitors displaying maps of the Middle East and Southern Europe. Two of the monitors tracked the incoming aircraft, showing lines inching from east to west, over the Aegean Sea.

"These two bogies are leaving Turkish air space and will soon be out of range of the Nike sites in Turkey," the USAREUR commander said. "We need authorization to take them out. The Turks didn't even have time to get their planes off the ground."

"We're waiting for the White House, General," the General in the Pentagon said. "The planes from the Abraham Lincoln are on their way. They'll be able to handle the Mirages. I don't think we'll need the missiles. The Greek Air Force already has fighters in the air. They'll provide backup."

"Yeah, but what if we do need them? What if there are more planes moving toward Greece, planes we haven't detected yet?"

"Let's not be melodramatic, General. I'm sure—"

Before the General at the Pentagon could finish, someone tapped the USAREUR Commander on the arm. The General turned while saying into the telephone, "Hold one second."

"We just got another call from one of the AWACS planes. They spotted a third aircraft."

"Where?"

"Coming in on the same azimuth as the first one they spotted. It appears it was flying directly below the first plane."

The USAREUR Commanding General turned back to the monitors and saw a third line pop up on one of the screens. "General, we got a third bogey."

The Pentagon General responded after a couple seconds. "Yeah, I see it here on our monitors. Give me a second."

The USAREUR Commander heard the Pentagon General order someone to put all three bogies on one screen. A half-minute passed, then he heard a moan, "Oh, my God, they're converging toward Athens." Pause. "The Olympics."

Now it made some sense, the USAREUR Commander thought. The target anyway. He couldn't figure out the Iraqi IFF signal, or from where the planes had originated. But he suddenly knew without a doubt some terrorist group had gotten hold of three French Mirage aircraft that had been sold years earlier to Saddam Hussein. He had a brief recollection that Saddam had moved some of his aircraft across the border into Iran; but that fact wasn't important at the moment. Stopping these fucking planes before they crossed the Aegean into Greece was what mattered.

"How many planes left the Abraham Lincoln?" he shouted.

"Two," the Pentagon General answered.

"Two! You've got to be kidding me. How the hell are two planes going to intercept three jets coming from different locations? Look at the flight paths of the Mirages. They won't join up until all three are right over Athens. And there could be more jets."

The silence over the line told the USAREUR Commander that what he just said resonated with the Pentagon General. When the man finally spoke, his voice was cold and steely. "I'm going to order our planes to take out the two southern-most Mirages. I'll get you authorization from the President to use the Nikes in no more than a minute. The missiles will have to take out the third bogey before it gets anywhere near Athens."

The USAREUR Commander said a silent prayer that there were no other jets approaching Athens.

CHAPTER EIGHTY-EIGHT

AUGUST 13, 2004

All the computer monitors at the CIA office in Glyfada were online with the War Room at CIA Headquarters at Langley. Additionally, Bob was on an open line to Jack Cole in the War Room.

When Bob learned that the White House had authorized arming the nuclear warheads on the Nike Hercules missiles at Greek sites, his heart felt as though it did a full gainer into his stomach. Michael's comment to him about the terrorists using a nuclear weapon already in Greece flashed before his eyes like a digital signboard. In all the years the U.S. had nukes in Greece, it had never gone to DEFCON 1 and had never authorized installing the arming plugs in the nuclear warheads mounted to Nike Hercules missiles. Bob's hands were vibrating like tuning forks.

Bob told Tony Fratangelo to try to raise Michael. Michael had called the Glyfada office after he and Barrows had completed each inspection at "D" Team and "C" Team. The last Bob had heard was that they were on their way to the "B" Team site near Koropi.

Tony tried Michael's cell phone number, but there was no answer. He called the 37th's headquarters and got the telephone number at "B" Team from a very stressed out soldier. He called "B" Team, talked briefly with Lieutenant Schroeder, and then yelled to Bob, "I've got a Lieutenant Schroeder on the line," he called to Bob. "He says Michael's there."

Bob motioned at Stacey Frederick and told her to pick up the line to the CIA War Room. Then he thought for a couple seconds about what he would say to Lieutenant Schroeder that would get the young man's attention. Saying he was Michael Danforth's father and that he was worried sick about him wouldn't get him very far, especially in the midst of a DEFCON 1 status. He hit the second lit button on his telephone console and said, "This is Bob Danforth. I'm Captain Michael Danforth's father and the senior Central Intelligence Agency Officer in Greece." He paused for a long moment and said, "Did all of that get through to you, Lieutenant Schroeder?"

"Uh-huh," Schroeder said, sounding overwhelmed and stressed. "Yes, sir."

"I need you to get Captain Danforth on the phone," Bob said.

"I can't do that, sir," Schroeder said.

"Why not?" Bob demanded.

"He and Captain Barrows and a squad of our men are outside the perimeter fence. Captain Danforth thought he saw movement there and went out to check on it."

"And?" Bob said.

"They signaled me about thirty minutes ago that they had seen the intruders. The next thing I heard was a couple explosions and automatic weapons fire."

Oh, Jesus, Bob thought. "What did you mean when you said 'they signaled you'?"

"On the radio, sir."

"So you're in contact with them?"

"Well, sort of. Captain Danforth told me not to break radio silence. He told me to call headquarters if we heard gunfire. I did that; but they can't send any men down here to help because of the alert status we're in. I tried the Greeks; but they've got the same problem, and I don't have enough men here to accomplish our mission *and* help Captain Danforth."

Bob could tell the pressure was starting to get to Schroeder. He modulated his tone and said, "Does Captain Danforth know we've gone to DEFCON 1?"

"How do you know we've gone—"

"Not now, Lieutenant. Just answer the question."

"No, sir. It happened after he and Captain Barrows left."

"Here's what I want you to do, Schroeder," Bob said. "Are you listening?"

"Yes, sir."

"Radio Captain Danforth and tell him he has to return to your location and call me immediately."

"He's not going to want to—"

"Tell him it's on orders from his father, and tell him it's not for personal reasons. It's business. National security business."

CHAPTER EIGHTY-NINE

AUGUST 13, 2004

The two-man plainclothes police team from the Ministry of Public Order sat in their vehicle and watched Dimitris Argyropoulos and his aide, Ari Stokolos, climb the steps of the residence in Syngrou, south of the Acropolis. It was 8:40 A.M. The two-story house was a massive affair, with white stone columns and a broad expanse of lawn, making it look more like an ancient temple than a residence. The man sitting in the passenger seat trained his binoculars on the Deputy Prime Minister.

When Argyropoulos and Stokolos were still three meters from the front entry, the door opened and a man stepped onto the porch. The man shook his visitors' hands. Then he led Argyropoulos and Stokolos inside.

"Who the hell is that?" the driver asked.

"I don't know," the other policeman said. "He looks familiar, though." He scratched his head and added, "Call in the address. Maybe the computer knows who lives here."

The driver called the dispatcher on his radio and gave the house address to the woman who answered. He told her it was important to have a quick answer.

The dispatcher returned the call in less than ten minutes. "Nicolaos Koufos," she said. "The house belongs to Nicolaos Koufos."

"Who in God's name is Nicolaos Koufos?" the driver asked.

"The head of the Economic Development Department in the Ministry of Finance," the second cop said before the dispatcher could answer the question.

"Thanks," the driver told the dispatcher and terminated the radio call. "How do you know Koufos?" he asked.

"I met him at a reception for our boss."

"You mean Serifides, the Senior Inspector?"

"No, I mean the big boss, Constantine Angelou. Nicolaos Koufos is Angelou's cousin."

The driver's jaw dropped. "Wait a minute; let me think about this for a second. We're following Argyropoulos because someone suspects him of being associated with *Greek Spring*. Argyropoulos visits Koufos. And Koufos is Angelou's cousin. So, if Argyropoulos is a terrorist, and Koufos is a terrorist, where does that put Constantine Angelou?"

The policeman in the passenger seat dropped the binoculars in his lap, covered his face with his hands, and groaned. "Equally important, where does that leave us?" He dropped his hands and stared at his partner. "In six feet of horse shit. And neither of us is close to six feet tall."

CHAPTER NINETY

AUGUST 13, 2004

Bob tried to hide his nervousness, but with each passing minute, he was finding it more and more difficult. It had been fifteen minutes since he'd talked with Lieutenant Schroeder, and still no word from Michael. He had sent his son out on what he thought was a boondoggle. It had turned into a dangerous, possibly life-threatening assignment.

He was starting another circuit of the office, when Tony came up behind him and said, "You got a minute?"

Bob stopped and turned. "What is it?"

"My contact at the Ministry of Public Order is on the phone. He said he's in a predicament."

"What sort of predicament?"

"He wouldn't say on the phone. He wants to meet with us."

"What do you want to do?" Bob asked.

"I trust this guy; I think we should have him come here."

"Then do it." Bob looked at his watch. "I'm only going to be here another hour before I have to go to the Olympic Stadium."

Tony walked over to a telephone and told the man on the line where he was located and to come over as fast as possible.

Then Sam Goodwin shouted, "Bob, Michael's on line two."

The office went dead quiet as Bob rushed over to his desk and punched the button for the second line. The members of his team knew that Michael had gotten into the middle of some action near a nuclear weapons site south of Athens. They'd watched Bob pace the floor for the last fifteen minutes and now stared in his direction while he lifted the receiver.

"Mike, are you okay?"

"I'm fine. We had visitors behind the missile site near Koropi. Two are now dead, two captured. What's going on, Dad?"

Bob realized he was holding his breath. He let it out of his lungs slowly. "Remember what you told me, about how you thought the terrorists might get a nuclear weapon?"

"Sure. I said they would have an easier time getting one that was already in Greece, than trying to import one into the country."

"What have you found at the sites you've visited?" Bob asked.

"So far, other than the armed men behind this site, everything's been fine. All the weapons are in place. The Captain who commands the 37th Detachment has been with me on the visits to three of the sites. He just called down to the fourth site and talked with both the American team leader and the Greek site commander. They said everything was okay there, too. All weapons accounted for."

"Besides the men you found behind the site you're at, has there been anything unusual at any of the sites?"

After a few seconds, Michael said, "Nothing I can think of. Hold on and let me ask Captain Barrows."

Bob heard a muffled conversation, and then Michael came back on. "Captain Barrows says he hasn't seen anything really unusual."

"Ask him to explain *really unusual*."

Bob heard another muffled conversation. Then Michael said, "He tells me it is very unusual for the Greek missile site commander to spend so much time up at the command and control area. At the other two sites he and I visited, and at the one he called a minute ago, the site commanders were inside the perimeter of the base where the missiles are stored. The commander at the site we're at hasn't shown his face since we got here."

"Where's the command and control area?" Bob asked.

"Each of them is on high ground," Michael said, "where the radar equipment can get line of sight on aircraft. This one is at least a couple miles away from the missile storage area. The firing of a missile is controlled by an officer in a command and control trailer on top of the mountain."

"So, the officer in the command and control trailer dictates when a missile is fired and where the missile goes."

"That's my understanding," Michael said, "but keep in mind that Air Defense Artillery isn't my specialty."

As minor as it seemed, the absence of the Greek base commander from the missile storage area, and his presence at the command and control area bothered Bob. It was just the sort of anomaly that couldn't be ignored. And now that the White House had authorized the use of nukes, his internal radar was thrumming. If a renegade Greek officer with control over missiles with nuclear warheads was in cahoots with terrorists, there could be a disaster in the making. And Bob knew he didn't have time to call in the cavalry. Besides, if he bumped this to the Greeks or to the U.S. higher military commands, he suspected it would take too long for them to react. It was already 9:00 A.M. Bob shook his head, as though to clear cobwebs in his brain. If the terrorists were planning an attack, and if the Olympic Stadium was the target, the timing was about right. The stadium would soon be packed with most of the Greek Government hierarchy, not to mention dignitaries from all over the globe, including the U.S. Vice President.

"I hate to get you more involved, Mike; but I have no other choice. You need to find out if there's something going on at the command and control area there."

"You think the Commanding Officer here—"

"I don't know what I think; but I can't afford to ignore any possibility."

"I understand, Dad. I'll get right on it. And don't forget that I've been trained for this kind of thing."

"No one's been trained for this, Mike. Keep your head down and your eyes open." Bob swallowed and said, "I love you, son."

CHAPTER NINETY-ONE
AUGUST 13, 2004

The two F/A-18Ds from the U.S.S. Abraham Lincoln followed the instructions relayed by the AWACS plane now circling the western coast of Turkey near Kushadasi and the ancient city of Ephesus. The AWACS plane had plotted the flights of two of the Mirages and sent the Iraqi planes' locations to the F/A-18Ds. The American jets screamed at over the speed of sound toward intercept points for the two Mirages. If all went as planned, the jets would pick up the southern-most of the Mirages off the tip of the Attican Peninsula.

At 0902 hours, the first F/A-18D raised one of the Mirages on its radar and the navigator radioed this information to the Abraham Lincoln.

"You have authorization to proceed," the Officer of the Deck radioed back to the American jet.

"It's a GO," the navigator told his pilot.

"Roger," the pilot replied. Just as he placed the crosshairs of his targeting radar on the Mirage, he heard his navigator release a little yelp and shout, "Holy shit! Another plane just popped up on the screen. One right on top of the other."

The pilot got tone indicating he was locked onto his target, and released an AIM 9 *Sidewinder* missile. He lost sight of the missile's trail after two seconds, but was able to follow its path on his radar screen. He banked his aircraft to the left and tracked the new aircraft his navigator spotted. He shot an IFF signal at this surprise airplane and got a bogey indicator. His radar screen bloomed and the first Mirage's heat signature disappeared. It took a minute to get a fix on the second aircraft—its pilot had taken evasive action. When he got tone on the second plane, he fired another *Sidewinder*, splashing this bogey as well.

"Splash two bogeys," the pilot said into his helmet microphone.

An almost identical scenario played out with the second F/A-18D and its Mirage. Except there was no surprise second aircraft.

The report of the destruction of the three Mirages swept across the communications systems of the U.S. military command and on to the White House and CIA War Room. Bob heard the news at the same time it reached the CIA facility.

"Three down and one to go," Tony said as the office erupted with shouts.

The shouting immediately died down as all eyes in the room followed the track of what they thought was the last Mirage. The plane had penetrated Greek air space about one hundred fifty miles north of Athens. It was speeding down the heart of the country toward the capital city.

"One of the F/A-18Ds is going after the last Mirage," Bob heard Jack Cole say into the telephone.

Someone else at CIA Headquarters said, "Sonofabitch, do our planes have enough fuel to go after that Mirage and make it back to their ship?"

"They can land in Athens, if necessary," Bob said. "Come on boys, get that bastard."

Then Jack's voice came over the receiver again. "A fourth Mirage is down; the F/A-18Ds are turning around."

"What happened?" Bob said.

"One of the Greek Nike Hercules sites took out the Mirage with a missile." Jack laughed and added, "They used a missile with an HE warhead; they never had to fire one of the nukes."

"Thank God," Bob whispered. "Thank God." One of the things that had been nagging at him all along was what the political fallout would be over a U.S. nuclear weapon being fired over Greece. Now it was moot.

"We dodged a big bullet this time, Bob," Jack said.

"Four big bullets," Bob said. "We have any idea where the jets came from?"

"Not yet, but we're working on it." He hesitated and said, "We just got word that the Nike sites in Greece and Turkey are being ordered to stand down. We're going from DEFCON 1 to DEFCON 2. I'm sure we'll be back to DEFCON 5 in less than an hour."

And then all hell broke loose.

A voice came over the War Room communications system. "We've got two more planes coming down the spine of the country. They're no more than fifty miles from Athens."

Bob felt his pulse explode in his throat. He knew without calculating that the American jets were too far south to deal with the two new bogeys. If the Nike sites didn't respond in time, the only chance remaining was that the Greek Air Force would be able to react.

Then the pain in Bob's head got even worse. What if one or more of the Iraqi jets got through the air defense net around Athens and dropped its ordnance on the Olympic venue? And what if those jets are carrying nuclear devices? Maybe Michael's theory had been correct in only one respect.

The connection to the CIA War Room seemed to have been lost. All was quiet. Then shouts went up as word spread from the Greek fighter pilots to their command headquarters, all the way through the U.S. military command structure, and to CIA Headquarters that the Greek Air Force pilots had taken out the two jets.

But Bob felt no elation. A sudden feeling of terror assaulted his brain, making his body go hot and his hands feel clammy. Time seemed to tick by in Bob's brain as though it was the metronome-like sound on some game show. Michael's theory about the terrorists possibly getting their hands on a nuclear device caused his head to ache and his throat to tighten. If the commander of the missile site at which Michael was located had gone over to the other side, then he could very well be planning to fire a nuclear warhead at Athens. Bob suddenly considered the possibility the Iraqi jets were decoys. They'd accomplished their mission—to get the Nike sites to go on alert, to trick the Americans into arming nuclear warheads.

"Jack," he shouted, "I need you to do me a favor," Bob said.

"Another favor? What now?"

"Could you arrange to have the two F/A-18Ds turn around?"

"Oh shit, what the hell is on your mind now? You already heard those jets are low on fuel. They can barely get back to their carrier as it is."

"I need thirty minutes, that's all, Jack. I need those planes circling Athens for the next half hour. In the meantime, you can get clearance for the F/A-18Ds to land in Athens."

"You either tell me what's on your mind, or you can forget about your little favor."

"There's something very strange about these Mirages. Those pilots never had a chance. Even coming in low the way they did wouldn't give them protection from satellite or AWACS surveillance. What did they think they were going to accomplish?"

"Those bastards came damn close to Athens, even with all our satellite and AWACS coverage. Besides, it wouldn't be the first time some Middle Eastern suicidal assholes blew themselves up for no reason at all."

"Maybe there *was* a reason," Bob said. "Maybe they accomplished their mission after all. Maybe all they wanted to do was to scare us into inserting the arming plugs into the nuclear weapons."

"You're reading too many novels, Bob."

"Just thirty minutes," Bob said.

"What's going to happen in thirty minutes?" Jack asked.

"Michael's checking out one of the Greek missile sites. We may have—"

"Did you say Michael?" Jack said, his voice a hoarse whisper, as though he was trying to make sure no one on his end of the line heard him. "What the hell are you thinking? You've got a U.S. Army officer running around Greece without orders. You ruined your own military career years ago with the same sort of cowboy tactics. Are you trying to ruin Michael's, too?"

"Jack, I had no other choice. It was either take a chance with Mike's career, or do nothing and see tens of thousands of people murdered."

"There's another choice," Jack said. "You could be hallucinating."

"I don't think—"

"Right, you don't think."

Bob had never heard Jack so angry, and his old friend had never talked to him like this before.

"I'll try to get your half hour, Bob; but if you're wrong, you need to think about putting in your papers. And, if you're wrong, I hope you haven't fucked up Mike's future, too."

CHAPTER NINETY-TWO

AUGUST 13, 2004

Bob saw Tony and another man coming across the bull pen area of the Glyfada office. He stood and greeted the man, Antonio Serifides. The three moved to Bob's private office. Bob pointed at the two chairs in front of his desk and said, "Please sit down."

Serifides was a pale, thin, almost emaciated-looking man with brown hair and amber-colored eyes. He was nattily dressed in a blue blazer, gray slacks, white shirt, and gold tie. But, Bob thought, the most obvious aspect of the man was the worried look on his face.

"You told Tony you had a possible problem," Bob said.

Serifides' Adams apple bobbed and he pulled at his shirt collar. "All the way over here I thought about just turning around and forgetting about my conversation with Tony," he said. "I don't know if I'm doing the right thing coming here."

"Why don't you tell us what's on your mind? Maybe we can be of assistance."

The man looked down at his feet for a few seconds, and then looked back at Bob and related what he had learned from the surveillance team he'd put on Deputy Prime Minister Argyropoulos. "Do you see why I was hesitant to come over here?"

"You're worried that your boss, Constantine Angelou, might be in with Argyropoulos, and, if you say something to him about following Argyropoulos to Nicolaos Koufos' house, you're afraid he'll try to divert you and your men away to protect Argyropoulos and Koufos."

Serifides nodded and said, "That's only part of what I'm worried about. If Argyropoulos is tied to the terrorists, as you believe he is, and if Koufos is in league with them as well, then my life could be in jeopardy. These people have murdered Greek law enforcement people before."

It struck Bob that there must be a lot of good men and women working in Greek law enforcement who had, for years, been afraid to do the right thing out of fear of retaliation. All because of traitors working in high positions in Greek Government.

"Do you really believe your boss, Angelou, might be allied with the terrorists, too? Maybe he's not."

"Yes, that's correct. But, at the very least, won't he try to protect his cousin, Nicolaos Koufos?"

"It's possible," Bob answered, "but maybe we should give Angelou the benefit of the doubt."

"I can't take this information to him; it's too risky."

Bob thought about the situation for a moment, and then said, "Tell me about this man Koufos."

"He's in the Finance Ministry. A brain. But he's a follower, easily influenced. I could see how a man like Argyropoulos could lead Koufos around by the nose."

"What's the history behind Koufos' relationship with Argyropoulos?" Tony asked.

"They were university students together and were part of the 1973 demonstrations in Athens. A lot of the leaders of our country rose from the ranks of students who opposed the junta. They have become heroes to a lot of our people."

"Where's Argyropoulos now?" Bob asked.

"My men are still following him. He's already at the Olympic Stadium."

Bob felt his career coming to an ignominious end. And what of Michael's career? Would Argyropoulos go to the Olympic Stadium if terrorists were about to attack it? "And how about Koufos?"

"He didn't leave his home after Argyropoulos left there. I assigned a second team to watch the house."

Bob looked at his watch. He had twenty-four minutes left of the thirty Jack had allotted him. He was already out on a limb; he might as well go all the way.

"Inspector Serifides, I think there is a conspiracy to attack the Olympic Stadium, and I believe the terrorists are going to try to use a nuclear weapon in that attack."

Serifides' face went white. "How is that possible, Mr. Danforth?"

"Not only do I think it's possible; I think it's highly probable."

"But that makes no sense." He looked at Tony. "You told me you were absolutely certain Argyropoulos was aligned with the terrorists. Would he be at the stadium if he knew it was about to be blown up?"

Bob saw Tony's face redden and came to his rescue.

"It does seem improbable, unless he isn't aware of the terrorists' plan. Maybe he will be just one more sacrificial goat."

"Gamo panageia," Serifides cursed. "What can we do?"

"There's one thing *you* can do. Call the men watching Koufos. Order them to go into his home with force. Tell them to say he's under arrest for terrorist acts. Put pressure on the man. If he's the follower you say he is, maybe he'll fold." Bob hunched his shoulders. "It's worth a try."

Bob stood and said he had to leave for the stadium.

"What are you going to do there?" Tony asked, his eyes wide and his face now white, too. "If you're correct about an attack, you'll be committing suicide."

Bob came around his desk and shook Serifides' hand and slapped Tony on the shoulder. "I've got two aces up my sleeve," he said. "One ace is your men at Koufos' home. Maybe they'll learn something that will put a stop to whatever the terrorists have planned."

Tony looked incredulous. "And the second ace?" he said.

"I'll let you in on that a little later. Right now I need to go to the stadium. Inspector, would you like to accompany Tony and me there? I may need your services."

Serifides' mouth dropped open and his eyes darted from Tony to Bob, and back again to Tony. He looked as though he was trying to come up with a reason not to accompany them to the Olympic Stadium. Finally, a resigned expression came over his face and he nodded.

CHAPTER NINETY-THREE

AUGUST 13, 2004

Major Lambros Petroangelos read the teletype message that had just come in and ripped it into postage stamp-sized pieces. He dropped the pieces to the floor of the command and control trailer. As he had anticipated, once the Iraqi jets were no longer a threat, his unit, along with all other military units in Greece, would be ordered to stand down. His main concern at the moment was how soon the Americans at the exclusion area would receive the same order. Once that happened, they would demand access to the exclusion area so they could remove the arm plugs from the warheads. He guessed he had no more than a couple minutes to act. He needed to launch the missiles while the warheads were armed and the missiles were elevated in firing position.

Michael and Barrows sat in the front of a pickup truck, while Sergeant Jackson and four men held on for dear life in the cargo bed. Lieutenant Kantelos followed in a second pickup truck, with two men in the cab and six more in the cargo bed. Barrows was taking the access road curves at breakneck speed.

"How'd you get Kantelos to agree to join us?" Michael asked.

"I asked him to call Major Petroangelos and tell him he had mail for the men and was about to bring it up to the top of the mountain. Petroangelos apparently went ballistic, ordering Kantelos to stay down at the missile storage area. When Kantelos told him it was no problem, since he had to make the drive for other reasons, Petroangelos screamed at him. Then Kantelos called the front gate at the command and control area and discovered that whoever answered the phone wasn't one of the two guards who were supposed to be on guard duty. The man who he talked with spoke Greek with a strange accent, according to Kantelos. Combined with everything else that has happened today, the Lieutenant didn't need much encouragement."

"Nothing like Iraqi jets, a fire fight on your base, going to DEFCON 1, and getting yelled at by your commander to make you see bogeymen behind every bush," Michael said.

"Especially getting yelled at by your commanding officer," Barrows said.

Michael laughed as he lurched against the pickup door. "You know, for a missile jockey, you're not half bad."

"Hah," Barrows said, "for an Infantry grunt, you're only half crazy."

"High praise," Michael said. "Okay, how are we going to play this?"

"A lot simpler than the plan you came up with. You would have had us drive to the top of the mountain, shoot our way through the gates, and then bust into the command and control trailer. Very Clint Eastwood-like."

"We Infantry types aren't nearly as smart as you Air Defense guys, but we do have a flair for the dramatic."

"Tell me about it." Barrows smirked at Michael. "All we have to do is disable power to the missiles."

"Where's the power cutoff switch?"

"That won't work," Barrows said, "unless we disable the generators. There are backup generators that power up the instant regular power is lost. The generators are locked up and Kantelos couldn't find the keys. I suspect Petroangelos hid them somewhere. We'll have to break into the generator room."

"You realize that if we hadn't taken out those guys behind the exclusion area, this part would have been a lot more difficult," Michael said.

"I've thought about that," Barrows said. "That's probably why those guys were hiding in the rocks, to keep anyone from interfering with the disabling of the launchers."

Barrows roared through the gate to the exclusion area. Kantelos' pickup stopped at the gate and dropped off half of his men to augment the pair of U.S. soldiers there. Then both drivers gunned their pickups and steered toward a steel building in a corner of the exclusion area.

Barrows leaped from the cab of the pickup and ran to the double doors on the steel building. He ripped a fire axe from its holding brackets on the front wall of the building. Michael was two steps behind Barrows as Barrows hefted the axe and began to raise it over his head.

"Hold it!" Michael shouted, causing Barrows to halt his backswing with the axe poised over his head.

Barrows lowered the axe and turned to Michael. "What?"

Michael shook his head and shrugged. "I don't know; this is too simple. If there is a plot to use a nuclear weapon against the Olympics, would terrorists sophisticated enough to devise a plan that complex have jeopardized the plan by ignoring the fact that the missiles could be so easily disabled by cutting electrical power?"

"We don't have time to screw around," Barrows argued, his voice sounding strained to the breaking point.

"Just give me a minute," Michael responded. "Just one minute." Barrows gave him a sour look, but nodded. Michael quickly moved to the generator building's door and inspected it. Nothing seemed to be amiss. He then walked around the building, looking for evidence that the building had been tampered with in any way. The only window in the building was a wired glass square set six feet high up in one of the side walls. He stood on his tiptoes and peered into the ten-foot by ten-foot enclosure. It was pitch black inside.

"Get me a flashlight," Michael shouted. One of Barrows' men ran over and handed one to Michael. He shined the light into the generator building and almost immediately sucked in a deep breath.

Someone had erected a steel plate between the generator and the door to the little building. Between the metal plate and the doors were at least six silvery wires. Michael couldn't see where all the wires began or ended, but he could clearly make out that a couple of the wires were connected to the inside door handles on one end and on the other end to two Claymore mines resting on the floor, pointing toward the doors. The minute the doors were opened, the Claymores would detonate, spraying thousands of lethal metal fragments at anyone in the doorway. The metal plate inside the building would protect the generator from being damaged.

Michael returned to where Barrows and Kantelos stood by the doors to the building. He explained the situation to Barrows and Kantelos. "We can't take the chance of forcing open these doors," he said. "I can't tell from outside how the building has been boobytrapped."

"Shit! Shit! Shit!" Barrows cursed.

"We'll lower the launchers," Kantelos said to Barrows. "Then you and your men can remove the cover plates and the arm plugs."

"That's going to take some time," Barrows said, but he gave Kantelos a thumbs-up sign and ran with his men to the nearest launching pad.

Michael felt the hairs on the back of his neck bristle. Each of the missiles rested on a launcher that had been raised to almost a ninety-degree angle. They looked ominous and beautiful at the same instant.

"We've got to lower the launchers," Barrows shouted at Michael. "Unfortunately, we have only enough men to lower one at a time."

Kantelos opened a box at the back end of the first launcher and appeared to press something. The launcher immediately descended with a loud whining sound. Then one of Kantelos' men disconnected a cable attached to the launcher, while one of Barrows' soldiers went at a cover plate on the missile itself with screwdrivers. Once the plate was removed, one of the Americans reached inside a small cavity and unplugged a colored device about the size of a coffee cup. He handed it to one of the other U.S. soldiers, who, along with a second soldier, ran it over to the exclusion area gate and handed it to one of the two American guards there. Michael watched the two guards rush inside the guard shack.

"They're putting the arm plug in the two-man safe," Barrows explained.

The second launcher had been lowered by this time and the Greeks were working on the third one. Michael guessed the whole operation would take about ten minutes.

The arm plugs from the first four warheads were in the two-man safe and the fifth launcher was nearly in a locked down position. Kantelos was directly behind the last missile, ready to open the control box to lower the launcher, when a strange sound came from the still-elevated weapon.

Michael looked at Barrows, who stood directly behind Kantelos, and saw fear etching the man's face.

"It's launching," Barrows shouted, as he grabbed Kantelos by the back of his uniform shirt and threw him to the side, just as the sound coming from the missile changed to a throaty roar, sounding like the revving motor of a giant hot rod. A blast of fiery air came from the rear of the missile and caught Barrows full in the face and chest, propelling him backwards about twenty feet. The missile moved a couple inches, as though in slow motion, while the noise coming from it gained in volume.

Michael saw Barrows take the full force of the blast from the cluster of four rocket motors. After a few seconds, the missile shot off its launcher and flew skyward toward the command and control area, and then cleared the top of the mountain. Michael leaped to his feet and ran for Lieutenant Kantelos, whose uniform was on fire. He stripped off his own fatigue shirt and pounced on the Greek officer, smothering the flames. He jumped back to his feet and looked toward the fence behind Kantelos. Barrows lay on the concrete. Smoke came off his body as though it seeped from every pore. The man had been burned beyond recognition.

Michael raced to the guard shack. He pointed at the telephone on the wall and demanded, "Can I get an outside line from here?"

One of the American guards answered in a quaking voice, "You have to go through the switchboard down at the headquarters building."

Michael snatched the receiver from its wall mount and waited for someone to answer. When Lieutenant Schroeder came on the line, Michael gave him his father's cell phone number from memory and told him to make the connection.

"What happened up there?" Schroeder asked breathlessly.

"Lieutenant, I want you to make that call right now. No questions."

"Yes, sir," Schroeder said.

Michael knew his voice was at least one octave higher than normal; but there was nothing he could do about it. "Dad," he yelled, "One of the missiles was fired. I couldn't stop it." His voice cracked. "I'm sorry, Dad."

CHAPTER NINETY-FOUR

AUGUST 13, 2004

Bob, Tony, and Serifides were speeding toward Olympic Stadium when Michael's call came through. After Bob cut off Michael's call, he hit the speed dial button for Jack Cole's phone at Langley. Jack came on the line after only one ring.

"Jack, they fired a missile at Athens. You've got to get word to the F/A-18D pilots. It's—"

"Hold on, Bob," Jack said, rare softness in his voice.

"Did you hear me, Jack; they fired a nuke at Athens?"

"We know, Bob. The F/A-18Ds picked it up the second it crested the mountain between Koropi and Athens. They got it before it detonated. They blew the damned thing to smithereens." Jack coughed out a strangled laugh. "Now we just have to deal with one hell of a fire that's raging near some ancient temple the Greeks and every archaeologist in the world hold sacred. Hopefully, we can keep the fact secret that there was a nuke involved."

Bob blew out a blast of air. He felt weak and nauseated. "Any danger of radiation or fallout?"

"Naw, that's a myth. Since the weapon didn't detonate, all we wound up with is a high explosive fire." There was an awkward moment of silence between the two men. Jack finally filled it. "I apologize for doubting you, Bob. I should have known better after all these years. If the F/A-18s hadn't stuck around, we would have had a disaster of unimaginable proportions. The Greek jets were already on their way back to their base. If it hadn't been for our planes—"

"Hold that thought," Bob said, "I'll get back to you." Bob turned to Serifides and pointed at the black limousine on the other side of the road to the Olympic venue. "Those flags on the limo," Bob asked, "whose car is that?"

Serifides looked out the window and stared for a second. "The emblem is for the Prime Minister or the Deputy Prime Minister."

Bob looked at the dashboard clock. The opening ceremony should have finished by now. Argyropoulos was on his way to Delphi. "You armed, Inspector?" Bob asked.

"Yes, why?"

"How about you, Tony?"

"I never leave home without it," Tony answered.

Bob explained what he was about to do and what he expected of them. He ordered Tony to call Grady McMasters' cell number and told him what he wanted Tony to pass on to the FBI man. He then spun the wheel of the Tahoe and cut across the median into the oncoming lane, barely avoiding a collision with another vehicle and setting off a mad melee of car horns. He dodged several cars and raced after the limo, which was cruising at thirty miles above the posted speed limit. Bob overtook the limo, passed it, and then cut it off against the curb. Tony and Serifides ran from the Tahoe, as Argyropoulos' two bodyguards leaped from the limo. Despite his limp, Tony was on one of the bodyguards before the man could raise his pistol. He grabbed the man's gun hand, twisted the pistol from his grip, spun him around, and plastered him against the limo, his pistol pressing against the bodyguard's temple. Serifides and the second bodyguard wound up in a Mexican standoff, each man pointing his pistol at the other.

Serifides held his ID wallet out and shouted, "Ministry of Public Order; I have an urgent message from the Prime Minister."

At that moment, Argyropoulos stepped from the vehicle, followed by Ari Stokolos. "What's the meaning of this?" Argyropoulos demanded.

"I have an urgent message from the Prime Minister," Serifides repeated, as he holstered his weapon and moved toward the Deputy Prime Minister. The second bodyguard relaxed and lowered his own weapon when he saw Serifides put away his pistol.

"Why didn't he call me on my—" He abruptly stopped talking when he saw Bob walk around the Tahoe. Then he caught a second wind and screamed, "Shoot that man."

But Serifides was quicker than the bodyguard. He brought his hand down on the man's wrist, knocking the pistol out of the body-guard's hand. Serifides scooped it off the pavement and pointed it at the bodyguard.

Tony frisked the man he was guarding and backed away from him. Serifides checked his man for other weapons, then pushed him over to where the other guard stood. Tony jerked his pistol toward the sidewalk and told the bodyguards to move over to it. Serifides followed them and used two sets of handcuffs to secure the men to a street sign. Tony and Serifides returned to where Bob was standing with his hands in his pockets, a smile on his face. Tony took Stokolos' arm and dragged him over to the Tahoe. Serifides did the same with Argyropoulos.

"What do you think you're doing, Danforth?" Argyropoulos shouted. He turned to Serifides sitting next to him in the backseat. "I'll have your job for this. You and your family will be ruined."

Bob climbed behind the wheel, while Tony got in the front pas-senger seat. Tony trained his pistol on Argyropoulos.

"Where are you taking us?" Argyropoulos yelled.

"You'll see," Bob said, pulling away from the curb and executing a U-turn. He drove the SUV at manic speed. He intermittently watched Argyropoulos in the rearview mirror and noticed that the closer they got to the Olympic Stadium, the more nervous the politician seemed to become. When the stadium came into sight, looming in the dis-tance, Argyropoulos tried to climb over his aide, Stokolos, jerking the door handle.

"Take it easy," Bob said, "the doors are locked. We're almost there. The Prime Minister doesn't want you to miss the rest of the ceremonies." The look on Argyropoulos' face was all Bob needed to see. The man was devolving into an emotional wreck. It may not have been a confession, but it was close.

Stokolos elbowed his boss back into the middle of the seat and muttered something under his breath.

"What did you say?" Argyropoulos screamed.

"I said you are a weakling; you make me sick."

Argyropoulos wrapped his hands around Stokolos' neck and started shrieking like a madman.

Serefides pulled Argyropoulos off Stokolos and planted his pistol muzzle against the man's cheek. "Try that again, and I'll shoot you right here."

Bob pulled into the stadium parking lot and drove to the main entrance. A cordon of uniformed police officers bracketed the entrance. Two of them came forward and opened the Tahoe's rear doors. Serefides got out and watched one of the men pull Argyropoulos to the pavement, while the other police officer did the same to Stokolos.

The policemen forced Argyropoulos and Stokolos to stand facing the entrance, down the line of other officers who suddenly came to attention. Out of the shadows of the arch over the entrance, Prime Minister Yiannis Ierides came forward. Grady McMasters and Constantine Angelou followed him.

"You left the ceremony so suddenly, Dimitris" Ierides said. "You and Ari are missing all the fun." The Prime Minister turned and started back into the stadium. He called over his shoulder, "Bring them along."

"No," Argyropoulos cried. Two policemen, one on each arm, began dragging Argyropoulos through the entrance. He tried to drop to the ground, but the officers supported him and pulled him along.

Argyropoulos was sobbing now. "No, no, please, no."

Ierides and Angelou suddenly turned back and approached Argyropoulos, who sagged in the arms of the two policemen. "What's wrong, Dimitris?" Angelou said. "You seem frightened."

"It's going to blow up," he whined. "A missile. Nuclear missile."

"How do you know that?" Ierides asked.

"*Greek Spring*," he cried. "They made me help them. They want to bring down our government."

"And you were willing to murder eighty thousand people or more, is that right, Dimitris?" Angelou said.

Argyropoulos' chin dropped to his chest. He had nothing more to say.

The Prime Minister turned to Stokolos. "And what was your role in this?"

Stokolos glared at Ierides, but didn't say a word.

Ierides grabbed Argyropoulos' chin, forcing his head up. "The missile was destroyed by American planes," he said. "And Nicolaos Koufos told us everything."

A supercilious look came to Argyropoulos' face. "That's impossible," he said.

"Why is that?" Ierides said.

Argyropoulos' mouth opened, then closed like a trap.

Ierides smiled. "Oh, you mean it's impossible that Koufos could have told us about your involvement with terrorists, or about the plan to attack the stadium, because you murdered him. You're right, he didn't say a thing to the investigators. Not with his throat slit from ear to ear. But you should have checked his safe. He'd written everything down for the past fifteen years."

Ierides growled to the policemen, "Take them away." He half-turned to the stadium entrance, but turned back and looked at Bob, Tony, and Antonio Serefides. "Gentlemen, I would be honored if you would join me in my box."

"I'm sorry, Mr. Prime Minister," Bob said, "I have something I have to take care of."

Ierides grinned and said, "I assume you're talking about your son, Michael."

Ierides statement shocked Bob. "How—"

"We may be a third world country, Mr. Danforth, but we're neither stupid, nor oblivious." He laughed. "And we have our information sources. Your son is on his way here. Why don't you come inside and wait for him?"

"What about the traitor at the missile site?" Bob asked.

Again Ierides laughed. Then his face set in a hard, angry look. "That too is being taken care of."

CHAPTER NINETY-FIVE

AUGUST 13, 2004

Lieutenant Alexandros Kantelos went from feelings of inconsolable sorrow, to deep remorse, to almost uncontrollable anger. Simon Barrows had died saving his life. But he didn't have time to indulge his feelings. He joined a Greek Army Special Forces unit that raided the command and control area. They drove through an open, unguarded entry gate and sped toward the top of the site as a Chinook helicopter lifted off from a flat area behind the command and control trailer. Kantelos thought he saw Major Petroangelos sitting near the open door to the cargo bay. The aircraft was out of range of the Special Forces soldiers' weapons by the time they reached the high ground.

Kantelos followed the assault team into the barracks where they found the bodies of twenty-two airmen. He found one airman inside a storage building. The young man was so traumatized, he was incoherent. He just kept babbling about Turks.

Kantelos was beside himself with sorrow and anger and felt as though he was losing his mind, when an idea hit him like a thunderbolt. He ran to the command and control trailer. The system was on. He searched the radar screen and immediately spotted an aircraft that was no more than twenty kilometers from the missile site. He fixed the Acquisition Radar's beam on the aircraft, then transferred the aircraft to the Target Tracking Radar. The console showed the exact altitude and location of the aircraft. What he wished he could do was fire one of his unit's missiles at the aircraft, but that was an impossibility with all the launchers disabled. He lifted the telephone receiver from its cradle in the console and called Greek Air Force Missile

Command Headquarters in Athens. He passed the coordinates of the helicopter's position to the Duty Officer there, who had already learned about the slaughter at the missile site. The man was more than ready to accept Kantelos' information as gospel.

The Duty Officer contacted his counterpart at Air Force Fighter Command. The news of the traitor at the Koropi missile site had spread like a wildfire through the entire Greek military community and to the Greek Prime Minister. Emotions were high, as was a universal need for revenge. The Fighter Command Duty Officer informed his commanding officer of the helicopter that had left the missile site. The traitor, Petroangelos, was aboard the aircraft.

The commanding officer issued an order to launch a fighter jet. There was nothing ambiguous about his follow up order: Blow the sonofabitch out of the air.

Major Lambros Petroangelos tried to relax in the back of the Chinook helicopter, but he couldn't seem to make it happen. Something had gone wrong. He had done what he'd been paid to do, but the missile had not reached the target. He knew that because he had watched the screen in the command and control trailer as the Missile Tracking Radar followed the missile. It had been on target until it suddenly disappeared from the screen. Things were coming apart. He hadn't heard from Demetrios Mavroyianni or any member of his team. They were supposed to radio him when they were ready to be picked up; but when Petroangelos hadn't heard from them, he tried to contact them. There had been no answer.

"Relax," Mahmoud Abdalan said across the cargo bay. "We'll be there in a couple hours and then you can enjoy your riches."

Petroangelos tried to smile, but he couldn't quite pull it off.

Mahmoud Abdalan was the first to see the Harrier jet approaching the helicopter. He had been about to throw Petroangelos into the sea, per his agreement with Giorgos Photos. But he now put aside the Greek officer's death, at least for the moment. At first, the Harrier was an object of curiosity. But now that it was coming closer to the Chinook, Abdalan felt a chill come over him. The jet came within about two hundred meters and then stopped, hovering at the same altitude as the helicopter, aligning its nose with the Chinook as it continued on its southeastern course. Then Abdalan screamed as a missile burst from a pod under the jet's left wing.

CHAPTER NINETY-SIX

AUGUST 13, 2004

The Greeks had put an amazing amount of pomp and ceremony into the Olympic Games' opening ceremony, but Bob wasn't able to concentrate on the last few minutes of the ceremony. Even when Michael arrived, he couldn't focus. He felt as though something had died inside him. What frightened him was that it might be his soul that had died. He had once again risked his life, his son's life, and his entire family's future. He realized he had made a difference, and had helped save thousands, perhaps tens of thousands of lives. But he didn't feel like celebrating.

"You don't look like you're enjoying yourself," Prime Minister Ierides whispered to Bob, who sat on the Prime Minister's right. Michael had been placed on the leader's left.

"I apologize, Mr. Prime Minister. I guess I'm getting too old for this much excitement."

"Perhaps you and your son would like to join your wives at the Grand Bretagne," Ierides said.

Bob raised his eyebrows and said, "You do have your sources of information, sir."

Ierides tipped his head in acknowledgement of the compliment. "My old friend Jack Cole called me the day before you arrived in my country. He asked me to keep an eye on you."

Now Bob was flabbergasted. "I don't quite know what to make of that," he said.

"Don't even try, Mr. Danforth. Some things have no explanation. But remember that Jack Cole is a friend you will never be able to replace." Ierides pressed Bob's arm and, tears forming in his eyes, added, "And I will be your friend for life. My people and I will never be able to repay you and your son for what you have done."

Bob held Ierides' gaze, and then shook the man's hand.

Ierides wiped a hand across his eyes and wagged a finger at one of his bodyguards. "Please drive Mr. Danforth and Captain Danforth to the Grand Bretagne Hotel."

Neither Bob nor Michael had slept in over twenty-four hours. They claimed opposite corners in the back of the Prime Minister's limousine. Bob watched Michael close his eyes and wondered at how quickly young people can fall asleep. Michael's breathing had become deep and regular in a matter of seconds. His boy's sunglasses had slipped down his nose and looked as though they would fall. Bob gently reached over and plucked the glasses off Michael's nose.

Michael surprised Bob when he spoke without opening his eyes.

"We make a hell of team, Dad," Michael said.

"I assume you have the sense not to mention any of this to your mother," Bob said.

"It'll cost you," Michael said. He laughed, then shifted in the seat and fell back asleep.

CHAPTER NINETY-SEVEN
NOVEMBER 17, 2004

Three months had passed since *Greek Spring* had been taken down, but Bob had only been back in the U.S. for a week. He and his team had helped the Greeks make a case against the terrorists and their friends in the Greek Government. Although they had accomplished a great deal, Bob couldn't get over the feeling that his mission had only been partially accomplished. He knew he would feel that way as long as Giorgos Photos was free.

Bob was back in his office, reading Intelligence data coming from a myriad of agencies about terrorist activities around the globe, when his secretary poked her head in his office and told him the DCI wanted to see him.

Jesus, what now? Bob thought. He was surprised that the Director of Central Intelligence, the big boss, would call him directly. Usually, this sort of summons would come through Jack Cole. The chain of command was alive and well at the CIA. And he wasn't happy about the prospect of seeing the DCI. The man was not only the Agency's top spy, he also had to be its top politician. And Bob had never felt comfortable around politicians. To make matters worse, the date was ominous: 17 November. Like the terrorist organization. When he arrived in the Director's reception area, he found Jack waiting there.

"What's up?" Bob asked.

Jack spread his hands in a "beats me" gesture, but Bob saw a glint in his friend's eyes that told him Jack was in on something.

The Director exited his office and greeted the two men. "You boys want to take a ride with me?" He didn't wait for a response and breezed through the reception area and out into the hall. Bob and Jack hurried to catch up.

The Director's armor-clad limousine was waiting outside the building. They all piled in and the driver took off without being given instructions. The Director picked up the telephone in the limo and made a series of calls all the way into the District.

Bob thanked Jack for recent personnel moves within the Agency. Bob had lobbied for promotions for the members of his Athens and Langley teams. Jack had seen to it that the promotions came through. But what Bob really had to push hard for was getting Tony Fratangelo appointed to Chief of Station in Athens. Tony was younger than most Chiefs of Station and, as a result, was less experienced than most. But Tony's performance finally won out in the end.

"Did you talk to Fratangelo?" Jack asked.

"Yeah, and I made sure he understood that the only way the job was his was if he took his family for a month-long vacation."

"Trying to relive your life through the Fratangelos?" Jack said with a mischievous grin.

Bob shrugged, but he knew that what Jack said was, at least, in part true.

Bob was dying to ask where they were going, but he knew better. The Director was a sober, close-mouthed sort. If he wanted them to know their destination, he would have already told them. And Jack could keep a secret. It wasn't until the limo pulled into the vehicle entrance at the White House that Bob began to get nervous. He was now one hundred yards from where the top politician in the world resided.

The Director led Bob and Jack into the White House. A Secret Service agent directed them through a metal detector and then preceded them down a hall and into an elevator. After rising two levels, they exited the elevator and followed the agent to a door where another Secret Service agent stood at parade rest. The second agent smiled at Bob for a split second and waved the three CIA men through the door.

"You ever been in the Oval Office before?" the Director asked.

Bob looked around the room and shook his head. "Not that I remember," he said, trying to use humor to relax.

"Oh, I think you would remember if you'd been here before," a voice said.

Bob whipped around and saw the President of The United States come through the same door they had just entered. Behind the President were Greek Prime Minister Yiannis Ierides, Liz, Miriana, and Michael. He forced himself to keep his jaw from dropping.

"Mr. Danforth, you seem surprised," the President said, obviously enjoying the moment.

"Mr. President, I would say that's the understatement of the millennium," Bob responded.

The President laughed and looked at Ierides. "Shall we proceed, Mr. Prime Minister?" he said.

"Of course, Mr. President," Ierides said.

The Director and Jack Cole stepped back while three Presidential aides entered the Oval Office. One of the aides brought Michael, Liz, and Miriana to the center of the room, next to Bob. Each of the other two aides carried a mahogany box and what appeared to be a citation in a gold frame under glass. One of the aides handed one of the framed objects to the Prime Minister and one of the boxes to the President. The Prime Minister read from the citation, which in glowing, but very general terms, recognized Michael for "great service to Greece and the Greek people." There was no mention of courage under fire, or terrorists, or nuclear weapons.

The President opened the box and dipped it so Miriana could lift the medal from inside. She took the medal and pinned it on Michael's uniform, kissing his cheek afterward.

The Prime Minister read from the second framed citation. The wording was identical to Michael's. Liz did the honors this time, pinning the medal on Bob's suit jacket. She wrapped her arms around his neck and kissed his cheek. But before she released him she whispered in his ear, "I don't suppose you'll tell me what you and my son did to deserve this."

Bob felt his face go hot. He didn't dare meet Liz's eyes.

The Prime Minister and the President shook Bob and Michael's hands. The President turned to one of his aides and said, "Please show the ladies to the dining room; we'll be right down."

Bob saw Liz's eyes narrow and held his breath out of fear she was about to tell the leader of the Free World to go jump in a lake. He expelled the air in his lungs when she left with Miriana and the three aides without making an incident.

The President closed the door to the Oval Office and congratulated Bob and Michael. "I assume you both understand we will need to collect your medals and citations before you leave here today, and that your experiences in Greece must remain state secrets."

Bob and Michael simultaneously said, "Yes, sir."

"Oh, by the way, Mr. Danforth," the President said, "I had a nice chat with the Secretary of the Army. I know you were concerned about negative reactions at the Pentagon about Captain Danforth's . . . escapades, shall we call them, in Greece. I made it clear to the Secretary that I have taken a personal interest in Captain Danforth's career, including making sure his name is added to the promotion list to Major. Do you think that ought to do it, or should I do something more?"

"No, Mr. President, I think that should do the trick," Bob said, smiling at his astonished son.

The President suddenly turned somber, looked at Michael, and said, "I wish I could have known Captain Simon Barrows. He appears to have been quite some man."

"Yes, sir," Michael said. "He was a real hero."

"That's why I've arranged for him to receive The Congressional Medal of Honor. I assume you all understand, as his parents have assured me they do, that the awarding of the medal will have to be kept secret."

The other men in the room all either nodded or said, "Yes, sir."

"Good," the President said. "Now let's go join the ladies for a cocktail. It's been a long day and I sure as hell need one."

CHAPTER NINETY-EIGHT
December 1, 2004

Photos was rattled. Everything was coming apart. His lifelong dream had been destroyed. The members of *Greek Spring* were either dead or captured. The police had set up checkpoints at all the exits from the Olympic Stadium and arrested half of them there. The ones who were arrested had given the police the names of the others. And the whole lot was singing like canaries. Between what the authorities got from his own people, what Nicolaos Koufos left behind in his safe, and what Argyropoulos and Stokolos gave up under interrogation, *Greek Spring* and most other terror groups in Greece had, at the very least, been emasculated. Even the terror organizations' moles inside the government had been ferreted out and arrested.

He had stayed ahead of the police and the counterterrorist agents for over three months now. He knew they would find him sooner or later if he remained in Greece. He settled on France, where he had lived so many years ago. The French were at odds with the Americans; he didn't think they would ever extradite him—if the Americans discovered his whereabouts. He changed his name, of course, and went underground. And he disassociated himself from his family. He didn't miss his wife—she had become fat and demanding. But he did miss his children and grandchildren.

Ruth Gordon, the U.S. President's Special Assistant for Islamic Affairs, prepared for her meeting with Rajavi Hashemi, the head of the Ideological Unit of the Iranian Supreme National Security Council. This would be their fifth in a series of meetings that began almost one year earlier, after the devastating earthquake that had leveled the ancient city of Bam, near Kerman in southern Iran. Over forty thousand people had died in the quake. The United States had sent millions of dollars of aid and a hundred rescue workers and medical professionals to assist the overwhelmed Iranian Government. This act of mercy, the U.S. hoped, would begin thawing relations between the two countries.

"You're going to antagonize the Mullah," the Special Assistant's American translator said, pointing at the woman's short, sleeveless dress. "If you were Iranian, they'd execute you for wearing that in public."

Ruth Gordon, at forty years of age, was still built like a beauty queen. She was also one tough piece of work and she was fed up with the dissembling and bullshit that the Iranian had thrown her way in their previous four meetings. "That's exactly what I intend to do," she told her translator. "Antagonize the crap out of that bastard." She smiled and added, "And this dress is going to be nothing more than minor aggravation when I tell him what I want from him."

The translator swallowed, his Adams apple bobbing. He wiped a palm across his forehead, attacking the sweat that had suddenly popped out there.

"Let's go," Ruth said, "we don't want to keep that chauvinistic, Stone Age asshole waiting."

She led the way from the hotel lobby to the limousine waiting under the *porte cochere*. The ride to the meeting place took less than five minutes. They were greeted by one of Hashemi's aides who escorted the Americans to gardens surrounding a government building that had once belonged to Reza Shah Pahlavi, the monarch overthrown by the Ayatollah Khomeini.

At the entrance to the gardens, Ruth instructed her translator to remain behind. "Rajavi Hashemi speaks perfect English. This meeting is going to be one-on-one." She followed the Iranian's aide to a table with four chairs that had been set up in the middle of a tennis court-sized lawn surrounded by ten-foot tall hedges. Hashemi and his translator were seated at the table. The translator rose as Ruth approached; Hashemi merely nodded.

"It is an honor to have you again as a guest in our country," Hashemi said, after Ruth took a seat.

"It never ceases to amaze me," Ruth answered, "how hospitable the Iranian people can be. I hope we can someday normalize relations between our two countries."

"As do I," Hashemi said.

Sure you do, you fanatical son-of-a-bitch. What you want is to blow the U.S. off the face of the map. "Thank you, your Excellency," Ruth said. "There is something your government could do to show your good faith in our negotiations."

The Iranian's face remained congenial, but she saw the man's eyes harden. "Of course," he said, "if it is in my power."

"Perhaps your translator could excuse himself," Ruth suggested.

The Mullah waved his hand, dismissing the translator.

Ruth then related a story about how United States Intelligence agencies had discovered the departure point from which six Mirage jets had taken off and flown to Greece, where they intended to attack the Olympic Stadium. She told him that a man high up in the Iranian Government had planned the attack.

"Who is this man?" the Iranian asked, his voice indicating he didn't like what he had just heard.

"Mullah Parviz Mirzadeh," she said.

The Iranian's eyes blinked and the American knew that her counterpart had been shaken. "How did you get this information?" the Iranian demanded, momentarily losing his calm demeanor. "Mullah Mirzadeh is a very important man in Iran. He is in charge of Asian Republic Affairs."

Ruth nodded. She felt exhilaration at having rattled Hashemi. The man had asked a question he knew she would never answer. He now knew without a doubt that she had Intelligence sources inside his country. He'd develop an ulcer trying to figure out who her sources were.

"It would be difficult for my country to restore relations with a country which elevates terrorists to high positions in its government," she said.

The Iranian sat statue-like for several seconds, staring unblinkingly into Ruth's eyes.

Ruth met the man's gaze. She uncrossed her legs and recrossed them, showing just enough thigh to cause any red-blooded man's testosterone to rebel. Hashemi was a fundamentalist zealot, but he was a notorious womanizer and pervert. He had been part of the Iranian leadership who had sanctioned the raping of female prisoners on the day before their executions.

Hashemi leaped from his chair, his face crimson, the sleeves of his robe flying around as though they were wings. "Parviz Mirzadeh is a hero of the Republic." He looked down at Ruth's legs and spat, "You dishonor Islam with your appearance and your false allegations about Mullah Mirzadeh. These meetings between our two countries are over." He spun around and stormed from the gardens.

Ruth bounced her crossed leg and tapped the tips of her steepled fingers together. Well, well, she thought, the Iranian Government is going to protect Mirzadeh. As we expected, Mirzadeh wasn't acting on his own. She had accomplished what she had set out to do—to determine if Mirzadeh was a rogue, or if the Iranian Islamic Republic had orchestrated the attack on Athens. The attack was one more part of the Iranian Mullahs' goal of *bast*, or expansion, of the fundamentalist revolution. Ruth took her cell phone from her briefcase and dialed 9-1-1.

"It's a beautiful day in Azerbaijan," a male voice answered.

"Do it," Ruth snapped and terminated the call.

CHAPTER NINETY-NINE

DECEMBER 3, 2004

Bob leaned over the bed and kissed Liz's forehead. "I'm going out for a walk," he said. "I'll meet you for breakfast in the dining room in an hour."

"Why don't you give me a couple minutes," she said. "I'll get fixed up and join you?"

Bob patted her shoulder. "Your idea of a couple minutes is more like an hour. We'll take a walk together after breakfast."

Liz gave him a suspicious look. "What's going on?" she asked. "This trip to Paris is supposed to be a vacation, remember?"

Bob smiled and said, "Jeez, can't I take a walk around the most romantic city in the world, full of gorgeous women, without you interrogating me?"

Bob could tell his attempt at humor hadn't placated Liz, but he had to go. "See you in an hour," he said over his shoulder as he left the room.

He walked through the lobby of the Paris Mirasol Palace Hotel and turned right along the sidewalk to a side street, and made another right turn. He walked quickly to a Peugeot parked at the curb and got inside the car. The driver handed him a copy of *Le Monde* and pointed at an article at the bottom of the front page.

"That was pretty quick," the driver said.

Bob read the article before responding. The story described the murder of a high-level Iranian Mullah, Parviz Mirzadeh, by unknown persons. Apparently, the Mullah and his seven bodyguards had been attacked and killed while driving to the Iran/Turkistan border.

"It was about time," Bob said. He didn't let on that Jack Cole had called him two days earlier to notify him of Mirzadeh's assassination. Bob looked out the side window, not wanting the driver to see the expression of pure joy on his face. A U.S. Special Forces team had flown in from Uzbekistan; met up with an Assyrian guide whose two daughters had been kidnapped, raped, and murdered on Mirzadeh's orders; and intercepted Mirzadeh. Bob knew that the Special Forces team had found ten million dollars in the trunk of Mirzadeh's car. Money probably intended for Islamic revolutionaries in the former Soviet Republics.

They drove in silence for a mile, and then the driver stopped on a street of three-story row houses. Bob left the car and went inside.

"Ah, *Robert*," one of three men inside the front room said.

"*Jean Paul*, it's been a long time."

"*Oui, mon ami.* Too long."

The Frenchman turned around and walked toward the rear of the house. Bob followed. He was surprised to find Stanton Markeson standing at the entrance to the kitchen.

"Stanton, you're looking well," Bob said.

Markeson patted his stomach. "One good thing came out of my being shot," he said with a laugh. "I've lost fifty pounds and gone on an exercise program."

"Good for you," Bob said. The two men shook hands, then Markeson backed into the kitchen, giving Bob a clear view of the room. A chair in the middle of the kitchen floor held a man whose head lolled to one side. From the man's color, Bob thought he was dead. He looked as though he'd been worked over by professionals.

"*Robert*, meet Giorgos Photos," Jean Paul said, with a flourish of his hand.

Bob stared at the man. Then he looked at Jean Paul Durand, a thirty-year veteran of the *Securite*. "*Est-il mort?*"

"No, no, *mon ami*, he is not dead, he is very much alive. It's the drugs that make him look dead." Durand made a clucking sound and added, "A quick death is not punishment enough for this monster."

"Did you learn much?" Bob asked.

Durand snapped his fingers and smiled. "Oh, *Robert, c'etait tres magnifique. Monsieur* Photos sang like a bird." The Frenchman blew air over his teeth, making it come out in a whistle. "This Greek has one incredible memory. Do you know how many Swiss bank account numbers he has memorized? Seventeen." He clapped his hands in glee. "We will track down the owners of the accounts through these numbers; and even if the names on the accounts are false, we will still be able to confiscate the funds because of the account owners' ties to terrorism." Durand looked over at Markeson for a moment, and then said to Bob, "*Monsieur* Markeson, as well as your people from Washington, were a big help."

Markeson's features went rigid for a moment. "This bastard identified the assassin who took down the Lambrakis Building." He seemed to need a few seconds to catch his breath before continuing. "He told us the guy, name of Musa Sulaiman, had settled in Brazil. He gave us Sulaiman's bank account number."

"He won't have much fun down there once you cut off his funds," Bob said.

"Oh, we're not going to do that until I make a quick visit to Rio," Markeson said, his eyes blazing with the fires of hatred and revenge. "No point in warning him."

Bob nodded. "What are you going to do with Photos?" Bob said to Durand.

The Frenchman smiled. "My good friend in Athens, Constantine Angelou, wants Photos in Greece. And, of course, England and the United States have reason to want him, as well. But the Greeks are still too soft on these bastards. And, in my opinion, sending him to

England or the United States will only bring unwanted attention to those countries."

A sudden groan from Photos caused the men in the room to look in his direction. The terrorist was regaining consciousness, although his eyes were barely open, and his head still hung to one side. Bob watched Photos until Durand began speaking again.

"The Turks have also expressed an interest in getting their hands on Photos, to try him for the murders of Turkish diplomats in Greece. I think they should be allowed to deal with Photos first."

"There won't be anything left of him after the Turks finish with him," Markeson said.

Durand bent over and grasped Photos' chin. "What do you think, *Monsieur* Photos? Do you want us to send you to the Turks?"

Photos still appeared groggy, but he was apparently lucid enough to understand Durand. His eyes popped open as though he'd seen someone rise from the dead. "No, no Turks."

Durand released Photos and turned toward the group of men. "Well, I think we have our answer. *Monsieur* Photos will be sent to Turkey."

CHAPTER ONE HUNDRED
DECEMBER 10, 2004

Bob left Durand and the others and returned to the hotel. He was already seated in the hotel dining room when Liz came down from their room. He stood as she reached the table and hugged her.

"How was your walk?" she said, giving him a narrow-eyed look.

He pulled out her chair and waited until she was seated. "It was great," he said. "But, you know something? I didn't see one woman half as beautiful as you."

Liz narrowed her eyes again. "What are you so happy about?" she asked. A fearful expression crossed her face and she said, "You've got that look you always get when you're about to go out on some mission."

Bob met her eyes and said, "I can't lie to you, Liz. I'm about to start the most important mission of my life. I don't know if you're going to be able to handle it."

Liz's expression went from fearful to angry. "Don't you dare—"

Bob interrupted her. "I just got off the phone with Jack Cole. As of five minutes ago, I became a retired government employee. Do you think you can deal with me being around all the time?"

Liz formed an "O" with her mouth, but made no sound.

"How do feel about extending our trip over here," Bob said, "now that I'm a man of leisure?"

Tears streaked Liz's cheeks.

Bob handed her his handkerchief. "I hope those are tears of joy," he said.

"Oh, shut up," she said, and then stood and moved to him. She sat in his lap and buried her head in his neck. "I love you, Bob Danforth."